Praise for the novels of Carla Neggers

"Worth the wait. Well plotted, with Neggers' trademark witty dialogue and crackling sexual tension, this is a keeper."
—*RT Book Reviews* on *The Whisper*

"[Carla Neggers'] books have that magical ingredient too—the ability to pick me up and transport me into another world for a few hours...a few days..."
—M. J. Rose, international bestselling author of *The Hypnotist*

"A haunting romantic story..."
—*Bookreporter* on *The Widow*

"Brimming with Neggers' usual flair for creating likeable, believable characters...she delivers a colorful, well-spun story..."
—*Publishers Weekly* on *The Carriage House*

"Well-drawn characters, complex plotting and plenty of wry humor are the hallmarks of Neggers' books. Jo and Elijah are very well matched, and readers will root for their romance."
—*RT Book Reviews* on *Cold Pursuit*

"Readers will be turning the pages so fast their fingers will burn.... A winner!"
—Susan Elizabeth Phillips on *Betrayals*

"Showcases the award-winning Ms. Neggers' unique blend of quirky humor, sizzling romance and engrossing suspense, which combine to produce irresistibly entertaining novels."
—*RT Book Reviews* on *Finding You*

Look for Carla Neggers' next novel
in the Swift River Valley series

A KNIGHTS BRIDGE CHRISTMAS

available soon from MIRA Books

CARLA NEGGERS

SECRETS *of the* LOST SUMMER

MIRA

Recycling programs
for this product may
not exist in your area.

ISBN-13: 978-0-373-40132-1

Secrets of the Lost Summer

This edition published by arrangement with Harlequin Books S.A.

For questions and comments about the quality of this book, please contact us at CustomerService@Harlequin.com.

Printed in U.S.A.

www.Harlequin.com

To Jennifer and Murray McCord

Chapter 1

Olivia Frost dribbled water from a measuring cup onto herb seedlings lined up in tiny pots on the windowsill above her kitchen sink. Parsley, dill, rosemary. The window looked out on the alley behind her Boston Back Bay apartment but received enough sunlight to grow a few herbs.

No sunlight today, she thought, setting the cup in the sink.

Just when New Englanders hoped they could put away their hats, gloves and boots, March had decided to turn into a lion again. The weather forecast promised the dreaded "wintry mix" by early afternoon.

Olivia sighed at the fresh green of the herbs. She didn't hate winter but she was ready for spring. March had less than two weeks to turn into a lamb and usher in April showers and May flowers. She couldn't wait to drive out to the hills and quiet back roads of Knights Bridge, her out-of-the-way hometown west of Boston, and plant her herbs at the early nineteenth-century house she'd bought last fall. The purchase had felt impulsive, but the owners, desperate to make a quick sale, had offered her a great deal. She had never been one for extravagant spending and kept her expenses as low as possible in Boston. Instead, she had saved her money and was able to snap up her historic house, as picturesque as her hometown itself.

Except for the eyesore just up the road, but that was a problem for another day.

She had enough problems for today.

"Challenges," she said aloud, turning from the sink. "Challenges, not problems."

She was already dressed for work, opting for a black skirt and blue merino sweater. She'd add what she needed to accommodate the weather, but she had a client lunch—a critical client lunch—and wanted to dress less casually than when she knew she'd be holed up at her desk all day.

She'd been too keyed up to sit at the table for breakfast, instead downing coffee and a bowl of oatmeal with walnuts at the sink. She liked her apartment, even if it was small and overlooked an alley. When she'd moved to the city five years ago, she had talked her landlord into letting her paint the walls and woodwork, choosing cozy, cheerful colors—misty-greens, rosy-pinks, summer-cloud whites—to offset the dreary light. On her way home from work last night, she'd picked up a dozen pink tulips and divided them between two glass pitchers and placed one on the kitchen table and the other on the dresser in her bedroom.

Tulips and herbs. Olivia smiled to herself. All would be well.

With a deep breath, she walked through the adjoining living room. The wood floor and her sofa were stacked with books on herbs, artisan soap-making, landscaping, old houses and painting furniture. All winter, she had half dreamed, half plotted how she could convert her historic house into a destination for weddings, showers, lunches and small one-day conferences—eventually, perhaps, into an overnight getaway.

She hadn't thought of her notes and plans as distractions, but maybe they were. Maybe, in part, they were the reason today's lunch was so critical.

She reached into the closet by the front door and reluctantly got out her scarf and coat, a full-length blend of black wool and cashmere that she planned to wear for years. She skipped gloves. She didn't care about sleet, snow and freezing rain. It was mid-March, and she wasn't wearing gloves.

Her iPhone dinged and she saw she had an email from Marilyn Bryson, another graphic designer and one of her best friends.

Hey, Liv. I can't get together while I'm in town after all. I'm so busy these days I can hardly breathe! I love what I'm doing. I look forward to getting up every morning. I can't wait to go to work. xo Marilyn

Olivia noticed Marilyn didn't mention when they might get together or ask about her, but she pushed back any disappointment and typed a quick response.

Glad to hear all is well. Have a fun time!

That was diplomatic, she decided, glancing in the small mirror she had positioned by the door after reading a book on feng shui. Her dark, shoulder-length hair was still slightly damp from her shower. She'd fussed with her makeup more than usual, but it was still understated. She would have to remind herself to put on fresh lip gloss before her lunch.

With another deep breath, she headed out, making her way down the steps of her building, a former single-family house, to Marlborough Street. Gray clouds had descended over the city, but there was no precipitation yet. Olivia tried to focus on her familiar routine. Her lunch was with Roger Bailey of Bailey Architecture and Interior Design, her biggest client. Something was off in their recent communications, and she was worried he was about to jump ship and had scheduled a face-to-face meeting.

The wind picked up as she walked to her building, a five-story brick bowfront just past Copley Square. Roger wanted to refresh the look for his company and she assumed—no, she thought, he'd *told* her—that he wanted her to take on the job. Landing his Boston-based firm as a client two years ago had been her first high-profile achievement as a graphic designer, and her work for them had won awards. She and Roger had hit it off from the start. Losing him as a client wouldn't be good.

Jacqui Ackerman, the slim, fifty-four-year-old owner of Ackerman Design, one of Boston's most prestigious studios, greeted Olivia with a quick "good morning," then disappeared into her first-floor office. Olivia tried not to read anything into Jacqui's behavior. She could be in a hurry. She could have a client on hold.

Olivia walked back to her own office and switched

on her computer as she pulled off her coat and scarf. She had several small projects that she could clear off her desk this morning, and she'd go over her Bailey Architecture and Interior Design files before lunch, so that everything would be fresh in her mind when she met with Roger.

Three hours later, as Olivia reached for her coat to head to her lunch with Roger, she received a text message from his secretary: Roger has an unexpected conflict and can't make lunch. He apologizes and will call tomorrow.

Olivia stood frozen by the coatrack. The secretary couldn't call? Did that mean the cancellation wasn't that big a deal—or that it was a huge deal?

In the past, Roger would have called or texted himself.

"This can't be good," Olivia said under her breath.

Bailey Architecture and Interior Design was not only her biggest and most prestigious client, it was one of the biggest and most prestigious for the studio. The last thing Jacqui would want would be for a defection of that magnitude to start a stampede out the door.

Taking a moment to pull herself together, Olivia put her coat on, anyway, then finally texted the secretary back: You caught me just in time. Thanks, and let Roger know I look forward to speaking with him.

She slid her iPhone into her handbag and left, grateful that she didn't run into Jacqui or anyone else she knew. It was just as well Marilyn couldn't get together while she was in town. Olivia had to admit she was too preoccupied with her own problems and wasn't in the mood to see her friend. Marilyn had worked hard to revitalize her own graphic design career—with Olivia's help. Marilyn had been stuck at a mediocre agency in Providence. She hadn't been bringing in clients—never mind top clients—and her work hadn't been setting anyone on fire. Last fall, she had asked Olivia's advice on how to break through, and together they had mapped out a Marilyn Bryson career revitalization plan.

It worked, too, Olivia thought as she crossed the street and walked toward Copley Square, not even certain where she was going. The wind was biting, bringing with it sprays of cold rain mixed with sleet. She pulled her scarf over her head and tucked in her chin, rushing with a small crowd across Boylston Street.

From November to mid-January, Marilyn had called almost every day and often emailed throughout the day and into the evening. She was focused, determined, hardworking and open to constructive criticism and advice from wherever she could get them. Olivia had admired her friend's resilience, her insights, her dedication to her work.

"When I'm successful," Marilyn would say, *"I'm getting all new friends."*

A joke, of course. An irreverent way for her to deal with her uncertain situation. She and Olivia had met at a graphic design and digital media conference in Boston not long after Olivia had started at Ackerman Design and had been friends ever since.

Not only did Marilyn revitalize her career, she opened her own studio in February, immediately wowing everyone. It was as if she had reached critical mass—a tipping point—and her success only brought more success. No longer in need of advice and moral support, enormously busy with her work, she got in touch with Olivia less and less frequently and took longer to respond when Olivia initiated contact. Visits to Boston and invitations to Providence for late-into-the-evening brainstorming ended. By early March, Olivia realized their friendship was in a lull if not in jeopardy, and she backed off, letting Marilyn take the lead.

Nothing happened. Marilyn disappeared, until the email two days ago that she would be in Boston this week and would love to get together. Then came this morning's email, canceling.

Olivia turned into the wind on Newbury Street and half wished she'd woken up with a sore throat and had just stayed home and planted more herbs, but it wouldn't have changed anything. She continued down the block, finally reaching one of her favorite restaurants. She descended concrete steps to a small open-air terrace that in warm weather would be filled with diners. It was empty now, a few handfuls of salt and sand scattered on the concrete. The interior of the restaurant, however, was crowded with people who had braved the lousy weather.

Lowering her scarf, Olivia pushed open the glass door. She would enjoy a pleasant lunch by herself and think about how to restart her own career if Roger defected. She couldn't deny reality any longer. He was on his way out. The signs were there.

The cold, wet wind followed her inside as the door shut behind her. Then again, maybe she'd just never mind her high-stress, competitive career for an hour and think about her herb garden and the color scheme for her house in Knights Bridge. She had never been one to stay in a rotten mood for long. Even if she wasn't as super-hot as she'd been two years ago, she was still an established, respected designer. Designers and studios lost clients all the time. It was the nature of the business. Why should she be exempt?

She unbuttoned her coat and pulled off her scarf. She was looking forward to warming up with a pasta sampler plate and salving her wounded ego with a glass of Chianti.

The bartender, a slender, black-haired man, waved to her as he filled three glasses in front of him with red wine. The restaurant was narrow, with small tables lined up along a brick wall on one side and a dark-red painted plaster wall on the other, both walls decorated with inviting black-framed prints of Tuscany. Five years ago, Olivia had celebrated her first night in Boston at a table in the far corner. She hadn't known if she would last six months in her graphic design job, but she was still there, still working.

She noticed that the far-corner table was open, but as she started to take off her coat, her gaze fell on a man and a woman seated across from each other halfway down the brick wall.

Olivia didn't need to look twice. The woman had her back to the entrance, but Olivia recognized Marilyn Bryson from her glistening pale hair and the way her hands moved when she was animated and trying to make a point. The man was even easier. He faced the entrance where Olivia was standing, coat half off. She only needed a glimpse to recognize stocky, grayhaired Roger Bailey.

She was positive that Roger and Marilyn hadn't seen her.

They *couldn't* see her.

Olivia had never been good at the small social lie

and knew she couldn't come up with one now, under pressure. Instead, she mumbled something unintelligible to the bartender, then fled, pushing past a couple coming through the door. Ignoring the icy conditions, she raced up the steps back out to the street.

Out of sight of anyone in the restaurant, she adjusted her scarf and debated her options. Just go back to work? How could she? She'd have to tell Jacqui what she'd just witnessed.

Unless Jacqui already knew.

Olivia headed up Newbury Street, not slackening her pace until she reached the corner. She paused to catch her breath and button her coat. Wind whipped sleet into her face and onto the clothes she'd carefully chosen for the meeting that had never happened. She shivered, blaming the tears in her eyes on the sharp wind and cold, even as a sudden sense of dejection and demoralization sank over her. Losing a major client to a stranger would be bad enough…but to a friend?

"Olivia!"

She pretended not to hear Marilyn behind her. The light changed, and she crossed the street at her normal pace, not wanting to look as if she were upset or fleeing from anything.

Marilyn caught up with her on the opposite corner. She hadn't grabbed her coat and already looked cold. "I thought that was you." She reached out a hand but didn't quite touch Olivia. "Are you okay? You ran out so fast—"

"I got a text message from a client," Olivia said quickly, hating to lie, suspecting she sounded phony. "It's nice to see you. I have to run, though." She faked a smile. "Just as well with this weather. Enjoy your lunch."

"It's with Roger Bailey, Liv. I should have told you but I didn't know what to say."

"He called you?"

Marilyn lowered her hand, and her eyes, their vivid blue enhanced by contact lenses, shifted back toward the restaurant, then focused again on Olivia. "We agreed to have lunch. This was the only place I could think of on short notice."

It was an evasive answer. Olivia forced herself to nod. "Tell Roger I said hi."

"I'll do that. It's good to see you, Liv. Everything's going so well for me right now that I just haven't had time—"

"I understand. I'm glad you're doing well, Marilyn. I have to go."

"Call me anytime."

Olivia didn't respond as she continued down the street. After half a block, she glanced back, but Marilyn was already out of view, in the restaurant that she knew was Olivia's personal favorite. Had Marilyn chosen it, risking that her friend might walk in, or just figuring she wouldn't?

Why had Marilyn chosen the restaurant and not Roger?

Did it even matter?

Olivia shoved her hands into her pockets, wishing now she'd worn gloves. She could see sleet collecting on the sidewalk and car windshields. She turned stiffly off Newbury toward Commonwealth Avenue.

Think about spring wildflowers. Trillium and lady's slippers, jack-in-the-pulpit, wild geraniums....

She lost her footing in a slick spot, dispelling any image of wildflowers trying to take form. She and Marilyn had developed a pattern in their friendship of focusing on Marilyn—her work, her problems, her accomplishments. Olivia hadn't felt any great need to talk about herself or break out champagne over her own accomplishments, but it was more than that. She saw that now, if too late.

Intellectually, she knew that her own situation had nothing to do with the turnaround in Marilyn's career. Every career, Olivia told herself, went through down-turns and she would get through whatever was coming at her. She rarely discussed her career with Marilyn. She tended to be more private, and Marilyn was busy, caught up in her newfound success and focused on herself and her own career. She had said repeatedly that she couldn't allow distractions. It was easy to think she had pulled back from their friendship once Olivia was no longer of use, but Olivia doubted it was that simple.

Until just now. Seeing Marilyn with Roger Bailey had Olivia reeling. Had Marilyn actually targeted a friend's major client?

The wind eased as Olivia came to Commonwealth, one of her favorite streets in Boston. She waited for the light, then crossed the wide avenue in front of a line of stopped cars, their headlights glowing in the gray, their windshield wipers grinding steadily against the unrelenting rain and sleet. Only the buds on Common-wealth's dozens of magnolias suggested that spring had, indeed, arrived and was just having a setback.

Olivia smiled to herself. "I can identify."

She had seldom taken time to celebrate when she was Boston's hot designer. Now she couldn't help but wonder if she would ever have another reason to break out the champagne.

Well, she thought, she would just have to make up a reason—like getting parsley, rosemary and dill to grow in pots in her city window. Wasn't that reason enough to open a bottle of bubbly?

The attempt at boosting her mood failed. She'd just walked into a restaurant and caught her biggest client blowing her off to have lunch with another designer—who happened to be one of her closest friends.

Not *happened to be*. Marilyn knew about Roger because of her friendship with Olivia.

Marilyn knew that what she was doing was unethical.

If Roger Bailey was in her orbit, who was next?

Olivia couldn't deny the reality of her situation. It wouldn't take many more Roger Baileys for her career to spiral into an outright tailspin.

She reminded herself that how she felt about today was for her to decide. Roger was making a business decision. The meaning she gave it was her choice. She was a professional, right? A positive person, right?

A dog walker, a graduate student who lived in her building, breezed past her with five tongue-wagging dogs of various sizes and breeds. He smiled in greeting but didn't pause as he and the dogs barreled toward Commonwealth, all of them looking unperturbed by the weather.

Olivia laughed as she watched them retreat.

Nothing like a quintet of happy dogs to lift the spirits. Her family had always had golden retrievers back in Knights Bridge.

Her father had warned her about Marilyn when he'd

met her on one of his rare visits to Boston. *"She's using you, Liv,"* he'd said, cutting right to the chase.

That was Randy Frost. He denied he was cynical, instead insisting he had a realistic view of human nature. Olivia hadn't listened. She was the one who knew Marilyn. Marilyn was driven and ambitious, but those weren't offenses in their world.

When Olivia reached her apartment, she shed her coat and scarf and left them in a heap by the door and walked in her stocking feet to her galley kitchen. She had pulled wool socks on over her black tights, but no one else could see them. She had wanted her lunch with Roger Bailey to go well. She had worked on fresh concepts and was ready to listen, get his thoughts on what he was looking for.

Instead, their lunch hadn't happened at all.

No, she amended. It had happened with Marilyn.

Olivia opened her refrigerator. She didn't have a bottle of champagne chilling, or anything she wanted to eat, either.

She wasn't hungry, anyway, she thought, shutting the refrigerator again. Her herbs looked cold on the windowsill. She raked one hand through her hair, damp from the sleet and rain. How could she go back to work and tell Jacqui Ackerman what had just happened?

She heard her iPhone ding and went back to the door and unearthed her handbag. She pulled her iPhone out of the outer pocket and glanced at the screen, hoping for a minor distraction—the latest from J.Crew or L.L.Bean—but, her day being what it was, she saw it was an email from Peter Martin, a digital marketing specialist she had dated last summer. He'd taken a job in Seattle in September, and that was that. He and

Olivia had never been that serious, but the thought of relocating to the West Coast had seemed as out of the realm of possibility as her signing up to be an astronaut.

She couldn't help but read his email.

Can you send me Marilyn's phone number and email? I have a client I'd like her to talk to.

Olivia started to respond, then realized she was out of her mind and deleted the email. Feeling faintly as if she'd done something wrong, she shoved the phone back in her bag. She dreaded going back to her office. She'd have to tell Jacqui what was going on. Olivia reached into the closet for a dry scarf. Last fall, when she and Marilyn were still regularly laughing and bitching over wine and takeout, plotting Marilyn's career revival, had her friend been envious, tapping Olivia for her contacts, expertise, insights and energy but secretly hating her for her success? Had Marilyn always planned to dump her as a friend once her own career took off?

Olivia wasn't sure she wanted answers. They were moot questions now, anyway.

"Make friends with a plumber or a kindergarten teacher or something," her father had advised. *"Forget other designers. They're your competition."*

It wasn't how Olivia viewed herself or the creative world in which she operated, but now she wondered if he didn't have a point.

She loved her little apartment and she loved Boston, but as she lifted her winter coat, she knew she was done. It was spring. The wintry weather would end. The magnolias would soon be in bloom on Commonwealth Avenue. All would be well, she thought as she put on her coat. She'd head back to work, but as she locked her apartment door behind her, she pictured the herbs on the windowsill and knew, deep in her gut, that it was time to make a change.

It was time to go home to Knights Bridge.

Olivia didn't wait. She got busy that night, packing her books and calling her sister to borrow her truck. The next morning, she gave Jacqui official notice. Jacqui asked her to stay, but she also indicated she was open to having Olivia freelance. Roger Bailey had finally called, first Olivia, then Jacqui, to explain his defection to Marilyn Bryson. He insisted it wasn't a reflection on Olivia's work. He just needed a fresh eye.

Jacqui was obviously disappointed but also philosophical. "You know this business, Liv. The only constant is change."

She did know.

A week later, when Jessica Frost arrived on Marlborough Street in her pickup truck, Olivia had what she wanted from her apartment ready to go. She and Jess would load everything into the truck themselves.

"I don't know how you lasted here all this time," Jess said as a cockroach scurried across the kitchen floor.

Olivia smiled. "It's only the occasional cockroach. I think it's because I stirred things up in here when I started packing."

"Oh, that's reassuring."

Jess, eighteen months younger, was blunt to a fault, as pragmatic as their father and as caring as their mother. She wore a faded blue plaid flannel shirt over jeans that were baggy on her slender frame. Her hair, as dark as Olivia's, was chin length but still managed to look wild and unruly. Her eyes were flat-out green, not Olivia's hazel mix. Her sister's one concession to not looking as if she had just stepped out of a barn was a silver Celtic-knot necklace, a present from Mark Flanagan, a Knights Bridge architect who specialized in historic preservation and restoration. Olivia, and no doubt everyone else in town, expected an engagement ring would be forthcoming.

It was Mark who had introduced Olivia to Roger Bailey in the first place.

"How long are you keeping your apartment?" Jess asked.

"Through April, at least. I'll be freelancing for a while, but my landlord won't have trouble finding another renter when the time comes."

"You'll miss Boston."

"It's not even two hours from Knights Bridge. I'm not moving to Tucson."

Jess lifted a box of dishes. "Have you decided on a name for this getaway of yours?"

"I have. I'm calling it The Farm at Carriage Hill. What do you think?"

"Love it." Jess headed through the kitchen into the living room with her box, but stopped abruptly at a large open box on the floor. She glanced back at Olivia. "Why do you have a hundred sets of sheets?"

Olivia smiled at her sister's exaggeration. It was at most fifty sheets—a lot, she knew, by most standards. "They're antique sheets. I've been collecting them at flea markets and yard sales and such."

"What are you going to do with them?"

"I don't know. Something will come to me."

Jess shrugged. "You're the one with the creative flair."

When they finished loading the truck, they threw a blue tarp over the back and secured it with bungee cords as best they could. Olivia could have hired a mover but why spend the money? She had always watched her expenses. A good thing, she thought, now that she wasn't drawing a regular paycheck. In the back of her mind, especially lately, she had known she would go back to her hometown one day and start her own business. Over the past week she had wondered if that was part of the reason she hadn't experienced the kind of explosive success Marilyn was enjoying. Then she reminded herself that she had enjoyed great success and was still a sought-after designer.

Her sister was frowning at her and Olivia forced herself to stop thinking about the past. She couldn't let Marilyn get to her. Marilyn was a superb designer. Her work was striking a chord with people. Olivia didn't want anything bad to happen to a friend, even if that friend had betrayed her trust and dropped her once she was no longer of use.

She'd just learn to watch her back.

"No one's here to see you off?" Jess asked.

"It's a workday and I'm not going far."

As she pulled open the passenger door, Olivia felt a sense of excitement tempered by no small measure of uncertainty at what lay ahead. Maybe on some level she was running from failure and disappointment, but she was also running *to* something. A new life. A new set of challenges.

"All set," Jess said, climbing in on the driver's side.

She gave her sister a sideways glance. "Are you sure you don't want to change your mind?"

"Positive."

"It's warmer here than at home. We still have snow on the ground."

Olivia settled into the passenger seat with her little pots of herb seedlings on her lap. The dill was tall enough to tickle her chin. "I know, Jess. I was just there."

"All right, then. Let's go." Jess was still obviously unconvinced. "Olivia, are you sure—"

"I'm sure."

"Nothing's wrong?"

"Nothing's wrong."

"Liv—"

"It's just time to make a change, Jess. That's all."

Her sister gripped the steering wheel. "It's Marilyn Bryson, isn't it? She's done something. Flaming narcissist. Never mind. You'll tell me if you want to. I'm not going to pry."

Olivia said nothing, watching out her window as urban sprawl gave way to rolling hills and fields.

The Farm at Carriage Hill...

It was perfect, she thought. Just perfect.

A winding, off-the-beaten track road led from the main highway to Knights Bridge, often cited as one of the prettiest villages in New England. Situated on the edge of the Quabbin Reservoir and its protected watershed, the village had changed little in the past century, at least in appearance. Olivia watched the familiar landmarks pass by: the white church, the brick library, the town hall, the general store, the school, the pristine town common surrounded by classic houses, the oldest built in 1794, the newest in 1912. When her historic house came onto the market in October, the idea of converting it into a getaway had seemed more like a fantasy than a realistic goal. Regardless, she had expected to keep her job and apartment in Boston for the foreseeable future.

Jess was silent as she turned onto a narrow road just past the village center and navigated a series of potholes as they came to an intersection with an even narrower road. Olivia grimaced at the run-down house on the corner. The whole place had become an eyesore. The house, built in 1842, was in desperate need of repair, its narrow white clapboards peeling, sections missing from its black shutters, its roof sagging. If possible, the yard was worse, overgrown and littered with junk.

Its one redeeming feature was its location, one of the most beautiful and desirable in Knights Bridge with its sloping lawn, mature shade trees, lilacs, mountain laurel, surrounding fields and woods—and, peeking in the distance, the crystal-clear waters of the Quabbin Reservoir.

Jess downshifted as she turned onto the quiet one-lane road. They were only two miles from the village center, but it seemed farther. "Mark says the house should be condemned."

"At least someone should clear the junk out of the yard. Grace hasn't seen it, has she? She'd be devastated."

"I don't think she's been back here since she moved out."

Olivia noticed a rusted refrigerator on its side amid brambles, melting snow and brown, wet leaves. Who-

ever had bought the house two years ago from Grace
Webster, a retired English and Latin teacher, hadn't
done a thing to it.

"How did a refrigerator end up in the yard?" Olivia asked.

"I don't know," Jess said. "Kids, probably. The house
has sat empty for two years. There's a washing machine, too."

Indeed there was.

Olivia had asked her friend Maggie O'Dunn, a local
caterer, to find out what she could about the absentee
owner. So far, Maggie had discovered only that it was
an older gentleman from out west. California, probably. Maggie, however, was sure that her mother, Elly,
who worked at the town offices, could produce a name
and address.

"Why would someone from California buy a house
in Knights Bridge and then disappear?" Olivia asked.

Jess shook her head. "No idea."

The Websters had moved to Knights Bridge more
than seventy years ago, after they were forced out of
their home in one of the Swift River Valley towns that
was depopulated and flooded for the reservoir. Grace
was a teenager then. She never married and lived in
her family home alone until a small assisted living facility opened in town and she finally decided to move.

Olivia pondered the situation as the truck rattled
down the road to her own house, a gem set among open
fields, stone walls and traditional, well-established landscaping. When the house was built in 1803, the road
wound into a pretty valley village, now under water.
These days the road led to a Quabbin gate, then through
what was now a wilderness and eventually straight into   .

the reservoir itself, a reminder that, as beautiful as it was, it was a product of both man and nature.

Jess pulled into the gravel driveway. "Do you want to wait for Dad and Mark to get off work, or shall we unload the truck ourselves?"

"We loaded it ourselves. We can unload it. Unless you have something else you need to do—"

"Nope. I'm all yours for the day."

"Thanks, Jess."

"No problem. It'll be great having you back in town."

Olivia got out of the truck, herb seedlings cuddled in her arms like little babies. The air was cold, clean, smelling faintly of wet leaves. "Home sweet home," she whispered, even as she felt a stab of panic at the uncertainty of her future.

Jess joined her on the driveway. "It's so quiet here. You're close to the village, but that way…" She paused and gestured down the road, toward Quabbin. "That way, Liv, it's nothing but wilderness and water for miles and miles."

Olivia smiled. "I know. It's perfect."

"So you say now. Wait until it's two o'clock on a moonless night, and it's just you out here with the bats, bears, eagles and mountain lions."

"There's been no confirmed sighting of mountain lions yet in Quabbin."

"I wouldn't want you to be the first to see one," Jess said with a grin.

They went inside before unloading the truck. The rustic, homey kitchen, in an ell off the original 1803 structure, was washed in the bright midday light. Her friend Maggie had left a lunch basket and a milk-glass pitcher of forced forsythia on the table, a square, battered piece of junk Olivia had discovered at a yard sale and repaired and painted a warm, cheerful white.

She felt some of her tension ease. It was almost as if the forsythia were smiling at her. Suddenly she couldn't wait to get her stuff from Boston into the house and make it feel like home.

Jess lifted chocolate chip cookies, apples and cloth napkins out of the basket. "Lunch first, or unload the truck first?"

Olivia opened the refrigerator and found sandwiches and a mason jar of tea. She grinned at her sister. "I'm starving. My question is whether we have the cookies first or the sandwiches first."

Jess handed her an index card she found in the basket. "Maggie left you a note."

Olivia glanced at her friend's messy handwriting: *Mom came through with info on the owner of Grace Webster's old house.*

Maggie had jotted down a name and address.

"Dylan McCaffrey," Olivia said, not recognizing the name. "Ever hear of him, Jess?"

Her sister bit into an apple. "Uh-uh."

It was a San Diego address. Far away for the owner of a wreck of a house in Knights Bridge to be living.

Olivia slid the card under the edge of the pitcher of forsythia. She didn't care where Dylan McCaffrey lived or why he'd bought the house up the road. She just wanted him to clean up the place.

Chapter 2

The note was handwritten on a simple yet elegant white card decorated with a sprig of purple clover. It came with a half-dozen color photographs in a matching envelope, also with a clover sprig. Dylan McCaffrey pushed back his chair, put his size-twelve leather shoes on his desk and contemplated his twentieth-story view of San Diego, which, on a good day, such as today, was nothing short of breathtaking.

Who the hell was Olivia Frost, and where the hell was Knights Bridge, Massachusetts?

Dylan read the note again. The handwriting was neat, legible and feminine, done in forest-green ink—probably a fountain pen.

Dear Mr. McCaffrey,

We've never met, but I'm your neighbor in Knights Bridge. I own the center-chimney 1803 house just down the road from your house.

Dylan stopped right there. What was a center-chimney house, and why was he supposed to care?

He gritted his teeth and continued reading:

You might not be aware of this, but your house is in rough shape. The structure itself isn't my concern, but the yard is. It's overgrown and strewn with junk, including, as you can see from the enclosed photographs, a discarded refrigerator.

He had lined up the photographs side by side on his dark wood desk. He glanced at the leftmost one. It did, in fact, show a rusted white refrigerator cast on its side amid brambles and melting snow. The fridge had to be at least thirty years old. Maybe older. He wasn't an expert on refrigerators.

He returned to the note:

I understand if you're unable to clean up the yard yourself and would like to offer to do it myself, with your permission. Of course, I'll waive any liability if I get hurt, and if I find anything of value, I'll let you know.

My family runs a small business in town that specializes in architectural reproductions and components—doors, windows, mantels and so forth. We've been in Knights Bridge for generations. I would hate to get the town involved in this matter. I look forward to putting it behind us and meeting you one day soon.

Thank you so much,

Olivia Frost

Whoever she was, Dylan suspected Olivia Frost thought the man she was writing to was old, or at least feeble. He was neither. He had to admire how she managed to offer help at the same time she threatened to sic the town on him, an outsider. His main issue with her note, however, was more immediate and direct.

He didn't own property in Knights Bridge, Massachusetts.

He dropped his feet back to the floor and tapped a few keys on his laptop, pinpointing the town on a map of Massachusetts. It was on the northern edge of what appeared to be a large lake, the largest by far in the small New England state.

He sat back.

Knights Bridge and Olivia Frost still didn't ring any bells.

He was about to zoom in for a closer view when Noah Kendrick entered the sprawling corner office. The door was open. Noah and Dylan had been best friends since first grade in a Los Angeles suburb. Noah, the genius geek. Dylan, the C-student hockey player. Now they were business partners, except it wasn't that simple. Dylan owed Noah his livelihood and maybe even his life. Noah said the same thing about Dylan, but it wasn't true and they both knew it. NAK, Inc., was Noah's brainchild, a four-year-old, highly profitable high-tech entertainment software company named for him—Noah Andrew Kendrick. Dylan had just helped put it together and keep it together. He knew how to fight. Noah didn't.

"What's up?" Noah asked.

Noah had on, as always, a black suit. He didn't care that he looked like an undertaker. He thought black made him look older and tougher. He was thirty-three, but even in his suit, he looked much younger. He was fair and angular and had to be coaxed into sunlight. He was deceptively tough and fit—a fencer and a brown belt in karate.

Dylan was the opposite. He was thirty-four but

looked older. He and Noah had met in first grade and graduated high school the same year, but Dylan had repeated kindergarten after his mother decided she should have held him back a year to begin with. The school didn't disagree. Everyone said it was because of his September birthday. Maybe, but he'd never been a great student.

He'd discovered ice hockey in fifth grade. No looking back after that. After twenty years on the ice, finishing up in the NHL three years ago, he was fit, scarred and lucky to have all his teeth. He could clean up a yard in New England if he needed to, even a yard with a refrigerator in the brambles.

Unlike Noah, Dylan wore jeans and a sweater. No suit, black or otherwise, today. He only donned a suit when necessary, such as when he had to be a fly on the wall for one of Noah's meetings and warn him that someone was a jackass who should be thrown out the nearest window.

Not that Dylan had ever thrown anyone out a window or ever would. He could give the heave-ho to most people he met. He knew how, and he had the strength. His gift, however, was his keen instinct—at least compared to Noah—for people who were looking to cause trouble.

He sighed at his friend. "I didn't buy a farm in Massachusetts when I was drinking Guinness one night, did I?"

"Not that I recall. Have you ever been to Massachusetts?"

"Boston Garden when we played the Bruins. Since then, I've visited Alec Wiskovich a few times. He's a former teammate. Otherwise…that's it."

Noah leaned over his shoulder. "Go to street view."

Dylan did, and in a moment a quaint village with clapboard houses and shade trees materialized on his screen.

"No horses and buggies, at least," Noah said. "Who's the letter from?"

"Louisa May Alcott." Dylan handed over the note card.

Noah gave a low, amused whistle as he read. "Do you have a great-uncle Dylan McCaffrey? Maybe Olivia Frost confused you with him."

"No."

Noah, of course, knew that Dylan had no family left on the McCaffrey side. His father, an only child, had died two years ago. His grandparents were gone, too.

"Maybe it's a long-lost uncle," Noah said, placing the note next to the photos lined up on Dylan's desk. "I bet Miss Frost will fly out here and smack your hand with a ruler if you don't clean up the place. What's The Farm at Carriage Hill?"

"The what?"

"It's on the card. See?"

Noah tapped a finger on the back of the note card, *The Farm at Carriage Hill* printed in dark purple lettering. Dylan had missed it. He did a quick search but nothing came up anywhere in Massachusetts, never mind Knights Bridge.

"I guess a farm would explain the chives on the front of the card," Noah said.

"I thought it was clover."

"Chives are more romantic than clover, don't you think?"

"I don't think I've ever thought about chives or clover."

Noah grinned. "Good luck. Let me know if you need my help."

"With moving the refrigerator or figuring out why Olivia Frost thinks I own this house?"

"Either one," Noah said.

He withdrew from Dylan's office. His own was just down the hall, at least for the moment. NAK had gone public late last year. He and Noah had both made a fortune in the process, but NAK as a public company was different from it as a private company. The tight team of the early years was transforming into something else, and Dylan wasn't sure what his new role would be, or if he'd have one. He'd always been willing to walk away when Noah no longer needed him.

He looked out at the view of his adopted city and dialed Loretta Wrentham, his lawyer and financial manager.

He worked for another two hours, then drove out to his house on Coronado Island, a two-story tan stucco built in the 1950s. Kidney-shaped pool out back, the Pacific in front. Loretta arrived thirty minutes later, glanced at the note card and photographs from Olivia Frost that he'd arranged on his coffee table, then walked straight across the living room to the beveled glass door that led onto his front porch. At five-nine, Loretta was almost as tall as he was, slender and impeccably dressed. Her silver curls were cut short, emphasizing her wide brown eyes, high cheekbones and strong chin.

"You inherited the house from your father," she said, cracking open the door. She wore expensive jeans, a silky top and heels that didn't seem to bother her but would kill most other women half her age. She glanced back at him. "I assumed you knew."

"How would I know?"

"He was your father, Dylan. Didn't you two talk about these things?"

"No. What about a mortgage?"

"There isn't one. He paid cash. It wasn't an expensive property."

"What about property taxes? What about upkeep?"

"I've paid property taxes on your behalf. They're not high. Upkeep..." Loretta grimaced. "No one's lived in the house for a while. It was unoccupied when your father bought it shortly before his untimely death. Upkeep is minimal, just enough to prevent the pipes from freezing."

"Who was the original owner?"

"A woman by the name of Grace Webster. I should say she's the most recent owner. The house was built in 1842. The original owner would be dead by now for sure."

"You're enjoying this, aren't you?"

Loretta grinned as she pushed the door open wide. "Oh, yes."

Dylan leaned against the back of the couch. His house, a few blocks from the famed Hotel del Coronado, was professionally decorated in shades of cream and brown. Restful and sophisticated, supposedly. The yard, too, was professionally landscaped. No junk.

"What do you know about this Grace Webster?" he asked.

"Not much. She's in her nineties." Loretta stepped onto the porch, her back to him as she took in the view of the Pacific. Finally she turned to him. "Her father

bought the house in 1938, after the state forced everyone out of their hometown to make way for the Quabbin Reservoir."

That had to be the lake Dylan had seen on the map.

"Quabbin," Loretta continued, still clearly amused,
"is a Native American word that means 'place of many
waters,' or 'meeting of the waters.' It refers to the Swift
River Valley, which was laced with three branches of
the Swift River and multiple streams—the perfect location for a reservoir."

"Loretta," Dylan said.

She waved a perfectly manicured hand at him. "Miss
Webster's ancestors settled in the valley in the mid-
1700s. Two hundred years later, she and her family were
forcibly bought out, along with everyone else in four
towns, so the state could dam the valley and let it fill
up with fresh water for metropolitan Boston. It's one
of the most egregious examples of eminent domain in
U.S. history. I'd love to fight that case now."

Dylan had no doubt, but he was lost. "How did you
find all this out?"

"Internet. Our Grace is quoted in an interview with
some of the last living residents of the valley before it
was flooded. She's a retired high school English and
Latin teacher. She never married."

Dylan considered his predicament, and the note from
Olivia Frost. He couldn't even guess why his father had
bought the house, or why there was a cast-off refrigerator in the yard.

He joined his attorney and friend on the porch. A vibrant sunset filled up the sky and glowed on the Pacific
across the street. "What do I do?" he asked.

"It's your property," Loretta said, gazing out at the

sunset. "You can do whatever you want. Sell it, renovate it, give it away. Move in."

"Move in? Why would I move in?"

"I don't know. You could take up chopping wood and picking blackberries." She crossed her arms in front of her in the chilly wind. "Those are blackberry vines in the picture of the old refrigerator, aren't they?"

"I have no idea what they are."

"Blackberry vines have thorns."

Other vines had to have thorns, too, but Dylan really didn't know or care. "What did my father pay for this place?"

"A pittance. He wrote a check. The house is a wreck but it sits on seven acres. Knights Bridge is out-of-the-way, in part because of the reservoir. It's not like the area grew up naturally around a big lake. Quabbin didn't exist when the towns were settled. Look on the map. You'll see what I mean."

He had, and he did.

"What's the name of this farm again?" Loretta asked.

"The Farm at Carriage Hill."

"Quaint. And the owner?"

"Olivia Frost." Dylan ignored the cool wind as he watched joggers on the beach. "Why did my father buy a house in Knights Bridge, Loretta?"

"That," she said, dropping her arms to her sides, "is your mystery to solve. If I were you, I'd let sleeping dogs lie and hire someone to clean up the yard, then quietly sell the place or give it away."

"You'll check out this Olivia Frost?"

"First thing when I get home. Right now, I'm going for a walk on the beach and enjoy the last of the sunset." She headed to the steps but stopped before descending, again looking back at Dylan. "You're not worried about this woman taking legal action, are you?"

"Not really, no."

"Good. An old refrigerator and whatnot in the yard aren't a serious concern."

"I think I saw a washing machine, too."

Dylan could hear Loretta laughing all the way down the steps and across the street to the water. He went back inside, shutting the door firmly behind him. The sunset was fading fast. He sat on his couch and picked up the note card from where he'd left it and the half-dozen photographs on the coffee table. Loretta hadn't asked to inspect them. No point, he supposed. He eyed the chives, or whatever the hell they were. They looked hand-drawn. The design, the use of color and the hand-writing were contemporary and stylish, not old-fash-ioned, yet they also conveyed warmth, hospitality and rural charm. He wasn't quite sure how his Massachu-setts neighbor had pulled off the effect but it worked.

He didn't care how she'd pulled it off, either. Olivia Frost had written to him to ask—or demand—he move junk and a rusted appliance off property he hadn't, until today, even suspected he owned.

He scooped up the photographs and took them and the card upstairs with him to his bedroom, the drapes still pulled from last night. He hadn't bothered open-ing them since he had left for his office before light, but it wouldn't have mattered. He wasn't spending a lot of time in his bedroom these days. A few hours for sleep, time to get dressed—that was it. He hadn't had a woman in his life in a long time. Too long, maybe, but he wasn't checking off days on a calendar.

Not yet, anyway.

He set the card and photographs on the end of his bed, then sat on the floor and rubbed his fingers over the black-painted hinges and latch of an old flat-topped trunk. A nomad at heart, his father had left behind few possessions. On his fiftieth birthday, he had quit his day job as a business consultant and spent the rest of his life—more than twenty years—as an adventurer and treasure hunter, tackling obscure mysteries on his own and with a small team of professionals and avid amateurs. He had never sought financial gain for himself. Prowling the world for lost treasures had been his passion more than a source of income. He'd just enjoyed the adventure.

In the months since his father's death, Dylan hadn't dug through the contents of the trunk. He and his father had had a contentious yet solid relationship, but first the NHL and then NAK, Inc., kept Dylan's schedule jampacked, allowing little time to try to understand why Duncan McCaffrey had made the choices he had, or to figure out what treasure hunts he had left unfinished. Dylan didn't need the money. Money was one thing he had in abundance, and how could anything in the trunk bring him closer to his father now that he was gone?

Dylan couldn't imagine how long it would take him to properly sort through all the files, boxes, envelopes and scrapbooks stuffed haphazardly in the trunk. Hours and hours, and even if he had the time, he didn't have the patience.

And there was no guarantee he would find one word about Knights Bridge.

He could send Loretta to Massachusetts to deal with the house and its offending yard, and with Olivia Frost.

He lifted out a tattered stack of a half-dozen manila folders, held together with a thick rubber band. He shook his head. "Leave it to you, Pop, to complicate my life."

The rubber band was so dry and brittle it broke when Dylan tried to remove it.

He welcomed the distraction when his landline rang. He rolled to his feet and picked up.

"Check your email," Loretta said. "I sent you some preliminary info on the woman who wrote to you."

"Are she and Grace Webster friends?"

"Maybe, but Olivia Frost isn't old. I can tell you that much."

Loretta was chuckling when she hung up.

Dylan checked his email on his BlackBerry. Loretta had produced a photograph of his tidy-minded neighbor. It was taken at a formal dinner in Boston and showed Olivia Frost accepting an award. Apparently the owner of The Farm at Carriage Hill and artist of chives was also a successful, accomplished graphic designer.

The picture was too small to see in any detail on his BlackBerry. He went back downstairs and fired up his laptop on the kitchen table.

Olivia Frost had long, shining, very dark hair, porcelain skin and a bright smile as she held her gold statue and accepted her award. He couldn't make out the color of her eyes. Green, maybe. She wore a sleek, rather businesslike black dress that came to just above her knees.

In another picture that Loretta had found on Facebook, Olivia was more casual, dressed in a denim jacket as she stood in front of an old sawmill. Loretta's email explained that the Frost family owned and operated Frost Millworks, a small, profitable company that did high-end custom work.

She provided a link. Olivia Frost had designed their website.

Dylan called Loretta back. Before he even had a chance to say hello, she broke in, "I can keep digging if you want."

"I'll take it from here. Thanks, Loretta. What's on the internet about me?"

"You beat up that Montreal defenseman—"

"It was a clean check. He should have gotten an Oscar for that fall."

"What about the ten stitches?"

Dylan hung up. He didn't care what was on the internet about him. He wondered if Olivia Frost had looked him up by now, or had even thought to, considering the condition of the property he owned in Knights Bridge.

He glanced at her Facebook picture again. It was more of a close-up than the one at the awards ceremony. Her eyes weren't green, he decided. They were hazel, a fetching mix of green and blue flecked with gold.

He shut off his laptop and called his assistant to book a morning flight east to Boston.

Chapter 3

Olivia raked the last of the fallen leaves from the raised herb bed by her back door. The overcast sky and chilly temperature didn't bother her. The snow had melted out of her backyard, if not in the woods, and signs of spring were everywhere. She loved finding shoots of green under their cover of sodden leaves. The physical work gave her a burst of energy. She was ready to head up the road to Grace Webster's old house and start hauling junk. Naturally its owner, Dylan McCaffrey, hadn't responded to her note.

What had she expected? After two years of ignoring his property in Knights Bridge, why would he care?

Elly O'Dunn, who'd provided McCaffrey's name and address, remembered meeting him when he'd stopped at the town offices. She told Maggie, who'd then told Olivia, that he was a good-looking man in his seventies, with thick white hair and intense blue eyes. She hadn't spoken to him, and she couldn't fathom why he'd wanted to buy Grace Webster's house.

Olivia couldn't, either. She took her rake with her to the front yard, just as her father pulled up in his truck. She'd almost forgotten she'd invited her parents to lunch. As he stepped onto the dirt driveway, she noticed he was alone. Randy Frost was a big, burly man who had transformed his father's struggling sawmill into a profitable enterprise, all while serving on the Knights Bridge volunteer fire department since his teens.

"Place is shaping up," he said, walking around to the front of his truck. He wasn't wearing a hat or gloves, and his fleece jacket was open over a dark blue sweater.

Olivia held on to her rake. "It is, isn't it?"

He glanced past her at the woods beyond the strip of yard on the garage side of the house. The area had been farmland before World War II, but hardwoods and evergreens had reclaimed much of the land, old stone walls that had marked fields now lacing a forest that stretched to the shores of the reservoir. Any open land was behind her house and up the road toward Grace's— Dylan McCaffrey's—house.

"Snow's almost gone," her father said, then sighed, turning back to his elder daughter. "This place is in the middle of nowhere, Liv, even by Knights Bridge standards. Do you really think people will come out here?"

"I do, Dad. No question in my mind."

"Maybe your sister can be your guinea pig."

Olivia almost dropped her rake. "She and Mark have set a wedding date?"

"No. She's waiting for him to come up with a ring. She's a romantic, but Mark…" Randy Frost ran a callused palm over his salt-and-pepper hair. "None of my business."

Olivia had graduated high school with Mark. She remembered him sleeping in the back of algebra class, but he'd gone on to become an architect. After ten years going to school and working in Boston and New York, he moved back to Knights Bridge a year ago and had no interest in living anywhere else ever again.

"If Jess had wanted a Byron-esque soul," Olivia said, "she and Mark Flanagan wouldn't be together. He's a great guy, though."

"Yeah. I guess. What have you been raking?"

"The herb beds. The lavender survived the winter. It's in a warm spot by the back door. I've decided to host a mother-daughter tea as a way to kick things off and get out the word that The Farm at Carriage Hill is up and running."

"Your mother told me. She says she and Jess are coming. You're not asking for money?"

"Right. It'll be like an open house."

"Makes sense. Then your guests can go home and decide to book their own event."

"I'll have meals catered and focus on smaller events at first—teas, bridal and baby showers, meetings."

Her father studied her a moment. "You sound excited. That's good."

"I've been dreaming about transforming this place ever since I learned it was up for sale. It's happening faster than I expected, but so far, so good."

"I don't have to tell you it'll be a lot of hard work. What kind of food are you offering?"

"I thought I'd base the menu on herbs."

"Herbal hors d'oeuvres, herbal bread, herbal soup, herbal dessert? Like that?"

Olivia grinned. "Yeah. Like that. People can wander in the gardens and woods, and I'll offer books and lectures on various aspects of herbs—cooking, drying, using them in potpourris and fragrances." She grabbed her rake and flipped it on end, pulling off wet leaves stuck on the metal tines. "I have lots of ideas. Right now I'm concentrating on cleaning out the gardens. You're staying for lunch, right? I thought Mom was coming, too."

"She's home planning her trip to California. She wants to do the coastal highway."

"Sounds beautiful."

"She'll never go, but don't tell her I said that." He seemed to give himself a mental shake and nodded toward the house. "How's Buster?"

"Staying. He refused to be persuaded not to dig up the lavender." Olivia was relieved at the change in subject. Buster, a large mix of German shepherd and who-knew-what-else, had shown up at her house unaccompanied by owner, collar or leash, and for the past ten days had gone unclaimed. "I was thinking in terms of getting a friendlier dog. A golden retriever or a chocolate Lab, maybe. Buster looks like he could chew someone's leg off."

"Good. Keep Buster. I'll feel better about you living out here alone."

She felt her father scrutinizing her again as she set the rake against the garage. "I should have worn gloves. My hands are cold, and they've taken a beating since I moved out of the city."

"It's only been a couple weeks. You got enough

money in the bank, Liv? You're not betting everything on this place, are you?"

"I have time to make it work before I go broke."

"A business plan?"

Sort of. She didn't like discussing her finances with anyone, including her well-intentioned father. She smiled at him as she headed for the kitchen door. "Blood, sweat, laughter and tears. How's that for a business plan?"

"Liv—"

"I'm still freelancing. Jacqui Ackerman gives me as much work as I can handle." Olivia pulled open the door. "Come on in. Lunch is ready."

"Where's Buster?"

"Cooling his heels in the mudroom. You're safe."

Not, clearly, that her father was worried. Olivia led him into the kitchen. She had set the table for three and felt a pang of disappointment and frustration that her mother had bailed on lunch. She probably *was* home planning her trip, but if she couldn't get herself out here for a visit, how was she going to get herself to California? After two weeks back in Knights Bridge, Olivia still hadn't seen a sign of her mother on her doorstep. So far, any contact was at the mill, her parents' house or her mother's usual haunts in the village.

Olivia watched as her father quietly stacked up the extra place setting and set it on the butcher-block island. Randy and Louise Frost had known each other since kindergarten and had been married for thirty-two years. Olivia was confident that whatever was going on between them—if anything—would sort itself out. After her experience with Marilyn Bryson, Olivia was resisting the temptation to help anyone, much less her parents. She was essentially working two jobs as it was with her freelancing and her efforts to turn her house into The Farm at Carriage Hill.

"What's that, Liv?" her father asked, pointing at the pot of soup simmering on the gas stove.

"Parsnip, turnip and apple soup."

"Ah."

"It's seasoned with a dash of nutmeg. I have chopped fresh parsley and grated Parmesan cheese for garnish. It sounds festive, don't you think?"

He picked up a wooden spoon and dipped it into the pot. "Sure, Liv. I'm game."

"I'm experimenting with different recipes."

He tasted the soup and set the spoon down. "Let's see what it tastes like with the parsley and Parmesan."

Olivia laughed. "That bad, is it?"

The parsley and Parmesan helped, but not enough. The soup was a little...earthy. Her father helped himself to two hunks of warm oatmeal bread, although he passed on the rosemary jam. "It's got cranberries in it," Olivia said. "I made it myself."

"All right. I'll try a little. For you, Liv."

She grinned at him. "Thanks, Dad. You're my test case."

"Guinea pig, you mean." He tried the jam and nodded. "Not bad. If you call it rosemary-cranberry jam, it won't sound like something out of a feedbag."

"Good point. I'll do that."

He made no protest about dessert, old-fashioned molasses cookies made from his mother's—Olivia's grandmother's—recipe. He took a cookie with him as he stood up from the table. "Let's have a look at your backyard now that the snow's melted," he said.

He'd been through the house last fall, after she'd said she was seriously considering buying it, but not since she'd moved in. He'd inspected the center chimney, the wiring, the furnace, the hot-water heater, any signs of potential water damage. The previous owners had done most of the infrastructure repair and renovation, allowing Olivia to focus on cosmetic changes and any adjustments to comply with local and state regulations in order to open up her house to the public. But the previous owners had thought of most of that, too, since they'd planned on starting their own bed-and-breakfast.

Buster barely stirred when they went out through the mudroom. Olivia left him inside. Her father wasn't one for gardens and yard work, but he nodded with approval at what she'd managed to accomplish in just two weeks. "It's a great spot, Liv," he said. "No trouble with wild animals wandering over here from Quabbin?"

"Not yet."

He pointed at the old stone wall that ran along the side of her property. "Beyond those woods are eighty thousand acres of wilderness. You're closest neighbor in that direction is miles and miles from here."

"I know, Dad. And my closest neighbor in the other direction is an old man from San Diego who hasn't done a thing to his property in two years."

Olivia didn't mention that she'd written to her absentee neighbor. When she and her father returned to the kitchen, Buster had knocked down the mudroom gate and was in the living room, asleep on the hearth in front of the low fire she had going.

"My kind of dog," Randy Frost said with a grin as he left.

He was on the road with cookies and soup for her

mother when she called. "Is your dad still there? There's freezing rain in the forecast. It's supposed to be bad."

"He just left." Olivia sat on the couch in front of the fire. "He'll be back before it starts."

"Right. Good." Her mother took an audible breath, obviously trying to control her anxiety. "How was lunch? Sorry to miss it, but some things came up here. I suggested we come tomorrow, but your dad—well, it doesn't matter. Did you have a good time?"

Her mother had been worried about the weather forecast, Olivia realized now. "Lunch was great. Dad didn't like my parsnip soup."

"But you got him to try it?" Her mother laughed. "That's an achievement right there. He doesn't always like to try new things." There was no hint of criticism in her tone. "I'll get out there, Liv. Soon. I want to help you with the place. Jess says you're raking and painting everything in sight. I can handle a rake and wield a paintbrush."

"That'd be great, Mom. I know you're busy planning your trip—"

"California," she interrupted, almost as if she were gulping. "I'm going. No matter what."

She made the trip—one she wanted to take—sound like an impending biopsy, but Olivia felt her own throat tighten at the prospect of her parents flying across the country. "I've seen pictures of California's Pacific Coast Highway. It looks beautiful."

"Yes. Right. I'll call you later, Liv. Be careful out there alone in this freezing rain."

"I will, Mom. I'm not that far from town, and I have Buster here with me."

"You've had the vet look at him? He could have worms—"

"Yes, and he got a clean bill of health."

"Your dad should be walking in the door any minute. Oh—I just looked out the window. I can see the ice forming on my car. Freezing rain is the worst."

"Do you want me to stay on with you until Dad gets there?"

"No, no. He'll be here any minute."

Her mother was close to hyperventilating as she hung up. Olivia took a breath, suddenly feeling anxious and unsettled herself. She jumped up from the couch and went into the kitchen. The freezing rain had ended her raking for the day. She'd clean up the lunch dishes and work on a design project.

She stood at the sink and noticed the raindrops on the window, the glistening film of clear ice on the grass, the gray mist swirling in the woods.

The house was so quiet.

"Buster," she said. "Buster, where are you?"

She checked the living room, but he was no longer asleep by the fire. She checked the cellar door, in case she'd left it open and he'd gone down there, but it was shut tight.

She called him again, but received only silence in return as she headed back to the kitchen.

She felt a cold draft and went into the mudroom.

The door was ajar.

She grimaced. "Damn."

Buster was gone, and she was going to have to go out into the freezing rain to find him.

Less than an hour after arriving in little Knights Bridge, Dylan found himself up to his calves in a patch of snow and mud next to a rusted, cast-off refrigerator and face-to-face with one seriously mean-looking dog.

The dog had bounded out of the trees as if he'd been lying in wait, planning his attack on the unsuspecting new arrival to his quiet country road. His wild barking had subsided to intermittent growls.

"Easy, pal," Dylan said. "Easy."

Olivia Frost had to be the dog's owner. Hers was the closest house; in fact, from what Dylan had seen, it was the only other house in the immediate vicinity. Freezing rain was coating everything in a film of clear ice. Prickly vines, pine needles, bare tree branches, exposed grass, last year's dropped leaves. The old fridge. The mean dog. Dylan.

"You should go home." Dylan pointed in the direction of The Farm at Carriage Hill. "Go. Go home."

The dog barked once, growled and didn't budge.

Dylan debated his options, none of them good. The freezing rain showed no sign of letting up. He was trapped out here in the middle of nowhere until it did. His flight from San Diego had been long but unremarkable, putting him in Boston late yesterday. He'd stayed with a hockey player friend, Alec Wiskovich, a Russian who had passed muster with Boston's discerning fans as a forward with the Bruins. Alec had never heard of Knights Bridge, either. Dylan rented a car in the morning, typed "Knights Bridge" into the GPS system and went on his way.

Whether it was jet lag, the freezing rain, the mean dog or thinking about his father, he felt at least slightly out of his mind. If he were sane, he thought, he would indeed have sent Loretta to deal with Olivia Frost instead of coming himself. He was a busy man. He could afford to pay someone to sort out a misunderstanding about an old house and junk in the yard.

"Buster!"

It was a woman's voice. Keeping the dog in the corner of his eye, Dylan shifted his gaze slightly and peered through the mist and rain at the one-lane road. The many potholes were filling with water and ice, but he didn't see anyone else out there.

"Buster!" the woman again called. "Buster, where are you?"

Dylan turned back to the dog. "You must be Buster."

A note of panic had crept into the woman's voice. Maybe with good reason, Dylan thought, noting that the dog was on alert, his head jerking up at the sound of her voice. She was probably less worried about Buster getting hurt than doing the hurting, although who she thought might be out here was a mystery.

Well. Dylan grimaced. *He* was. But he hadn't told her he was coming.

A slim figure materialized around a slight curve in the road.

Olivia Frost. Had to be. She was hatless and coatless, as if she'd bolted out of her house in a hurry—probably when she realized her dog was missing. Dylan wasn't wearing a hat or gloves but he had on a canvas three-quarter-length coat.

As she stepped off the road into the patches of snow and soaked, cold, muddy brown leaves, the big dog again became agitated, snarling and growling.

Dylan figured he had seconds to live unless he thought fast.

He put up his hand in front of him in a calm but assertive gesture that stopped any advance the growling dog had in mind, then called to the woman. "Buster is right here."

"So I see," she said, coming closer, freezing rain visible on her dark hair.

"He and I just met. He seemed surprised to find anyone here."

Olivia came to an abrupt stop. She was obviously surprised to find him there, too. Up close, Dylan could see her eyes were definitely hazel, and even prettier than in the photographs Loretta had sent him. Incredible eyes, really, with their deep blues and greens and flecks of gold. Maybe they stood out because of the bleak surroundings, or maybe because he was just happy to have survived his first hour in Knights Bridge.

She frowned at him as her dog trotted to her side. "Did you decide to pull off the road and wait out the freezing rain?"

"No, although it sounds like a good idea." With Buster visibly calmer, Dylan dared to lower his hand. "I'm your neighbor. You wrote to me about the junk in the yard."

"*You're* Dylan McCaffrey?"

"I am."

"I'm Olivia Frost. I thought—" Her frown deepened as her eyes narrowed on him. As cold as she had to be in her black corduroy shirt and jeans, she wasn't shivering. "Are you sure you're the right Dylan McCaffrey? I didn't get in touch with the wrong one? You own this place?"

"Right McCaffrey, and yes, I own this place."

He was obviously not even close to what his Knights Bridge neighbor had expected. Buster growled next to her. She made a little motion with her fingers and he quieted. She recovered her composure and nodded to the refrigerator in the muck. "Then you'll be cleaning up this mess. Excellent. It's turned into quite a junkyard, hasn't it?"

"No argument from me."

He glanced at the mess behind him. The cast-off washing machine was farther up the slope, in more prickly vines. Between it and the fridge were tires, hubcaps, a rotting rake with missing tines, bottles, beer cans and—oddly—what was left of a disintegrating twin mattress.

"There was never a report of a break-in," Olivia said. "We suspect kids partied out here and got carried away."

"Hell of a place to party."

She seemed to take no offense at his comment. "As I explained in my note, I live just down the road."

"The Farm at Carriage Hill," Dylan said with a smile.

"More like The Soon-to-be Farm at Carriage Hill." She brushed raindrops off the end of her nose, then motioned vaguely up the tree-lined road, toward the village. "My family lives in town. They'll be checking on me with this nasty weather. It's not as remote out here as you might think. People come by at all hours."

Dylan realized her comment was a warning—a self-protective measure, given that the two of them were the only ones out on the isolated road. He didn't want to unnerve her, but he didn't think he looked particularly threatening standing there in the mud, mist and freezing rain, especially when she was the one with the big dog.

Nonetheless, he made an effort to give her an innocuous smile. "You're lucky to have family close by in this weather."

She returned his smile. "Spring can't come soon

enough, can it? As I mentioned in my note, I can help with the yard if you need it." She glanced at his rented Audi parked on the partially washed-out driveway, then shifted back to him. "I also have access to a truck."

"Good to know."

"I should get Buster back to the house. You're not..." Olivia grabbed her dog's collar. "I thought you'd be older."

"You were expecting my father, Duncan McCaffrey," Dylan said, figuring it was a good guess. "He died a few months after he bought this place. I didn't know about the property and didn't realize he'd left it to me until I received your note."

"Really? How could you not know?"

"Long story. You're not wearing a coat. Why don't you take mine? You don't want to get hypothermia—"

"I'll be fine. Thanks, though."

"Are you sure you don't want to come inside and dry off? Looks as if I won't be going anywhere for a while."

"That's nice of you to offer, but Buster and I will be on our way. He's not good with strangers."

Another warning, Dylan decided as he watched Olivia turn with her badass dog and head through the ice-covered patches of grass, snow, dead leaves, mud and muck. He noticed she was wearing close-fitting jeans and had mud splattered on her butt and the backs of her thighs. She must have tripped or stumbled in the freezing conditions while chasing Buster up the road.

It was sunny and seventy-five degrees when Dylan had left Coronado yesterday.

He hadn't been kidding; he wasn't going anywhere until the weather cleared, and he certainly wasn't hauling junk. He didn't entirely understand Olivia Frost's fuss over her neighbor's makeshift dump and over-grown yard. Her place wasn't visible through the trees. It wasn't as if she were right next door. Managing not to slip, he made his way to his nondescript little New England house. Loretta had given him the keys. He'd done a quick walk-through already. The front door was on the left side of a roofed porch and opened into an entry with green-carpeted stairs leading up to three small bedrooms and one bathroom on the second floor. To the right of the front door on the first floor was a living room with tall windows and a double doorway to an adjoining dining room with a bay window over-looking the side yard opposite the spot with the junk.

Off the dining room was the kitchen, with doors to the cellar and backyard.

That was it.

The house was modestly furnished with a couch, a cupboard, a dining room table and chairs, and old player piano. Bookcases upstairs and in the dining room were filled, but otherwise, there were no personal belong-ings. It was as if Grace Webster had left behind what-ever she couldn't find room for in her new residence or just didn't want or need.

Dylan flipped a switch on a dusty overhead in the living room.

The power was out.

He sighed. "Great."

Naturally the house didn't have a landline, and he couldn't pick up a signal on his cell phone. He glanced out the front window and saw the power lines were drooping with the ice that had formed on them.

What about his neighbor? The power had to be out at her place, too.

Dylan wondered if he should check on her. Small towns looked after their own, didn't they?

Olivia Frost's family and friends wouldn't be able to get out here. No one and nothing would be moving in these conditions.

Dylan buttoned his jacket and stepped back out to the porch. As far as he could tell, the precipitation was still freezing rain—it fell as rain and landed as ice, creating treacherous "black ice" conditions.

"Miserable," he said, pulling up the collar to his jacket as he ventured down the slippery porch steps.

Slipping and sliding, Dylan made his way down the road to The Farm at Carriage Hill. Clear ice and a film of rainwater covered everything, including the sand that was supposed to help with traction.

He heard a branch snap somewhere in the woods, then nothing.

The silence was downright eerie.

He reminded himself he liked ice. He had been a natural on skates. These weren't rink conditions, but he was good at keeping his balance, or so he told himself as he considered that if he fell, he was on his own. No one would find him.

Unless Buster sneaked out again, he thought with a grim smile, pressing on.

Smoke was curling out of the chimney of his only neighbor's cream-colored house. An ice-and-rain-coated walk took him to a wide stone landing, and he knocked on the front door, painted a rich blue. There was another door to his right, to a newer addition. This was obviously the oldest part of the house.

"Miss Frost?" he called. "It's Dylan McCaffrey."

She opened the door. Her hair was still damp, and her cheeks were pink from the cold—or warmth, Dylan realized suddenly. Even from his position on the landing, he could tell that her house was toasty. She obviously had a fireplace or woodstove going. Hence, the smoke coming out of the chimney.

With his dripping coat and wet, muddy pants and shoes, he felt marginally ridiculous coming to her aid. It probably should have been the other way around. He was the unprepared stranger.

"I thought I'd check on you," he said. "The power's out at my place."

"Here, too. I called the power company and notified them. Power's out all over town. We'll be among the last to get it restored."

"The power company doesn't like you?"

He was joking but Olivia gave him a cool look. "We're on a sparsely populated dead-end road."

"It's just the two of us out here in the sticks?"

"I have my dog," she said.

"Buster. He's—"

"Asleep out by the fire at the moment. It wouldn't take much to wake him."

Dylan wondered if his presence was making Olivia nervous. That wasn't his intention, but he could be thickheaded at times, or so Noah Kendrick, various hockey coaches, teammates and an assortment of women had told him. Often.

He attempted to look amiable and easygoing, not half frozen, hungry and out of his element. "If you need anything, I'm right up the road in the cold and the dark."

"You weren't expecting to spend the night in Knights Bridge, were you?"

"I thought I'd figure that out once I got here. I wasn't counting on an ice storm."

"Do you have food? I have homemade parsnip soup and oatmeal bread from lunch that I'd be happy to send back with you."

Parsnip soup. He felt a fat, cold raindrop splatter on the back of his neck. "Thanks, but I brought some basic provisions with me, just in case."

"I remember Miss Webster had a woodstove. Did she leave it behind?"

He hadn't even considered a woodstove. "It's in the dining room."

"You'll want to check to make sure a bat or a squirrel hasn't taken up residence in the chimney." Olivia leaned out of her warm house and pointed a slender finger vaguely in the direction of her garage. "You can help yourself to some dry wood if you'd like."

Dylan figured he would only be able to carry enough for a few hours' fire. There wasn't much point. At the rate he was going, he'd die of hypothermia before he reached his house, anyway.

It was only a slight exaggeration.

He thanked his neighbor and noticed she didn't press him to take wood or offer him a spare bedroom. "Thanks for stopping by," she said politely, then shut the door quietly behind him.

He half skated back to the road, which was even more treacherous. What had his father been thinking, buying a house in this backwater little town? There couldn't be lost treasure in Knights Bridge, or even clues to lost treasure. Impossible.

Then again, Duncan McCaffrey had been a man who relished taking on the impossible.

When Dylan arrived back at his inherited house, he examined the woodstove that was hooked up in a corner in the dining room. It looked like an oil drum. It couldn't be that efficient, but it was better than a cold night in the dark. He found dry wood in an old apple crate in the kitchen and hit the stovepipe chimney with a log to warn any critters before he lit matches.

He wasn't worried about a buildup of creosote. If the house burned down, so what?

The wood was dry enough that he needed little kindling and only one match to get the fire started. As the flames took hold, he checked his cell phone and walked around the house until he got a weak signal by the back door.

He dialed Noah in San Diego. "Tell me there's been an emergency and you need me back there," Dylan said.

"All's well. What's happening in New England?"

"Freezing rain. No heat, no electricity. I've turned into Bob Cratchit."

"What's the house like?"

"It's a dump."

"Have you met Olivia Frost?"

"I have." Dylan pictured her pink cheeks and hazel eyes. "She's warm. I wonder if she has a generator."

"Not sharing her heat?"

It wasn't a bad quip for Noah, who wasn't known for that particular variety of verbal quickness. "She offered me cordwood. I'm not going anywhere for a while. We're in the middle of an ice storm."

Noah burst out laughing.

Their call got dropped just as the ceiling in the kitchen started to leak.

Dylan slid his phone back in his pocket and watched water pool on the wide-plank floor.

"Well, hell."

What could he do? He was stuck here.

He hoped Grace Webster had left behind a bucket.

Chapter 4

Olivia's house had come with a generator for nights just such as this one, but she only turned it on for an hour before she decided to wait out the power outage. She had little food to worry about spoiling, and she didn't like generators. In storms, people too often misused them and died of carbon monoxide poisoning. She had dutifully read all the instructions and had her father do a dry run with her, but the thing still made her nervous. She wanted to be positive she knew what she was doing before she ran it for any length of time.

As she snuggled under a soft wool throw in front of the brick fireplace, she told herself it was decent of Dylan McCaffrey to check on her. He hadn't meant anything by his visit except to make sure she was all right in the midst of a nasty ice storm.

The wind picked up, and a spruce tree swayed outside the front window, casting strange shadows in the living room. She heard the crack of a branch breaking off in the old sugar maple in the side yard. Right now, the branches and power lines were weighed down with ice, but once the temperature rose above freezing, the ice would melt as if it had never been. Spring would resume its steady march toward daffodils, tulips and lilacs in bloom.

The fire glowed, the only light in the darkening room. A chunk of burning wood fell from the grate, startling her, but she quickly told herself it was nothing. She had lived alone in her Boston apartment, but she had to admit that living alone in her antique house in Knights Bridge was taking some getting used to. The creaks, the groans, the shadows, the dark nights— anything could fire up her imagination. At first, she'd slept with her iPod on, playing a selection of relaxing music, but she was beginning to develop a routine and was getting used to the sounds of the old house and country road.

Tightening her throw around her, she turned her attention back to her neighbor. Elly O'Dunn must have run into Duncan McCaffrey, Dylan's father. When Olivia had written to Dylan, she hadn't expected him to show up in Knights Bridge, and she certainly hadn't expected to meet him the way she had, muddy, yelling in panic for her wandering dog.

She especially hadn't expected the new owner of Grace Webster's house to be a man close to her own age, with a sexy grin, sexy broad shoulders and sexy black-lashed deep blue eyes.

The McCaffreys had no ties to Knights Bridge that Olivia knew of. Because of the massive Quabbin Reservoir, her hometown was out-of-the-way, not an easy commute to any of the major cities in Massachusetts. The University of Massachusetts Amherst, Mount Holyoke College, Hampshire College, Smith College and Amherst College—the Five Colleges—were a more reasonable commute. A number of people from town worked at the different schools. She had no idea what Dylan McCaffrey did for a living but supposed he could be a college professor.

She pictured him standing in the snow and mud.

He wasn't a college professor. She knew some rugged-looking professors, but Dylan McCaffrey didn't strike her as someone who could sit in a library carrel for more than ten minutes before he needed to get moving.

Olivia heard a gust of wind beat against the windows. The truth was, she hadn't given her neighbor much thought once she wrote to him. She just wanted his place cleaned up. She had so much to do before her mother-daughter tea. She swore she had lists of lists of things to do to get ready.

She wished the power would come back on before nightfall. She didn't look forward to sitting there in the pitch-dark.

Her landline rang, startling her. Buster barked but settled down, spent from his romp up the road. She reached for the phone on an end table, a flea-market find that she planned to paint. It was on one of her lists, she thought as she picked up and said hello.

"Hey, kid," her father said. "You and Buster okay out there? Everything's at a standstill but we'll be through the worst of it soon."

He didn't sound concerned, and Olivia assumed that

her mother had put him up to calling. "The power's out but we're fine here."

"Are you using the generator?"

"I did for a while but not right now. It's okay. Buster and I are nice and cozy by the fire."

"Cozy. Right. If you need anything, call. I'll find a way out there."

He would, too. Olivia debated a moment, then said, "My neighbor's here."

"Neighbor?"

"Dylan McCaffrey. He's the guy who owns Grace Webster's old place."

"I thought he was dead."

"You did? I should have asked you about him. That was his father."

"I met him a couple of years ago. Ran into him at Hazelton's." Hazelton's was the general store in the village. "I didn't ask why he wanted to buy a house in town. Why's his son here?"

"I wrote to him about the junk in his yard. He lives in San Diego. I didn't expect him to actually come out here. I offered to do the work. I figured he'd jump at the chance since no one's touched the place in two years."

There was a moment's silence on the other end of the phone. "I hope he doesn't mind freezing rain," her father said finally.

After she hung up, Olivia got out a sketch pad and colored pencils and, curled up in front of the fire, worked on a color scheme for the interior of her house. She had narrowed down her choices to three different palettes. For each, she drew a large rectangle, then drew smaller rectangles of various sizes inside it. She filled in the large rectangle with her main color and the smaller rectangles with secondary colors and accents. She had decided against a traditional New England look, as much as she loved it. She wasn't sure exactly what colors she wanted, but she definitely wanted a palette that was lively, vibrant and welcoming, with a touch of rustic charm.

Intrigued by the play of the flames in the fading natural light, she chose a golden yellow lightened with white for her first large rectangle. For the smaller rectangles, she used two shades of aquamarine, a watery blue, a creamy linen, a splash of red. She wanted to choose colors and paint finishes that worked with the sharp differences in New England seasons—from the frigid temperatures of winter to the hot, humid conditions of the dog days of summer. She would have to pay attention to the orientation of her different rooms. An eastern room that received the cool light of morning might need a different shade or tone than a western room that received strong afternoon light.

Buster rolled over, his back to Olivia, as if to tell her how boring he thought paint palettes were. She stayed in front of the fire and continued working. As darkness descended, she liked having him there, close to her, rather than in the kitchen or locked up in the mudroom. Soon the fire provided the only light in the house. She hadn't lit any candles or turned on her flashlight. She put away her colored pencils and left them and the sketch pad on the floor.

The power still hadn't come on.

More trees creaked and groaned in the wind. The fire flared in a backdraft in the chimney. She shuddered, a ripple of irrational fear running up her spine. She had locked the front door after Dylan had left and was positive she had already locked the other doors. She *knew* no one was in the kitchen and mudroom, or in the garage—or hiding upstairs.

She dreaded turning on her small flashlight and walking up to her bedroom.

"What's the matter with you?" she asked aloud. "Nothing's up there with the power off that isn't there with the power on."

The living room glowed in a flash of lightning followed by a rumble of thunder.

It was an *ice* storm. Why was there thunder and lightning?

Never mind, Olivia thought, grabbing another throw off a chair. She wasn't going anywhere. She curled up with the two throws on the thick rug in front of the fire, staying close to warm, mean-looking Buster. She had no reason to be afraid alone in her country house, but the occasional bump in the night nonetheless could get her heart racing and her mind spinning with possibilities.

She wondered how Dylan McCaffrey was doing up the road. Grace's house wasn't in good shape, especially after sitting empty for so long. People in town speculated that the new owner had bought it for the land, not for the house itself. After receiving the note about the yard, had Dylan decided to head east to check out his newly discovered inheritance and put it on the market? Olivia would love to have the seven acres to add to The Farm at Carriage Hill, but she couldn't afford them right now and had her hands full getting her own house in shape.

Wrapped up in her warm throws, she noticed the wind was dying down and the one flash of lightning and rumble of thunder seemed to be all the storm had in mind. The power didn't come back on, but she suspected it would soon now that the weather was improving.

She grabbed a pillow off the couch and placed it under her head. She doubted Grace had left behind blankets and sheets, never mind a bed, or if she had that any of them were usable. Was Dylan sleeping on the floor, too? He probably hadn't planned to spend the night in a house on the verge of being condemned.

A run-down house, a yard filled with junk, a confrontation with a big dog, an ice storm and a power outage—not an auspicious first day in Knights Bridge. Olivia shut her eyes, imagining what her neighbor thought of her hometown and if he'd be there in another twenty-four hours.

The power came back on just after two in the morning, the floor lamp popping on, the refrigerator cranking into gear, startling Olivia out of a deep sleep. She left the lamp on, letting the glow of the low-wattage bulb settle her heartbeat. She didn't go upstairs to bed and instead stayed under her throws. Buster got up and stretched as if he thought it was morning, then settled down again in front of the fire, just a few hot coals now.

By morning, the sun was shining and any ice from the storm had already melted. That, Olivia reminded herself, was one of the key differences between early spring and the dead of winter. In winter, the ice would still be there, with more on the way. She could safely hope that last night was the end of any freezing precipitation in her part of New England until next winter.

She switched off any lights that didn't need to be on and went upstairs to shower and get dressed, figuring she'd head into the village after breakfast. The house, although not large, felt huge in comparison to her apartment in Boston. Back downstairs, she made coffee and toasted some of her oatmeal bread, spreading it with peanut butter. She ate at her table overlooking the herb gardens. Even without checking her palettes from last night, she knew she'd reject the watery colors. She wanted earthy colors that still felt light, inviting, vibrant.

Picking out colors, she thought, was the fun part of opening The Farm at Carriage Hill. The uncertainties and the sheer amount of work that needed to be done were the hard parts.

She finished her toast and coffee and cleaned up the kitchen, wondering what her neighbor was doing for breakfast. She watered her rapidly growing herbs and decided that Dylan McCaffrey was perfectly capable of looking after himself. The roads were clear. He could get out now, and Knights Bridge had a restaurant, run by family friends, that served a great breakfast.

If he wanted her help, he'd ask.

She walked Buster and left him in the mudroom with his bed and bowls of food and water. She didn't put up the gate. He seemed calmer, more at home. "Back soon, my friend," she said, and headed outside. The air was sharply colder than yesterday, but it'd warm up to the fifties by midafternoon—another difference between winter and spring.

She started her car, a Subaru in serious need of body work, and turned onto the road.

When she came to the Webster house, Olivia noticed Dylan's Audi—undoubtedly a rental—was still there. A rivulet of rainwater was running down a split in the

dirt driveway. A massive, overgrown forsythia, however, was about to burst into yellow blossoms, a telltale
sign of spring in New England.

Which also meant her opening day mother-daughter tea was getting closer, and she had much to do before it arrived.

She was surprised to see Dylan down by Grace's old
mailbox at the bottom of the driveway. He had a long-
handled shovel and stood it up, leaning into it as Olivia
braked and rolled down her passenger window.

"Morning," he said. "Quite an ice storm last night."

"We're lucky the temperature rose as fast as it did.
Everything all right here?"

"Just fine. The driveway didn't wash out into the
road. The leak in the kitchen stopped. Life is good."
There was only the slightest trace of sarcasm in his
tone as he picked up a take-out coffee he had set atop
the crooked mailbox. "I've already been out for breakfast. Nice little restaurant in town. I suppose you know
the owner."

"The Smiths. Sure. I'll tell them you liked your
breakfast."

Olivia watched him sip the coffee. Even in sunlight,
without the adrenaline of yesterday's storm, her missing
dog and the surprise of discovering Dylan McCaffrey
wasn't in his seventies, she still found him incredibly
sexy. She probably should have just waved on her way
past him.

"I see you found a shovel," she said.

He set his coffee back atop the mailbox. "It was in
the kitchen, interestingly. I'm not even going to try to
guess why. The drainage culvert down here got filled
up with leaves and ice, and the water was diverting

onto the road. I figured I'd dig it out." He picked up the shovel again, his eyes on her as he smiled. "Then I'll get the junk removed."

"I have to run out for a little while, but I can help when I get back. Feel free to check my garage for any tools or materials you might need. It's unlocked. There might be work gloves in there that would fit you."

"Good to know."

His tone suggested he hadn't considered work gloves. Although he was from Southern California, the chilly morning temperature and stiff breeze didn't seem to bother him.

Olivia suppressed a shiver when the cold air coming in the open window overtook the warm air blowing out of her car heater. "You aren't planning to do all this work yourself, are you?"

He stabbed the tip of the shovel into the gravel and squinted at her in the bright sunlight. "Not if I can help it."

Maybe, she thought, she should mind her own business. "I'll leave you to it."

"Where's Buster?"

"Who knows. I threw caution to the wind and let him have the run of the house instead of locking him in the mudroom."

Dylan's deep blue gaze settled on her. "Is that fair warning?"

Olivia laughed. "If you want to look at it that way."

She rolled up her window and continued into the village and on to Frost Millworks, located on a wide, rock-strewn brook. The building was just ten years old and occupied a section of flat land above the brook, its exterior designed to fit with the rustic surroundings, its interior modern. Jess lived in an apartment in the original nineteenth-century sawmill overlooking the rock dam and millpond. It was one of the few surviving sawmills that had once dotted the streams and rivers of the region. As kids, Olivia and her sister used to swim in the millpond. The water was clear, clean and ice-cold, even on a hot August afternoon. They'd grown up a half mile down the road in the same house where their parents still lived.

By the time Olivia parked in the small lot, she had decided she didn't have the whole story about Dylan McCaffrey and his intentions in Knights Bridge. Whatever they were, her reaction to him was perfectly normal. He *was* sexy, and there was no point in denying otherwise, at least to herself. His presence up the road from her was her doing, and if he complicated her life, it was her own fault.

She found her mother at her cluttered rolltop desk in the office just inside the mill entrance. Louise Frost smiled brightly at her elder daughter. "How's your road?"

"Not a problem, except for the potholes. They're brutal this year."

"Do you keep a bag of sand in your trunk, just in case?"

Olivia shook her head. "I figure I can always call you or Dad if I get stuck."

"That's true, but sand makes sense."

Her mother stood up from the desk. At five-five, she was shorter than either of her daughters. She worked out most days and was in good shape, wearing a fleece vest over a thick turquoise corduroy shirt, jeans and mud boots. She had dyed her hair auburn about five years ago and kept it cut short and, with her green eyes and round face, reminded Olivia of her younger sister. She tended to favor their father.

She peered at a new photograph taped to the top edge of the antique desk, this one of palm trees, sandy beach and ocean. It joined a dozen others her mother had printed off the internet of the famous 123-mile Pacific Coast Highway in central California: Monterey, Carmel-by-the-Sea, San Simeon, Cambria, Morro Rock, sea otters, sunsets, surf crashing on sheer rock cliffs.

"That's the beach in Santa Barbara," her mother said.

"It's beautiful."

"We're going to fly into Los Angeles and spend the night in Beverly Hills or Malibu, then head up to Santa Barbara for at least one night. I'm investigating hotels and inns. I haven't made reservations yet. I'd do a bed-and-breakfast, but I don't think your father would like it."

Olivia smiled. "You could try. It'd only be a couple nights, right?"

Her mother nodded, staring at the pictures on her desk. "They say driving south-to-north isn't as unnerving with the cliffs and water as north-to-south, but people do both. Driving south you hug the coast. You see more, I guess. I think we'll see plenty."

"Are you going as far as San Francisco?"

"I think so. It depends on how much time we have." She shifted from the photographs to a map of California she had tacked to the wall, with pushpins marking various stops she wanted to make. She seemed transfixed, then took a slow, deep breath and turned to Olivia, obviously forcing a smile. "It'll be fun. I can't wait."

"When do you leave?"

"We haven't set a date yet. Depends on the work here. Your father is overdue for a vacation."

"You are, too," Olivia said.

"I suppose. I started dreaming about this trip a few years ago when we did the custom windows for that house in Carmel. Remember, Liv? It was outside our usual area, but the family used to live in Boston and knew about us. They sent pictures…" She sighed, standing back from the desk. "It's beautiful here. I don't want to live anywhere else, but I knew I had to go to California, see this part of our country."

"Good for you, Mom."

"Yeah." She seemed a little shaken, as if she'd said too much. "Thanks."

Olivia heard the main door open. In another moment, Jess appeared in the office doorway, tightening the belt to her tan raincoat. "I'm on my way to Boston and thought I'd stop in. I'm meeting with clients. Want to come, Mom?"

"I should mind things here."

"It's quiet today. There's nothing to mind—"

"There's always something. I'm never bored."

"You haven't been out of town in weeks," Jess said, impatient. "It'd do you good."

"I have plans, Jess."

Olivia could see their mother wasn't about to budge and would only get her back up and go on the defensive if Jess kept pushing her. "I'm heading over to see Grandma. Care to join me?"

"You go, Liv," her mother said, dropping back to her chair at her desk. "Tell your grandma I said hi. We're having her out to the house this weekend. I'm doing a Sunday dinner for a change. You two will both be here?"

"Of course, Mom," Jess said with a sigh, then left.

Louise Frost stared at the spot her younger daughter had vacated, then finally said, half under her breath, that she needed to get to work and started tapping keys on her computer. Olivia said goodbye and headed back out.

She found her sister standing on the rock wall at the edge of the millpond. "You can't enable her, Liv." Jess shoved her hands in her coat pockets and watched the rushing water, high with the spring runoff and yesterday's rain. "It won't help."

"Arguing with her isn't going to change anything."

"What will? Medication? Therapy? Some herbal potion?"

"There are a number of herbs that can help alleviate anxiety, but she has to want to do something about it."

"Planning a trip she'll never take…"

"Maybe she will take it," Olivia said.

"Dad doesn't think so. It's pathetic, Liv. She didn't used to be this bad."

Olivia watched a dead leaf float over the small dam into the rushing stream below. "I think she's trying, Jess."

Jess didn't respond at once. The only sound was the rush of the water over the old dam. "I'm worried I'm catching it," she said finally.

"Catching what, Jess?"

"Mom's anxiety. I woke up last night in a sweat and couldn't go back to sleep. I was ready to jump out of my skin. The power was out…." She pulled her hands out of her pockets and raked her fingers through her hair. "I turned on a flashlight and just sat there, trying to calm myself."

"The weather was nasty."

"Freezing rain, clouds, fog, darker than the pits of hell…" Jess shuddered. "I felt closed in. I couldn't breathe."

"We're all feeling closed in after the long winter. Green grass and daffodils will help. What about Mark? Was he—"

"He wasn't here. He never stays past sunup. We're old-fashioned that way, with Mom and Dad right up the road, working here." She squatted down suddenly, picked up a stone and flung it into the millpond as she stood again, the ripples spreading across the clear, coppery water to the opposite bank. "What if I was freaked out at the prospect of going to Boston today?"

"Did that run through your mind?"

"*Everything* ran through my mind."

"Who are you seeing in Boston?"

"The manager of a small law office in the North End that wants to redo the interior of their building, the owners of a house on Beacon Hill, a hole-in-the-wall library that specializes in early New England history. It'll take all day."

"You're feeling the stress," Olivia said.

Her sister almost laughed. "I hope that's all it is. I hope I'm not…" She didn't finish. "There's so much I want to do, Liv. I don't want to be afraid to leave Knights Bridge. What about you? You won't fly."

Olivia averted her eyes. "I'll fly."

"Ha. You're not a good liar." Jess abandoned the subject and spun away from the dam. "Mom's driving us all crazy. She's driving Dad crazy, too, but he'll never admit it. Mark hasn't said anything but I know he's getting impatient."

"Jess, is anything going on between you two?"

"Nothing, no—" She stopped, turned back to Olivia. "I don't know. This California trip has taken on a life of its own. I sometimes wonder if Mark's waiting to see how it turns out, if he looks at Mom and sees me in twenty or thirty years. She's a mess, Liv. You haven't been around day to day. You haven't seen her."

"I know but I'm here now."

"We all are so busy. You, me, Mark, Dad, Mom. My hours have been insane since January. It's a sign business is good, which is terrific, but I have to do almost all the off-site client meetings. Dad does what he can, but he and the crew have their own work here. It doesn't make sense to hire someone just because Mom's gotten to the point she'll hardly go anywhere."

"Have you talked to them? Told them you're feeling overburdened?"

"Wouldn't do any good."

Her sister, Olivia realized, was in a mood to vent, not to work on solutions. "I can always help."

"You have your hands full as it is." Jess sighed, calmer. "It's going to be a long day."

"Why don't you stay in Boston and not kill yourself to get back here tonight? You can stay at my apartment. I have it until the end of the month. I left the couch. It's not bad to sleep on."

"That'd be great." Jess gave a wry smile. "What if I run into your friend Marilyn?"

"You won't run into her."

"I know she did something to you—"

"She looked after herself. That's what Marilyn Bryson does. Maybe we should, too."

They walked up to the parking lot together, the mill's handful of employees arriving for the day. Olivia noticed green shoots on the bank of the brook and remembered that her mother had planted a hundred daffodil bulbs there last fall, turning down help from anyone. She'd wanted to do the work herself.

Jess stopped at her truck, one hand on the driver's door as she squinted back at her older sister. "You love Boston, Liv. Are you sure you'll be happy living in Knights Bridge full-time?"

"So far, so good, Jess. Really. I'm fine."

"You have big plans for Carriage Hill. Between it and freelancing you're already working long hours. Unless you're very lucky or get some major backing, this first year's going to be tight financially and grueling in terms of workload. I can help—I want to—"

"You have your hands full with your work here." There was also whatever was going on with Jess and her almost-fiancé, Olivia thought. The last thing Jess needed right now was to worry about her sister. Olivia gave her a reassuring smile. "Don't worry about me, okay? I was ready to make a change or I wouldn't be here."

"Dad says Dylan McCaffrey's shown up. Your note about the mess in Grace's yard must have gotten to him."

"It's his yard now," Olivia amended.

"He reminded you of that, did he?"

"That's one old house that should be condemned," Mark Flanagan said, emerging from behind an SUV. He was angular and long legged, his dark blond hair cut short. He wore pricey jeans and a black windbreaker over a flannel shirt, his usual outfit even through a good chunk of summer. "There's no point in sinking money into trying to renovate it." He stood next to Jess. "Sorry. Didn't mean to eavesdrop."

"When did you get here?" Jess asked, regaining her composure.

"A few minutes ago, but I'm not staying. I just need to check on an order. I saw you two talking and figured I'd say hi."

She yanked open the door. "What were you doing, sneaking up on us?"

He gave Jess a mystified look. "You probably couldn't hear me over the water." He left it at that and turned to Olivia. "I ran into Dylan McCaffrey at breakfast this morning. I understand he's the new owner of Grace Webster's old house, but I can't believe he's staying there. That place is a dump. I'm not sure it's even safe there."

For no reason that could possibly make sense to her, Olivia felt her cheeks flame. "He looked alive and well an hour ago. He was digging out a drain, and the house was still standing."

"What's he doing here?" Mark asked.

Jess either hadn't noticed his mystified look or was pretending she hadn't. "Olivia wrote to him."

Mark raised his eyebrows at Olivia. "You wrote to him? Why?"

"I asked him to clean up the yard," she said, trying not to sound defensive. "It's an eyesore. It sends a bad message to people passing by—"

"What people passing by?" Mark asked, amused.

"No one now, but I am opening a business. My clientele will want a picturesque country setting. They won't want to go by rusted appliances and cast-off mattresses."

"Relax, Liv," Mark said. "People who want to eat chive soup won't mind passing the Webster place. You can tell them it's authentic country."

"Not funny, Mark," Olivia said good-naturedly as he continued across the parking lot to the mill entrance. "Not funny at all. And it's not chive soup. It's potato-leek soup sprinkled with chives."

He laughed. "I feel so much better."

Jess watched him disappear inside the mill. "Don't mind him, Liv. He's getting to be as big a stick-in-the-mud as Dad. I can't wait to try your soup."

"Thanks, but he was just teasing. Jess—"

"I have to get going. I'll see you later. Good luck with McCaffrey."

She climbed into her truck. Olivia shook her head with bemusement and returned to her car. She drove the short distance into the village, turning onto another of Knights Bridge's narrow roads, this one dead-ending at a popular gate that fishermen and hikers used to access Quabbin. She pulled into Rivendell, a small assisted living facility situated on open land dotted with sugar maples and white pines, with views of the waters of the reservoir in the distance. Audrey Frost, Olivia's grandmother, lived in a one-bedroom apartment down the hall from Grace Webster.

Grace had been entirely unhelpful in tracking down the new owner of her house, which Olivia had attributed to her advanced age. Grace was, after all, in her nineties. With Dylan's arrival, Olivia was no longer as sure age had anything to do with it. The story of how he'd ended up with the house had too many unanswered questions.

Maybe Grace was hiding something. Maybe whatever she was hiding had brought Duncan McCaffrey to Knights Bridge—and now his son.

"Or maybe I didn't get enough sleep last night," Olivia muttered under her breath as she passed the sunroom. She spotted Grace in a chair, alone in front of a wall of windows, and went in. "I thought that was you. Good morning, Miss Webster."

Grace beamed, her eyes sparkling at her visitor. "So good to see you, Olivia. You know you can call me Grace now. I was always 'Miss Webster' to my students, but I'm no longer a teacher. We live in a more casual age than when I was younger." She set a small but powerful pair of binoculars on her lap. She was a tiny woman with snow-white hair she kept neatly curled, and light blue eyes that added charm to what could be a stern demeanor. Her attention was on birds fluttering at feeders outside. "I just saw a male cardinal. We'll have to take the feeders down soon, though. Now that the weather's warming up, they'll attract bears and mountain lions."

"Mountain lions, Grace?" Olivia asked with a skeptical smile.

"Darn right," she said, clutching the binoculars with her arthritis-gnarled fingers. "I heard that catamount scat was discovered in Quabbin. Mountain lions are shy animals. They stick to the wilderness and avoid human contact. Who would have thought bald eagles and moose would return to the area? But they have, so why not mountain lions?"

Olivia wasn't arguing about mountain lions in Quabbin. There had been periodic reports of their return to the back areas of the protected, limited-access wilderness surrounding the reservoir, but no confirmed sightings.

"The bird feeders are a nice touch," she said.

Grace sank into the cushions of her high-backed chair. "We take care of them ourselves. How are you, Olivia? Your grandmother and I have yoga class together in a little while. She's younger than I am, but I hold my own."

Of that, Olivia had no doubt. "I'll stop by and say hi, but I also wanted to see you. I'm wondering if you've thought more about the man who bought your house."

She gazed out the windows as three chickadees darted at the feeders. "I haven't, no."

Stonewalling, Olivia thought. "Apparently he died and left the house to his son in San Diego. He's here."

That got Grace's attention. She peered up at Olivia. "He's in Knights Bridge?"

"He arrived yesterday and spent the night at your old house."

"You asked him to clean up the yard?"

Olivia nodded. "I told him it's become an eyesore since you sold the house."

"Hoodlum teenagers. I left the washer and refrigerator on the back porch for the new owner to get rid of. That was part of our deal. I didn't want to be bothered with taking them to the dump…" Grace sniffed, a touch of the old-fashioned, formidable teacher coming out in her. "I wish I'd been there to catch the little devils having their fun. I'd have had every one of them arrested for criminal mischief."

"Just as well you weren't there, Grace."

"That's why kids run wild these days. There's no one to take a firm hand. We don't want to be bothered. Look at me here, holed up in an old folks' home, watching birds…."

"You did your bit for the youth of Knights Bridge."

Grace loosened her grip on her binoculars and raised a hand, pointing one finger at Olivia. "I don't believe for one minute the brats who vandalized my house were from Knights Bridge."

By their own account, some of the adults in town who had been students of Grace Webster back in her days as an English and Latin teacher were still afraid of her. Olivia could understand why. Grace in her prime must have been something.

She was something now, Olivia thought, and steered the conversation back to her reason for being there. "The son—the man who inherited your house—is named Dylan McCaffrey."

Grace lowered her hand, her brow furrowed as she waited a moment before speaking. "McCaffrey. Yes, I remember now. His father was also a Dylan?" She shook her head, stopping Olivia from responding. "No, it was something else."

"Duncan," Olivia said.

"That's right. Exactly so." Grace kept her eyes on the bird feeders. "This Dylan McCaffrey—he's a scoundrel, isn't he?"

Scoundrel? Olivia bit back her surprise, as well as a smile. "Why would you think he's a scoundrel?"

"His father was a treasure hunter."

"A what? Grace—"

She raised her binoculars again. "Spring's here despite last night's storm. I've seen robins. I'm sure I saw a bluebird, too, but your grandmother isn't so sure."

"Grace," Olivia said, "if you know of any reason I should be wary of Dylan McCaffrey, you need to tell me."

"I would think you would be wise to be wary of any man who mysteriously inherited a house on the other side of the continent from a dead father." She set her binoculars back in her lap and fixed her gaze on Olivia. "Is this Dylan McCaffrey single?"

Her blunt question didn't surprise Olivia. Grace Webster was famous in town for being probing, straightforward and, if herself a private woman, interested in her friends and neighbors in Knights Bridge.

Noticing the cardinal had returned, Olivia said, her voice even, "I don't know anything about him. I didn't get the impression he was married, but I don't really know."

"Why would a single man bother with my old house? Why doesn't he just sell it?"

"I don't think he's planning to move in. He's just checking it out after I wrote to him and he discovered he'd inherited it from his father. I only met him for a few minutes in the freezing rain. Did you meet his father?"

"Yes, I met him. I didn't want to."

"Why didn't you want to?"

"Because I didn't want a picture of the man who was buying my house stuck in my head." She again raised her light blue eyes to Olivia. "Then I discovered that he was a treasure hunter. All treasure hunters are scoundrels."

"I don't know much about treasure hunters. What 'treasure' could anyone hope to find at your house?"

"None," the old woman answered without hesitation.

Olivia's head was spinning. "Then what difference does it make that he was a treasure hunter? If it wasn't the reason he bought your house—"

"I don't know why he bought my house."

"What was he like? Do you remember?"

"Of course I remember. Just because I didn't tell you doesn't mean I don't remember. He was charming." Grace watched the bright red cardinal flutter at the feeders. "I've written a book."

A book?

"Did your father tell you?" Grace asked, matter-of-fact.

"No, Grace, he didn't."

"I told your grandmother, and I gave her permission to tell him."

"I haven't heard about your book. What's it about?"

"My life. I wrote it by hand before I moved out of my house and then I typed it onto a computer here in the computer lab. It took forever. I had ten copies printed, but I don't want anyone to read it until I've passed. I've set aside one for Audrey, should she outlive me, and one for the library. I'm not sure what to do with the rest of them." She smiled. "You could always sell them at Carriage Hill. Your grandmother tells me that's what you're calling it. People love local color, and I'm one of the last residents left from the lost valley towns."

"That's a little morbid, don't you think?"

She gave Olivia a cool look. "If I were getting married, would you think it morbid to plan my wedding?"

"Of course not, but—"

"Then it's not morbid to plan my passing. I didn't say I was going to drink hemlock or sprinkle monkshood on my oatmeal. You know monkshood is poisonous, don't you?" She didn't wait for an answer. "You'll want to be careful about planting any near children."

"I will," Olivia said. "Does your book have anything to do with the McCaffreys?"

"No. Nothing at all to do with them."

"Treasure?"

"It's about a long-ago summer," she said. "A lost summer of my lost youth."

"Grace…"

Olivia didn't go on. The older woman's eyelids were drooping, and the binoculars fell out of her hand into her lap as she nodded off. She woke up almost immediately, but Olivia said goodbye and headed down the hall to see her grandmother.

"Oh, she worked on that book for months," Audrey Frost said as she rolled up her yoga mat in the living area of her little apartment. Her hair was snow-white and cut short, and she had on a dark pink tunic over black ankle tights and Nikes. "She locked the copies in her safe-deposit box at the bank."

Olivia noticed a slender vase of forsythia on the small dining table. Her grandmother almost never cooked. She liked to tell people she'd have moved into assisted living sooner if she'd realized she didn't have to cook unless she wanted to.

"Grace said she won't let anyone read it until she's gone."

"She means it, too. She wouldn't let me near it when she was writing it. I'd stop by, and she'd shut her notebook the minute she saw me. Then when she was typing it up after she moved here, she would only use one of the computers near the door, so no one could sneak up on her or peek over her shoulder." Audrey Frost looked just like her son, Olivia's father, when she rolled her eyes. "You would think she was writing the secret biography of the Queen of England."

"Do you think she told secrets? About herself? About other people in town?"

"I don't think anything."

Olivia considered the news of Grace Webster's book as her grandmother, eighty-six, clasped her hands behind her and did a quick stretch.

She raised her arms above her head for another stretch. "Some secrets are best taken to the grave. Not that I have secrets," she added quickly. "How could I in this town? And your father. You know him, Liv. He doesn't believe in secrets. He doesn't go around telling people intimate details about his life or putting his bank account numbers up on Facebook—but those aren't secrets."

Olivia smiled. "Surprisingly enough, I know what you mean. Do you think Grace has secrets?"

"She's lived alone all these years, and the people she grew up with were scattered when the valley towns were depopulated to make way for Quabbin. She could just have bottled-up memories, and now they've become secrets."

"How long have you known her?"

"She moved to Knights Bridge before the war. I was thirteen or fourteen, but I didn't get to know her until I started to work at the school. I was the bookkeeper there for forty-two years. Some days I can hardly believe I've been retired for twenty years."

"But you and Grace Webster were friends—"

"All these years, yes, but I couldn't tell you if she has anything to hide or not."

Olivia pictured the old woman looking at birds in the sunroom. "If Grace does have secrets, I don't know if I can see her revealing them in a book for people to read after she's gone."

"Good point." Her grandmother glanced at the clock on her spotless stove. "I have a few minutes before yoga class. Come. Sit. Tell me about this man who's moved into her house."

"It's temporary, and how did you know?"

"People talk and I listen. He's very good-looking, I hear."

Word about Dylan's appearance at breakfast must have spread to the assisted living center a mile away. "Grandma, I didn't come to bug Grace because Dylan McCaffrey is good-looking—"

"So he is?"

"He's strongly built and… I don't know. Yes, I guess you could say he's good-looking in a rough-and-tumble sort of way."

"You're blushing. Whatever happened to that man of yours in Boston?"

"Peter moved to Seattle." Olivia wasn't going further than that. "I should go. I have a million things to do. It's good seeing you, Grandma. Enjoy your yoga class."

By the time Olivia drove back through the village and onto the road to her house, the temperature had risen into the fifties. Dylan's car was still in his driveway, but he wasn't outside. He—or someone else—had gathered some of the smaller pieces of junk from the yard and stacked them at the end of the driveway. Slowing to a crawl, Olivia saw that the washer and refrigerator were still in the blackberries. Even as strong as he looked to be, Dylan would need help moving them.

She picked up speed and continued down to her house. As she got out of her car, she noticed that a cluster of a dozen purple crocuses had opened up by her kitchen steps.

Buster greeted her at the door, eager for a walk. Luckily, he hadn't torn up the place. She snapped on his leash and headed out, deliberately turning down the road toward Quabbin, away from Grace's old house. She didn't want to run into Dylan. Not right now. She needed to think. She wanted to know more about him and his treasure-hunting father, but without doing anything that would upset Grace, who clearly remembered more about the man who'd bought her house than she'd initially let on.

Time, Olivia thought, to figure out a game plan.

Maggie O'Dunn's mud-splattered van was parked out front when Olivia got back to the house with Buster. Her friend was crouched in front of the crocuses, but she pointed at several healthy mounds of chives. "Wow, no wonder you went with chives on your stationery," she said, rising. "You could supply half of Knights Bridge with just this lot. More out back?"

Olivia smiled. "Tons more."

"This place looks fabulous," Maggie said, tightening a long, silky, deep teal scarf in her curly strawberry hair. She had taken off to the city herself for a few years but was back in Knights Bridge with her two young sons, running a catering business out of her nineteenth-century "gingerbread" house in the village. "Right now everyone's talking about your neighbor. What do you know about him?"

"Next to nothing."

Her turquoise eyes gleamed with mischief. "Shall we do a little investigating?"

They made a pot of tea, grabbed Olivia's laptop, set it up on the kitchen table and hit the internet.

"Oh, my," Maggie said after a few minutes, pointing to a page she'd found through Google. "He's a former defenseman with the NHL."

"As in National Hockey League?"

"Uh-huh." Maggie clicked a few keys on the laptop. "Here's a picture of him in his hockey uniform. He was with L.A. then. Whoa, huh? Studly. Same guy who's up the road?"

Olivia stood behind Maggie with a mug of tea and leaned closer to the laptop screen, studying a smiling Dylan McCaffrey in uniform and skates, hockey stick in hand. "Same guy," she said.

"Let's see if we can figure out what he's up to now."

Two minutes later, they had the answer. Dylan helped run childhood friend Noah Kendrick's NAK, Inc., which had gone public a few months ago.

Maggie gave a low whistle and poured more tea. "Noah's worth a billion. Even if Dylan's worth a tenth of that—"

"That's higher math," Olivia said lightly.

"No, it's not. It's a hundred million. Even if Noah's net worth is exaggerated, it's still got to be a lot more money than either of us has ever seen. Why is Dylan bothering with a crumbling house in Knights Bridge?" Maggie sat back with her tea, the midday sun streaming through the kitchen windows. "Because of you, Liv?"

"That's what he said."

"Liv?"

"Because I wrote to him," Olivia amended.

"And he came, just like that?"

"I'm being careful, Maggie." Olivia sighed, averting her gaze from the laptop screen. "Do I tell Mom and Dad about him, or do I just keep my mouth shut?"

"Are you kidding? They probably have a dossier on Dylan on their desk by now. You know how they are."

Olivia did, indeed. She wanted to find out more about Dylan's father but she didn't want to keep Maggie from her work. They shut the laptop, cleaned up the tea dishes and headed outside.

"I can't believe how much you've got done in such a short time," Maggie said as she opened the door to her van. "It's shaping up even better than I thought it would. You'll get people to come out here, Liv. No question. I'll bet you have your own kitchen soon, but let's have fun in the meantime, shall we?"

"My mother-daughter tea seems awfully close."

"It'll be great. I'll come by in the next day or two and we'll nail down a menu. In the meantime, I have two rascals to pick up from school. Wait until they hear a hockey player's in town."

"Maggie—"

She laughed. "Kidding. Mum's the word until you figure out what Mr. McCaffrey's really up to. I doubt it's just to move an old refrigerator."

As Maggie climbed into her van, Olivia debated, then said, "I saw Grace Webster this morning. She's doing well. She's into bird-watching and she's taking yoga with my grandmother."

"Good for her. I saw her a few weeks ago when I catered a hundredth birthday party for one of the residents. She looks great."

"Did she tell you she wrote a book?"

Maggie's eyes sparked with interest and humor. "Oh, yes. She won't let a soul read it until she's gone. Makes you wonder what's in it, doesn't it? ~~Probably~~ not just essays on Latin verbs and Shakespeare."

"Probably not," Olivia said, watching her friend pull the van door shut and start up the road back toward the village.

Chapter 5

My name is Grace Webster, and as I start this book, I am ninety years old, living my last days in my adopted town of Knights Bridge, Massachusetts. I was born in the back bedroom of my family's house, gone these many years, torn down to make way for the vast Quabbin Reservoir. The house's foundation is all that remains, and it's now under fifty feet of water. It was made of rocks my great-grandparents and their neighbors collected when they cleared the land for farming. It's just one of the countless old cellar holes in the woods and under the waters of Quabbin, silent reminders of the lost towns of the Swift River Valley and the people who lived there.

The valley towns of Prescott, Dana, Enfield and Greenwich were already doomed when I was born, and so was my mother. She died in childbirth. I don't *know what happened but I remember stains on the worn floorboards. I expect she hemorrhaged. We didn't discuss such things in my family.*

As a teenager, I watched as our house was razed by strangers, but that gets ahead of my story. My grandmother—my father's mother—was the first to explain to me what would happen. Dottie Webster was a gentle soul, a self-educated woman who had never known another home and seldom left the valley. My father, Isaiah Webster, was her only surviving child. She'd lost two babies before he was born. She would only say they died of a fever. My father was the strong, silent type who hid his pain and anger with work and a kind of mental toughness that a young girl can find unforgiving.

I was ten when Gran and I were snapping beans in the shade of a sugar maple her ancestors had planted and she told me about the reservoir. It was a hot summer afternoon, and we'd spread an old quilt on the grass. We'd picked the beans ourselves that morning.

"The state wants the valley for the reservoir—for water for Boston," Gran said.

I grabbed a handful of beans, still warm from the sun. "The valley? You mean Greenwich?"

"Not just Greenwich. They want Prescott, Dana, Enfield, several villages, parts of other surrounding towns. Everyone and everything has to go. People, houses, shops, mills, churches. Even the trees will be ripped out of the ground. The work's already started—"

"Then it has to stop. It's not fair, Gran."

"Fair or not, we don't have a choice. The state can take the valley by what's called eminent domain. It's for the public good."

"What about our good?"

"*The people in Boston need drinking water. It's a big city, Grace. We can't stand in the way of progress.*" *Gran's tone was firm and pragmatic, but her eyes misted with tears.* "*I don't know how long before we'll have to move. Some people are already taking the state offers for their homes and leaving the valley.*"

"*Where would we go?*" *I asked.*

"*Most people will move to one of the surrounding towns that aren't being flooded. The engineers have calculated to the inch where the water will go. Many of the hills in the valley will become islands as the reservoir fills.*"

I flicked an ant off the quilt. "*I hate engineers.*"

"*It's not their fault, Grace. They're decent men doing the best they can. They're charged with building a safe reservoir that will provide clean water to Boston for the foreseeable future. There's nothing we can do.*"

As Gran and I snapped beans, she told me about the two dams that would plug the valley like a bathtub and allow it to fill with water, creating the largest lake in southern New England and one of the largest man-made reservoirs in the world. An aqueduct almost a hundred miles long would take the water to Boston.

"*Where we are sitting now,*" *Gran said,* "*will be under fifty feet of water.*"

I couldn't listen to another word. I jumped up and ran to the stream behind the house, plunging in to my knees. I imagined everything around me gone, under water. I couldn't breathe. It was as if I were drowning along with everything I knew. I'd never left the valley. I'd only seen pictures of other places.

Gran stayed in the shade, snapping beans as if nothing would ever change.

A few days later, I followed her as she walked to the small cemetery where my mother and multiple genera-tions of the Websters were buried. I hid behind a tree while Gran sank to her knees at the graves of her hus-band and babies. She didn't know I was there, or she pretended not to know. Later she told me that the state was moving all the graves in the valley, most to a new cemetery on the southern edge of the reservoir. It was supposed to be a beautiful place. Gran would still be able to be buried with her family.

I was horrified but I didn't say anything. Gran would only tell me that we mustn't be bitter, and we must bear with dignity what we had no other choice but to bear. I didn't want to hear it. I don't think my father did, either, because he never talked about the coming of the res-ervoir, at least not in my presence in those early days.

I just wanted everything to stay the same, even as the world was changing around me.

Chapter 6

Dylan called a private trash removal outfit to come by for the junk he'd collected and heaped at the bottom of the driveway. If Grace Webster had sold her house just two years ago and the refrigerator and washing machine had belonged to her, she wasn't one to update appliances for the fun of it. Apparently if they still worked, they stayed.

The trash removal outfit turned out to be a big, middle-aged guy named Stan. As Stan loaded the junk into the back of his truck, Dylan tried to engage him in conversation. "Do you know Grace Webster?"

"Miss Webster? My dad had her for English. Said she was tough."

"She lived out here alone?"

"It's not that far from the village."

Depended how one defined "far." Dylan could walk

to shops, restaurants and the beach from his place on Coronado. "Any family in the area?"

Stan shrugged. He had broad shoulders and wore a Red Sox cap and a Bruins shirt. "I don't know. She never married. She's from one of the Quabbin towns."

"Brothers, sisters, nieces, nephews?"

"Don't know."

Stan didn't seem to care why Dylan would want to know, either, which was good, because he wasn't sure himself—except that the previous owner's family might provide clues as to what his father had been after when he'd bought the house.

"What about Olivia Frost?" Dylan asked casually as he tossed a tire into the truck.

Stan pointed a gloved hand down the road. "She lives about a half mile that way."

It was pulling teeth to get the guy to talk. Dylan lifted an old toaster oven he had found under some soggy brush and added it to the accumulating junk in the truck. "She asked me to clean up this place."

Stan grinned. "That sounds like Olivia."

For a split second, Dylan thought Stan would continue, but he didn't. "She has a lot to do before she opens The Farm at Carriage Hill to the public."

"Yeah."

"Think it stands a chance?"

"We'll see."

"Any old stories about this house?"

"What?"

"Old stories. What's its history?"

Stan paused and adjusted his baseball cap. "It's just an old house."

"I understand Grace Webster moved here when Quabbin was being built."

"Yeah, the state took their house. She lived here with her grandmother and father. Then they died. She's just a normal person. Tough teacher but everyone I know who had her appreciated how tough she was after the fact. You know how that is."

Dylan had had a tough algebra teacher. He still hated him. He'd had a few tough coaches he appreciated, though. "I get your point."

"They say Miss Webster mellowed some after she retired. She took up bird-watching."

Bird-watching. Dylan nodded to the run-down house. "Who tossed this place?"

Stan dumped the rotting mattress into the back of the truck. "Punks."

"Were there any arrests?"

"Nope."

"Were they looking for anything or just trashing the place?"

"Drunk." He turned to Dylan. "Anything else you want hauled out of here?"

"Not for now."

Dylan paid him in cash and watched the truck rumble down the road. All in all, the place looked better, but it still needed landscape work. He had a feeling he could call Stan, and he'd come with a shovel and weed whacker and get that job done, too.

Unsettled and restless, Dylan found a pair of clippers in an attached shed that smelled faintly of mud and axle grease.

Knights Bridge wasn't growing on him.

He made his way down to a tangle of brush at the

back of the house and started cutting briars. There was no snow there, at least. He came to a slender tree sporting what he thought might be pussy willows. He'd had no idea where or how pussy willows grew, just that people liked it and regarded it as a pleasant harbinger of spring.

He rubbed his fingertips over the smooth gray buds.

"You have to get out of here," he said to himself.

Nonetheless, he cut several thin branches, spacing the cuts so that they didn't warp the look of the tree, then stood back, sinking into mud and wet leaves. What would his former hockey teammates think of him standing out here in the woods holding a bouquet of pussy willows?

What would Noah and Noah's enemies, who were Dylan's job to identify and keep at bay, think?

"Damn," he said with a laugh and headed down the road to The Farm at Carriage Hill. He found his neighbor sweeping off her front walk. He held out the pussy willows. "I don't have a vase, but I thought you might enjoy them."

Olivia smiled as she took them. "Ice one day, a sure sign of spring the next. Thank you." She nodded toward the door to the ell, not the front door he'd knocked on last night. "Would you care to come inside? I can give you the grand tour."

"Where's Buster?"

"In the mudroom. He decided to dig up my lavender. He only adopted me a couple of weeks ago. We're learning, but it'll take time and patience."

"Does Buster have time and patience?" Dylan was teasing but Olivia's hazel eyes darkened, and he could see something else was on her mind besides her misbe-having dog. "I'd like that grand tour if you—"

"Sure. Let's go."

They entered a cozy kitchen with butcher-block counters, a rustic island and dark green painted cupboards. Buster barked from behind his gate in the mud-room but without the snarls and growls of yesterday. Olivia let him out, and he bounded over to Dylan as if they were now best friends.

"You must have made an impression on him," she said, retrieving a blue pottery pitcher from an open shelf.

"A good one, I hope."

She placed the pussy willows in the pitcher and added water at the porcelain sink, then set the pitcher on a square table in front of a double window that looked out on the backyard. Dylan noticed a large garden, half raked clean, the other half still covered in fallen leaves and small branches that had been whipped out of nearby trees over the winter.

Olivia followed his gaze. "I bought this place last fall. I didn't have a chance to clean it up the way I would have wanted to before winter. It was a cold one. Most of the perennials survived. The chives in particular have come back with a vengeance."

"So my friend Noah was right and those were chives on your note card?"

Something in her expression told him she knew just who he meant by "my friend Noah." She nodded as she turned from the table. "That's right. Chives."

"I thought they were clover. I'm not much of a gardener."

"I tried various herbs, but I liked the chives best."

"Then you drew them yourself?"

"Yes, with watercolor pencils. I'm a graphic designer, but I can manage a drawing of chives."

"What are those in the window?"

"Parsley, rosemary and dill. I started them at my apartment in Boston and took them with me when I moved in here. Long story." She cleared her throat but showed no sign she regretted inviting him in. "This part of the house was added on in the 1920s."

"Where's the center chimney you mentioned in your note?"

"In here."

She led him into the adjoining living room and dining room, both with painted wood wainscoting and brick fireplaces. The furnishings were sparse and obviously not new, but fabric swatches and paint chips were laid out on a coffee table.

"There are five fireplaces off this one chimney," Olivia said. "Three downstairs and two upstairs. The wainscoting and wide-board floors are original. My family's mill did replacement windows for the previous owners—they look just like the original windows but are considerably more energy efficient."

"They're also not rotted and don't have cracked panes."

"As is the case with your house?"

Dylan gave her a wry smile. "As is the case."

Olivia took him through a library, which had one of the five fireplaces, and a small study that was obviously her main workspace. He noted the computer, calendar board, filing cabinet, art supplies and stacks of graphic design books. She winced at the clutter. "I just shoved everything in here and figured I'd organize bit by bit. I left a full-time job to start Carriage Hill."

From the tightness of her expression, Dylan guessed her departure from her job hadn't been without stress, but she rallied as she explained that she planned to use the downstairs rooms for her get-togethers, arranging tables as necessary depending on the size and type of event.

"Money's tight," she said, "but I can do so much of the work myself—painting, slipcovers, decorating. My sister, Jess, will help. You met her boyfriend this morning at breakfast."

"Mark Flanagan. Architect specializing in old buildings."

Olivia brightened. "Very good. You're getting to know the locals."

They returned to the kitchen. Buster had flopped on the floor under the table. Olivia scooped up a bit of bark or something that had fallen off the pussy willows. "You were an NHL hockey player for ten years—a defenseman. Now you work with Noah Kendrick, one of the tech-world geniuses."

"We're friends. Did you look me up on Google yourself, or did someone else in town do it and give you the results?"

"My friend Maggie stopped by and we couldn't resist. I didn't have any reason to check you out. I just wanted you to clean up your yard or let me do it. Then…" Olivia walked over to the table. "Then someone said something, and I decided to look into your background."

"Ah. 'Someone said something.' Small towns."

"Your father was a treasure hunter."

"You and your friend Maggie looked him up, too?"

"Not yet. Maggie went home and I haven't had a chance—"

"Then how do you know he was a treasure hunter?"

"That's the something I heard that got me to fire up my laptop and look into you." Olivia walked over to the counter and flicked the bark into the sink. "Do you think your father bought Grace's house because of lost treasure? Is that why you're here?"

"I don't care about lost treasure." Dylan kept his tone even as he watched her from the kitchen door. "I never got caught up in my father's adventures. I didn't pay much attention to what he was up to, and he didn't tell me."

"Did you two get along okay?"

"Leaving me the house wasn't a way to get back at me, if that's what you're thinking. We butted heads from time to time but we got along fine. We didn't see that much of each other. I guess we both thought he'd have more time."

Her changeable eyes seemed bluer in the midday light. "What happened? Do you mind if I ask?"

"He had a heart attack on some adventure in Portugal. He fell, but almost certainly because of the heart attack. It's how he wanted to go out. He told me he wouldn't have wanted to live past the time he could travel and do things. He wasn't destined for a rocking chair."

"I'm sorry for your loss," Olivia said quietly.

Dylan was surprised when he felt his throat tighten. "My father was a good guy. That doesn't mean he was perfect, but I hope everyone in town knows he wasn't responsible for throwing that junk in the yard."

"Everyone I know says that it was definitely kids. This house was empty at the time. Two unoccupied houses on a quiet country road must have been too much to resist." She leaned back against the sink and angled him a look. "Do you have any reason to believe Knights Bridge or specifically Grace's house had anything to do with your father's treasure hunting?"

Dylan shook his head. "No."

"But you think it's possible. You're curious, aren't you? That's why you came out here yourself. You can easily afford to have sent someone to check out the town, your property—me."

Dylan shrugged, his eyes half-closed on her. "I wanted to come here myself."

"Because of your father. You're an only child?"

He nodded. "My parents divorced when I was five."

Buster got up from under the table and sniffed Dylan's hand. Dylan petted him, the softness of his coat surprising him given their meeting. Somehow a snarling dog and a soft coat didn't go together. He glanced up at Olivia, still by the sink, a ray of sunlight shining through the window striking her hair. He noticed golden highlights. They were a surprise and matched the gold flecks in her eyes.

Time to get out of there.

He yanked open the door, welcoming the brisk air as he stood on the threshold. A night on a makeshift bed in the pitch-dark listening to water drip into a bucket had left him ragged. Hauling junk and digging ditches hadn't helped. He was bound to overfocus on his neighbor's feminine qualities, as his friend Noah would put it.

Olivia wasn't giving up. "Did your father have a connection to Knights Bridge?"

"He grew up in a Chicago suburb and moved to Los Angeles after college. He had no connection with Knights Bridge, or with New England, that I know of. He did well in business, but he was a nomad at heart, especially in his later years."

"He never lived on the East Coast?"

"No."

Olivia joined him at the door. "Have you decided what you're going to do with the house?"

"I haven't thought beyond cleaning up the yard. Where will you live once this place is up and running?"

"Here. Eventually I want to open up to overnight guests—not as a bed-and-breakfast. I'm thinking in terms of dedicated getaways for small groups. Mini reunions, girlfriend weekends, weddings, small conferences. I might hold my own workshops and conferences."

"On what?"

"Herbs, furniture painting, design. Lots of possibilities. I can enlist friends who are experts in different areas. It'd be fun but I'm being careful, since it's just me and I have to make a living."

"You're a successful graphic designer." Dylan smiled. "I looked you up on Google, too. Why give that up? Is opening The Farm at Carriage Hill a dream of yours?"

"In a way, yes, although I didn't think about giving up Boston until recently." She averted her eyes and pointed toward the mudroom behind her. "Would you like to see the gardens?"

Why not? He shut the front door and smiled. "Sure."

He and Buster followed Olivia outside. The air was still, almost warm with the resurgent sun. Green shoots poked out of the wet dirt in cleaned-out beds carved between muddy paths that, she explained, she would soon be mulching. "I thought about small rocks, but then I decided they'd never stay in the paths and I'd end up with them everywhere." She glanced back at Dylan with a smile. "And Buster likes to chew rocks."

Buster would, Dylan thought. He found himself picturing his house on Coronado. He and Olivia Frost lived very different lives.

She bent down and pulled sopping, dead plant matter from a corner of one of the beds, leaving it on the path. She pointed victoriously at frothy green sprouts underneath. "There. Purple sage."

"Ah."

She grinned at him. "You don't care about purple sage."

"I can see that it's not chives."

"It's easy to think nothing happens until all the snow has melted and the trees have leafed out, but look at the signs of spring. Seeing the new growth puts everything into perspective, doesn't it?"

Her mood had shifted, and she seemed more pensive as she stood straight. Dylan was beginning to suspect that something had happened in Boston, and whatever it was, it wasn't good. She didn't want to talk about it with him—maybe not with anyone. Olivia Frost, he was discovering, was straightforward but also reserved, and proud. He thought the contradictions made for an intriguing combination.

And whatever had brought her back to Knights Bridge to convert her little house into a getaway had also prompted her to contact him.

If she could guess what he was thinking, she pre-

tended not to and proceeded down another path. "I envision having a destination herb garden, one that people
will want to see. The previous owners gave me a good
start, especially with kitchen herbs. They loved cooking and gardening. I want to add beds for medicinal
herbs, aromatic herbs, maybe do an entire section of
meditative herbs."

"Herbs meditate?"

She rolled her eyes but was clearly amused. "You
know what I mean."

He didn't, actually. "How are you going to do everything? Gardening, mulching, painting, slipcovering,
freelancing—it's a lot."

"I'll manage." She gave him a bright smile. "I love
this work."

Dylan had another dozen questions he could ask her
just off the top of his head. Did she have a business
plan? Was Carriage Hill incorporated? Did she have
an attorney? What about loans, investors, partners, employees?

Three tiny foxgloves that had returned for the season
caught her eye. After she pointed them out, she led him
across sodden grass to an old fieldstone wall. On the
other side of the wall was an open field, with a wooded
hill beyond another field and another stone wall.

"That's Carriage Hill," Olivia said, pointing.
"There's a trail to the top. It has amazing views of the
reservoir and the valley. You and I own the field and
the woods at the base of the hill. The rest is state forest. Quabbin's on the other side. You can see part of it
from your house. I'm too low here. How long are you
staying in Knights Bridge? Will you have time to see
any of the area?"

"I leave tomorrow," Dylan said.

She continued to look out across the field, no patches of snow in sight. "That doesn't leave you much time to figure out why your father bought Grace Webster's place."

"I won't be surprised if I never know." He squinted out at the hill rising across the field. Had his father hiked to the top? What, exactly, had he been doing in Knights Bridge? Dylan put aside his questions and smiled at the woman next to him. "I'd like to hike up Carriage Hill. I have time. Care to join me?"

"I would," Olivia said, almost as if her answer surprised her.

Twenty minutes later, Dylan was climbing over a stone wall with Olivia. "This was all farmland in the nineteenth century," she said as they walked across the field, its tall grass matted down from winter but starting to show signs of life. "If you see a stone wall in the woods, you know the land around it used to be cleared. Imagine hauling all those rocks."

"It must have been backbreaking work."

"There's something to be said for physical work. You do it, and it's done." They came to a trail that led into the woods, the ground soft and muddy from last night's rain and the spring runoff. "Rocks don't grumble or stab you in the back."

Dylan thought he heard an undertone of regret, even anger, in her voice, but she kept her eyes on the trail as it curved past a gnarly evergreen—a hemlock, she said. He noticed the shape of her hips in her cargo pants and the mud crusted on her functional trail shoes as she moved with energy and confidence up the hill. She wasn't wearing a hat, and the intermittent breeze would catch the ends of her long dark hair.

"So, Olivia," he said after a few yards, "did you get your ass kicked in Boston?"

She spun around at him. "Did you learn to be blunt as a hockey player, or working with Noah Kendrick?"

He shrugged. "I came that way."

"Sometimes things sort themselves out the way they're meant to."

"True, but it's also true, as the saying goes, that sometimes you're drinking the wine one day and picking the grapes the next."

"Was that you and the NHL?"

"You're changing the subject."

She took a steep section of the trail at a fast clip, then stopped and waited for him. "We're technically in the Quabbin watershed right now. The understanding of how to ensure water purity has changed somewhat since the 1930s, but the basic approach is to use the land as much as possible as a natural filtration process."

"No chemicals needed, then," Dylan said, deciding not to push her further on her reasons for leaving Boston.

"Not for water treatment. Fluoride and a small amount of chlorine and lead suppressant are added at the end for health reasons. Building Quabbin was a decades-long process. Boston engineers and politicians started talking about flooding the Swift River Valley as far back as the 1890s." Olivia climbed onto a small boulder near the top of the hill and squinted out at the view. "You can see why."

Dylan stood next to her and looked out at the sprawling valley, a finger of the reservoir sparkling in the afternoon sun. More hills dotted the landscape, and not a house or a boat or a road was in sight. "It's beautiful," he said.

"This area is part of the New England uplands. We're higher than the land on the coast. Even the floor of the valley under Quabbin is higher. Engineers realized they could easily dam the Swift River, build an aqueduct and let gravity take pure, unfiltered water to the residents of Boston."

"The locals were outnumbered."

"Badly. A hundred years ago, we'd be looking out at small New England villages instead of water and wilderness. Dana, Prescott, Greenwich and Enfield, and several villages—Doubleday, Packardsville, Millington—were wiped off the map. The reservoir takes up about forty square miles. There's over a hundred miles of shoreline. For a small state like Massachusetts, that's a lot."

"And none of it's occupied?"

"There are offices, a visitors center and a lookout tower in Quabbin Park at the south end of the reservoir. That's where Winsor Dam and Goodnough Dike are— they keep the water in the valley." She sighed, her hair blowing in her face with a gust of wind. "This is Daniel Shays country. Have you heard of him?"

Just barely, Dylan thought. "Some kind of revolutionary, wasn't he?"

"He was a hero of the American Revolution who came home to chaos after the end of the war. He organized local farmers and led a controversial revolt against unfair and impossibly high taxes. They were routed, but their revolt helped lead to the Constitutional Convention."

"Sounds like one of those damned-if-you-do, damned-if-you-don't situations."

She hopped down from her boulder, one of countless hunks of granite scattered among the bare trees and evergreens on top of the hill. "His original homestead was on the bank of the western branch of the Swift River. It had to be torn down. The plans for Quabbin called for obliterating a number of major roads, so the state built new highways, including one on the western edge of the watershed—Daniel Shays Highway. Ironic, isn't it?"

Dylan glanced at her. He wondered if she had a clue how attractive she was, even now—maybe especially now—up here in the wind, talking about revolutionaries, a lost valley, this place where time seemed to have stopped but, in reality, hadn't. "I can see that you love this area," he said.

"It's home. I love Quabbin, too. I might have fought tooth and nail against it if I'd been in one of the towns marked for destruction, but it's an incredible place now. People call it the 'accidental wilderness.'"

"I understand that Grace Webster came from one of the valley towns."

"Her house wasn't that far from here. It's under water, but not all the houses that were taken and torn down were in the flood zone. Some were just in the watershed, but they had to go, too. A number of the people who were displaced moved to Knights Bridge."

Dylan shook off an image of his father, shook off his questions about how an adventurer and treasure hunter had ended up here, and turned from the view, facing Olivia as another gust of wind, colder than the last, blew through her hair. "My father was always one for living in the present, and he's gone now. He bought his house here for his own reasons."

Her eyes narrowed as she stood back from him. "So you'll put it on the market and dust the dirt of Knights Bridge off your feet once you leave?"

"I wouldn't put it that way, but—"

"But it's what you'll do. I can't say I blame you. I assume you'll be flying back to San Diego?"

"It's a hell of a long drive across the country."

"Yes," Olivia said half under her breath, then, with a sudden panicked, pale look, burst back down the trail.

Dylan watched her retreating figure a moment before he headed down the trail himself, catching up with her. "You don't like to fly?"

"Does anyone these days?"

"I don't mind. I don't think about it. It's just a means to get where I want to go."

She moved quickly, seemingly oblivious to the steep, wet conditions. "Do you fly on private jets?"

"Not often. Olivia, what's wrong?"

"Nothing. I'm just curious." She stepped over protruding tree roots. "The air feels good, but it's still early to be out on the trails. I have to head straight back. I almost forgot that my parents are coming for dinner. You're welcome to join us."

Dinner with the parents. Dylan didn't think so. "Thanks, but I might go for a drive and see the area before it gets dark."

"There are stories of ghosts in Quabbin but I've never run into one."

She drifted into silence as they continued down the hill. When they reached the first of the two fields, he said, "I'm glad you wrote to me about the house."

"I didn't realize you didn't know about it. I thought I was writing to your father." She climbed over the stone wall and jumped into the second field, her breathing shallow, rapid, her face pale. She turned to him with a strained smile. "I suppose I won't see you again before you leave tomorrow. It's been a pleasure to meet you. If I can do anything to help with your house here, don't hesitate to let me know."

Something was off with her. Dylan couldn't pinpoint what it was. "Thanks."

She tucked wild strands of hair behind her ears. "That's what neighbors are for."

"Olivia, what's wrong?" he asked again.

She pointed a shaky hand toward her house across the field. "I'm going to pick up my pace." She tried another faltering smile. "You're an athlete. You'll keep up."

Before she could get two steps, Dylan caught an arm around her middle. "Whoa. Hold on." He turned her to him. "What's going on?"

She swallowed, licked her lips and took in a shallow breath. "Nothing. I'm fine." She cleared her throat and looked up at him. "I got to thinking about too much at once. Boston, freelancing, all I have to do before my mother-daughter tea…"

"My flying back to San Diego set you off. When's the last time you flew?"

"It's been a while."

"'A while' for me would be a few weeks. What's 'a while' for you?"

She stiffened but was noticeably calmer. "I don't like to fly."

"Ah. This was a bit of a panic attack?"

"It was a bit of an 'I'd better get the roast out of the freezer' attack."

He grinned. "All right. Let's go get the roast out of the freezer. I might have to stay for dinner after all."

She shifted her gaze to him. "Sure. That'd be fine."

She wriggled out of his arm and resumed her course across the field, if at a less manic pace. Dylan watched her, thinking about their conversation, her body language—thinking past his attraction to her to what she was communicating. Being nervous about flying was one thing, but he had a feeling he was on the right track about her and her reasons for returning to Knights Bridge.

He ambled next to her. "Who screwed you over in Boston?"

"What?" She cut him a shocked look. "What are you talking about?"

"A client? A coworker? A friend or boyfriend?"

Her chin snapped up. "I don't want to talk about it."

"I'm right, then."

"And you love being right."

She was obviously trying to divert his attention, but he said, "Yes, I do. It pays the bills and most of the time it feels good. Not always. Like right now. I don't want you to be here because you're running from someone."

"I'm not running from anyone or anything. I'm taking the bull by the horns and realizing a dream."

"The timing's not on your terms. It's on the terms of this person who hurt you. I'm guessing…" He slowed his pace deliberately, letting her get ahead of him. "I'm guessing it was a friend."

She kept going as if he hadn't said anything.

"A colleague—someone who worked at the same design studio as you?"

He watched her jump over a soggy patch in the field, then caught up with her again. She angled a look at him. "Nobody did anything to me. It was just business."

"It's always 'just business' when you're getting screwed. When someone does you a good turn, it's because they love you. It's not because you deserve it."

Olivia raised her eyebrows at him. "That's cynical, don't you think?"

"Nope."

"Eye of the round," she said abruptly. When Dylan frowned at her, she let her smile broaden. "It's the roast I'm thawing for dinner tonight."

He realized he wasn't getting anything more out of her and stopped trying. Instead, he decided to enjoy being attracted to her as she led the way back over the stone wall to her house. Somehow she'd gotten more mud on her butt. He didn't mind. Not at all.

Chapter 7

After finishing her last meeting, Jess window-shopped at the expensive stores on Newbury Street, taking the opportunity to appreciate Boston's slightly warmer temperatures. She was looking at a display of jewelry when her cell phone buzzed and she saw that her sister was calling. "Hey, Liv, what's up?"

"You have to get back in time for dinner," Olivia said.

"Why?"

"I'm cooking. I have a roast thawing. I never cook a roast, and here I am… Mom and Dad were supposed to come, but they just called. They had to bail."

"They did? Why?"

"Problem at the mill. They said it's nothing serious. Jess, I accidentally invited Dylan McCaffrey, and he's coming."

"How do you accidentally invite someone to dinner?"

"I don't know. I just did." Olivia gave a mock groan. "I'm not sure I want to be alone with him."

"Oh, come on, Liv. He's not a criminal."

"He's a rich ex-hockey player," her sister said, then ran down what she and Maggie O'Dunn had discovered about him. Olivia sighed, calmer. "You're right. He's harmless. Never mind. He's heading back to San Diego tomorrow. The chances of him returning to Knights Bridge are somewhere between slim and none. I'm making myself nuts over nothing."

"It's because you saw Mom this morning. Those pictures of California get me going every time. I swear I pick up her anxiety."

"She's looking forward to going—"

"Liv, there isn't a chance in the world she's making that trip. You know there isn't. She won't even drive to Boston. Flying across the country?" Jess moved from the jewelry story to a window decorated with spring clothes on skinny mannequins. "You haven't been around her that much until lately. It's bound to get to you."

"Maybe that's it."

"Relax, Liv. Being alone with Dylan McCaffrey can't be that big a chore. Enjoy having him in town while you can."

Jess thought Olivia laughed as she hung up. Even if her sister's laughter was just so Jess wouldn't worry about her, it was a relief to hear. Bad enough that she had her own wild thinking to deal with—she didn't want Olivia going down the same path. Olivia couldn't let herself be influenced by their mother's anxieties, if such a thing were possible.

"Poor Mom," Jess said to herself as she turned off Newbury toward Marlborough Street and Olivia's apartment.

The buds on the magnolias that lined Commonwealth Avenue were almost ready to burst into bloom. Jess noticed clusters of cheerful daffodils in tiny, formal yards in front of the elegant residential buildings and felt her own tension ease. She loved springtime in Boston— springtime anywhere, she supposed, but the city felt so energetic, as if it were coming to life after the long New England winter.

She let herself into Olivia's apartment using keys she'd given to her.

Big change, she thought, from the fancy jewelry shops on Newbury. The late-afternoon sun wasn't reaching the apartment. Despite the cheerful colors and the good scrubbing she and Olivia had given the place when she'd moved out, it felt dingy and depressing without her personal items and most of its furniture.

Jess stifled a sudden rush of claustrophobia and opened the window above the sink.

Maybe it was her imagination, but she swore she could smell garbage in the alley. Not just trash, she thought, but actual garbage.

Wrinkling her nose, she walked back into the living room, where she'd left her tote bag on the floor by the couch, one of the few remaining pieces of furniture. She had brought work with her but supposed she could head to a coffee shop or a hotel bar to do it. The apartment seemed so lonely, and wasn't the idea of spending time in the city to be around people? She wanted crowds. Strangers. She knew almost everyone in Knights Bridge. She wondered if Dylan McCaffrey realized what a big deal his presence was in her little hometown—if Olivia even realized it, since she'd been away for so long.

A rich, good-looking stranger in their midst. A man alone.

A man with secrets.

No wonder Olivia was torn about having him to dinner, Jess thought as she stood in the middle of the near-empty room. At least she couldn't smell garbage anymore, she thought as she contemplated her options.

She grabbed her tote and headed out again, locking the door behind her. She didn't have a plan. She just didn't want to stay alone in her sister's apartment.

As she ran down the front steps, she noticed a dark gray truck double-parked in front of the building.

Mark.

He rolled down his window. "Hey, good-looking. Where you headed?"

She grinned at him, hoisting her tote onto one shoulder. "Be careful. Someone could be calling 911 now. What are you doing in Boston?"

"I ended up meeting some engineers in Cambridge and decided to cross the river and see if I could find you. I was just going to call, and here you are."

"Go park," she said. "I'll whisk you off to dinner."

Feeling less agitated, less unfocused and restless, Jess waited by a black lamppost, but Mark got lucky and found a spot at the end of the block. She watched him park and then walk toward her with his long, confident stride. He wore a full-length raincoat but left it open.

"You look like you belong here," she said. "Mr. Urban."

"I don't miss the city."

"Did you hate living here?"

"Not hate." He winked at her, coming closer. "Disliked."

"A country boy at heart," she said lightly.

"Heart and soul. You, too, Jess. A country girl at heart. What do you have in mind for dinner?"

"There's a restaurant Olivia likes on Newbury. It's early. Why don't we see if they have a table? I'm staying at her apartment tonight. That means I can have wine."

Mark slung an arm over her shoulders. "I'm meeting the engineers again tomorrow. I thought I'd drive back home tonight, but maybe I'll stay in town. I can have wine, too."

"And where were you planning to stay, Mr. Flanagan?"

"Your sister's apartment—"

"There's no bed. Just a couch."

"Pullout?"

"I don't know."

He drew her to him and slid his arm to her waist. "Either could work."

Jess felt warm as they headed back to Newbury Street, then a couple of blocks to the restaurant. They were seated at a small table in the back corner. Jess felt herself beginning to relax. She and Mark settled on an inexpensive red wine—she barely paid attention to what it was—as she marveled at the way her evening had changed.

"How was your day?" Mark asked her.

"Busy. Good. Yours?"

"Dull." He smiled, then added, "Until a few minutes ago."

The waiter arrived with their wine, a basket of soft, crusty bread and a bowl of olive oil. They ordered appetizers of spinach gnocchi and eggplant with smoked mozzarella and shared a main dish of fresh seafood over house-made linguine. As she reached for bread, Jess pictured her sister here, meeting clients, enjoying life in the city.

She dipped her bread in the oil. "I've never lived anywhere but Knights Bridge," she said.

Mark eyed her over his wineglass. "Lucky you."

"I know. I love it there. It's home. I don't want to live anywhere else. I just…" She ate a bite of her bread as she watched another young couple enter the restaurant and wondered what their lives were like. Were they engaged? Just getting to know each other? She shook off her questions and picked up her wineglass. "Never mind. I can see us buying land in Knights Bridge. Then you'll design us a wonderful house—"

"If that's what you want," Mark said quietly.

Although not officially engaged, Jess realized that they often talked comfortably about a future together. "It's what I want. Of course." She stopped herself, suddenly out of sorts. She didn't understand why. This man she adored had found her in Boston, and they were having a lovely dinner together—and she was impatient and irritable. She drank some of her wine. "I'm sorry. I don't know what's got into me."

He shrugged. "Nah. You're fine. Long day."

"You don't have to make excuses for me, Mark."

"Okay. You're a crazy bitch—"

She laughed. "All right, all right. Let's change the subject."

He settled back with his wine. "What's up with Olivia and this Dylan McCaffrey?"

"I don't know. He's going back to San Diego in the morning."

"He's rich. You know that, right? I don't care one way or the other, but I wouldn't have expected a partner in a high-tech entertainment company to take a personal interest in an old house in Knights Bridge."

"His father left it to him. Maybe that's why. Olivia's having him over for dinner tonight, but I doubt we'll ever hear from him again after tomorrow." Even as Jess spoke, her words didn't feel quite right. She couldn't put her finger on why not. "Have you ever been to San Diego?"

"Once."

"Did you like it?"

"Yeah, sure." Mark smiled over his wineglass at her. "You have wanderlust, Jess."

Their appetizers arrived, and she tried the gnocchi, relishing the mix of flavors. "I want to travel," she said. "That doesn't mean I don't love Knights Bridge. I don't fantasize about living somewhere else—"

"Yes, you do."

She stabbed more gnocchi and said without looking at him, "Don't tell me what I think, Mark."

"Sorry. That's not what I meant to do. I just want you to say what's on your mind. Don't pretend to feel something you don't feel. If you want to try living somewhere else, we can figure that out."

"I'm glad you said 'we.'"

His eyes narrowed on her for a moment, then he tried the eggplant. "You picked a good restaurant."

Jess tried the eggplant, too. "No wonder Olivia loves this place. She never saw herself staying in Boston forever. I think she's leaving sooner than she planned, but she was so thrilled when her house came on the market and she could afford to buy it."

"It's a risk giving up her job."

"I'm not sure she had a choice, but she won't talk about it." Jess tried more of the gnocchi and eggplant, drank more wine, listened to the murmurs of the other diners as the restaurant filled up. "I've never wanted to live anywhere else, but sometimes I think I should want to. Do you know what I mean?"

She half expected him to say no, he didn't, or to make a joke, but instead he nodded thoughtfully. "I think I do. I left Knights Bridge because I had to—for school. Then I stayed away because what I wanted to do was in the city. I discovered at heart I'm a hometown guy." He glanced down at his plate. "I thought that's what you wanted."

Jess reached across the table and touched his hand. "I want you, Mark. That's all."

He grinned at her. "I'll go with that."

"I don't have to try living somewhere else, but I do want to travel."

"You're not afraid to? You're not using me as an excuse, putting words in my mouth so that you don't have to admit that you're as nervous about traveling as your mother is?"

"No." Jess waited as the waiter delivered their main course. She loved the smell of the rich, spicy sauce but wasn't sure she was that hungry anymore. The appetizers, bread and wine had filled her up, and she could feel her stomach churning at the thought of her mother and her pictures of California taped to her desk. "I'm determined not to let any fears stop me."

"You're not just dreaming, then—"

"Like my mother, you mean?" Jess didn't wait for him to answer. "I want to travel. I'm willing to get on a plane. I haven't had a reason to fly anywhere since my friend's wedding in Chicago two years ago, but I did it."

Mark scooped up a chunk of steaming lobster. "You make it sound like a root canal."

Jess stared at the seafood, vegetables and pasta and resisted the urge to jump up and run out of the restaurant. "I want to go to Paris," she blurted.

"Paris? When?"

On their honeymoon, she thought. Wouldn't that be nice? But she didn't know if there'd be a honeymoon. Mark liked the status quo of their relationship. They were comfortable. Why would he rock the boat with talk of marriage, a wedding, a honeymoon?

Jess finished off the gnocchi, thinking, and said finally, "I don't know. Soon. Before the end of the year."

"Paris is great. I've only been there once but I liked it."

"That doesn't mean you want to go again."

He shrugged and didn't rise to the bait. "Do you have your passport?"

"Not yet. I'm getting one," Jess said, feeling defiant—as if somehow Mark were doubting her, challenging her. "Is your passport current?"

"I think I've got a couple of years left on it. I'll check."

"Then you'll go with me?"

"Jess Frost and Paris... I suppose if I have to."

She was ready to be offended but saw the twinkle in his eyes and the play of a smile at the corner of his mouth and laughed. "If we weren't in a restaurant, I swear I'd throw something at you."

He laughed, too, and any frustration, anxiety and defiance Jess felt fell away as they chatted and enjoyed the rest of their dinner.

Out on Newbury, Mark slipped his hand into hers. Jess glanced back at the restaurant. "I wonder if Olivia misses Boston. I'm not sure she's told us everything about why she's back in Knights Bridge."

"Maybe not."

"I think something happened with her work and a friend of hers—Marilyn Bryson. Have you met her?"

"Not that I know of. What about Roger Bailey? Is she doing freelance work for him? I introduced them, but I haven't talked to him in a couple months. Everything okay?"

"I don't know," Jess said.

"Olivia's not one to discuss her work, especially if there are problems," Mark said. "I can call Roger, see what I can find out."

"I just hope she's okay."

"She seems happy and excited about what she's doing, but she has to be careful not to let her pride and stubbornness keep her from asking for help when she needs it, or even just getting a little moral support."

Jess looked over at him. "Is that what you think I do, too? I'm her sister—"

"But you have me," he said, his voice low, sexy.

They continued down the busy street. Jess found everything around her energizing. The crush of people, the traffic, the lights. Whatever problems she had were back in Knights Bridge—and she wasn't. She was here, walking in the city on a cool, early-spring night with the man she loved. For now, she thought, Paris could wait.

Chapter 8

Olivia decided to have dinner in the kitchen, not in the dining room, which would have seemed too intimate, too romantic. She lit candles on the kitchen table and got out her good dishes, white china she had found at a Boston yard sale. Dylan arrived with a bottle of wine and let her be the one to say that the roast was awful. It'd been a while since she'd cooked one, and it was tough and stringy. The sides were decent, though—mesclun salad with a few snips of fresh herbs, roasted Brussels sprouts and butternut squash with a dash of nutmeg.

They talked about design, Boston and her family's custom millwork business. Dylan deflected questions about himself, not necessarily, Olivia thought, because he had anything to hide but because he wanted to know about her, whether she could help him understand why his father had bought Grace Webster's house.

Or he was just bored and curious.

He switched on an overhead light in the dining room of Grace's—*his*—house. They'd walked up the road after dinner, dusk making the surrounding fields and woods seem even quieter, more isolated.

"Grace left a lot of books behind," Dylan said as they entered the dining room.

Olivia ran her fingertips along a row of musty books on a shelf of one of Grace's old bookcases. "Latin readers, English grammar books." She smiled back at Dylan. "A little midnight reading for you."

He eased his jacket off his broad shoulders and hung it on the back of a dining chair. Olivia left her own jacket on. She didn't expect to stay long, wasn't even sure why she'd come.

He withdrew a slender volume from another shelf and read the spine. "*Scaramouche* by Rafael Sabatini. Have you read it?"

"When I was a teenager. It's a lot of fun."

"It's about a swashbuckler during the French Revolution, isn't it?"

"The main character is a fugitive who becomes a master swordsman."

Dylan flipped open a page. "Noah might like it. He's a master fencer."

The mention of Noah Kendrick only reminded Olivia how little she knew about the man next to her. She abandoned the grammar and Latin books and checked out his shelf. She read a line of titles. "*The Scarlet Pimpernel, Jane Eyre, Rebecca, The Count of Monte Cristo, The Three Musketeers*. We must have stumbled on the action, romance and adventure section."

"You seem surprised."

"I guess I am. The Latin readers seem more in Grace's character."

"Most of these books look as if they're in decent condition. They could be sold or donated. Why would she leave them here?"

"Good question," Olivia said, glancing at the bottom shelf, which held more titles in a similar vein. "She's in her nineties. Maybe she just didn't want to bother, or she thought your father would enjoy them."

Dylan slid *Scaramouche* back onto the shelf and pulled out a thick, warped copy of *The Count of Monte Cristo* and opened it. A yellowed bookplate was stuck to the inside cover, with *Grace Webster* printed in neat lettering under a sepia drawing of a cat sitting on a stack of books.

"Is there a date?" Olivia asked, then pointed, her arm brushing against his. "There. In the corner—*1938*. She must have had this book since she was a girl."

He turned a page. "'Chapter One, Marseille, The Arrival.'"

"Hooks you right into the story, doesn't he? Have you read it?"

"I saw the movie," Dylan said with a wink, replacing the book on the shelf.

"Your father was into adventures, although I suppose not ones in the pages of an Alexandre Dumas novel. He didn't buy this house because Grace liked swashbucklers, but if she thought of him as a swashbuckler…" Olivia stopped herself. "She asked me if you were a scoundrel."

Dylan laughed but seemed surprised as well as amused. "A scoundrel, huh?"

Olivia ran her fingertips over the row of adventure

novels. "Your father was a treasure hunter. He could have stirred up her teenage soul."

"That wouldn't explain why he landed here in the first place. He loved looking into old mysteries and lost ships and such, but he lived in the present."

Olivia watched Dylan return *The Count of Monte Cristo* to its spot on the dusty shelf. He was out of place here, in this leaking wreck of a house, she realized, but she couldn't picture him in San Diego. Where did he live? What was his life there like? Finally she said, "This all must seem so foreign to you. You have a life in San Diego. You'll go back to it tomorrow. Right now you're trying to reconcile yourself to never knowing exactly why your father bought this place, aren't you?"

He turned to her, pushed a few stray strands of hair out of her face. "Not even close. My father left me a trunk filled with files and God knows what else. I want to have a closer look." He skimmed a knuckle across her cheek. "Then who knows."

Her skin tingled from his touch, and she fought an urge to sink against him at the same time she fought an urge to run. "You can afford to do whatever you want with this place. Sell it, keep it, give it away. You have the means, and you don't have any emotional attachments."

"Do you? To this place?"

Olivia shook her head. "I guess it'll always be Miss Webster's house to me, but no—no emotional attachment."

"It's not a historic center-chimney farmhouse?"

"Are you making fun of me, Dylan McCaffrey?"

He leaned closer to her. "You're not the starchy Yankee I expected Olivia Frost of The Farm at Carriage Hill to be." He placed his hands on her shoulders. "Olivia…" He sighed. "Well, damn." He spoke half under his breath, then kissed her, a quick, intense kiss that said he wanted more even as he stood back from her. "I've been thinking that was bound to happen. I suspect you have, too."

She waved a hand, feeling a little breathless even from that brief contact. "Maybe." She steadied herself. "Maybe in the back of my mind."

"Hmm. I hope that means you're not going to sic Buster on me." He reached for his jacket. "Come on. I'll drive you back down the road."

"I can walk. The air will do me good. I walk Buster after dark all the time." Olivia glanced around the sparsely furnished dining room. "Where do you sleep? I can't imagine you brought an air mattress with you."

"I made a bed out of old blankets. It's not too bad."

"Not quite the five-star accommodations you're used to."

"Softer than a skating rink."

Before she could consider what she was doing, she said, "I have spare bedrooms if you want a proper bed."

Dylan took a second too long to respond, the pause getting her heart racing. "Thanks for the offer. I should camp out here again tonight. I have an early flight."

"Right. Well. At least you have your choice of reading if you can't sleep."

He walked out with her, giving her instructions on how to reach him should his property require more work and wishing her luck getting ready for the opening of The Farm at Carriage Hill.

It was as if their kiss had never happened. Of course, he lived a very different life from hers. He was worth millions. Sneaking a kiss probably wasn't that big a deal for him.

Olivia figured a for sale sign would go up within days of his return to San Diego.

She had grabbed *The Three Musketeers* to take with her. She doubted she'd sleep well tonight, home alone, with scoundrels, swashbucklers, treasure hunters and one incredibly sexy ex-hockey player on her mind.

Dylan watched Olivia head down his driveway and onto the back road they shared before contemplating his situation. What did he know now that he hadn't known the day he'd received her note?

Nothing more about why his father bought this place and didn't tell him about it. But he had learned he didn't particularly like hauling old appliances out of snow, mud and dead leaves...and that a certain brunette looked even better in person than on the internet. Kissing her might have been a mistake but it didn't feel like one.

Turning down a bed in her house felt like the mistake.

His house was quiet and still.

He returned to the dining room and went through more of Grace Webster's books. He didn't know what he had expected to find. A treasure map? A forgotten letter describing lost treasure?

He found nothing.

Taking *The Count of Monte Cristo* with him, he went upstairs to his makeshift bed. He couldn't pinpoint why he hadn't accepted Olivia's offer of one of her spare rooms, except that it hadn't felt like the right thing to do—for her sake, at least.

He pulled back a wool blanket that smelled like mothballs.

This house, this place, his father, his pretty neighbor. He wasn't accustomed to his head spinning with emotions, but he had to admit it was.

He plugged in a small lamp on the floor next to his pallet and adjusted the shade so that the dim bulb was pointed at his book. Had his father ever spent a night here? Olivia had raised a good point, Dylan thought. What if he never knew why his father had come to Knights Bridge?

He opened his book to page one, and, putting everything else out of his mind, started reading the tale of Edmond Dantès and his adventures.

Chapter 9

By the summer of 1938, the state had "disincorporated" the towns of Prescott, Dana, Enfield and Greenwich. Officially, they no longer existed. The valley emptied out slowly, painfully, one family and one business at a time. Work on the reservoir went on, as relentless as a summer storm. I watched graves being dug up, and I watched trees getting chopped down and houses—some of the nicer houses of the valley—being dismantled and moved on trucks to other places.

I learned about the baffle dams that would turn the water of the east branch of the Swift River north again, so that it wouldn't enter the aqueduct that would take it to Boston too soon and would have time for the reservoir's natural filtration process to occur. Engineers had made precise calculations about every aspect of the massive project. Winsor Dam and Goodnough Dike—

two massive earthen dams—would impound the waters of Beaver Brook and the three branches of the Swift River.

The modern world had come to our quiet valley, and my father could no longer pretend it hadn't.

He didn't like it. Not one bit.

The letter we had received from the state was to the point:

"You are hereby notified that the Commonwealth of Massachusetts acting through its Metropolitan District Water Supply Commission requires the land and buildings now occupied by you."

Our home, in other words.

Gran tried to put the best face on the inevitable. "At least we have a chance to move. We're not being wiped out by a tornado or an earthquake."

"No," my father said, "we're being wiped out by our fellow citizens."

I ran out of the house. It was a bright, clear, early-spring morning, and I knew our last days in the valley were upon us, but with the sunlight dancing on the stream bubbling along the lane, I pretended that everything would stay the same. The sugar maples that my great-grandfather had planted would leaf out, just as they had for as long as even Gran could remember. I'd pick wildflowers in the woods, and Gran and I would snap beans in the shade.

My vision ended, proven to be the delusion it was, when a truck lumbered past me, filled with the belongings of a family down the road. The dad was driving. He kept his eyes pinned straight ahead and didn't smile or wave. I don't think he even saw me.

I veered off the lane and followed a stone wall on the

*edge of a hayfield that no one had tended last summer
and no one would tend this summer. When I came to a
giant elm tree, I climbed over the stone wall and took a
path to a small pond. Carriage Hill Pond, it was called.
In the distance, I could see Carriage Hill itself. On the
other side was Knights Bridge; Daddy and Gran were
considering buying a house there. I hated the idea. I
didn't want to move.*

*A one-room cabin was perched on a hillside a few
yards from the water. It used to belong to a family who
had spent summers on the pond. The state had bought
them out last year, and the cabin would eventually be
demolished. I went inside. I still remember the stillness
as I stood in the doorway. I would create my own little
haven in the abandoned cabin. It would be my secret.
No one else need ever know.*

*The family had left behind a cot, a chest of draw-
ers and a table, and I gathered up blankets and linens, added cheerful curtains, found a hooked rug for
the bare wood floor. There was no kitchen or bathroom, just an outhouse, which wasn't that unusual in
those days.*

*It was perfect. While Gran and Daddy figured out
where we would go, while workers ripped apart our valley, I would sneak off to Carriage Hill Pond and escape
into the world I'd created in my tiny hideaway cabin.
I'd bring food in a basket and stay there for hours.*

*One summer morning, I escaped to my cabin after I
overheard Daddy discussing the imminent razing of our
house with two workers. I was breathing hard, my chest
tight with emotion. I kicked off my shoes, climbed under
the blankets and quilts piled on the cot and grabbed a
book from the stack I'd left on the floor. Using money*

I'd earned selling vegetables, I'd bought books at a sale our library held when they had to shut down for Quabbin. The building was gone now, only the foundation left.

For next to nothing, I bought The Scarlet Pimpernel, The Three Musketeers, Scaramouche, The Count of Monte Cristo, Jane Eyre, Wuthering Heights *and so many others. The librarian, one of Gran's friends, gave me a Latin primer and a grammar book for free. I'd come to the cabin whenever I could and read and study and try not to think about the future. If I got married, I knew I would die in childbirth, like my mother. So I wouldn't get married. I'd become a spinster teacher like Miss Johnson, my teacher. But where?*

Not here, I thought. Not in the valley of my childhood. It would be under water.

We would have to move soon. We had no choice, but I didn't want to live among strangers.

I opened my book and realized I'd grabbed Ivanhoe. *I'd read it already but happily started it again. I'd fallen in love with spies, swashbucklers and adventurers. I knew I'd never meet one in real life, but I wished I had a romantic name, like Marguerite or Rowena. Grace was so plain in comparison.*

I read the first page under my covers, but I had to go back and read it again; I kept hearing my grandmother sobbing last night, alone in her room.

"Where will we go? What will we do?"

Poor Gran, I thought. She was stoic and pragmatic during the day, but at night, her fears and her sense of loss would overwhelm her. These were hard times. The modest payout from the state wouldn't make a fresh start elsewhere easy.

"And I'm old," Gran would cry, alone in her room.

Everyone said the evictions were hardest on the old people. Some of the younger people were excited about having the chance—the excuse—to make a fresh start somewhere else.

I put Ivanhoe in my lap and looked out the cabin window at the pond. The water glistened in the sun, and I saw a lone duck in the shade on the opposite bank. Every day, I tried to etch bits and pieces of the valley in my mind. I'd have my memories forever. No one would take them away.

Of course, that was before I wished someone could.

Chapter 10

Olivia was out back contemplating the design and location of her aromatic herb garden and trying to put Dylan's departure out of her mind when Jess stopped by after lunch. "How was Boston?" Olivia asked, joining her sister on the terrace.

"Great. Thanks for letting me use your apartment. I left the keys on your kitchen table. Liv..." Jess hesitated, then said, "Why aren't you working at the studio anymore? I was right, wasn't I? It's because of Marilyn Bryson."

"Why do you ask?"

"I ran into Mark in Boston. He talked to Roger Bailey this morning and Roger said he was working with Marilyn now. Is that true? Did you introduce them? Did he jump ship before you left?"

"Design's a competitive business. Marilyn's hot."

"She went after Roger? Isn't it unethical to steal clients from a friend?" Jess made a face. "I knew I didn't like her."

Olivia appreciated the sisterly solidarity even as her pride and natural reluctance to discuss her problems with her younger sister stopped her from saying more. "I'm happy freelancing."

"You're doing okay with it—making enough to pay the bills?"

Just barely, but she said, "Yeah. It's fine. I like making my own schedule, and I like being here."

"You'll have the last laugh when this place opens."

Olivia noticed a lone daffodil, not quite in bloom, by a small lilac off the end of the terrace. "I'm not here because I'm running from anything, Jess. Marilyn was in a downturn last fall—"

"And you helped her turn her career around. Now she's stealing your clients."

"She's a friend, or she was. She's in high demand. I thought I could have it all—stay on with the studio and still work on this place—but I had to choose. My only regret is that I didn't have more money in the bank before I quit full-time work."

"Do you think you'd still have Roger as a client if you hadn't helped Marilyn?"

"Jess…"

Her sister gave an exaggerated shiver in a sudden breeze. "I can't wait for spring to really get here. You don't have to tell me anything you don't want to, Liv. We all have things we contemplate while we're weeding the oregano and trying out recipes for lemon tarts."

Olivia smiled. "When have you ever tried out a lemon tart recipe?"

"Ah, yes, good question. Hey, I didn't see a car in Grace's driveway. Your good-looking neighbor's on his way back to San Diego?"

"First thing this morning, or so he said. I didn't see him leave."

"Will he be back?"

"He didn't say."

Jess tightened her heavy sweater around her. "At least he's a nice distraction. Not that you're looking for distractions. I wonder if Mom is, and that's why she's planning this trip to California."

"She wants to go, don't you think?"

"I want to go to Paris," Jess mumbled, "but it doesn't mean I'm looking for a distraction—or that I'll ever get there."

Olivia tried to ignore a sick feeling in her stomach as she envisioned her mother on a plane flying west across the continent and her sister on a plane flying east across the Atlantic while she stayed in Knights Bridge.

"Olivia?"

She heard the note of concern in her sister's voice and forced a smile. "Would Mark go with you to Paris?"

"I'm lucky I can get him to go to Boston for a Red Sox or Bruins game once in a while." There was no edge to her words, or she hid it well. "I found some old chairs and a couple of small tables at the sawmill that might interest you. I can help paint them. We can have our own little painting party."

Olivia loved the idea and they started making plans as they walked around to the front of the house. After Jess left, she stood in the driveway and noticed the quiet, noticed how alone she was out on her dead-end road, but she reminded herself that the location, not just the house, was part of the attraction of The Farm at Carriage Hill.

There was just no broad-shouldered ex-hockey player up the road to whisk her off for a hike or come to dinner.

A week later, Olivia hadn't heard a word from Dylan. Not that she'd expected to hear anything. His life was in San Diego, not in little Knights Bridge. At least the house Duncan McCaffrey had mysteriously left his only son wasn't looking as shabby with the landscape greening up in a stretch of warm weather. She headed to Boston for her first face-to-face meeting with Jacqui Ackerman since her departure almost a month ago.

"Marilyn's starting work with us," Jacqui said when she and Olivia sat down at a table in the small conference room.

"Marilyn Bryson? She's moving to Boston?"

"That's right, Olivia. We're thrilled she's decided to join us. Thank you for paving the way. She's bringing Roger Bailey back, plus she'll bring in new clients."

"I'm sure she will," Olivia said dully.

"She starts on Monday. We're all excited. It's the right move for us."

"That's great. What does it mean for me?"

Jacqui hesitated, then said, "Nothing for the moment. You're doing a fabulous job freelancing. You and Marilyn are friends. This can be a positive for everyone."

Olivia mumbled something agreeable. What else could she do? She needed the freelance work. Jacqui seemed relieved, and they moved on to a discussion of designs, which ultimately was what they both loved most about what they did. Afterward, Olivia skipped her plan to have dinner with friends and spend the night at her apartment. Instead, she drove back to Knights Bridge. As the city gave way to the quiet winding roads of her hometown, she decided to do what she had to do to meet her expenses but to concentrate on making The Farm at Carriage Hill a success.

When she arrived at her house, her father's truck was in the driveway, and he was out front with Buster.

He threw a stick across the front yard. "No word from your neighbor?"

"Nope."

"I didn't realize he was *that* Dylan McCaffrey. Jess told me. She thought I knew."

"There was no reason for me to say anything, Dad."

"I saw him play against the Bruins when he was a rising star. He had some great years, then some okay years after injuries. He was a solid player, well liked. Funny he'd end up owning Grace Webster's old place."

Buster went after the stick but immediately flopped down in the grass and started chewing on it. Olivia laughed. "He's not a golden retriever. So, do you like Dylan better now that you remember you saw him play?"

Her father toed loose a rock in the driveway. "I don't know. Should I?"

She changed the subject. "Grace says she met Duncan McCaffrey. Could she be mistaken?"

"I doubt it."

"There's not much that goes on around town that you don't know about. And if you don't know, Mom does. Where is she?"

"Home. She's working in the garden. She says she's coming out here to help paint those chairs and tables Jess found."

"We're having a painting party, sort of a girls' night out."

Her father tossed the rock over to Buster. "I'll contribute the wings and beer."

Olivia laughed again, feeling less stressed after her trip to Boston. After he left she extricated the rock and stick from Buster and went inside. She started a fire to take the chill out of the air, then sat in front of the flames with Buster's head on her lap. But she was restless, her mind spinning with worries, possibilities, questions about Duncan McCaffrey and his good-looking son, and what had happened between her and Dylan on his trip to Knights Bridge.

"Nothing," she muttered, jumping up and heading into the kitchen. "Nothing happened."

What was one little kiss to a man like Dylan? Ex-hockey player, multimillionaire business executive.

She watered the herbs in the window and rummaged in the fridge, but she wasn't hungry.

She went up to bed early and read more of *The Three Musketeers,* imagining Grace immersing herself in tales of swashbucklers and adventurers as a teenager, her world changing around her.

In the morning, Olivia took herself to breakfast at Smith's, Knights Bridge's only restaurant, tucked on a side street off the common in the heart of the village. She sat at a booth across from Albert Molinari, the real estate agent, she'd discovered, who'd handled the sale of Grace's house to Duncan McCaffrey. Al was in his early sixties and semiretired, having left a law practice in Worcester several years ago and moved to Knights Bridge. He spent most of his time biking and kayaking.

"McCaffrey blew in and out of town. A lot of energy. I remember that about him."

"Did he look at a range of properties?" Olivia asked.

"Just the Webster house. It was the only one that interested him."

"Why?"

"He didn't say. I didn't ask. No one else was going to buy the place. I was worried Grace would get stuck with it and sit out there until the roof caved in around her."

"Did he give you a hint of his plans for the property?"

"I tried, Liv, but I didn't get a thing out of him."

After breakfast, she headed over to Rivendell and found Grace on her feet in the sunroom with her binoculars. "I was just going out for a walk," she said.

"Would you like some company?"

"That would be lovely."

They went through a glass door out to the yard. Grace explained that they hadn't refilled the bird feeders now that spring was on the advance, not in full retreat as it had been when Dylan had arrived in town.

"I've been reading *The Three Musketeers*," Olivia said as they walked past a bank of forsythia, their yellow blossoms waving in a light breeze. "When Dylan McCaffrey was here I borrowed the copy you left behind in your house."

"I love that book. I've read it many times. The library here has a copy."

"You're not going to let me read the book you wrote?"

"After I'm gone."

Olivia smiled as they circled back toward the sunroom. "Do you reveal any juicy secrets?"

"We all have our secrets," Grace said quietly.

"Would yours have anything to do with the McCaffreys?"

Grace stopped, gazing out at the surrounding hills, the reservoir glistening in the distance. When Olivia was born, Quabbin was already well-established, already a fact of life in her part of New England. She saw its beauty and had only old photographs and stories to imagine life there before the valley was flooded. When Grace looked at Quabbin, what did she see? The houses, lanes, farms and gardens of her childhood? The friends who'd moved to other towns? Post offices, ice-cream shops, sawmills and Grange Halls that no longer existed? Even the dead, Olivia thought, had been cleared out of the valley.

"I don't know the McCaffreys," Grace said finally.

Olivia didn't want to push the older woman to say anything she would later regret, or to upset her. They returned to the sunroom. Her grandmother had arrived to take Grace to one of their exercise classes. Olivia got out of there, not sure why she'd stopped in the first place. She only knew that she was now madly curious about Duncan McCaffrey's reasons for turning up in Knights Bridge.

His son had to be, too.

Olivia started her car. Dylan would be back. Even if their kiss had been a passing moment not to be repeated, he had unanswered questions about his father.

He wasn't finished with Knights Bridge.

After a long run on the beach, Dylan met Noah and Noah's date, an aspiring actress, at the Hotel del Coronado down the street from his house. They had drinks on the sundeck behind the romantic landmark hotel, with its red-shingled Victorian domes and white-on-white exterior. Dylan stayed through a glowing sunset over the Pacific, then left Noah and his date to enjoy dinner on their own and walked back to his house.

He ate a sandwich and dragged out his father's trunk again. His search wasn't as cursory this time, and he wasn't as impatient. He'd spent his first few days back putting out fires for Noah and trying to convince himself that he didn't need to know any more than he already did about his father's house in Knights Bridge.

"Just get rid of that house," Loretta had told him upon his return from Massachusetts. *"Get rid of it and forget about Knights Bridge."*

Not so easy to do, Dylan realized now. Dreaming about kissing Olivia Frost again didn't help. He'd woken up thinking about her every night since he'd been back in San Diego.

He dug his father's old laptop out of the trunk and fired it up out on the porch. The night was warm and still, the tide out as couples walked hand in hand on the silver sand of the beach. Dylan stifled an unbidden image of himself with Olivia and focused on the laptop screen. He'd never wanted to dip into his father's life. He'd died suddenly, with no time to prepare—no time to burn the classified papers, as it were. Dylan had quickly discovered he needn't have worried. If his father had secrets, he hadn't bothered to write them down or put them onto his computer. His "official" treasure hunts had all been taken over by his partners and colleagues. He wasn't the type to get bogged down in details. He would gather what information he needed, then establish a clear mission and take action.

Dylan had checked with his mother when he'd arrived back in San Diego, but she was of little help. During their brief marriage, she and his father had focused on the present. *"I wasn't meant to be part of his life forever,"* she'd told Dylan. *"I think I always knew that."*

He noticed a file cryptically named "1938" and sat up straight as he opened it and scanned the brief entry:

In early September, 1938, a private luxury hotel on Arlington Street in Boston was broken into and an aristocratic stash of three rings and a necklace, some or all reputedly given to the Ashworth family by Queen Victoria, were stolen. The owner of the jewels, Lord Charles Ashworth, was knocked unconscious but later brushed off the theft, offering only a modest reward for return of "several family heirlooms."

Rings: diamond-and-sapphire; diamond cluster; diamond-and-ruby. Necklace matches the diamond-and-sapphire ring.

A major hurricane struck New England three weeks after the theft. Then came the Munich Pact, the Nazi German invasion of Czechoslovakia and the start of World War Two.

Ashworth survived the war. The Ashworth jewels have never been recovered.

Dylan put his feet up on the porch railing. "Well, well."

He couldn't remember his father ever going after stolen jewels, but why not? The Ashworth jewels had to be worth a fortune. He did a quick internet search of Lord Ashworth. He was a British viscount who'd died forty years ago. One marriage, no children.

No mention of the jewels, never mind the heist in Boston. Too distasteful? Too obscure? They didn't exist?

A quick search wasn't going to do it and he needed to do more digging.

Dylan reread the file as Noah walked up the porch steps, his black suit coat hooked on one finger over his shoulder. He nodded back toward the Hotel del Coronado. "I took her home. She said she had to read *Alice in Wonderland* for a graduate course. You don't think she was blowing me off, do you?"

"She's a graduate student?"

"English."

Dylan supposed it was possible. "Does she know you're rich?"

"No. At least I don't think so. *Alice in Wonderland,* Dylan?"

He grinned. "She was blowing you off, whether or not she knows you're rich."

Noah sighed and sat up on the porch rail, draping his coat next to him. He had on a black shirt, too. "I think I'm depressed."

Noah wasn't depressed. Dylan gave him a beer.

"How the hell old is that laptop?" his friend asked.

"It's an original. Still runs."

Noah took a long swallow of the beer. "What's on your mind, McCaffrey?"

Dylan handed over the laptop and let Noah read.

Noah set the laptop on a small porch table. "How did old Duncan come across the news of this heist?"

"No idea. I don't know of any other unsolved jewelry thefts that caught his eye."

"Why do you think this one did? The history of the jewels? The amount they're worth? The Ashworths? Could they have hired him to find the jewels?"

"He wasn't a private detective."

"What's a jewelry heist in Boston in 1938 got to do with a falling-down house in Knights Bridge?"

"That's what I want to know."

"And the reason would be…what?"

A good question, Dylan thought, suddenly restless as he dropped his feet back to the porch floor.

Noah drank more of his beer and studied his friend. "Let's be honest here, Dylan. You don't care about an obscure jewelry theft. You care about your father, and you're attracted to this woman, Olivia Frost."

Dylan didn't argue with him, but he didn't explain himself, either. He thought of Grace Webster's collection of novels. "Maybe I'm just ready for my own adventure." He rose, welcoming the breeze off the water. "You're in good shape here, Noah. You have a team you can trust in place. You can manage without me."

Noah was philosophical. "We've worked hard, and we've been lucky. Time to get our personal lives in order."

"My personal life's just fine."

"But you are going back to Knights Bridge?"

Dylan looked out at the ocean, dark under the night sky. "I am."

Fifteen minutes after Noah left, Loretta Wrentham breezed up the porch steps. Dylan had texted her about the laptop file. "I haven't had any air all day." She grabbed the last of the three beers Dylan had brought outside with him, one of which he'd drunk. She uncapped it and sighed at him. "You McCaffreys know how to drive a woman to drink. Not that I ever worked for your father. Just you."

"Lucky you," Dylan said with a wry smile.

She angled a skeptical look at him. She had on a crisp white shirt, slim jeans and red heels, as if she were coming from or going to dinner. "You aren't getting into treasure hunting, are you, Dylan?"

"Not if I can help it. I just want to know about this property in Massachusetts."

She glanced back at the beach, then again at him as she took a swallow of the beer. "I don't have anything to add to what I've already told you. I wasn't involved in your father's purchase of the Knights Bridge house."

"But you knew about it."

"After the fact. He told me—because of you."

"Because you're my lawyer and financial manager."

She eased out of her red heels and stood barefoot on the porch. "Correct."

Dylan rose, facing the ocean. "What about the Ashworth jewels, Loretta?"

"You've been busy, I see." She sank against the rail, next to him, her back to the water. "More nonsense. I didn't know much about your father's treasure hunts. While you were in Massachusetts I did some checking. Ninety percent of what he pursued came to a dead end—nature of the beast—or he just lost interest—nature of Duncan McCaffrey."

"Whatever he was up to in Knights Bridge was different," Dylan said.

Loretta studied him as she drank more of her beer. Finally she said, "Are you speculating or do you know?"

"Half and half."

She set the beer bottle back on the table. She'd drunk maybe a third. "He never mentioned the Ashworth jewels. Not to me."

Dylan shifted his gaze from the ocean and nodded

to the old laptop, still open on the table. The screen had gone blank. "You can have a look at the file if you want."

"Dylan…"

When she didn't go on, he filled her in on what he'd discovered on his father's laptop.

Loretta shook her head. "Dylan, I don't know what to say. A 1938 Boston robbery, missing jewels—I can't help you."

"My father's interest in Knights Bridge feels personal," Dylan said, turning again to face the water. "I don't think he bought the Webster house on a whim."

"Maybe not." Loretta turned with him, the porch light catching the lines at the corners of her eyes. "It's a beautiful night, isn't it?"

Dylan didn't answer. It was obvious it was a beautiful night. "My father didn't involve any of his usual partners and investors in whatever he was after in Knights Bridge."

"No, he didn't." She stared out at the water. "Sometimes it's best to let sleeping dogs lie. You have a life here, Dylan. Your father's gone. You can afford to walk away from this house." She shifted her gaze, leveling her dark eyes on him. "Maybe you can't afford not to walk away."

"The roof leaks but there are all these musty old books. Have you read *The Count of Monte Cristo?*"

Loretta frowned at him as if he'd lost his mind and finally sputtered into laughter. "I'm not even going to ask what *The Count of Monte Cristo* has to do with any of this. I've seen the movie. That's enough for me."

Dylan grinned at her. "Ever been to New England?"

"No."

"This is the New England of historic houses, town greens, rolling hills—"

"I like San Diego," she said stubbornly. "You live in paradise. If you want, I can take care of this house in Knights Bridge for you. You don't have to think about it again."

It wasn't her tone that got his attention. It was the way she fidgeted, closing the laptop, lining up the beer bottles on the table, then twisting her hands together as if she were cold. She wasn't cold.

Dylan narrowed his eyes on her. "Loretta?"

"Nothing. Never mind. I have to go." She scooped up her shoes and bolted for the steps. "Let me know what you decide to do."

"I've already decided."

She glanced back at him. "You're going back to Knights Bridge."

He smiled. "All the snow and ice should be melted by now."

She descended the stairs, muttering to herself as she disappeared down the walk.

Dylan collected the laptop and bottles and went back inside. Before he headed east again, he'd go through every file on his father's laptop and every scrap of paper in the trunk. He wanted to know what his father hadn't told him, and what Loretta knew and wasn't telling him about his run-down little house by Carriage Hill. She wasn't herself. Stalling, parsing her words, changing the subject—probably trying to avoid lying to him.

Near the bottom of the trunk, he found a small-press history of Quabbin tucked in a letterbox. *The Day Four Quabbin Towns Died* by J.R. Greene. It proved his father not only knew about the massive reservoir but had

wanted to read about its history. Dylan flipped through
the pages of the slender volume. A yellowed newspaper
article about the Ashworth robbery fell out onto his lap.
He carefully unfolded it. There was handwriting in the
corner—a woman's handwriting, he thought. It was as
if someone had torn the article out of a Boston newspaper and jotted a note to herself.

Isaiah Webster, Knights Bridge.

Was it Grace Webster's handwriting?

Who was Isaiah?

Dylan refolded the article and slipped it back into the
book. He reached for his phone. He'd be on a plane tomorrow, with no answers, just a fresh set of questions.

Chapter 11

Olivia told herself that a trio of daffodils blooming by the front steps had lured her into Dylan's yard, but she knew better. She loved daffodils and the ones at her house were in a cooler spot and not yet in bloom, but it wasn't their cheerful welcome that had prompted her to head up her neighbor's driveway. It was curiosity.

On another walk that morning with Grace, the older woman had said something that had been on Olivia's mind ever since. *"A house is not a home. I didn't mind leaving my house and moving into my apartment here at Rivendell. If Duncan McCaffrey thought I left behind clues to a lost treasure..."*

Grace didn't go on, but Olivia had prodded her. *"Did you?"*

"Of course not. Where would I get a treasure? This," she'd said, dramatically gesturing toward the nearby

fields and woods, with Quabbin in the distance, *"is a true treasure."*

Maybe so, Olivia thought, but as she mounted the sagging steps to the back porch, she had the feeling that Grace had deliberately played the sentimental card to change the subject.

Olivia realized her heart was pounding. She didn't know why she was so on edge. It wasn't as if she had to worry about passersby or a police cruiser catching her sneaking into her neighbor's house. No one ever came out here.

She found a mud-encrusted key under an empty, cracked flowerpot and scraped it clean, then tried it on the back door. The door opened, and she went inside, heading straight for the dining room. She sat on the floor in front of one of the bookcases and emptied it, examining each volume before she returned it to its shelf. Had Dylan done the same before he flew back to San Diego?

After almost an hour, she'd gone through every one of the books Grace had left behind in the dining room.

No treasure map with an X marking the spot, no cryptic notes, no hollowed-out pages with gold coins inside.

Nothing at all of interest to a treasure hunter, Olivia thought with a sigh as she rolled to her feet and stretched out her lower back. There could be more books in the living room or upstairs. She supposed it was crazy to think she'd find anything in them.

She heard a car on the road and crept to the front window in the living room. A dark blue Audi similar to the one Dylan had rented was pulling into the driveway.

Could it be Dylan?

Whoever it was, Olivia didn't want to have to explain why she was inside his house. She ran into the kitchen and slipped out the back door, shutting it quietly behind her. She tiptoed down the steps to the overgrown yard, dozens of violets mingling with the grass in the late-afternoon sun. She could make a break for the stone wall, then sneak through the woods back out to the road and walk innocently to her house.

She got halfway to the stone wall before Dylan caught up with her, hooking a strong arm around her waist. "I wonder if I could get anyone in Knights Bridge to arrest you for breaking and entering."

"I didn't break in. I had a spare key." In fact, she thought, she still had it in the right hip pocket of her jeans. "I saw Grace this morning—"

"Grace doesn't own this place anymore."

Olivia could see he was enjoying himself. "I didn't expect you," she said, aware her fleece shirt was askew, his arm settling on bare skin just above her hips. "Why are you back?"

"Maybe because of you."

She wriggled loose from him and adjusted her shirt. "Did something happen?"

He didn't answer. His canvas jacket was unbuttoned over a dark brown shirt that fit closely to his chest. Olivia felt a rush of warmth and suspected it showed in her face, but she hoped he'd assume it was due to the cool air or her mad dash across the yard.

She nodded toward the house. "I wasn't snooping. I was just curious. Because of your father."

"Were you hoping to find lost treasure?"

"Clues, maybe," she said lightly. "How long are you staying this time?"

"For a while."

"'A while' meaning forty-eight hours or forty-eight days?"

"A few days, at least. I've already been by the general store and stocked up on basics. Food, a camp bed, a refrigerator—"

"A fridge? It's in the back of your car?"

"It's a dorm-size fridge." He started back across the yard. "I have some planning and thinking to do, away from any distractions in San Diego."

"Wine, women and song? Maybe no song." Olivia kept up with him as he headed for the back porch. "You don't seem like the singing type."

He glanced sideways at her. "How did you learn about my father's work as a treasure hunter? You were vague when I asked you before. Was it Grace? She knew?"

"She told me after you turned up here and weren't seventy. Then I looked him up on Google. Why?"

"How many people around here know?"

"I have no idea. It's not a secret, is it?" Olivia studied Dylan, noticing a seriousness about him that hadn't been there before. "I'm a graphic designer, Dylan. Up until recently I had a busy, demanding career in Boston. I got in touch with you because of junk in your yard. I didn't look up you or your father because of any treasure."

He nodded but said nothing.

She stopped abruptly. "You don't believe me?"

He went a few steps ahead of her, then turned, his blue eyes dark, unreadable, as they settled on her. "I didn't say that."

Something, she realized, had happened in San Diego.

"I didn't expect to stir anything up when I contacted you. I thought you'd tell me to go ahead and clean up the yard myself. If I hadn't written to you, where would you be right now?"

Some of his tension seemed to ease. He winked at her. "Running on the beach, probably, or drinking beer on my front porch. It doesn't matter. I'm here." He looked over at the porch steps. "Where's the key?"

She dug it out of her pocket and handed it over. "It was under the flowerpot. You probably should hide it somewhere else. If I'd known you were coming, I'd have mopped the floors. I didn't have time to do the windows."

"Funny, Olivia." He tucked the key into a jacket pocket. "Imagine if I'd caught you upstairs instead of out here."

It was exactly what she'd been imagining since she'd made a run for the woods. She smiled at him. "You move fast. I thought you'd need skates to cross a yard that fast."

He grinned. "I was highly motivated."

"No wonder Grace thought you were a scoundrel."

"You have dust in your hair," he said, coming a bit closer to her.

"At least it's not mouse droppings."

"I'm not sure I'd want to kiss you with mouse droppings in your hair. Dust, though… I don't mind dust." He tucked a finger under her chin. "I'd come back here for you. I don't need lost treasure."

"You're making my head spin, Dylan McCaffrey."

"Good." He lowered his mouth, brushed his lips across hers, then drew back. "Say hi to Buster for me."

"Dylan—"

"I'll try out my new camp bed tonight with Grace's musty blankets. Safer." He smiled. "I'm on California time. I don't want to keep you up late."

Olivia breathed again. "Must have been a long flight across the country."

"Hell of a long flight."

Now wasn't the time to try to talk to him about what was going on between them. Too much adrenaline. Too much testosterone, she thought, glancing at her ex-hockey player neighbor. She could see him hip checking an opponent, no question.

"If you need anything," she said, "you know where to find me."

"Thanks."

"Not a lot of neighbors out this way," she added, as if he needed reminding.

As she walked back down the road, Olivia noticed daylight was lasting later into the evening, a sure sign that spring had arrived. Once back at her house, she dragged out one of the tables Jess had found and set it on a drop cloth in the back room, where she did all her painting. A deep, rustic gold with a sponged finish would be nice, she decided, trying to focus on her work and not her sexy neighbor, her tingling skin and lost treasure.

She set up her painting supplies and wiped down the table. She wanted everything in the house to look as if it belonged, had been there awhile. She opened a window for ventilation. She still could feel Dylan's mouth on hers and sighed, wondering if she should have gotten a few friends together and cleaned up Grace's old yard and not bothered contacting the owner. He'd never have been the wiser, and she wouldn't be thinking about when she'd get to kiss him again.

She opened the can of paint.

Wherever Dylan was sleeping tonight, it was just as well it wasn't under her roof.

Dylan had ordered breakfast and was drinking his first cup of coffee of the day when Olivia eased onto the stool next to him at the counter at Smith's. His neighbor looked refreshed and energetic, he thought, but then again, she'd spent the night in a real bed. He'd spent the night on his new camp bed. It was more comfortable than his pile of musty blankets but he hadn't slept well. He wouldn't have, even if he'd been in a proper bed. He'd tossed, turned and stared at the ceiling, asking himself what, if anything, Grace Webster, Olivia Frost and the rest of the population of Knights Bridge knew about Lord Charles Ashworth and the missing Ashworth jewels.

"The omelets here are great," Olivia said cheerfully. "No caviar, though."

"I ordered the one with local cheddar, peppers and onions. What would you like?"

"Just coffee."

"Did you follow me?"

Her changeable eyes sparked. "Maybe." She waited for the waitress to deliver a mug of coffee, then added cream and glanced at him next to her. "You look more like a hockey player this morning than an executive for a major corporation."

"I'm not an executive. I'm Noah's friend from first grade. I have his back."

"You're a glorified bodyguard?"

He couldn't help but smile. "Not exactly."

She added more cream to her coffee. Evidently she liked it very light, or she'd forgotten she'd already put cream in it. "Don't underplay your role because you think we can't handle the truth out here in Knights Bridge."

Dylan shrugged. He had the feeling Olivia had been reading more about him, Noah and NAK, Inc. on the internet. "Okay."

She snapped up her mug with such force that hot coffee splashed onto her hand. She grabbed her paper napkin and blotted the spill. "Do you have that effect on everyone?"

He suppressed a smile. "What effect?"

She muttered something under her breath that he couldn't quite make out.

His omelet arrived. It was damn near perfect and came with homemade toast and a little bowl of home-made strawberry-rhubarb jam and another little bowl of soft butter. At home on Coronado, he'd be having Cheerios and a banana.

At home on Coronado, it was five o'clock in the morning. He'd be asleep.

He decided to satisfy Olivia's curiosity about him. "I helped Noah with people and structure so that he could focus on what he does best. We took a few risks that paid off. Yes, I've done well. Yes, I can afford caviar, but I don't like it."

"You've tried it, though."

"Once. At a party in L.A."

Olivia swiveled on her stool so that she was facing him. She had on a marine-blue corduroy shirt over cargo pants and trail shoes with wool socks. April, he thought, and still wearing wool socks. Her hair was pulled back in a loose ponytail, strands of gold-streaked dark hair falling into her face. He doubted she even noticed.

"A party for what?" she asked.

"Just a party. Noah likes parties, or he says he does."

"He's known for having a string of women in his life. Actresses and models and such. I read that on some gossip page on the internet."

"Noah's single—"

"As are you."

"Don't believe everything you read on the internet."

"I don't, but I saw a picture of Noah with a babe on his arm. I doubt she was his sister."

"Noah's trusting."

"And you?"

Dylan handed her a triangle of toast. "Eat. You look hungry."

"I'm not—"

"Yes, you are. That's what I bring to my work with Noah—I'm pretty good at reading people."

"You can tell I'm hungry? That's just a lucky guess." But she took the toast and bit right into it. "You keep unpleasant people at bay in order to let Noah focus. Is that right?"

Dylan spread another triangle of toast with the jam, the tiny chunks of strawberry and rhubarb just the right size, and grinned at her. "'Unpleasant people.' That's a polite way to put it."

"I don't mean to be intrusive. What you do and how much you're worth are none of my business. Did you investigate me before you came out here?"

He laughed. "I threw caution to the wind after seeing your picture and came out here without a complete dossier on you." He was enjoying himself and couldn't quite explain why. "How's everything coming along for opening day at The Farm at Carriage Hill?"

"Everything's going just fine, thanks. I don't need you to warn me off any jerks and scumbags. That would have been handy when I was still in Boston."

She seemed to think she'd said too much and jumped down from the stool. She started to reach for her bag, but Dylan put his hand on her arm and leaned close to her. "I'm not worth a billion, but I can afford to buy you a cup of coffee."

"I can pay my own way."

"You can, but sometimes you don't have to. Sometimes you can just say thanks and let it go."

She smiled. "Thanks."

"I still want to know what happened to you."

"I came home to Knights Bridge."

After she left, Dylan had a refill of coffee and finished his breakfast, feeling as if he might have just landed from Mars and had nothing in common with Earth's population. An out-of-the-way New England town, a stubborn, independent, attractive woman with secrets? What the hell was he doing here?

He drove over to Frost Millworks. Olivia's sister, who worked in the family business, lived in the picturesque original nineteenth-century sawmill by the old dam and millpond. The Frosts had converted it into a residence. Dylan hadn't needed to do any digging to find out that tidbit. All he'd had to do was sit at the counter at Smith's and listen to his fellow patrons, then put the bits and pieces of different conversations together.

He entered the surprisingly modern mill building. He'd also gathered from his eavesdropping at Smith's that Randy Frost was well liked and something of a force of nature in town. Dylan found him in the toasty warm front office, eyeing a row of photographs taped to the top edge of the rolltop desk.

"That's Cambria," Dylan said, pointing to one of a familiar street in the small town on California's scenic Pacific Coast Highway. "Nice spot."

"You've been to Cambria?"

"Many times."

"They say the road can be downright scary."

"Depends on what scares you, I guess."

"You weren't scared," Randy Frost said, making it a statement.

"Nah. Are you planning a trip west?"

"My wife is. She says she wants me to go with her, but I don't know. She's not one to travel. She might want to slay this particular dragon on her own." Randy pointed to a large sheet of white sketch paper on the desk. "I just unfolded this. I thought it was something work related. Louise will kill me dead if she walks in here and sees me with it, but what do you think it is?"

Dylan took a closer look. In the middle of the page was a blue dot, probably done with a crayon. It was surrounded by other crayon dots in various colors, with a few stray dots farther from the blue dot.

"It looks like dots," he said.

"That's what it looks like to me, too." Randy refolded the paper and stuck it under a magazine with an enticing photograph of Malibu on the cover. "Keep your mouth shut, all right?"

No worries there, Dylan thought. "Sure."

"Damn. What a mess. I shouldn't have said anything,

but what the hell. You didn't come here to listen to me talk about dots. What can I do for you?"

"Just thought I'd stop by. Mind if I look around?"

"Sure. Here, I'll go with you. Are you thinking about renovating Grace's place?" Randy asked as he followed Dylan out to the showroom.

"I'm not sure that's possible."

"Most people around here thought she wouldn't be with us before her house had to be condemned. Kind of morbid, but that's the truth."

"It needs a wrecking crane. I can't see putting any money into it."

"You won't get an argument from me." Randy walked over to a large window that looked out on the stream; next to him was a display of an assortment of moldings and trim. "We like to save our old houses around here, but Grace's house wasn't much even when it was built. It's gone to hell in the meantime. Have you figured out why your father bought it? Is that why you're back here?"

"My father died before I even knew I owned a house in Knights Bridge."

Randy grinned. "Cagey answer, McCaffrey. Come on. I'll show you the rest of the place."

They went into a workroom, where a small crew of skilled craftsmen was getting set up for the day at their various machines. They seemed comfortable with Randy Frost, and respectful. He greeted them each by name and introduced Dylan. Most, but not all, were from Knights Bridge. Randy explained how the family sawmill had transformed into a company that provided quality custom millwork to builders, architects and homeowners, predominantly in the New England area.

"Grace Webster's father worked at the old sawmill for a few months before he died," Randy said as he and Dylan returned to the showroom. "I think it was his last job."

"Does Grace have any family left in the area?"

"Not anymore, no. She's an only child. Her mother died in childbirth. Her father and grandmother raised her. My mother remembers them. They were never the same after the state took their home for Quabbin. I was fishing a few years ago and realized my boat was right over the spot where the Websters used to live. It was downright eerie."

"I didn't realize fishing is allowed in Quabbin."

"March through October. There are restricted areas but they're clearly marked, and you can't go out on the water unless you have a fishing license. Pleasure boats aren't allowed. I don't fish very often. Louise gets nervous when I go alone, and most of the time I'm too busy. Some of my buddies fish, but they're more serious about it than I am."

"I don't think I've ever even picked up a fishing pole."

"Gee," Randy said with a grin, "what a surprise."

"Did you have Grace as a teacher?"

"English my senior year. They say she'd mellowed some by then, but I'd have hated to see her when she was in her prime. She was tough. She was one of the best teachers I ever had, though."

"She left a lot behind when she moved out of her house."

"Shook the dust off her feet and moved on. I can admire that, but there's not much room in her new place."

"I'd like to meet her."

"That's up to her."

"Understood."

"I'll give my mother a call. She and Grace are tight. I'll see what she says."

The front door opened, and Olivia entered the showroom with two other women. Dylan immediately could see a family resemblance as Randy introduced his wife, Louise, and Jess, their younger daughter. Jess gave him a frank once-over, as though she suspected he might be an issue, if not a problem. Could she have found out he'd kissed her sister?

"Good to meet you finally," Jess said, then headed to the workroom.

Randy motioned for Dylan to follow Olivia and her mother to the office. Dylan noticed Olivia's expression tighten as she glanced at him, as if he were spying on her family, then turned her attention to the map of California tacked on the wall.

Louise Frost settled at her rolltop desk. She looked up at her pictures of the coastal highway. "Have you visited any of the Central Coast wineries, Dylan?" she asked.

He didn't mention that Noah owned one. "Several. Beautiful country."

She swiveled around to him. "Randy says you were with the NHL. We do an ice rink on the town common every winter. If you stay in Knights Bridge, maybe you can give the kids a few pointers."

"It won't be winter again for a while, I hope."

Louise laughed and nodded to her husband in the doorway. "You gave Dylan a tour of the place?"

"The five-minute version," Randy said. "He'd like to meet Grace. I thought I could run him over there and ask Ma to introduce him—"

"I can take him," Olivia said; she turned from the map and addressed Dylan. "We can go in my car. I can drop you off back here."

Meaning she wanted to keep an eye on him. Well, he thought, that was a two-way street. He smiled. "Sounds good."

She led the way out to her car, not glancing back to see if he was following her. He climbed in on the passenger side. "No dog hair," he noted.

"Buster doesn't like cars."

Fabric swatches were stacked in the backseat, the range of colors and patterns reminding him that Olivia was a graphic designer, a woman with a creative flair. "I don't have a creative bone in my body," he said.

She started the car and backed out into the parking lot, then turned on the road that would take them back into the village. "I'll bet you do. You have to think creatively to be a hockey player and a successful businessman, don't you?"

"Those are learned skills."

"I've learned my skills, too. We need both—inspiration and craft." She continued along the quiet road. "Money helps, too."

Dylan frowned at her. "You look tired, Olivia. Not enough coffee?"

"I should have stuck around longer at breakfast. I was up late last night working on a project."

"Freelance or for Carriage Hill?"

"Freelance. It's not one I'm enjoying."

He considered her comment. "Because of the client or the job itself?"

"The work is fine. I always enjoy the work. It's a leftover job for a longtime client who decided to go with another designer."

"So you did get your ass kicked in Boston," Dylan said, matter-of-factly.

"I didn't say that."

"You didn't have to."

"There are some sharp curves ahead. I should concentrate on my driving."

He shrugged. "By all means."

The road wasn't that twisty, and Olivia obviously knew it well. She could have just told him to mind his own damn business but that, he realized, wasn't her style. After another mile, he could see a rolling field with a low-slung building situated among stone walls, gardens and a sprawling lawn dotted with a mix of deciduous trees and well-maintained evergreens.

"This is Rivendell, our local assisted living facility," Olivia said. "The original residents named it when it first opened a few years ago. Mark Flanagan, Jess's boyfriend, did the design. It's small, but Grace and my grandmother love it here. It was a surprise for us as much as them, I think. They both get out, but Grace less so. My grandmother has her own car. Grace doesn't drive anymore."

"She was retired by the time you were in high school?"

"Yes, but she tutored until her mid-eighties."

"Did she tutor you?"

"Not me, but I know she tutored Mark Flanagan. He didn't tune into schoolwork until college. No one ever thought he'd become an architect."

"Did Grace do him any good?"

"He read Shakespeare because of her," Olivia said. "He wouldn't have otherwise."

"That's good."

"Othello dies in the end, you know. So does King Lear." She turned off the car engine and shifted to him, her eyes sparkling with humor. "I hope I'm not giving anything away."

Dylan grinned at her. "That's better. You have a lot on your mind. You're opening a new business, your sister's exhausted and your parents are planning a trip to California that's a source of tension—"

"Are you profiling us?"

"Just getting to know my neighbors."

She shot out of the car. He joined her on a brick walk to the main entrance. "I'm trying to keep everything in perspective," she said. "I admit I'm a little tense. If Carriage Hill fails—"

"It's not going to fail."

"I hope not. Did you consider failure when you played hockey?"

"What's failure? I gave a hundred percent every time I got out on the ice and did my best, tried to learn from my mistakes and build on my strengths and not think about what I couldn't control." He eyed the attractive woman next to him, her ponytail loosening even more in the wind. "Why are you back in Knights Bridge, Olivia?"

"You don't give up, do you? It was perfect timing to pursue a dream."

"Did you leave behind a broken heart as well as a backstabber in Boston?"

She didn't answer and quickly went ahead of him and buzzed the intercom.

Dylan eased in next to her. "Or did you take a broken heart back with you to Knights Bridge?"

She gave him a cool look. "You're the one who's the good judge of people. You tell me."

An attendant opened the door, sparing him having to respond. He walked with Olivia down a wide corridor, past various rooms devoted to exercise classes, arts and crafts, board and card games, and reading. There was even a computer room.

They entered a sunroom with floor-to-ceiling windows overlooking the beautiful scenery. An elderly woman was settling into a chair with a pair of binoculars. "Olivia! Well, how nice to see you."

"It's good to see you, too." Olivia said. "Grace, this is Dylan McCaffrey. He's—"

The old woman narrowed her gaze on him. "You're the son of that rogue who bought my house."

He bit back a smile. "I understand you met my father."

"I think I told you, Grace," Olivia said quickly. "Dylan flew out from California after I wrote to him about the trash in the yard."

Grace Webster held her binoculars in both hands, her gaze fixed on Dylan. "Your father agreed to take the place as-is, with all my ancient appliances and anything I left behind. He didn't ask me to do repairs or pack up so much as a dish I didn't want to take with me to my new apartment here at Rivendell."

"Why do you think my father was a rogue?" Dylan asked.

"Because he was. He was a treasure hunter. I read about him after he came by. I'd already moved. What lost treasure did he think was in Knights Bridge? Did he tell you?"

"I didn't know he'd bought your house until Olivia wrote to me and I realized he'd left it to me."

Grace's expression softened. "When did he die?"

"It'll be two years in June."

"Not long after he was here, then. I'm sorry for your loss, Mr. McCaffrey."

He was more affected by her words than he expected to be. "Thank you, Miss Webster."

"You can call me Grace. Everyone here does. I was Miss Webster to hundreds of students for more years than I can count."

"And I'm Dylan."

"Dylan," she said, as if trying out the pronunciation. But she was clearly agitated and distracted, and Olivia gave him a sideways glance. She'd noticed, too.

He backed off. "Your house is located in a beautiful spot, Grace. Olivia and I hiked up Carriage Hill."

"I remember hiking up there when we first moved to Knights Bridge. I'd look out at Quabbin as it slowly filled with water. It took eight years for it to reach capacity. It's a lovely place, so quiet and peaceful, but I can still see the houses, the people who lived there." Grace stared out the window. "I have so many memories. My grandmother and my father, but especially my father, never got over the loss, that they couldn't go home again. The lanes and farms and shops they'd known all their lives were gone forever. We weren't as mobile in those days as people are now. The valley was all we knew."

"I can't imagine," Olivia said.

"We were never in physical danger. What happened

to us was a deliberate act designed to benefit others. 'The greater good,' as Gran used to say. When I sold the house, I wanted to be able to walk away and make another home, here, even at this late date." Grace's cheeks were still flushed as she looked up at Dylan. "Where's your home, Mr. McCaffrey?"

"Coronado. It's an island near San Diego—"

"Where the Navy SEALs train," Grace said.

Dylan smiled. "That's the place. I've been there three years. It's the longest I've lived anywhere since I was a kid."

"What about your father?"

"He never stayed in one place for long. He loved being on the go."

"That might be difficult with a child at home."

"My parents divorced when I was young."

Grace raised her binoculars, her hands visibly trembling. "There." She pointed out the window. "There's my cardinal. He comes by every day. His bright red color attracts the female to him."

"Ah," Dylan said. "Maybe I should watch more cardinals."

Grace laughed, but she looked tired as she placed her binoculars on her lap. "I just came from yoga class. Are my cheeks still flushed, Olivia?"

"They're rosy," she said, smiling. "You look healthy. It's good to see you, Grace. You'll come to my opening day tea?"

"It's a mother-daughter tea. I'm not a mother, and my own mother's long dead—"

Olivia leaned over and gave the old woman a quick hug. "I want you there, Grace."

"I'll come, then, of course."

Halfway down the hall, Olivia said, "That was decent of you to distract her."

"She knows something about why my father came to Knights Bridge."

"You're not going to ask her."

It wasn't a question, but Dylan said, "No, I'm not going to ask her."

"Because she can't possibly know anything about some crazy treasure hunt your father was on."

They passed the arts-and-crafts room, where a half-dozen senior citizens were setting up easels. Dylan glanced at them as he spoke. Could a retired teacher in her nineties know anything about a fortune in missing British jewels? It seemed unlikely. "I meant what I said, Olivia. I don't care about lost treasure."

She spun around at him. "Then what do you care about?"

He didn't answer, if only because he didn't have an answer. Not an easy one, anyway. She went ahead of him and didn't say another word until they were back in her car. She looked at him in the seat next to her. "Dylan…" She sighed. "Never mind."

"Does Grace always tremble?" he asked.

"No."

"Were her cheeks flushed from yoga class?"

"I don't know. Maybe."

"She definitely knows something, Olivia."

"She's been around for nearly a century. I imagine she knows quite a lot."

And that was that. Dylan noticed that Olivia had no trouble navigating the twisty road back to the mill.

Chapter 12

After she dropped Dylan off at his car, Olivia returned to Rivendell and found Grace bundled up in front of the windows, as if she couldn't get warm. Her pink cheeks were ashen now. "Grace, are you all right? Should I call the doctor?"

"I'm fine. Did you come back just to check on me?"

"I did. You were looking upset—"

"Don't worry, Olivia. I promised your grandma I'd have dinner with her tonight. She keeps me going." Grace seemed to drift off. "McCaffrey. I never knew any McCaffreys. I'm sure I didn't."

"In Knights Bridge, or when you were growing up?"

"Anywhere. Where are Dylan's people from?"

"I don't know. Grace…"

But she was vague, lost in her own thoughts. "I have no one in my life," she whispered. "My family's gone. My home's gone. So many of my friends are gone."

"Grace, maybe you shouldn't sit here alone."

"Why not? I *am* alone." She looked up at Olivia and smiled. "You go on. I'm fine. I'll take it easy the rest of the day."

On her way out Olivia asked the manager to keep an eye on Grace.

Dylan's rented Audi wasn't in his driveway when Olivia passed his house. The day had warmed up nicely, and when she reached her own house, she grabbed Buster and headed down the road with him. By the time she got back, Maggie O'Dunn's van was parked out front, Maggie sitting on the kitchen steps with a glass of iced tea. "I helped myself," she said, squinting up at Olivia. "Did you forget we had an appointment?"

"I'm sorry, Maggie. I didn't forget. How long have you been waiting?"

"Hours and hours." She grinned, tossing her head back, her strawberry-blond curls catching the midday sun. "Seven minutes. I figured you were off with Buster. How is the big brute?"

"Acclimating," Olivia said, just as Buster decided to stick his nose in Maggie's face.

She stood, gently pushing him aside. "Shall we?"

They went into the kitchen. Olivia wiped Buster's muddy paws and gated him in the mudroom while she and Maggie went over the menu for the mother-daughter tea. Scones with clotted cream and local jam and a variety of little sandwiches, tarts and teas. They would do herbal potpourri sachets for favors. Maggie suggested having a table of goodies and teapots for sale, focusing on locally made items, but Olivia wasn't sure. "I don't want anyone to feel pressured to buy anything. This is supposed to be an open house."

"They'll want to buy things," Maggie assured her. "You could do a hutch that's part of your decor."

"If I could find an old one to paint, that would be great."

"I might have one in my cellar. I'll have a look. *Everything's* in that cellar. I'll be old and gray before I can go through it all."

She left samples of goodies and appetizers for Olivia to try. Instead of feeling overwhelmed by her to-do lists, Olivia envisioned her house and garden filled with guests enjoying themselves on a spring afternoon. Buster barked, and she noticed Dylan at the door. She let him in.

He glanced at the goodies on the table. "You've been busy."

"My friend Maggie was just here. She's a caterer. These are all her doing."

"Tough to resist."

"Impossible. I just put on tea. It's warm enough to eat outside. Care to join me?"

They gathered dishes, tea and goodies and headed out back to the terrace, setting everything on a round wood table, grayed from the weather. Olivia helped herself to a mini currant scone, aware that the intensity and sparks between her and Dylan, so evident last night, hadn't disappeared. They were just banked, ready to flare up again with the least provocation.

She broke open the scone and ate a bite plain, without jam or clotted cream. "I checked on Grace on my way home. She was quiet, in her own world."

Dylan reached for a tiny cucumber sandwich. "I won't do anything to upset her. If I can't get answers without her, then I won't get answers."

Olivia believed him. He might be a lot of things, but a man who would sacrifice the peace of mind and health of an old woman wasn't among them. She dotted the other half of her scone with clotted cream. "Tell me about your life in San Diego. What's Coronado like?"

"Paradise," he said lightly. "Have you ever been to San Diego?"

"Not yet, no."

"Does your mother plan to stop there on her trip?"

"I don't think she's getting that far south. I've seen pictures of a huge, curving bridge. It leads to Coronado, doesn't it?"

He nodded. "The San Diego-Coronado Bridge. That's what I take to and from my house."

"Every day?"

"Most days. It's a different lifestyle from here, but Coronado is a small town in its own way."

Olivia tried one of the smoked salmon sandwiches. She'd never liked smoked salmon that much, but if anyone could make her, it was Maggie. One nibble, though, and she set it aside. "Still not a fan of smoked salmon. Does your house have a view of the water?"

"The Pacific, yes. I go for runs on the beach. My office is in the city."

"I can map out a running route here if you'd like. There should be some great days for running now that the weather's warming up." She settled back in her chair with a lemon tart that, she hoped, would get the smoked salmon taste out of her mouth. "Assuming you're staying long enough to bother with runs."

"As I said, I don't have a set date to go back to San Diego."

"You're taking a vacation?"

He smiled at her. "Time off."

"What's Noah Kendrick like?"

"I don't know. He's a friend."

"And that covers it? 'He's a friend.'" Olivia pushed back an unwelcome image of Marilyn. "What will you do here? You'll be bored after a few days. A hockey player, a mover and shaker—you won't sit still."

He tried a ham salad sandwich and a lemon tart. The tarts and scones were the size of a fifty-cent piece, the sandwiches no bigger than a folded dollar bill. His dark blue eyes leveled on her with a mix of intensity and humor that she found sexy, unsettling and utterly intriguing. Finally he said, "No, I won't sit still."

Olivia ignored a surge of heat and kept her voice light. "Do you need to borrow a shovel to start digging for buried treasure?"

He leaned back. "I already have one. Grace left a shovel, hoe, rake and a whole host of tools."

"Where are you going to start? Are you going to knock out walls, crawl through the cellar? It's a dirt cellar. There are probably snakes and mice down there."

"A garter snake and a couple of mice aren't going to throw me off the trail."

"There is no trail," Olivia said.

"Not much of one."

"Are you trying to get closer to your father?"

Dylan kept his gaze on her, but his expression was unreadable. "The time to get closer to my father has passed."

Olivia looked out at her garden, the herbs and flowers bursting into life after the long New England winter. "My grandfather on my father's side died when I was fifteen," she said, thoughtful. "I know that's different from losing a father, but I've found my relationship with him has continued. He lived in Knights Bridge his entire life. He loved to garden. I talk to him when I weed the herbs."

"Your mother grew up in town, too, I gather."

"Her father moved here when he got married. My grandmother's from here. He worked at Amherst College. It's a long commute, but he didn't mind. My uncles both moved out there but my mother stayed."

"Because of your father?"

"As far as I know, neither one of them wanted to live anywhere else."

"Were you ever involved in Frost Millworks?"

"I worked there in high school, and I designed the logo and website. Now that I'm in town, I suppose I can do more, but I'm focused on getting this place open and making enough to stop freelancing." She glanced across the table at him. "How did we end up talking about me?"

"Just making conversation." Dylan looked out at the yard, the view of Carriage Hill across the fields. "It's a good life here, Olivia. Do you miss Boston?"

"Sometimes, mostly at night. Knights Bridge doesn't have a lot going on at night."

His gaze again settled on her but he said nothing. Olivia felt herself grow hot and jumped to her feet. "I have a second coat of paint to put on some chairs," she said, not even sure if she did.

They gathered the dishes and remaining goodies and headed back to the kitchen. Olivia had forgotten about Buster and for a moment thought he might have escaped again, but he was curled up in the living room, asleep.

"I do have a good life here," she said, turning to

Dylan, startled by his effect on her. Her attraction to him hadn't lessened with his return; if anything, it was more intense, impossible to ignore. She cleared her throat. "I'll help you in any way I can, short of upsetting Grace."

He pulled open the front door. If he could tell that her insides were churning, he didn't say. "It's okay. I'm not sure what the hell I'm doing here. My father could have dropped whatever he was after once he realized real people were involved."

"It's not like he had to worry about the crew of a sunken sixteenth-century Spanish galleon turning up. Here…" Olivia pictured Grace in the sunroom with her binoculars. "Grace has some good days ahead of her."

"I hope so." Dylan's eyes were distant as he changed the subject. "Thanks for the treats. You and your friend Maggie know what you're doing."

"We've been friends since first grade—like you and Noah Kendrick."

After Dylan left, Olivia rousted Buster and walked out to the field with him. She had to burn off tarts, scones and an hour sitting on her terrace with her sexy neighbor. He definitely wasn't one to sit still. When she spotted him going for a run on their quiet road, she wasn't surprised. Never mind tarts and scones. He had energy to burn off.

She returned with Buster and went into the back room, where she was doing most of her painting. She did have chairs to paint. *Good,* she thought, and got busy.

* * *

Grace Webster's former bathroom didn't have a shower. Dylan had to stick his head under the faucet in the claw-foot tub, which he didn't actually mind as much as he thought he would. He even rinsed his hair with cold water. Why not? It might help him think straight.

He couldn't tell Olivia about the Ashworth jewels. Not until he knew more.

Not until he was sure no one in Knights Bridge knew anything about them.

He toweled off, put on a clean T-shirt and pair of jeans, and headed to the bedroom he'd chosen to make his. It didn't feel like his. It felt like a guest room in an old lady's house. His camp bed was a step up from blankets on the floor, but he doubted it was nearly as comfortable as a bed in one of Olivia's guest rooms.

A dangerous thought, there.

He checked his BlackBerry for messages and saw that he had just enough of a signal to call Noah. His friend picked up on the first ring. "How's life in the land of the chives?"

"I just went for a long run. I saw a bald eagle."

"You're scaring me, Dylan."

"Are you sure you don't want to order me back to San Diego?"

"Have I ever ordered you to do anything?"

"Where are you right now?"

"Your office, actually. Pining for my co-conspirator in this crazy-assed business."

"Good one, Noah. Funny. No fires, earthquakes, sons of bitches, financial emergencies?"

"Nothing. Dare I ask where you are?"

"I'm standing in a bedroom with peeling wallpaper and a creaky floor—"

"Nice view?"

He hadn't noticed and glanced out the window, taking in the buds on the trees, the green grass, scattered daffodils in front of the stone wall and, across the fields, Carriage Hill. "Nice enough," he said. "Different."

"Olivia Frost?"

"Dying to meet you," Dylan said as Noah hung up. His friend was in one of his bounce-on-the-surface-of-life moods, which usually meant he did have something on his mind. Even if Dylan was there, it wouldn't make any difference. Noah wouldn't necessarily be able to pinpoint what he was thinking about. He'd just wander around, mulling, all but walking into walls.

Dylan went across the hall to the smallest of the three bedrooms and found a stack of books and old files on the floor by a nightstand. He sat on the threadbare rug. He needed to borrow a vacuum from his pretty neighbor. He opened the top book, an illustrated version of J.R.R. Tolkien's *The Hobbit.* Inside the front cover was a handwritten note: *To Miss Webster, From your grateful students, The English IV Class of 1975.* They'd all signed it. Dylan remembered his own high school years. He'd squeaked through his classes, doing just enough to stay out of trouble and be able to continue playing hockey.

His father had loved Tolkien. Had he sat here, under this same floor lamp, on a similar dark night, reading about Bilbo Baggins?

The next book was a local church cookbook, with recipes by church members. Several were from Grace Webster. There was one from an Audrey Frost. Olivia's grandmother? A great-aunt? A cousin? How many Frosts were there in the area? Then there was the mother's family, too.

In the back of the cookbook were black-and-white photographs of the lost towns of Quabbin. Barefoot schoolchildren, a horse-drawn wagon stacked with wood, men harvesting ice on a local pond, young women dressed up for portrait day, country roads and farmhouses now gone forever. One was of a young Grace Webster, or so was noted in the caption. She wore a simple dress and was standing alone in front of a clapboard house. Dylan was surprised he recognized her, but the teenager's eyes and those of the elderly woman he'd met earlier were the same.

He put aside the cookbook and picked up a third book, surprised when he saw that it was relatively new.

It was a guide to Portugal.

He opened it carefully, as if his father had just walked into the room and was standing over him. A page was bent back—it described the area where his father had died. He must have planned that final trip while he was here in Knights Bridge. He always had a number of projects going at once. Whatever his reasons for buying this house, he hadn't displayed any sense of urgency, at least none that Dylan had noticed.

He shut the book and got to his feet. His father had been in this room. He'd gone through Grace's books.

"Why, Dad?" Dylan asked aloud. "What did you want here?"

Maybe Olivia was right and he was in Knights Bridge to get closer to his father, the elusive Duncan McCaffrey.

Chapter 13

Jess rolled out of bed in her apartment in the old saw-mill far too early, her heart racing, sweat pouring off her, the walls and ceiling closing in on her. She gulped for air and bolted down the narrow stairs and through the side door, into the morning mist. She felt as if the clouds themselves were holding her down, choking her.

Mark had to be in the city again today and hadn't stayed through the night, but he always left before her parents arrived at the mill. It wasn't that they didn't know that she and Mark were sleeping together—they were all but formally engaged, after all—but he was self-conscious. Jess supposed she was, too, but not right now, she thought. Right now she just wanted to calm down.

Sunlight pierced the mist. It would burn off soon and turn into a glorious day, with temperatures into the sev-enties by afternoon. She wanted to enjoy it.

She did a few deep-breathing exercises and focused on her surroundings, the present, as she walked over to the millpond. The smell and sounds of the clear water rushing over the dam soothed her anxiety. She loved this place but could understand why her mother dreamed about going somewhere else. Traveling, visiting museums, seeing different sights—different people.

Jess sometimes wondered if her bouts of crawling claustrophobia had to do with knowing every damn person in town. Some days she thought she knew every tree, too.

She headed up to the shop and made coffee in the office. Her mother arrived first, alone. She set her bag on the rolltop desk and spun around at Jess. "Did your father ask about the dots?"

"The what? Mom…" Jess couldn't deal with it. Dots. What the hell?

Her mother showed her an 8½-by-14-inch sheet of plain white sketch paper. "I'm talking to someone. Not a psychiatrist. I'm not on pills." Her tone was more combative than defensive. "I'm working on…things."

"Things? Mom, I don't need to know."

She plopped down in the chair at her desk. "I have anxiety issues, Jess. It's not a secret. You, Liv, your dad—you've all noticed. Everyone in town's noticed."

Jess concentrated on the dripping of the coffee.

Her mother smoothed the paper out on the desk and pointed at a cluster of multicolored dots centered on the page. "That's me. The blue dot in the middle."

"The blue dot," Jess said, wishing the coffee would finish brewing and she could have an excuse to get out of there. She was interested in what her mother had to say, curious about what the dots were all about, but she'd just bolted out of bed in a crazed panic herself.

Olivia arrived, standing in the doorway. She started to back away, but Jess held up a hand, keeping her there.

Olivia didn't say a word, and their mother either didn't see her older daughter or pretended not to as she continued, "The therapist gave me a sheet of blank paper and asked me to make a dot that's me and then to put dots where everyone in my life would be in relation to me. You're the red one, Jess," she said, pointing to a dot close to the blue dot that represented her. "Liv's the purple one right next to you. I tried not to fuss too much with which colors to use for each person. I had a nice fresh box of Crayola crayons to choose from."

"Mom…" Jess cleared her throat and tried to make her voice sound less strangled. "Mom, you don't have to tell me about your session with your therapist."

"Your dad's the dark gray one. Then there's his mother, my folks, Mark—"

That got Jess. "Why is Mark on your page?"

"Shouldn't he be? He's a little farther away from me but close to you."

"All right, all right."

"I have dots for my brothers, my nieces and nephews, the crew here, the church, friends."

"That's a lot of dots, Mom," Jess said.

"I was afraid I'd forget someone important. Notice how the dots are all crowded at the center of the page, near my little blue dot. That's because they all represent people I care about."

It was Olivia who spoke next. "What did the therapist say?"

Their mother sat back in her chair and sighed. "She said, 'It's a big sheet of paper, Louise.'"

Jess stared at her mother. "Mom?"

"It made sense to me. I can give myself space, and everyone can still be on the page with me. I keep everyone so close, especially you two." She shot to her feet. "Jess, Liv, am I suffocating you?"

"Not at the moment," Jess said lightly. "Right now I need coffee and here you are with a coffeepot right in your office. I have a ton of work to do today—"

"Jess."

She raked a hand through her hair. Coffee first, then she'd brush her damn hair. If she hadn't leaped out of bed so quickly, she might have missed her mother's talk of dots, but it couldn't have been easy for her to explain their meaning. Finally Jess gave her mother a reassuring smile. "I'm glad you did this. I want you to be happy. That's all."

"Me, too," Olivia said. "It's great you're talking to someone, Mom. I hope it helped to do this assignment."

"My happiness isn't your responsibility," she said. "Nor is your happiness my responsibility. That doesn't mean we don't love each other and aren't there for each other."

Jess wasn't one for heart-to-hearts and tried not to cringe. When she heard the outer door creak, she looked past Olivia and almost jumped in relief when she saw her father enter the building. "Dad's here. Mom, have you told him about the dots and the therapy?"

"No, but it's not a secret. If you want to—"

"No way. I'm not telling him for you."

Her mother swiveled around in her chair, quickly

folded the sheet and hid it away in one of the nooks and crannies in her desk.

Olivia backed out of the doorway. "I just remembered something. I'll see you all later."

Jess didn't believe her for a second. Her sister was making her escape, although Jess couldn't blame her. She poured coffee and headed for her desk in the show-room as her father entered the office. He and her mother were a pair. They could work out whatever was going on between them without her help.

Breathing in the steam and rich smell of the coffee, she switched on her computer and settled at her desk by a window overlooking the brook. She remembered when she was six and had gone to look for their golden retriever after he'd wandered off. Her mother had found them at the edge of the brook. It was the first time Jess had noticed that her mother didn't exactly have nerves of steel. She supposed any mother would be panicked, but even as a small child she had recognized that hers had gone into a state of near hysteria.

She remembered her father saying, *"Look at Jess, Louise. She's okay. You can relax. All's well that ends well."*

He'd been reassuring, protective. In those days, she hadn't let her worries impede her. Then came her daughters' teen years and a car accident that would have challenged any parent's nerves.

It didn't do much for mine, either, Jess thought, all at once faintly irritated with her mother.

"We're fine," she said aloud, as if to convince herself. "We were fine then and we're fine now. We were lucky."

She didn't want to think about the accident, but she was proud of her mother for recognizing her problem and doing something about it. Jess had often wondered if she'd stayed in Knights Bridge just to avoid upsetting the applecart with her mother. She was twenty-seven and had never lived in another zip code.

Was that why she'd fallen for Mark? Because he'd keep her in Knights Bridge, and she wouldn't have to confront her own anxieties?

Jess gave herself a mental shake. Was she out of her mind? She loved Mark.

She drank her coffee and reviewed a complicated order of doors and windows for the restoration of a Maine museum. She loved working for her family's business. She loved living in her hometown. Was it wrong not to want to do anything else, live anywhere else? Should she live in Boston or New York—or Paris—before she settled down in Knights Bridge? She and Mark had talked about starting a family right away. How long before they could afford to travel? If she didn't go to Paris now, when?

Her mother materialized behind her. "I'm going to California, Jess. I don't want you and Olivia to trim your dreams because you worry about me. I want to be an example to you."

Jess rose with her coffee. "Don't go to California for our sake, Mom. Do it because it's what you want."

"I am." Her eyes brimmed with tears even as she smiled. "I am, Jess. I'm making this trip. I don't care if I have to have someone knock me out with a brick to get me on the plane. It's not flying that gets to me so much as…going. I didn't know that for a long time. I rationalized my fears."

Jess noticed her father had left. "Did you tell Dad you're seeing a therapist?"

Her mother waved a hand in dismissal. "It's none of his business."

"You and Dad…"

"We're fine. Don't worry."

"I'll worry if I want to worry," Jess snapped, immediately regretting her impatience. "Sorry. I got up too early."

When her mother returned to the office, she shut the door behind her, which she almost never did. Jess called Mark on his cell phone but hung up before he could answer.

He called her back. "Everything all right?"

Jess hesitated. How could she explain that her mother was seeing a therapist and marking dots on a page over a trip that most people would jump at the chance to take? "Mark, Olivia and I are strong, independent women, aren't we?"

"What? Yeah. The strongest and most independent. Why?"

"Anxiety isn't a weakness. It's a condition that can be treated."

"Jess?"

She stopped short of telling him about her attack of claustrophobia. "I'll see you later?"

"Yeah," he said. "Jess—"

"I'm fine, Mark. Sitting at my desk going over an order for reproduction twelve-over-twelve windows."

"I'll be back in time for dinner." He paused, then added, "We can plan Paris."

"Do you mean that?"

"I wouldn't have said it if I didn't mean it."

He hung up, and Jess looked out the window at the familiar scene of brook, trees and rocks. The broad, sweeping branches of the old sugar maple by the entrance were leafing out, creating dappled shade now that the sun, as expected, had burned off the morning mist.

Paris…an entire ocean between her and Knights Bridge. Between her and her family.

Her stomach twisted. Her mother would worry even if she said she wouldn't.

Jess pictured the Louvre, the Seine, croissants. A week alone with Mark in one of the most romantic places in the world. They wouldn't have to think about someone they knew popping in or driving by.

She smiled, loving the idea. Whatever had awakened her in a panic this morning was gone, and had nothing to do with Paris.

By evening, Olivia and Maggie had moved the hutch out of Maggie's cellar at her gingerbread house in the village and into Olivia's back room, where she'd set up her painting supplies and lined up her to-be-painted furniture. The hutch was made of pine, scarred and weathered, absolutely perfect for painting and then displaying anything from teapots and herbal teas to artisan soaps and potpourri sachets. After Maggie left, Olivia cleaned it off and now was debating her options for painting it, whether to do a smooth, glossy finish or go with layers of colors. Clouds had moved in, and the warm, sunny spring day had changed quickly into a drizzly evening, but she didn't mind. Best she stayed in tonight. She didn't need to be tempted to check on her neighbor and see what he'd been up to all day.

"Olivia—Olivia, it's me," Jess said, bursting into the kitchen, a large sketch pad tucked under one arm. "You're game, right, Liv?" Without waiting for an answer, she set the pad on the table and tore off two sheets. She glanced back at Olivia. "You must have crayons or something."

Olivia saw that her sister was agitated and determined, and didn't argue. She went into the living room and returned with a box of oil pastels. "I came in late to Mom's explanation about the dots."

Jess dumped the pastels out on the table and pointed to the two sheets of blank white paper. "First you take a crayon or whatever and make a dot that represents you."

"Middle of the page?"

"Anywhere that works for you. I think deciding is part of the process. Then you pick out colors for the people in your life and make a dot for them in relation to you."

Olivia considered the assignment. "Okay, Jess. I can do that."

"I want to be green, though. A rich, deep-forest green. We can't be the same color. That'd be too weird."

"I'll be magenta, then."

They grabbed pastel crayons. Jess angled her shoulders so that Olivia couldn't see her page, but she stood straight and frowned. "It'd probably be more effective if we were doing this not knowing the point of the exercise," she said.

"I'm not sure I *do* know the point."

"It's a physical demonstration of where the people are in your life in relation to yourself. Mom keeps us all very close. She has everyone clustered around her one little dot. Never mind what it does to us, what does it do to her? She can't move. She can't breathe. You can keep everyone on the page and still give them all and yourself room."

"Jess, have you had wine?"

She grinned. "Just do the exercise, will you?"

Olivia looked at the array of pastels and considered all the different people in her life. This could take forever, she thought.

"Marilyn Bryson doesn't get to go on the page," Jess said. "You put her there and I'm going to erase her or white her out or something."

"You're interfering with my page."

"I guess my dot's going close to you?"

"Right. You're suffocating me."

They laughed but drifted into silence as they did the exercise. Olivia debated what to do with Roger Bailey—should he go on her page? What about future guests of Carriage Hill? But she was getting ahead of herself. First came family—her parents, Jess, her grandparents.

Mark Flanagan?

Olivia glanced at Jess, no engagement ring yet on her finger, and picked out a sturdy brown for Mark and made a dot close—but not too close—to her sister.

She had dots for Maggie O'Dunn and a few other friends in town and in Boston.

As instructed, she had no dot for Marilyn Bryson. She put a faint yellow one high up in a corner for Jacqui Ackerman.

A steel-gray crayon made her think of Dylan. She cleared her throat. "We're not going to tell each other who our different dots are, right?"

Jess nodded. "Right. That would never work. You don't even have to show me your sheet."

"Okay, good."

Olivia picked up the steel-gray pastel and placed a dot near her dot. It felt too close, and yet at the same time not close enough. She was surprised the effect the exercise was having on her. Definitely a strange experience.

"I'm running out of colors," Jess muttered. "We have a lot of family and friends."

Olivia had just been thinking she had far more colors than she needed. "You're doing a dot for everyone? Cousins, uncles, aunts?"

"They'd be offended if I didn't, wouldn't they?"

"Jess, we're not showing our papers to anyone. We can burn them in the fireplace after we're done."

"Oh. Maybe I should rub out Uncle Richard."

They laughed, and when they finished, they silently folded their sheets into squares, hiding the dots. Olivia got down glasses and poured chilled pinot grigio.

"Where's Buster?" Jess asked.

Olivia thought he was in his bed in the mudroom but he was gone. She groaned in frustration. "He must have slipped out when you came in, or when Maggie and I carried in the hutch she gave me. For a big, noisy dog, he can be very quiet when he wants to be."

"Old habits from his life before he adopted you," Jess said.

They started out back with their wine, the drizzle now a light but steady rain. Dylan was at the mudroom door with her soaking wet, muddy dog. He got Buster inside, pulled the door shut and let go of her misbehaving dog's collar.

He stood straight. Olivia saw that he was almost as wet and muddy as Buster, just a lot better looking. "I'm sorry," she said. "I had no idea he'd sneaked out."

"Look at it as an opportunity. Wolf dog and I are

getting to know each other. We didn't come back here with my left arm in his teeth."

Jess leaned against the counter, observing Dylan, Buster and Olivia as she sipped her wine. "Where was he?"

"I spotted him in the field and caught up with him in the brook."

Olivia frowned. She hadn't yet touched her own wine. "I didn't think he liked water."

"He was after a rock." Dylan glanced from her to Jess and back again. "I don't want to interrupt a sisterly wine-and-laugh session."

Buster bolted past him and shook off in the middle of the kitchen. Jess set her glass on the counter and subtly held her page of dots at her side. "I should get going before I have too much wine. I'm meeting Mark for dinner, anyway. The place looks great, Liv. The Farm at Carriage Hill is just what this area needs. Before long you're going to have more bookings than you can handle."

She breezed out through the front door, shutting it firmly behind her. Olivia suspected her sister wouldn't have stayed even without Dylan arriving with Buster or her dinner with Mark. The dot exercise had gotten to Jess.

Dylan sighed. "Buster and I are tracking mud. I'll clean it up."

"No muddy woods at home on Coronado Island."

"Not like here."

"Don't worry about the mud. I'll let it dry and sweep later." Olivia took her wineglass with her and set it on the table as she put away the pastels. "What's up, Dylan?

You look as if you have more than muddy paw prints on your mind."

"I have to go back to San Diego for a few days on unexpected business. I've been on the phone most of the day. It can't wait."

"When do you leave?"

"I head to Boston tonight for an early-morning flight."

"You fly as if you were driving."

He shrugged. "It's safer than driving, statistically. I don't think about it."

"That's good. You had to fly all the time as a hockey player. It must have become routine for you. Your father was a world traveler. Flying is what you know."

He picked up a dark blue crayon. "It gets me where I'm going."

"When I was growing up, flying was a big deal, at least among the people I know. They would plan trips for months. They didn't just buy a ticket one day and fly the next. They still don't."

"You're spooling up, Olivia," he said, setting the crayon in her box.

She shut the lid, set the box back on the table and sipped her wine. He was right. She could feel the anxiety building in her. She wanted to blame Jess and her dots, but she knew if they were playing a role, it was only a small one. "Sometimes just thinking about flying gets me going." She ignored the tight twist of anxiety in her stomach. At least her hands weren't shaking and she didn't spill any wine. She gave a small, fake laugh. "I know wine doesn't help."

Even with the gloom and fading daylight, her house felt cozy and cheerful. The colors and furnishings she'd chosen so far worked, creating just the right atmosphere, she thought, trying to focus on anything except the panic mounting inside her. She was aware of Dylan watching her as if she might fall into pieces at any moment.

"Thanks for fetching Buster," she said. "If there's anything I can do, let me know."

"Don't call the fire department too fast if my house catches on fire." Dylan gave her an irreverent smile. "Not that I've deliberately left any fire hazards."

"You wouldn't want the place to burn down if any treasure is there. Imagine a volunteer firefighter bashing down a wall and discovering a fortune in gold."

"I don't think that's likely to happen."

"And you don't need a fortune in gold," Olivia said, then immediately wished she hadn't.

Dylan didn't seem to take any offense. "If my father was on some kind of treasure hunt, there's a good chance he figured out whatever he was after was a lost cause."

"That could explain why he more or less abandoned the house and never mentioned it to you."

"Or he just ran out of time."

"Dylan, if you discovered something new—you'd tell me, wouldn't you?"

He gave her a quick, unreadable smile. "Hypotheticals get me in trouble every time. I should get rolling."

"Nice sidestep." She let it go, at least for now. "You'll let me know if you decide to stay in San Diego? Who knows, I might want to buy your house." She added lightly, an attempt to ease her own tension, "I could use the acreage for more herbs."

"Just what you need. More herbs."

"Whatever you decide to do, I'll still be right here." She finished off her wine a little too quickly and took the glass to the sink. "I'd like to visit San Diego one day. I wonder if I'll end up like my mother, planning trips…" She turned back to him. "Safe travels, Dylan."

The rain shifted to a heavy downpour, lashing at the windows. His expression—unsmiling, his eyes narrowed, his jaw set—hinted at the intensity of a man who had been a top athlete, who had helped grow and manage a successful corporation.

Then the intensity was gone, a smile playing unexpectedly at the corners of his mouth. "Does that mean you don't want me to kiss you?"

She did. She definitely wanted him to kiss her, but not as a means to avoid talking to her. "Your house here is a wreck and it brings up unresolved issues with your father."

He grinned and walked over to her. "Unresolved issues?"

She blamed the dots, the wine and the thought of flying for her pensive mood. "Not terribly introspective, are you?"

"Sometimes. Not right now." He covered her hands with his, hooked his fingers into hers. "Right now I want to kiss you. What do you say, Liv?"

"You want my permission to—"

"Lots of Frosts and people related to Frosts in this town. I'm all by myself here."

"Isolated and alone, huh?"

He tightened his fingers around hers and smiled. "You don't feel sorry for me, do you?"

"Not even a little. It's not what you'd want, anyway. It's not what I want, either. About my thing with fly-

ing—" Olivia felt the warmth and strength of his hands
and forced herself to concentrate and make her point
"—I'll figure it out."

"You have plenty to keep you occupied here."

She took a shallow breath. "You could tell Noah
you're staying to help me paint walls and furniture and
pull weeds."

"Noah's a friend and I owe him, but I don't jump
whenever he snaps his fingers. He'd hate that and I
couldn't do it." Dylan slipped his hands out of hers and
planted them on the counter on either side of her, more
or less pinning her against the counter. "I'm coming
back, Olivia. I promise you. I'm coming back."

"I won't hold you to that." She realized she was arch-
ing her back over the counter, as if to get farther away
from him when it was the last thing she wanted. She
gave a small laugh. "I'd have to get on a plane to hold
you to it."

"You could send Buster," he said, lowering his mouth
to hers.

She lost her balance and shot out a hand, grabbing
hold of him, steadying herself. She inhaled sharply at
the feel of the hard muscle above the waistband of his
jeans and knew immediately she was lost. She wrapped
both arms around him, her lips parting for their kiss.
The taste of him set her on fire. She let her hands course
up his back. He responded, probing deeper with the kiss,
lifting her off her feet.

The wind picked up outside, and she realized she'd
left the window above the sink open. Cool air and a
spray of rain hit her overheated skin. She hooked her
legs around his hips and he pressed himself into her as
if they were naked.

They could be, she thought. In a few seconds, she and Dylan McCaffrey could be making love against the kitchen sink. All the anxiety of earlier fell away. She just wanted him inside her.

"Dylan…"

She didn't know if it was the sound of his name or her moan of out-of-control desire, or the wind and rain, but Buster was on alert, charging out from the mudroom, barking and growling as he circled her and Dylan.

"Hell, Buster," Dylan muttered.

Olivia sputtered into laughter, shushing her dog as she came to her senses and all but jumped out of Dylan's arms and stood on the wide-board floor. "I guess I have my own bodyguard," she said, more welcome rain blowing onto her.

Dylan patted her on the hip. "Definitely coming back."

In a few long strides, he was out the door. Olivia took a breath and shook her head at her dog. "You've got to learn better timing, my friend."

She shut the window, the house somehow instantly feeling quieter, lonelier. Dylan's departure was abrupt, but deliberately so, she thought. It was as if he'd realized he had to get out of there—not because he didn't want to make love to her, but because he did. And he couldn't, because he *was* hiding something.

Something to do with his father and lost treasure.

"No doubt in my mind." Olivia turned to her big dog, still damp from the rain; she was glad she had a hutch to paint tonight. "Well, Buster, looks as if it's just you and me again. Come on. Let's get you dried off and go build a fire."

Chapter 14

It rained the next day and the day after. Olivia holed up at her house and worked. She finished several freelance design projects, finished painting the hutch, rearranged furniture, threw out her page of dots and, during lulls in the rain, planted spinach, lettuce and green onions and cleaned out a patch of rhubarb behind the potting shed.

By nightfall on the second day, she was beat, and still thinking about Dylan, what he hadn't told her, when—if—he'd be back.

She was heating up leftover chili for dinner when her phone rang. "I'm working late," Jacqui Ackerman said. "I thought you might be, too."

"I just poured wine," Olivia said truthfully as she sat at her kitchen table.

"Good for you. Mine's waiting for me. Listen, I wanted to talk to you. I just got off the phone with

Roger Bailey. He's hiring a new manager for his interior design department. They're expanding. He says there'll be more work for us. We're trying to figure out what to do."

"That's a nice problem to have."

"Roger says he always liked what you did for them, especially for the interior design arm of the business."

"I appreciate that," Olivia said, watching out the window as rain puddled in a low spot in the front yard.

"Any chance you might consider coming back to work full-time?"

"In Boston?"

"That's right." Jacqui hesitated. "We've changed a few things here but you'd have your same job. Your workload was too intense in the months before you left. I threw too much at you. You never cracked, but with this new position, you'll have more time to focus on actual design work."

"What changes have you made, Jacqui?"

"Well, you know we hired Marilyn Bryson. She's heading up a design and digital media team focusing on our biggest clients. You'd be a part of that. Come into town, and let's all sit down together. You're a good designer, Olivia. Your freelance work has been top-notch. This is a great opportunity for you. Think it over."

"I will, Jacqui. Thanks for calling."

As she hung up, Olivia pictured herself back at the studio. If she missed anything about Boston, it was the camaraderie of going into work every day. She marveled at Jacqui's timing, managing to call when she'd hardly been out of the house for two days.

She wouldn't be returning to her old job. Not really.

Marilyn was there now, and Olivia would be reporting to her instead of directly to Jacqui.

Know your worth was a mantra she'd learned early in her career. In retrospect, she could see that she'd helped Marilyn increase her worth while not paying enough attention to her own. That wasn't Marilyn's fault. It was her own fault.

Olivia grabbed her wineglass and stood up. She turned the heat off under the chili. Blaming herself, blaming Marilyn, rehashing the past, fighting regrets and second-guessing herself wouldn't accomplish anything. She was lucky, she reminded herself. One of Boston's most prestigious studios wanted her back on the payroll. At the same time, she was doing well freelancing. She was limiting the number of projects she took on only because she also was focused on transforming her house into a getaway.

She had chosen to move back to Knights Bridge. She *was* a good designer, but Roger Bailey's defection and Marilyn's behavior had forced her to examine what she really wanted.

I want this, she thought, looking around her as darkness gathered on her quiet road. Her muscles ached from painting, planting and hauling. She felt great. Her vision for Carriage Hill had started to form when she and Marilyn were still close friends, talking every day. It wasn't a reaction to anything Marilyn had done.

Olivia smiled, relaxing. She wasn't going back to work for Jacqui or anyone else. She was taking everything she'd learned during her years in Boston—about design, color, marketing, client management, herself and business—and putting it to work on creating The Farm at Carriage Hill.

Her life was here, in Knights Bridge.

She abandoned her wine and got Buster onto his feet. She clipped on a leash, not wanting to risk having him run off in the dark. She imagined her house filled with people enjoying a getaway, whether for a few hours, a day or a weekend. Every aspect of her work energized and challenged her, from drawing up a business plan for the bank to weeding the chives. She wanted The Farm at Carriage Hill to succeed.

She had to be "all in." Half measures wouldn't do it.

Buster pulled on his leash as they headed outside. The rain had let up, and she could feel the front moving in, bringing with it dry, clear air. The contrast between her life in Boston and her life in Knights Bridge couldn't have been more dramatic. There were no upscale shops and fancy restaurants, no lights and crush of people, hardly anyone she didn't recognize. Marilyn had pretended to disdain the attention and perks that came with being in high demand as a designer, but, deep down, she'd wanted them. She just couldn't admit it, maybe even to herself, when she'd been struggling.

The night was so quiet that Olivia could hear the crunch of small stones under her shoes. Jacqui's call had stirred her up. She couldn't just let it go. When she'd first conceived of The Farm at Carriage Hill, she hadn't expected it to be her livelihood, at least not so soon. She'd thought she'd have time to make it happen. Now if it failed, she would have to start over.

It won't fail.

Buster pulled on his leash all the way to Grace's old house.

Olivia saw an owl swoop through the trees where the kids had dumped the refrigerator, now gone.

What if Dylan didn't come back? What if he'd gotten sucked back into his life in San Diego?

Their kiss didn't have to have any deeper meaning. He'd been chasing Buster. His blood was up, and she'd been there, emotions raw, wine poured.

She tugged on the leash. "If not for you, Buster…"

He lurched off down the road, and she laughed and trotted alongside him. Whatever betrayal of friendship and professional ethics Marilyn had committed, somehow she had helped Olivia get here, to this moment. She knew she was where she wanted to be, doing what she wanted to do, and she knew, without a doubt, that she was a damn good designer.

And she knew that Dylan would be back.

Olivia got out of the house in the morning. It was one of those fresh, clear, perfect spring days, the air washed clean, the trees budding. Everything seemed green and new. She pulled into the mill and found her father down by the dam. With feigned nonchalance, he drank his coffee and watched the water sparkling in the sunlight. "Your mother tell you about seeing a therapist?"

"Dad…"

He held up a hand without looking at her. "It's okay. I'm not asking you to betray a confidence. I know. And those damn dots. I figured it out. We're crowding her, Liv. All of us."

"I don't think it's that simple, Dad."

"I just don't want her to be afraid. Her, you, Jess."

"You've always tried to protect us." Olivia wasn't sure what to say. "Sometimes we have to fall and get bruised, or even if we don't have to, we will."

He made a face and finally turned to her. "What happened in Boston, Liv?"

She shivered in a cool breeze. She'd let the sunshine fool her and hadn't worn a sweater. "Nothing I can't handle."

"I didn't say you couldn't handle it."

"I know, Dad. It's behind me." She smiled. "I'm not afraid or hurt."

He dumped the last of his coffee into the dirt. "What about this guy McCaffrey? He's gone back to San Diego?"

"For now. If he thinks his father was after lost treasure here, he'll be back."

"There's no treasure in Knights Bridge, Liv."

She seized on the change in subject. "What about Quabbin? Do you remember any stories about treasure from when you were a kid?"

"The valley was flooded before I was born. I knew some of the old-timers who moved here from the lost towns." He bent down and picked up a loose rock and rubbed the dirt off it with a thick, callused thumb. "There was some bitterness about what happened, but people moved on, lived their lives. I didn't know any rich people, Liv. The people I knew owned farms and small shops, worked in the mills. I can't imagine any of them having the kind of treasure that would have interested Duncan McCaffrey."

"He was a legitimate treasure hunter. I have no reason to think he did anything sleazy or unethical." Olivia sighed, the water on the millpond rippling in a stiff breeze. "I don't know if he was even after treasure, never mind if it had anything to do with the building of Quabbin. It feels as if it was so long ago, but then I see Grace with her binoculars…"

"Hell, it *was* a long time ago, Liv. Grace is older 'n dirt."

"Dad!"

He grinned. "You were getting awfully serious."

"Aren't you even a little curious?"

"No. I have to deal with the here and now. Rich treasure hunters like Duncan McCaffrey and his son can fool with this stuff. Grace had nothing to do with whatever they're after."

"Would Grandma know anything?"

"Doubt it. You can ask her but you'll get the whole town talking. Do you want that? Do you want Grace to hear you're looking into something in her past?"

"You make it sound like I'm being nosy."

He arched a brow. "Well?"

He walked up to the mill to work. Olivia didn't follow him and instead drove into the village and stopped at the library, a small brick building just off the town common. She wasn't even sure what she was looking for but the library seemed like a good place to start. The main reading room had framed black-and-white photographs on the walls of the Swift River Valley before and after Quabbin. She wondered if Dylan's father had figured out that the treasure he was after was now under water. Not long ago, divers had surveyed the former valley floor, discovering interesting tidbits but no sunken treasure.

She found the librarian, Phoebe O'Dunn, one of Maggie's sisters, shelving books in the children's section. Olivia came straight to the point. "Do you have much on Knights Bridge during the building of Quabbin?"

Phoebe gathered up books off a cart. Her strawberry-blond hair was a tone darker and six inches shorter than her sister's, but just as curly. "Are you looking up something because of your house? It's the last one on an old road that leads right into the water."

That hadn't occurred to Olivia. What if Duncan McCaffrey had bought Grace's house because it was next to *hers?* What if whatever he had been after was there?

"Do you get a lot of requests for information on Knights Bridge and Quabbin?"

"Rarely. It's been a couple of years, at least. Most people specifically curious about Quabbin visit the Swift River Valley Historical Society in New Salem or the Visitors Center at Quabbin. They don't come here."

"Do you remember who was here a couple of years ago?"

"Yes, definitely—it was the man who bought Grace Webster's house. I don't remember his name. I remember he said he was from California."

"He died not long after he was here."

"Oh, how sad," Phoebe said, pausing to shelve several of her armload of books.

"What did he want, do you remember?" Olivia asked.

"He didn't go into detail. He was up there." Phoebe pointed to black-painted metal stairs that led to a small balcony. "That's where the local papers from the 1930s are located. He didn't say why he wanted them, but he was up there for a long time."

Olivia thanked her and headed up the narrow stairs to a row of neatly dusted dark wood shelves. She imagined

Dylan's father in the Knights Bridge library, searching for...what?

She found a bound copy of papers dated *Summer, 1938*. She had no idea what she was looking for. An article about a train robbery? An armored car robbery? Stolen paintings? Duncan McCaffrey had varied interests. He could have been after anything.

Or nothing, she reminded herself, although that seemed unlikely at this point.

She sat cross-legged on the floor and flipped through the newspapers from 1938.

Within five minutes, she had her answer.

It wasn't so hard after all to find out what Duncan McCaffrey had been up to—and now what his son was up to.

"Jewels," Olivia whispered, stunned.

In early September of 1938, a British aristocrat—Lord Charles Ashworth—was robbed at his hotel in Boston of a fortune in jewels that he had inherited upon the death of his sister.

Olivia might have sailed right past the article but for the business card marking it. The card belonged to Duncan McCaffrey. It included his name, cell phone number, email address and a California post office box.

The Ashworth heist wasn't front-page news in Knights Bridge. It was just an interesting filler tucked on an inside page two days after the robbery; police were still looking for whoever had made off with three rings and a necklace. No precise description was provided. At least one of the rings had been given to Lord Ashworth's great-grandmother by Queen Victoria herself.

Nothing like jewels with a British royal connection to spark the imagination.

Had Duncan McCaffrey suspected Knights Bridge held clues to the whereabouts of the Ashworth jewels?

Her hands shaking, Olivia slipped the card into her pocket and replaced the bound papers on the shelf. The metal steps clattered as she ran back down to the main floor. She waved to Phoebe and didn't slacken her pace until she was outside, on the sidewalk in front of the library. She took a moment to catch her breath and calm herself, then crossed the quiet street to the common and called Dylan, using the number he'd left her the first time he'd gone back to San Diego.

He answered on the second ring, but she didn't let him say a word. "Do you think we're thieves out here?"

"What? Olivia…" He sounded half-asleep. "I just rolled out of bed. Who's a thief?"

It would be just after seven on the West Coast. Olivia pushed back an image of him in bed. Unshaven, shirtless. More than shirtless. "Jewel thieves, specifically," she said. "Do you think one of us stole the Ashworth jewels?"

He sighed, fully awake now. "I don't think anything."

She took in a breath. "How long have you known?"

"Not long. My last trip back here."

At least he wasn't denying it, she thought as she stepped into the cool shadow of a granite statue of a Union soldier. "I see."

"What did you find, Olivia?"

"I just came from the library. Your father was there before me. I found an article about a jewelry robbery in Boston in 1938. Dylan…" She swallowed, controlling her emotions. "Why didn't you tell me?"

"I didn't know enough. I figured the last thing you all needed was some wild story about missing jewels."

"Your father left a card in the newspapers. I'll give it to you when you're back."

"Olivia…"

But Dylan seemed at a loss, and she remembered that Duncan McCaffrey was his father, not a stranger. "I should go, let you go back to sleep or get on with whatever you're up to today—"

"Where are you?"

"Standing in front of our Civil War statue."

She thought she heard him chuckle before they disconnected.

She went home and worked on the hutch. She'd decided to add stenciling; being creative always settled her mind and helped her think. The Ashworth jewels would be worth millions, if they existed, if they were genuine. She could suddenly understand why Dylan hadn't mentioned the 1938 robbery.

The hutch loomed above her as she carefully hand-painted a flower motif to a small door at its base. She thought the flowers added a needed bit of bright color and contrast to the light blue of the hutch but also looked modern. As she worked, doubts assaulted her. Maybe she was fooling herself after all. She loved how the house and landscaping were shaping up, but had she done enough? What wasn't she doing that she didn't even know she wasn't doing? Where were the gaps, the weaknesses, the problems in her plans and vision for Carriage Hill?

Was she insane not to take Jacqui's offer and return to work in Boston?

Even more so, was she insane to still be thinking about Dylan McCaffrey?

Chapter 15

"Holy hell," Noah said when he and Dylan arrived at the Webster house. "It's a bigger dump than I imagined."

Leave it to Noah to be blunt. "It used to be a cute house."

"For an old Latin teacher."

"Did you take Latin?"

"Uh-huh. Four years."

Dylan parked in the driveway. For once, Noah wasn't wearing a black suit. He was in his idea of wilderness clothes: black jeans and an L.L.Bean hiking shirt. He'd felt mildly guilty at pulling Dylan from his mission in Knights Bridge and had insisted on flying east with him.

"It's beautiful here, though," Noah said as he got out of the car and breathed in the clean country air. "What a spot."

"But you're not staying," Dylan said. It was more like an order than a question. The last thing he needed to do was to find a place for his friend to sleep in the crumbling house. Noah had been particular about his comforts even when he'd been broke.

"Not a chance. Relax."

"Olivia Frost is highly annoyed with me."

"Like you're not used to people being annoyed with you." Noah motioned toward the woods behind the house. "Do all these trees make you claustrophobic?"

"No."

"Not even now that they're leafing out?"

"No. There are fields, too, Noah. You're just focused on the woods."

"I don't think I'm cut out for New England. I don't need four seasons. Let's take a walk. I want to stretch my legs."

In other words, he wanted to see The Farm at Carriage Hill and meet Olivia Frost. Dylan didn't dissuade him, and they headed down the narrow road. He explained what he could about the Quabbin Reservoir and what the area must have been like in 1938 when Lord Ashworth was being robbed in Boston to the east.

Noah was quiet. "Have you considered that your father might have been scammed by these people?"

"How? He got a good price on the house. The land alone would sell for what he paid."

"That's because the house is worthless. It should have been a negative. Think of what you'll have to pay to have it torn down."

"I haven't thought that far ahead."

Noah glanced at him. "You know where you're headed but you focus on where your feet are planted right now. It's why you don't get blindsided by jack-asses."

"We all get blindsided by jackasses."

"This jewelry heist. Suppose these people lured your father to their quaint little town in order to manipulate him into finding the missing jewels. What if he found them, and they're hidden away in this old lady's bank vault, or the Frost family vault?"

Dylan had told Noah about the robbery because he was his friend and was good at patterns and connections. Now he regretted opening his damn mouth.

Noah took a few more long strides. "You might want to keep your eyes open for anyone with a sudden influx of funds."

"That's conspiratorial even for you, Noah."

Dylan had discovered long ago that Noah Kendrick tended to be naive. At the same time, he had a conspiratorial mind. The two weren't as mutually exclusive as people often thought but played off each other, the naïveté fueling the conspiracies and vice versa. He didn't think in straight lines. Dylan could cut to the chase with people. Love, greed, fear, sex, violence. Motivations were everything. He had met people who acted out of a sense of honor, integrity, courage, but his sole focus was whether they were okay or not okay for Noah and his business.

"You're a guy's guy, Dylan," Noah said, matter-of-fact. "Your father was, too. Women like you. They liked him. This Olivia Frost never met him?"

"No. What are you getting at?"

"Nothing. Just taking a walk on a fine spring day. I'm waiting for a cloud of blackflies to descend. I read about them. They can be nasty this time of year."

They came to Olivia's house. Dylan felt as if he'd been gone for weeks instead of just a few days. Purple, white and yellow tulips blossomed beneath a sign she'd put up for The Farm at Carriage Hill, painted with chives like the ones on the card she'd sent.

Noah gave a low whistle. "Very nice. It's more upscale and tasteful than I expected. Not cutesy. Does that describe your Liv Frost?"

"She's not mine, and you tell me," Dylan said as she came out the door, obviously not expecting them. Her hair was pulled back, and she had on jeans and a dark green top that brought out all the colors in her eyes. He smiled. "We were just admiring your new sign."

"Thanks." She brushed her hands off on her jeans. "I've been digging in the dirt since first thing this morning. For some reason I thought it'd be fun to plant a hundred yellow pansies out back."

Dylan noticed her muddy knees but realized he was starting to stare and jerked himself back to the business at hand. He introduced Noah. "Olivia, this is Noah Kendrick. Noah, Olivia Frost, proprietor of The Farm at Carriage Hill."

She came forward on the stone walk, smiling graciously. "It's great to meet you, Noah. Welcome to Knights Bridge."

"Great to meet you, too, Olivia. This place is fantastic."

"I'm glad you like it. I'm hosting a mother-daughter tea tomorrow. It's sort of an unofficial opening day."

"Terrific. A tea. That's just what I expected from the note card you sent Dylan, but Carriage Hill itself isn't as unfinished and rustic as what I expected from his description."

Olivia glanced at Dylan with an unexpected spark of humor. "We'll have to work on your talking points."

Noah winced. "Dylan was enthusiastic about the place—"

"Mmm. I'm sure." She was clearly not insulted at all, but she added, her tone more guarded, "Dylan didn't bring you here to help him dig for buried treasure, did he?"

"You mean the long-missing Ashworth jewels," Noah said, innocent.

Dylan grimaced at his friend's bluntness, but Olivia didn't seem surprised that he'd told Noah the story and not her. She motioned toward her house. "Can I offer you gentlemen something to drink?"

"That'd be great," Noah said. "I'd also like to see your gardens, if you don't mind."

"I'd love to show them to you."

She seemed genuinely pleased and started up the walk. Noah hung back and gave Dylan a tentative look. "I'm not screwing things up for you, am I?"

Dylan shook his head. "Just be yourself. Don't worry."

The ground was soft and moist as they followed Olivia around to the back of the house, but Noah was dressed for the conditions. Dylan was, too, but that was nothing new. He watched Olivia leading his friend through the parsley, chives and such, her easy manner slowly wearing down Noah's self-consciousness. He was less awkward, and genuinely interested in the various herb, flower and vegetable gardens and, especially, for reasons only known to him, the potting shed with its bags of soil, fertilizer and compost, mounds of small stones and stacks of old pots.

"My sister found this one in back at the mill," Olivia said, pointing to a blue-glazed pot that came to her knees. "Isn't it great? I'm loading it up with red flowers and putting it on the terrace. The red should attract hummingbirds. I love finding old things that I can make new again. I look clever when I'm just pinching pennies."

"You're very talented," Noah said. "Dylan, would you know what flowers to plant to attract hummingbirds?"

"Probably not," he replied, teeth clenched. Was Olivia deliberately turning on the charm with Noah, or was he just bringing it out in her?

"You have a decent garden at your place on Coronado," Noah said.

"The house came with landscaping. I didn't plant anything myself."

"Got an urge to dig in the dirt at your house up the road?" his friend asked, amused.

Dylan gave him a sharp look, but Noah was oblivious and asked more gardening questions as Olivia led them inside. She pulled a large mason jar out of the refrigerator filled with what Dylan assumed was tea. Noah took it upon himself to get glasses out of the cupboard, add ice to them and set them on the counter.

Olivia poured the tea. "It's regular old black tea, in case you're wondering."

Dylan was. He took a glass, remembering their kiss in the kitchen. He noticed her cheeks color, as if she could read his mind.

For all he knew right now, she could.

"I'm trying a new vegetable soup recipe," she said, handing Noah a glass of tea. "You're welcome to stay.

I have some homemade bread. I've been experimenting. It's all good, though. I've tried everything—well, not the soup, but you can't go wrong with vegetables."

She was as unselfconscious as Noah was self-conscious. He tried his tea and gave Dylan a pointed look. "Knights Bridge is full of surprises."

"We don't have to stay," Dylan said.

"I'm going to resist homemade vegetable soup and homemade bread? I don't think so."

"Olivia has a big day tomorrow—"

"I can give you some to take with you," she said.

She had the windows open and the house was cool, the temperature dropping with the waning afternoon. Everything about Carriage Hill exuded her personality, her taste, her warmth, but Dylan could also see just how much work she had to do before The Farm at Carriage Hill was a profitable business. He remembered what it was like to be working night and day toward realizing a dream while at the same time knowing deep down it might not happen despite his best efforts.

She wrapped the bread in foil and put it and a container of soup into a brown paper bag for him and Noah to take back with them.

"Good luck tomorrow," Noah said.

Olivia thanked him, obviously taken in by the founder and chairman of NAK, Inc.

Dylan carried the bag and scowled at his friend when they reached the road. "When did you go to charm school?"

"What? I was trying to make a good impression. I figured if I was a jerk, she'd be more likely to think you're a jerk."

"She does think I'm a jerk."

"Because you didn't tell her about your father's interest in this 1938 jewelry robbery." Noah continued up the road, finally shaking his head. "You're in trouble, Dylan, my friend. Big trouble."

"I don't belong, do I?"

"You're the stranger in quiet and quaint Knights Bridge."

"It's not that quiet and quaint."

"It is compared to our world. Time stopped here when the buggy whip went out of style."

"I suspect we underestimate these people at our own peril. They're as much in this century as you and I are."

"Maybe, but I know you, Dylan. You won't stop until you figure out what happened with your father and this place—why he bought it, these missing jewels, Grace Webster, the Frosts, Quabbin Reservoir. You're relentless."

"Maybe Olivia wants answers as much as I do."

"Your presence threatens this little town. Hers doesn't."

"She lived in Boston for several years."

"And she's here now. So is her family. It's her home. She has roots here. Now she has a business here. You're a nomad like your father, and…" Noah frowned. "And there are blackflies."

"What are you saying?"

"I'm saying falling for her could be a big mistake."

Dylan nodded. "I know."

Noah waved a hand, swiping at the tiny flies. "I'm also saying there really are blackflies. Damn." He slapped at a gnat on his cheek. "Olivia won't hurt you. You're tough as nails, Dylan McCaffrey. You could hurt her, and you could hurt the people she cares about, even if you don't mean to."

"Trying to get me back to my desk?"

"As if you ever worked at a desk for more than twenty minutes at a time. I'm speaking as a friend, Dylan, not as a business partner."

"I thought you were the one who didn't notice things."

"Well, out here in the woods, a beautiful brown-haired woman is bound to get my attention."

"She's too good for me?"

Noah grinned. "Damn straight. You're caught, my friend. You can't have Olivia Frost if you pursue the Ashworth jewels, and you can't have peace of mind if you don't."

"What if the jewels have nothing to do with her or Knights Bridge?"

"That's why you found that file on your treasure-hunter father's laptop and why he bought the house of an old woman who was in turmoil in the 1930s. That's why your father's card was in the Knights Bridge town library."

"There's a reason you're a billionaire."

"Yeah. Luck, and at least one person on this planet I trust. Now, if you don't mind, I'm heading back to the land of concrete and five-star hotels."

Dylan was silent a moment, taking in the quiet, the lush green of the landscape. "Think I could settle down here?"

"And what, grow beans?"

"I could coach youth hockey. My father and I used to talk about getting into adventure travel. Knights Bridge would be a good base."

"You're out of your mind," Noah said, "but if anyone can figure this out, you can."

Dylan grinned at him. "I'll take that as encouragement."

A black Lincoln pulled into the driveway—Noah's hired car. He wasn't staying. He'd never planned to stay. He had meetings in New York. As the driver got out and opened the back door for him, Noah hesitated and looked at Dylan. "I'm used to having you at these meetings, Dylan."

"You'll be fine. You've built a team you can trust."

"No, you built a team I can trust. You played hockey. You're the team type. I'm not." Noah glanced down through the trees toward Olivia's house. "Neither is Olivia Frost. We're solo operators. Teamwork doesn't come naturally to us. It takes some effort for us to learn how to build a team, trust a team—trust ourselves. I don't have good instincts about people, but I can recognize someone else who gets burned because they can't see a son of a bitch coming down the road."

It was probably the most Noah had said at once since eighth grade. Dylan frowned at his friend. "Think she's here licking her wounds?"

"Count on it," Noah said. "I'm sorry I'll miss her soup and bread."

He climbed into the car and was gone. Dylan went inside and set the bag in his little refrigerator. He wasn't hungry yet. He was restless, not quite sure what he was supposed to do next, which wasn't like him. He changed into running clothes and took off in the opposite direction of The Farm at Carriage Hill. Blackflies found him, which he figured served him right for the thoughts he was having about his neighbor down the road.

When he returned, he tackled the claw-foot tub again and put on clean, dry clothes, as if somehow that would help him make a fresh start. He went back downstairs and, restless and out of sorts, searched through a cupboard in the living room and found a stack of old maps. He took them into the dining room and spread them on the table. One was a copy of a 1903 map of the Swift River Valley. It showed the towns that were disincorporated with the building of the Quabbin Reservoir thirty years later. He noted the three branches of the Swift River, roads, a railroad, tiny black dots marking where houses had been. It was a topographical map, and he could see the shape of the valley that ultimately had filled with water and the surrounding hills and ridges.

There was no way to know if the Ashworth jewels had ended up somewhere in the eighty-thousand acres of limited-access wilderness, or under water altogether.

What if Lord Ashworth had made them up?

Noah was right, Dylan thought. Either he had to leave Knights Bridge now and give up on getting answers, or he had to stay and try to dig into the reasons his father had bought this place and let the chips fall where they may.

If he left, would Olivia forget what she knew, or would she look for answers herself?

She would look. She wouldn't forget.

Dylan smiled and got out the soup and bread. At least he and his hazel-eyed neighbor had something in common.

Chapter 16

*O*n a hot afternoon in early September, toward the end of that long, lost summer of 1938, our last summer in the Swift River Valley, I read about a jewelry robbery in Boston in my hideaway cabin. My spot by Carriage Hill Pond hadn't changed, not yet, but work on the reservoir continued everywhere for miles and miles around me. Cutting, chopping, ripping, digging, burning. It went on all the time. The land was being scraped clean, creating a pristine bottom for when Beaver Brook and the three branches of the Swift River finally had nowhere else to go.

The story of a British aristocrat robbed of valuable jewels at his expensive hotel was a welcome diversion. I read about it in a newspaper already several days old. Lord Charles Ashworth and his fortune in missing jewels captured my imagination. I wondered if the thief had been caught already. Was he British? I couldn't imagine he would come all the way to our valley. Daddy had finally taken the state's offer and bought a house in Knights Bridge but he didn't want to start over there or anywhere else. He wanted to pretend the politicians would change their minds and the valley could go back to the way it had been.

He must have known that was impossible. The valley towns no longer officially existed. They'd been "disincorporated" in April. Most of the residents had moved out. We were still living in Gran's house, but Gran had started packing for our move to Knights Bridge. I was like Daddy. I didn't want to pack until the last minute.

Safe in my little cabin, I reread the article on the jewelry robbery. I had to force myself to breathe calmly. I'd had drowning nightmares for months and would wake up gasping for air, but lately I often had trouble breathing during the day, too, just thinking of water inundating everything I knew. I didn't tell anyone. We had to bear what we had to bear for the sake of progress, and millions of people would benefit from our sacrifice. Boston would have pure, unfiltered drinking water for the foreseeable future.

As I pictured the missing Ashworth jewels, I could smell the clean water of the pond and tried to pretend the rest of the valley was unchanged, still filled with people, homes and businesses. It was getting harder and harder to pretend. People said that in ten or twenty years, we would all come to love Quabbin. I hoped so. I wanted the destruction to end and the scars to heal.

That evening I slipped out of the house at dark. In the distance I could see the glow of the fires from the burning of brush and trees. When I got home, I cried *until I couldn't cry anymore. Daddy and Gran didn't like me to cry. We were to carry on. I expected one of them to come to my bedroom door and tell me to hush, but neither did. I thought they didn't hear me, didn't realize I'd sneaked out. Now, with the benefit of time, I think they knew. I think they heard me and said nothing, did nothing, because they, too, were grieving for all we were losing. I don't know if things would have been different if we'd talked. I pulled the curtains that night and crawled into bed, still seeing the glow of the fires.*

The next day, I returned to the cabin. It was a sad walk from Gran's house. So few houses were left. Trees I'd walked under for as long as I could remember were gone. I held back tears and by the time I reached the pond, I wanted to keep going, running until I came to a place where no one would ever tell me I had to leave my own home. I sat on my boulder and put my feet in the water, and when I was sure I wouldn't cry, I went inside the cabin. I never cried in there. It was my one rule.

The cabin would go soon, too. It was in the watershed that had to be protected so the natural filtration process could occur. A drop of water entering Quabbin, they said, would take four years before it came out of a tap in Boston.

There was no running water at the cabin. I would get water from the pond or from a shallow, hand-dug well, probably from one of the valley's original settlers, that was in the woods not ten yards behind the cabin.

I had grabbed my bucket to fetch water from the pond for dishes when I heard a noise in the woods. It sounded like a deer stepping on fallen branches. Instead, a man staggered out of the trees. He was bloody and filthy and hadn't shaved in several days. "I need help," *he said in a hoarse whisper.*

I gasped at his English accent. "Who are you?"

"My name's Philip. I'm not..." *He went very pale and almost sank to his knees, but he managed to stay upright and even give me a faltering smile.* "I won't hurt you. You're—"

"Grace." *I believed he wouldn't hurt me; it hadn't occurred to me that he would.* "We need to clean those wounds. Are you hungry?"

He attempted another smile. "Starved."

I got him inside and onto my cot. He didn't moan or complain but I could see he was in pain. I found a pan and soap, and I heated water from the well on the wood-fired kitchen stove. Philip was shivering under the quilts, and I realized he must have a fever. I touched his forehead. His skin was fiery hot.

"I can run and fetch my grandmother," *I said.*

"No. Don't tell anyone about me. Please, Grace. I promise I won't hurt you."

"I know you won't."

I cleaned his wounds. He had superficial cuts and scrapes on his hands and arms and a small gash on the left side of his face. He was lean and muscular, but I knew he wasn't one of the reservoir workers.

"No one will bother you here for now," *I said.*

"Thank you, Grace."

I saw then how handsome he was. He had a strong jaw and clear, deep blue eyes. "Is there anything else I can do for you?"

He touched a book I'd left on the cot. "I see you like your swashbucklers. I'm more of a scoundrel." *He sank into the thin mattress.* "Will you read to me, Grace?"

I know I blushed. "Latin verses or The Scarlet Pimpernel?*"*

He smiled. "Not Latin."

His eyes were shut but I could tell he wasn't asleep. I opened The Scarlet Pimpernel *and read to him.*

Chapter 17

Olivia couldn't sleep and got up at four to finish her Carriage Hill website. She wouldn't go live with it until after her mother-daughter tea. As night gave way to dawn, she wandered through the downstairs rooms, still and quiet in the dim light. There was still so much more to do, but the place looked good. The colors, the fabrics, the flow and style of the furnishings had all come together the way she'd envisioned. She would add more artwork and make adjustments as she went along, but she was satisfied with what she'd accomplished in such a short time.

If people decided they wanted ultratraditional New England, then what?

She pushed back the doubts and went into the kitchen. Buster stirred on his bed in the mudroom. She smiled at him. He had settled down since he'd adopted her. She trusted him not to scare off guests. Everyone coming today liked dogs, even a big, homely mutt like Buster. With the sunrise just peeking over the hills, she took him for a quick walk, turning back before she got to Dylan McCaffrey's house on the corner. She hadn't mentioned the decades-old jewelry robbery to anyone since reading about it in the library, especially not to Grace.

Maggie O'Dunn arrived early, as cheerful and relaxed as ever. How she pulled off everything without breaking a sweat amazed Olivia, who tended to agonize over details.

All the mothers and daughters were friends and family. Maggie's mother was the first guest to arrive, but the rest followed soon after, curious about Carriage Hill—and, of course, the man up the road. Both Olivia's grandmothers were there. Grace had declined to come, instead sending an opening-day gift, a set of binoculars so that Olivia could watch the birds.

She wasn't sure her own mother would turn up, but Louise Frost arrived with Jess. Olivia hugged them both, finally convinced that she'd chosen the right event for her opening day.

The tea went beautifully. The only problems were so minor as not to be real problems. She needed a quieter lock in the downstairs bathroom, and she needed to double the number of cloth napkins she owned. As the mothers and daughters left, several asked about bookings for a baby shower, a garden club meeting and a one-day training workshop for a local business.

Jess lingered on the terrace while Olivia saw Maggie off. Her friend was tireless, calm even after helping to serve a full tea to a dozen people. After she rattled off in her van, Olivia joined her sister out back.

Jess was on a yellow-painted bench, staring at the lavender. "Do you have a passport?"

Olivia kept her expression neutral as she sat at the table. "Yes."

"When did you use it last?"

"When I drove to Montreal last summer on business."

"I've applied for one. My first passport at twenty-seven."

"Good for you," Olivia said, meaning it.

"My passport picture is awful. Everyone says that, apparently. I want to go places, Olivia."

"You should, then."

"Don't you want to dust off your passport? Go to London, Paris, Ireland, Tuscany? Australia?" Jess looked down at her hands. "Mom wouldn't sleep a wink."

"That's her problem. Don't make it yours."

"What about you?"

Olivia felt the familiar tightness in her stomach at the prospect of flying but smiled through it. "I think it'll be Mark going with you not me."

She followed Jess out to her truck, the afternoon temperature the warmest yet that spring. "I left a bottle of champagne in your refrigerator," Jess said, climbing in behind the wheel. "Everything went great today, Liv. Time to celebrate."

Olivia watched her drive up the road, then decided her sister was right.

It was time to celebrate.

* * *

The air was cool and still, the sky clear, when Dylan walked down the quiet road to his neighbor's house. It was dusk, and he was finally certain that all of Olivia's guests were safely on their way. He found her sitting on the kitchen steps with her legs stretched out.

"I didn't want to interrupt your tea," he said. "How were the mothers and daughters?"

"Terrific. Everything went well. I've already had champagne. Of course," she added, "everyone was curious about you."

He grinned as he headed up the stone walk. "I love small towns. Do they know Noah was here?"

"I didn't get that impression, no."

"He likes you. He thinks you're a lot like him."

"A genius-tech type?" She laughed and leaned back against the step. "I don't think so."

"People who give too much of themselves and end up getting burned. Would that describe you, Olivia?"

"Sometimes. I think sometimes that would describe any of us."

"You're probably right about that. Noah asked about your tea. He had business in New York but he's on his way back to San Diego now. Flying," Dylan added, coming closer. "Noah likes to fly."

Olivia averted her eyes. "I'm sure that's a plus given his lifestyle."

"You, on the other hand, don't like to fly. A lot of anxieties percolating in the Frost family." He left it at that; he was standing at her toes now, noticing that she just had on wool socks, as if she'd come outside expecting to stay only for a few minutes. She didn't make a move to get up. "Your future brother-in-law stopped by to see me."

"Mark? Why?"

"I asked him to. I wanted to talk to him about the property." Dylan deliberately didn't say *his* property but wasn't sure why.

"About tearing down the house, you mean."

"About my options."

"Dylan, Grace understands she sold the house. She was ready to make a move. She knows it's in bad shape. You won't be making enemies here if you tear it down and have Mark design a great house for you to build in its place."

"Is that what you envision?"

"It's not my property. I suppose you could build a house and sell it. This area isn't the draw Cape Cod and the Berkshires are for wealthy second-home owners, but there are some. They tend to be people who want a genuine small-town atmosphere and don't mind that we don't have a five-star restaurant tucked away on a side road." She paused, and Dylan watched her as she shoved a hand through her hair. In the gray light, her eyes took on more of the blues than the greens and gold. "Never mind. Mark and I were in the same class in high school, did he tell you?"

"He mentioned it."

"No one ever thought he'd come back to Knights Bridge, but now no one can imagine him living anywhere else, least of all him."

"He's worried Jess thinks he's boring because he doesn't care about going to Paris, that she'll go off and have adventures without him."

"Then he should talk to her about it."

"I suspect he's the sort who doesn't talk to anyone. He didn't tell me in so many words. I put the pieces together. He likes a quiet life."

"We've all assumed he and Jess are more or less engaged. A friend of hers who was at the tea wants to throw her bridal shower here." Olivia jumped up suddenly, strands of dark hair flying into her face; she pushed them back with one hand. "You don't like a quiet life, do you?"

Dylan shrugged. "I wouldn't know. I've never had one."

"Rest my case," she muttered, then spun around and yanked open the door.

Dylan hesitated for a fraction of a second before he followed her into the kitchen. He glanced into the living room and noticed that she had a low fire burning in the old fireplace; Buster was asleep on the hearth. "How many nights around here are warm enough for you not to want a fire?"

Olivia glanced back at him from the counter. "I like fires. Is it cold at your house? My offer of a room here is still open. I don't want you going back to San Diego and telling all your friends that Knights Bridge is an unfriendly little town with old houses with leaky roofs. Maybe one of them will want to book an event here."

"Maybe." He walked over to the counter. "You're freelancing to make ends meet until this place provides a stable income."

"I have plenty of projects. I focus on my work, my clients—"

"You were the talk of the town for a while. One of the hottest designers in the Northeast. Don't forget, I looked you up before I flew out here. What happened?"

"Nothing happened. I kept working. I still am working. I just bought this place and decided to move back to Knights Bridge."

Dylan shook his head. "Something happened."

She turned away from him and grabbed a small saucepan soaking in the sink. Nothing like doing dishes to end a conversation, but he wasn't letting her off the hook. Whatever was going on with her design work had been eating at her for a long time. He could see it just in the way she moved.

"Do you want to tell me about it?" he asked softly.

Her back stiffened visibly. "No."

"Have you told anyone?"

"Jess."

"Not all of it," he said.

Olivia dumped water out of the pan. "Right. Not all of it." She glanced back at him. "Did you take classes in reading body language, or are you just a natural?"

"I've been paying attention to the Frost family and Knights Bridge dynamics. You're a proud, tight-lipped bunch." He leaned against the butcher-block island; she turned away from him again and flipped on the faucet, filling the pan with fresh water. "So, what happened? Who screwed you?"

"She didn't screw me. She just…she took care of herself and I didn't take care of myself."

"She's a designer? A friend?"

"We're friends but we aren't as close as we once were."

"What does that mean?"

"Just what I said." Olivia shut off the faucet, steam rising from the soaking pan. Without looking at him, she said, "Actually, I had an email from her just before you got here. That's why I went outside. I needed to think. She's very tapped in to what's going on, and she heard a former NHL player and Noah Kendrick had been here."

Dylan frowned. "Noah doesn't keep a low profile even when he's keeping a low profile."

Olivia's tension seemed to ease, at least for a moment. "I can see how that would work after meeting him just for a short time. You two—"

"You're changing the subject."

"Trying to."

"What's this woman's name?"

She sighed and turned once more to face him. Her expression was unreadable, intentionally so, he thought. Finally she said, "Marilyn Bryson. She's from Providence but she just moved to Boston and started as a senior designer at the same studio where I worked."

"Ah."

"She's a very good designer. She's hot right now."

"And you're…what?"

"Established but not that hot," Olivia whispered, then jerked her chin up as if he wasn't supposed to hear. "I don't feel sorry for myself."

"What did you do, take a victory lap and let things slide?"

"No! I've always worked hard. Marilyn and I had been friends for several years and her career was floundering. Nothing she was doing was working the way she wanted it to. She asked me what I'd do in her position. We put our heads together and mapped out a strategy. She took my advice and added her own talents, ambition and willingness to roll up her sleeves and get the job done."

"That was decent of you. So, what happened? She steal your clients?"

"One client," Olivia said, her voice almost inaudible.

"Your biggest client?"

She nodded. "I think he was restless, anyway. It happens. I hadn't seen or heard much from Marilyn in months, so it wasn't the slap in the face you might think."

"It could have been worse, you mean. It was bad enough."

"Yes," she said. "I was doing a good job for this particular client but I wasn't…as cutting edge and unique as he apparently thought I should be."

"And there Marilyn was. She called him?"

"That's right. I'm not jealous, Dylan. That's not how I operate."

He stood up from the counter. "What did she do, dump you as a friend once her career took off?"

"That sounds like first grade, I know."

"Nah. Sixth grade."

She managed a small laugh and reached for a towel on the island. "I wanted to celebrate her success and wish her well, but she disappeared. I got over that, more or less, and then in mid-March I stopped at my favorite restaurant…" Olivia looked down at her hands as she dried them. "Marilyn was there having lunch with my biggest client."

"What did you do?"

"Got out of there. Then I looked at my life and what I wanted and decided to get this place off the ground. I never expected Marilyn to do what she did. Or Roger Bailey, for that matter—"

"The snake-in-the-grass client."

Olivia set the towel back on the island, a spark of humor in her eyes. "He's not a bad guy. He just—"

"Relax. People can be jerks. Even good people. It's not a sign of weakness or pettiness to say so. We're not all that evolved. Maybe Roger was just looking after his business and didn't know the rules of yours. This Marilyn woman used you, dumped you and stabbed you in the back."

"That's a little blunt."

"Is it accurate?"

"I let her—"

"Not what I asked."

"I put her in the freezer," Olivia said abruptly.

Dylan angled a look at her. "You what?"

"I was drinking wine alone one night, which is never good, and I let everything get to me. So I wrote Marilyn's name on a slip of paper and stuck her in the freezer." Olivia pointed at the refrigerator on the other side of the island. "She's still in there. I feel like a four-year-old."

Dylan couldn't help himself. He grinned. "Wait, what? You put her in your freezer to freeze her career?"

Olivia reddened and turned back to the sink. "It was meant as a ritual to help me. I don't mean her any harm."

"Why not? If you'd been in her shoes, what would you have done if a friend went out of her way to help you turn your career around?"

"I didn't go out of my way. Not really. She was a friend. It was fun. We had a good time. I didn't expect her to disappear and steal my biggest client. When I didn't hear from her, at first I told myself she was just busy."

"Then you ran into her and this Roger character having lunch together." Dylan pictured the scene. "Ouch. Tough way to figure out what was really going on."

Olivia took in a deep breath and shifted back to him. "That was difficult and painful, but I'm here because of it. I've reevaluated, and I don't blame Marilyn, or myself. I have no regrets about our friendship."

"Easier with her in your freezer. It's okay to get mad, Olivia. It's okay to be hurt. No one likes to be a victim, but sometimes we pick the wrong damn friends, or friends go their separate ways."

"I know I don't have to like everyone and everyone doesn't have to like me, but this was tough. Anyway, Marilyn and I aren't like you and Noah Kendrick."

"No. Not at all. I have no idea how Noah's brain works and he and I aren't competitors."

"I don't see myself as Marilyn's competitor."

"How do you think she sees you? You're both designers. Noah and I are business partners, not business rivals. You and Marilyn weren't after the same guys, too, were you?"

"Guys?"

"Not clients. Guys. Men. Romance."

Olivia yanked open a small drawer and pulled out a folded white towel. "No, never."

Dylan tilted his head back. Now, this was interesting. "But there was a guy?"

"He's gone. I don't know that he ever—we ever—" She sighed and unfolded the towel. "We were never serious."

"Where'd he go?"

"He's in Seattle." She laid the towel over a plate of tiny tarts obviously left over from the mother-daughter tea.

"You weren't going to fly to Seattle to keep the relationship going."

"There wasn't much of a relationship."

Dylan grunted and walked over to the refrigerator and pulled open the freezer. The slip of paper with the traitor friend's name was tucked into a tray of ice cubes. Olivia wasn't leaving anything to chance, he thought with amusement.

He took the paper into the living room.

Olivia followed him. "What are you doing?"

"Throwing Marilyn here in the fire. That's a better ritual. She'll be ashes. Gone."

"That sounds so brutal."

He grinned at her. "Freezing her doesn't?"

"Freezing her career. This is burning her. And I wasn't serious."

"I'm serious. I want you to stop thinking about this woman. I want you to let her go and trust yourself again."

"I trust myself—"

"Not the way you did before this happened. Am I right?"

Olivia sat on the chair in front of the fire, on the edge of the cushion. Buster stirred and rolled over, then heaved a sigh and went back to sleep. "I second-guess myself more than I ever used to."

Dylan looked at the slip of paper. The name was written in thick red marker. He wondered if that had any significance, or if a red marker just was what was handy when Olivia decided to pop her friend into the ice-cube tray. He sat on the rug next to Buster. "You can't let your experience with her undermine your confidence in your own judgment. You can't lose faith in yourself."

"Did Noah lose faith in himself?"

"This isn't about Noah."

"He did, though, didn't he?"

"He's never had any faith in himself when it comes to people. I'm his friend. I was his friend at six, I'm his friend now and I'll be his friend at eighty. It's just the way it is. It wasn't that way with you and Marilyn Bryson."

"Maybe so." Olivia looked past him at the fire. "I don't want to be too hard on her, or on myself. Sometimes friendships aren't meant to last forever. I don't regret ours. She's a lot of fun, energetic, optimistic."

"Would you ever have stolen one of her clients?"

"No, of course not. Maybe Marilyn didn't know that she shouldn't—"

"Yeah, right," he said, skeptical. "Don't start making excuses for her just because you admitted you had her in your freezer."

"You have a poor view of human nature, don't you?"

"Realistic." He stood again, his eyes still on Olivia. Whatever she was telling herself now, her experience with Marilyn had eaten at her. "This woman looked after herself, and maybe she got too busy to call, but if she behaved unethically and that hurt you, then I'm glad you put her in your freezer."

"I'm not a mean, vindictive person, Dylan. Marilyn isn't, either. I don't think she calculated any of this."

"Her bad behavior will bite her in the butt, or it won't. Not your call. Your call is to act out of your own sense of integrity and honor, and to forgive yourself your own mistakes." He glanced again at the paper. "I bet she spreads lies about you."

Olivia bit back a smile. "Every now and then our

inner eleven-year-old does come out. I can only imagine what all you deal with in your work. People must spread nonsense about Noah from time to time."

"Yep. Not everyone, and you start to recognize the self-absorbed, self-serving, entitled SOBs after a while. You have a good thing going here. If some bad as well as some good got you here, so be it."

He tossed Marilyn into the fire. Olivia watched the flare of the flames as the little slip of paper quickly burned.

"It's not her success that upset you," Dylan said. "That has nothing to do with you. It's the loss of her friendship. It's misjudging her, and yourself. Maybe you were ready to shake things up."

She nodded but was obviously on the verge of tears.

Dylan kissed her on the top of the head. "I'll get out of here and give you some time to yourself. Your father said that fishermen can go right over the cellar hole to the Websters' former home. I was thinking about getting a fishing license and renting a boat, seeing for myself."

"Tomorrow's supposed to be beautiful."

"You could come with me."

"I could."

"I found a couple of old fishing poles in Grace's shed. See you bright and early."

She caught his arm as he started to leave. "I have one en suite bedroom if you want to stay here. That way you won't risk running into me in the hall."

"Just in the morning when your hair's tousled from sleep and you're especially irresistible."

"I'd be sure to get dressed first."

"No fun in that."

She let go of him and laughed, even as her eyes filled with tears. "I've lost some confidence in myself the past few months. Normally I'm more fun to be around."

"Pour yourself another glass of champagne and celebrate opening day and freeing yourself from the grip of a lost friendship. Take a hot bath. I'll see you in the morning." Dylan opened the main front door, hating to leave but knowing he had to. He looked back at her, saw that she was still fighting the tears. He smiled. "I'll bring the poles. You bring some of those leftovers from your tea."

Chapter 18

Jess ran down from the mailbox the next morning and burst into the mill office. "It came! My passport. It's here."

Her mother pushed back her chair at her desk and eyed the stiff new passport in Jess's hand. "Good for you."

"Thanks, Mom. I'm so excited." Jess smoothed the front of the passport with her thumbs. "It was easier than I thought it would be. Getting the photo was the hardest part. Now I have no more excuses. Honestly, Mom, I want to go to Paris as much as you want to go to California."

"Does Mark want to go?"

"He says so. It doesn't matter. *I'm* going. If I wait—I won't get there for another twenty years. I want to see Paris before Mark and I have kids." Jess tucked her passport into her handbag. "Assuming... I don't want to jinx anything by speaking too soon."

Her mother got to her feet. "Has Mark..."

"I shouldn't have said anything. He and I—" Jess broke off abruptly. "No, Mom. No ring yet. Go ahead and make your plans for California. I'll work Paris around them if I'm needed here."

She looked over at the map on the wall. "Maybe I'm fooling myself, Jess. Maybe I'll never go to California."

Jess slumped. Louise Frost could be the biggest wet blanket in Knights Bridge without even putting her mind to it. "Mom...come on. Don't say that."

She seemed to make an effort to smile. "I love my life here. Why would I want to leave, anyway?"

"Because you want to go places and see new things. Why wouldn't you?"

"You're right. Don't worry about me." She gave Jess a quick hug. "I have to make some calls. Enjoy your passport. It's great."

Jess ran outside and down to the old sawmill, so frustrated with her mother that she kicked stones into the water. She immediately felt guilty and forced herself to focus on the sounds of the water rushing over the rocks, the twitter of birds, the rustle of the breeze in the trees. She wasn't just frustrated with her mother. She was frustrated with Mark. With herself. With her life. Who was she kidding? She had a million things to do. When would she have time for Paris?

Her father joined her at the edge of the dam. "You showed your mother your spanking-new passport? She just threw up."

"I didn't need to know that, Dad."

He looked at her. "Sorry. Just kidding. She's fine. When are you going to Paris?"

"I wanted to go for our honeymoon." Her eyes misted. "That's not going to happen."

"Why not? Don't tell me Mark's afraid to fly."

"No, he's just not interested in Paris—or a honeymoon. I can tell. He's been to Paris. He doesn't care about going again."

"I don't know if I can blame him for that."

"Dad!"

"But I bet he's interested in going to Paris with you. I'm not getting involved in whether the trip's a honeymoon or not, but he'll want to show you Paris."

"That's what he says but I know he's had his fill of cities."

"So? Do five days in Paris, then five days hiking in the Alps or kayaking somewhere."

Jess stared at her father. "That's so easy. Simple. Why didn't I think of it?"

"Because you're too close to the situation. I won't even call it a problem. Not being able to afford food is a problem. Paris or no Paris—not a problem. See what Mark says. Don't tell him I thought of it in case he hates the idea."

"Have you ever wanted to go hiking in the Alps?"

Her father winked at her. "I'll be hiking the California Pacific Coast Highway soon."

"Mom's getting cold feet. Dad, I don't know—she's planning this trip to the minute. What if she doesn't go? She avoids driving to Boston. How is she going to fly to California and then drive a hundred-plus miles up a winding, unfamiliar road?"

"Sometimes it's easier to make a big change than a little change. She's trying, Jess."

"I know, Dad."

"We live in a beautiful place and yet we're all thinking about other places."

"Olivia isn't."

Jess considered her older sister a moment. "I think she wants to know she can get in an airplane, at least."

Her father picked up a smooth, flat rock and tossed it into the millpond. "If she doesn't want to, she doesn't have to."

"Maybe she could use a push, Dad. We can encourage her. I know you want to protect us all but sometimes we just need support, not protection."

"I'm supportive."

"You want to be. You're protective."

"When did you get your shrink degree?"

She laughed but felt a twinge of uneasiness. Her father obviously had his suspicions, but he still didn't know for sure that one Louise Frost was seeing a therapist. Jess knew that he would do anything to keep them all safe, emotionally as well as physically. He was a bear of a man who was unconditionally on their side. Seeing a therapist wasn't a criticism, or a sign he wasn't doing enough or there was something wrong with him.

"Never mind." He gave her a quick hug. "Get back to work."

"Dad, what would you have done if Olivia had followed Peter Martin to Seattle?"

"That was never happening. That guy wasn't for her. She knew it."

"But if she had."

"I'd have wished her well."

"Mom?"

He didn't hesitate. "She would have, too."

Jess was skeptical. "Her older daughter living on the other side of the country?"

"Yes. We're not hemming you two in. Whatever's going on in your heads, that's not what we're doing."

"You don't want to get rid of us, do you?"

"You both are grown."

"Dad, you know your lines, but what comes out of your mouth isn't what you feel. You and Mom don't want either of us moving out of New England. Seattle…" Jess grinned at him. "It's another place I want to see."

"Your mother, too. She says I'd love some open-air market there."

"Maybe you're the stick-in-the-mud."

"Maybe I am." He picked up another stone, the breeze catching the ends of his salt-and-pepper hair. "I see Dylan McCaffrey's back in town. What's he up to?"

"I have no idea," Jess said.

"He's rich. He's not as rich as his friend Noah but he's still worth a fortune, more than anyone around here. Probably more than the whole town combined."

"Just because he has money doesn't mean he's up to anything."

"Doesn't mean he's not, either. He doesn't need to stay out there in Grace Webster's old house. It's a wreck. What's he doing for furniture? Appliances?"

"He has his reasons for being there, I'm sure."

"Is Olivia one of them?"

Jess gave her father a wry grin. "Who knows, maybe Dylan doesn't need to worry about furniture and appliances because he's staying with her."

"Is he?"

"It's possible."

Her father grimaced and plopped his rock into the water. "Some things I don't need to know—"

"Kidding, Dad. Kidding. I have to lock up my passport, then get back to work."

Jess ran back to her sawmill apartment. Talking first with her mother and then with her father had both energized and unsettled her, but she smiled when she slipped her new passport into her dresser drawer. She suddenly couldn't wait to show it to Mark.

She headed back to the mill and got to work, forgetting about Paris and her passport…at least for the moment.

After work, she drove out to Olivia's house. For the first few weeks, she hadn't wanted to get too invested in having her sister back in town, since she could decide it wasn't for her, or a getaway was an impossible dream, and return to Boston. Now, though, Jess was almost convinced that Olivia was in Knights Bridge to stay.

Almost.

Olivia had picked up their grandmother and Grace Webster for the afternoon. Jess found them on the terrace. The two older women were sitting on chairs in the sun, chatting while Olivia worked on clearing out an untouched corner of her yard. "Need some help?" Jess called to her.

"I'm good," Olivia said. "I've started a compost bin."

Jess had never been much of a gardener. She noticed the wheelbarrow parked next to her sister, overflowing with cut brush and raked leaves.

"That man is getting to her," Audrey Frost said as

Jess sat next to her. "The one living in Grace's old house."

"He owns it now," Jess said.

Her grandmother sighed. "Something's going on between those two. I think it has to do with the father. Duncan McCaffrey. The treasure hunter."

Grace tightened her thick sweater around her. "Sometimes it's best to let the past be."

"You wrote a book about your past," her friend reminded her.

"About my life. There's no one to remember me when I'm gone. I have no children, grandchildren, brothers or sisters."

"Don't you have a cousin in Chicago?"

"Minneapolis," Grace said. "We haven't seen each other in years. I think he might be dead."

Jess was relieved when Olivia returned with the now-empty wheelbarrow. Grace eased to her feet. "I'd like to see my old house," she said. "Can you take me there, Olivia? Jess can stay here with your grandmother while we scoot out."

Audrey Frost snorted. "I don't need a babysitter."

"Come on, Grandma," Jess said. "We can go see how the rhubarb is coming along. I still want your recipe for strawberry-rhubarb pie. It's my favorite."

Mollified, her grandmother got to her feet. "We used to eat rhubarb like celery. We loved puckering."

"Grace and I won't be long," Olivia said.

"Is Mr. McCaffrey there?" Grace asked.

"I imagine so."

The old woman frowned. "He doesn't have enough to do, does he?"

Olivia laughed. "Not nearly enough."

* * *

Olivia drove Grace the short distance to her former house. She parked as close to the steps as she could, but Grace got out of the car and walked up to the porch on her own, not waiting or asking for help. The sun was rapidly giving way to clouds, a hint of rain in the air. Olivia needed a quiet evening. Her excursion with Dylan on Quabbin that morning had frazzled her nerves. They'd been alone on the water, not another soul in sight. The reservoir and the surrounding wilderness were so quiet that she'd found herself barely able to imagine that the area had once been filled with towns and villages.

"Are you coming?" Grace asked, pausing at the bottom of the porch steps.

She nodded and smiled. "Right behind you."

Dylan would be there, she thought. She didn't know how being out on the water—being with her—had affected him. He'd turned off the engine of their rented boat and sat for a while, fishing, listening to the birds and the wind on the water and in the trees on the shore. For miles and miles, there was nothing but wilderness. They'd spotted an eagle nest high in a spruce tree. Olivia wanted to see a moose. Maggie O'Dunn had said she'd seen a moose in Quabbin last fall.

Using an island—once a hill—to orient themselves, they located the area where Grace had grown up. The water was deep, impenetrable, no old foundations or anything else visible on the bottom.

"Olivia," Grace said quietly.

She snapped out of her thoughts. "Sorry. Dylan and I went out in a boat today. We wanted to find the spot where you grew up."

She smiled. "Did you catch any fish?"

"Not a one."

Dylan had seemed taken in by both the history and the beauty of Quabbin. Olivia had been taken in by him. He wasn't just a sexy jock or just a hard-driving businessman. Out on the water, those stereotypes didn't hold, and, she realized, they had nothing to do with him. He was who he was. He didn't play games. He was, she thought, completely authentic, and would stand for no less from the people in his life. It was why he and Noah Kendrick got along. Noah couldn't be anyone but who he was.

Grace mounted the steps slowly but without hesitation. She straightened when she reached the porch. "This place looks seedier than I remember. Was it this seedy when I sold it to that rogue Duncan McCaffrey?"

"I wasn't in town when you sold it," Olivia said.

Grace sighed at the cracked, warped front door. "I suppose one's eye gets used to certain things. In my last years here, I was terrified that I wouldn't notice bathroom odors as I aged. I was staying home for longer periods. One's senses adjust. It's like people who don't notice pet odors." She glanced at Olivia. "I made your grandmother promise to tell me if she walked in here and the place smelled like pee."

Olivia laughed in surprise. "Grandma probably would have told you even if you hadn't asked her to."

The door opened and Dylan greeted them. "Hello, Grace, Olivia." His tone was polite, neutral, as he stood back and motioned for them to come inside. He'd obviously showered since fishing on Quabbin that morning. The ends of his dark hair were damp and he'd changed into a warm gray sweater and canvas pants that fit closely on his athletic, muscular frame. "I was restless and cleaned this afternoon," he said with a smile as they stepped past him. "Don't forget to notice the floors. I mopped."

Olivia suppressed an image of him with his sleeves rolled up, cleaning house. She had to get her attraction to him under control. If Grace noticed, she made no comment. She entered the living room, placing a hand tentatively on the door frame. The floors did look better, and the room smelled fresh, not as dank and musty.

After a moment's hesitation, Grace walked through the living room to the dining room. "I used to grade papers here," she said, rubbing her fingertips over the newly polished table. "You can see the marks from my red pencil. I always used a red pencil."

"My folks remember," Olivia said.

"Your father enjoyed Shakespeare but he pretended he didn't like reading. He could have made the honor roll all through school, but he didn't want to put in the effort. Your mother was different. She pushed herself to do well."

"She wasn't as smart as Dad?"

"I didn't say that. Randy could get by with no work. Louise couldn't, not because she wasn't smart. She would get paralyzed if she wasn't prepared. Your father didn't mind winging it."

Dylan stood in front of the bay window. "Were they artistic like Olivia?"

"Randy liked to draw but I wouldn't know about artistic skill. I taught Latin and English. It was a long time ago but I remember him and Louise well, perhaps because Audrey and I were friends."

"No secrets in a small town," Dylan said.

Olivia followed his gaze as he glanced out the window. No rain yet, but it was gray, blustery.

Grace looked past him to the overgrown yard. "I beg to differ. Small towns have their secrets, possibly more so than the city because we in small towns have reason to keep them. The city can afford more anonymity. What difference does it make if a stranger discovered your secret? You can just blab away and go home, knowing you're unlikely ever to see them again."

"Do you have any secrets?" Dylan asked.

She ignored him. "The house is clean but it's so rundown. I suppose I'm spoiled. Everything at Rivendell is new." She moved over to one of the bookcases. "I didn't do much when I was here. I kept it clean, but I hated to spend money on anything but the most critical repairs. I loved the view, the gardens, my favorite chair and my books. I tidied up but I never saw any need to redecorate or to replace anything that still worked. My family…" She paused, deep in thought. "Gran liked it here well enough, but my father never felt at home. I did, but my idea of home changed after the state took our land."

"Who owned Olivia's place before she did?" Dylan asked.

"There were several owners during my time here. The most recent—the couple who sold her the house—planned to convert it into a bed-and-breakfast but ran out of money. They put a lot of work into the place. A new roof, new furnace, new wiring."

"Which helped me," Olivia interjected. "I can concentrate on cosmetic work instead of infrastructure."

"Did you always live here alone?" Dylan asked, standing by the piano.

"After both my father and grandmother died, yes. I

often considered taking in a boarder, but I never did. I would see students and teachers all day." Grace ran her fingertips over a row of books. "I'd go to church, and to dinner and the movies with friends. I loved the quiet here and I appreciated my solitude. I'd watch the birds, work in my garden, read, build puzzles. I'd listen to the radio but I seldom watched television. I got a DVD player when I couldn't get out as much anymore."

"A good life," Olivia said.

Grace turned from the books. "It still is a good life. Since I never married and have no close family, I never had the illusion that I would have someone else around to take care of me in my late senior years." She laughed, her light blue eyes sparking with sudden humor. "Although I never thought I'd live this long."

Dylan nodded to the shelves of adventure novels. "You've left me some good reading."

A little unsteadily, Grace touched the copy of *The Scarlet Pimpernel*. "I loved these books. I have no room for them in my apartment. When I get a hankering to read about swashbucklers and such, I borrow a copy from the library."

"These don't have sentimental value?" Dylan asked.

She looked up at him. "They have great sentimental value. I left them for your father to enjoy. I'm sorry he didn't get that chance. I hope they're not too far gone for you."

"Not at all. I'm reading *The Count of Monte Cristo*."

Grace smiled. "That's a good one. You're enjoying Knights Bridge, then? Have you had a chance to hike up Carriage Hill yet?"

"I have," Dylan said.

She walked over to the bay window, pulled back a

sheer curtain, then craned her neck as if to get a view of the hill. "I haven't been up there in years. There's a pond on the other side. Carriage Hill Pond. When I was a girl..." She seemed to struggle to find the right words as she let go of the curtain and stood straight. "I used to read books in a small cabin there, before it was torn down for Quabbin."

Grace was visibly tired, and Olivia exchanged glances with Dylan. He slipped an arm around Grace. "Will you allow me to walk you back to the car?"

She beamed a smile up at him. "You *are* a scoundrel."

He laughed. "I think I prefer swashbuckler."

Once Grace was safely into the passenger seat, Olivia returned to her house and collected her grandmother, then took both women back to Rivendell. A half-dozen residents were gathered around a large television, cheering on the Red Sox against the Yankees. Olivia's grandmother joined them, but Grace wasn't interested. "I'm going to have hot chocolate, read and go to bed early," she said, pensive.

"Sounds good," Olivia said cheerfully. "I might go home and do the same."

"Are you happy being back in Knights Bridge, Olivia?" Grace asked as they came to her apartment door.

"Yes, absolutely. I was never far away in Boston. In some ways it's as if I never left."

Grace unlocked the door and pushed it open, then turned to Olivia, her steady gaze a reminder of her reputation as a stern teacher. "Dylan McCaffrey is a nomad at heart, isn't he?"

"Maybe. I don't know him that well. His father was, at least from what I can gather. Dylan must have been on the go all the time as a hockey player. Nowadays, he has the means to do whatever he wants."

"He can even wash floors if he so chooses," Grace said with unexpected levity.

Olivia left her to her hot chocolate and drove back to Carriage Hill. She had deep roots in Knights Bridge. Dylan had none, but it wouldn't have mattered. She'd seen that morning that new things—new discoveries, new adventures—energized him. His work and his lifestyle opened the world up to him. He could get on a plane in a heartbeat if he wanted to go somewhere.

Her hands shook, and she felt light-headed, early signs of a full-blown panic attack at the thought of flying. Buster didn't seem to notice her agitated state. He wandered into the mudroom and lapped the water in his dish.

"Let's go for a walk," Olivia said, grabbing his leash.

She welcomed the cool air and light rain as she and Buster headed out the driveway and down the road. Dogs weren't allowed in Quabbin but they wouldn't go that far. She just wanted to give the exercise and quiet surroundings a chance to soothe her. It wasn't just the thought of flying that had frayed her nerves, she realized. It was Grace. It was her mother, Jess, Mark Flanagan. The uncertainties of her own life and work. Duncan McCaffrey and the Ashworth jewels.

And it was Dylan, she thought.

She smiled as she and Buster rounded a curve. Mostly it was Dylan.

He was strolling toward them in the mist as if he'd lived in Knights Bridge his entire life.

Olivia did her best to cover for any lingering visible effects of her moment of panic. "The rain's nice right now, isn't it?" She didn't wait for an answer. "I think Grace appreciated seeing the house again. Thanks for doing that, but don't you wonder what she isn't telling us?"

He nodded. "Whatever it is might not have anything to do with my father or the 1938 robbery."

"Weird to think Grace could know anything about a fortune in missing jewels."

"Maybe she doesn't." Dylan patted Buster on the head.

"How far do you two plan to go? The rain's supposed to get worse."

"Not far. We can turn back now and walk with you, unless you'd rather be alone."

"I'm alone enough at that house."

Olivia let his comment go at that but no sooner did she get Buster redirected than the rain picked up. Within a few seconds, they were in a downpour. She hadn't brought a jacket and was just in a lightweight sweater. She was drenched almost immediately.

Dylan grabbed the leash from her. "Want to run?"

Olivia figured she was soaked no matter what she did. "Just remember who's an athlete and who's not an athlete."

He laughed and jumped over a pothole rapidly filling with water, then picked up his pace. Buster got right into the spirit of things and trotted alongside him. Olivia kept up as best she could, but not only was Dylan a trained athlete, he was taller. She tended to take almost two steps for his one.

When they reached her house, it was practically raining sideways, water streaming down her driveway in cracks and splits in the dirt. She and Dylan were both soaked to the skin. He hooked Buster's leash over his wrist and then caught her by the waist, lifting her off her feet.

She gave a little whoop of surprise and pleasure. "What are you doing?"

"Carrying you."

She knew that much. She could tell because her feet weren't on the ground but her body was still moving up her walk. He kicked open her front door and set her on the floor. He wasn't winded. He wasn't even breathing hard. He got Buster's leash off and let the big dog shake off in the middle of the kitchen, rainwater flying everywhere.

Dylan grinned. "Guess I'll have to get acquainted with your mop now."

"Getting caught in a chilly rain is a cardinal sin," Olivia said with a shiver. "We're lucky we don't have hypothermia."

"I'll build a fire. You should get out of those wet clothes."

"You, too." She still could feel his arms around her. Every stitch of her clothing was completely drenched. With a shaking hand, she pulled off her soaked shoes and socks and left them by the kitchen door. Her heart was racing, her blood pounding as she manufactured an easy smile. "Amazing how you can be dry one minute and soaked to the bone the next."

"Uh-huh. Amazing."

Olivia was aware of his eyes on her, then realized that her thin, wet sweater was clinging to her skin from the waist up, revealing more than she was prepared for him to see. She took in a shallow breath. "I'll get changed upstairs. Feel free to borrow a towel. There's a half bath down here and a full bathroom at the top of the stairs."

Dylan gave her a head start, at least. She was up the stairs and on the landing before she heard his first step below her. He moved deliberately, in no apparent hurry, but she doubted he was tired after their morning on Quabbin or their run in the rain. She stood back, not sure if she was pausing to catch her breath or just waiting for him. She was freezing now and wanted to get dry and warm and by the fire.

He didn't look cold at all when he reached the top of the stairs. She noticed his broad shoulders, his slim hips, his muscular thighs—he'd obviously kept in shape since his peak hockey days.

She pushed back her wet hair and searched for something to say. "Why are you so interested in an old jewelry robbery? You can't possibly care about any reward or profit from the jewels themselves. Is it the hunt, or is it because of your father?"

"Maybe it's because of you and your note."

"Ah." Her senses were on overdrive, tuned in to his presence, reacting to his sexiness. "It was the chives, then. On my card."

He smiled. "*The Farm at Carriage Hill* got me, too." He curved two fingers and wiped water from her hair off her cheek. "You're not what I expected."

"As the owner of Carriage Hill pestering you about your yard?"

"That, and this." He lowered his mouth to hers, just skimming her lips with his, then staying close. "I didn't expect I'd come out here and fall for you."

"You came because of your father. Otherwise you'd have just hired someone to deal with me."

"Aren't you glad I didn't? Go on. Change before you freeze."

"I'm not likely to freeze now," she said half under her breath as she slipped into her bedroom.

Dylan leaned in the doorway. "Will I turn into a toad if I step over the threshold?"

"You're the big risk-taker. Try it. See what happens."

She pulled open an oak wardrobe she'd found at a yard sale last fall and had painted a warm, restful cream, never imagining she'd be living here come spring. Pretending to have nothing else on her mind, she grabbed dry wool socks, jeans and a shirt, then subtly tucked underwear between them. As she turned, she remembered that she'd had some of her antique linens out first thing that morning, before Dylan had whisked her off to Quabbin. They were laid out on her bed, sorted according to color, fabric or edging.

Dylan had stepped onto the wide-board pine floor. He was fine. He was, she thought, more than fine. Just looking at him made her tingle with desire.

"You probably don't have lace-edged pillowcases in San Diego," she said.

"Not probably. Definitely."

She suppressed a touch of self-consciousness and set her clothes on the foot of the bed. The room overlooked the backyard, and on warm mornings, with the windows open, she could hear the birds and smell her gardens on the breeze. That morning, she'd imagined Dylan with her.

He planted his hands on her hips from behind and turned her to face him. "Olivia."

"I collect them." Suddenly she was having a tough time forming a coherent thought. "Antique linens. I thought I could use them here, especially when I start taking in overnight guests. I can make things out of some of them. Sachets, pillowcases. The lace on one is so fine, so beautiful, I can actually cut it out of the rest of the pillowcase, which is a disaster, and frame it."

"Good. Excellent. You're an amazing woman with an amazingly creative eye."

She draped her arms over his shoulders. "You don't care about antique linens, do you?"

"I do because you do."

She smiled. "I actually like hockey."

He'd had all he could take. She could see it in his eyes, feel it in the tightening of his hold on her. He eased his arms around her and lowered his mouth to hers again, and in the split second before his lips touched hers she knew this wasn't going to be a soft, gentle kiss. As if just to torture her more, his palms somehow found the bare skin of her lower back, eased under her wet sweater and up her midriff to just beneath her breasts. When she gave a little gasp, he deepened their kiss as he let his thumbs ease up and under her soaked bra.

Emboldened, aching with anticipation, Olivia coursed her hands over his shoulders and down his back, drawing him tightly to her. When she came to his leather belt, all she could think of was unbuckling it, stripping off his wet clothes, and her own.

He gave a ragged moan, then raised her sweater. "Time to get this off," he whispered, kissing her again before he pulled back just enough to get the sweater up over her head. He tossed it onto the floor. His gaze swept over her. "You're beautiful, Olivia. You're so damn beautiful."

"Dylan…"

In the next two seconds, her bra was off, on its way to the floor with her sweater.

He took her hand, placed it on his jeans, under his belt buckle, so that she could feel the size and shape of him. He kissed her again, then lowered his mouth to her breasts.

She was melting, aching, dying for him to be inside her.

If she hadn't slipped in her wet feet, on the wood floor, anything could have happened. *Everything* could have happened. Instead, she found herself on her bed tangled in antique sheets and pillowcases.

Dylan's blue eyes seemed darker, grayer in the late-afternoon light. The rain had stopped as abruptly as it had started, and now a ray of bright sun raked across her simple, attractive bedroom. Olivia realized she had linens scrunched in front of her, as if she were trying to cover herself. Dylan helped her up, giving her a soft kiss on the lips. "Go ahead and get on dry clothes. I'll meet you downstairs." His voice was slightly hoarse, but he cleared his throat and grinned. "Still want that fire?"

She threw a pillowcase embroidered with tiny violets at him as he left.

As she reached for the dry clothes she'd left on the bed, she caught her reflection in the mirror above her dresser. The short-lived sunshine was gone, but her eyes, her skin, her expression all seemed brighter. She wanted to credit her run in the rain but she knew it was mostly one Dylan McCaffrey.

She tugged off the rest of her wet clothes and got dressed.

"I think your father is the only reason you're here," she said when she returned to the living room. "You didn't come here because of a run-down house you didn't know you owned, the junk in the yard or missing jewels. You came here—and you came back—because of your father. He died suddenly, and too soon."

Dylan stood back from the fireplace. He had a small fire lit and he'd dried Buster off and let him flop on the hearth. "You don't think I came just to be a good neighbor?"

"You could have been a good neighbor by calling Stan to move that junk by himself. Or asking me to call Stan, or whomever. You wanted to see for yourself this mysterious property your father had left you."

"Maybe my father got me here but you'll keep me here."

"How? By tying you up in the attic?" Olivia was only half kidding. "Not that I have an attic. Dylan, you don't trust us. At least not yet."

"Us?"

"Grace, my sister, my parents, me—any of us in Knights Bridge."

"I don't even know you."

"My point exactly. How did your father learn about the jewelry heist?"

Dylan stirred the fire with a poker, set the screen back in place and settled onto the floor next to Buster. Finally he said, "I found notes about the robbery on my father's laptop."

"He left you his laptop?"

"It was in an old trunk he left me." Dylan stretched out his thick, muscled legs as if he belonged there and glanced up at her. "I opened the trunk once right after he died, shut it and didn't open it again until I got your note and discovered that I owned a house out here."

Olivia lifted a log out of her wood box and set it on the fire. She was too restless to sit. "Tell me about the notes you found on his laptop," she said.

"I didn't find them until this last trip to San Diego. They describe the Ashworth robbery but don't explain why it caught my father's attention. I finally dug through the trunk and sorted every piece of paper, every file, every book, brochure and folder."

When he paused, Olivia turned to him, noticing the play of the flames in his eyes. "What else did you find, Dylan?"

"A newspaper article about the robbery. It was tucked in a book about Quabbin."

"From the Knights Bridge paper?"

"A Boston paper. *Isaiah Webster, Knights Bridge,* is written on the margin of the article. It looks like a woman's handwriting. Who's Isaiah Webster, Olivia?"

"Grace's father. Do you think it's her handwriting?"

"I can't tell if it matches the handwriting on Grace's bookplates. She could have put it into one of her books as a bookmark and forgot about it."

"Then how did your father end up with it?"

"He could have found it after he bought her house and was going through her old books."

"That would have been after he came to Knights Bridge. It wouldn't explain why he was interested in her house in the first place."

Dylan shifted his gaze to the fire. "No."

He didn't continue. Olivia frowned at him. "Dylan?"

"I think my father had the article before he bought the house. I think the article is why he came to Knights Bridge." He shot to his feet, the explosive force with which he moved a reminder of the athlete he was. He touched her arm, a gentle, brief touch. "I'm sorry if I had no business coming onto you like that."

"I didn't exactly object."

"No, you didn't. That's good. Olivia..." He lowered his hand, his expression serious, tortured. "I should see if the roof at my house leaked in that rain."

"What's wrong, Dylan?"

"Noah said my presence here could change everything for all of you. He's right. I have to let this go—"

"You can't."

"Not if I stay, no. I know myself, but I'm also getting to know you. You won't let it drop, either, and I'm starting to wonder if either of us really is ready for what we'll find."

As she followed him to the front door, Olivia noticed she was warm now, if also drained from her mini panic attack, running in the rain, getting soaked and now nearly making love to this man. She touched his hand. "We can talk to Grace. She could be waiting for us to ask her what she knows. Maybe we're not protecting her by not saying anything."

"Maybe. I'll see you in the morning." Dylan kissed her again, just a brush of his lips on hers. "Sleep well."

After he left, Olivia stood by the door and listened to the fire crackle in the quiet house. She would let it die down for the night.

She groaned. What was she thinking?

She headed for the door and yanked it open, the cool draft unexpectedly reenergizing her. There were no streetlights on her road. She couldn't see Dylan in the dark but he couldn't have gotten too far. "Don't you even want to borrow a pillow?" she called to him.

She heard the crunch of small stones and then saw

his silhouette out on the road. "I bought one at the general store."

"If you change your mind about the guest room, call. Unlike everyone else in Knights Bridge, I lock my doors."

A moment's silence. "What about your windows?"

Olivia laughed as she shut the door. They both needed time and they knew it. Whatever was going on between them was intense and exciting, but also real, not just some opportunistic, fleeting attraction that they knew would go nowhere.

That didn't mean it couldn't easily unravel.

She went upstairs and cleared off her bed, discovering her wet sweater on the floor.

She let out a long, slow breath. "Maybe I should lock the damn windows," she said, smiling to herself as she crawled between the cool sheets and tried to think about something else. Fresh herb recipes, designs for potting sheds and walled gardens, moving the astilbe—anything except Dylan getting on an airplane again and leaving her behind in Knights Bridge.

The kitchen ceiling was leaking onto his clean floor when Dylan returned to his house. "To hell with it," he muttered, and headed upstairs. His bed was cold, hard and lonely, but he was where he needed to be—at least, he thought, for tonight.

Fortunately during his hockey years he had learned how to sleep anytime, anywhere. He'd also learned that sometimes he made good plays and bad plays, and sometimes the refs made good calls and bad calls. It was all part of the game and he'd had to figure out how to deal with success, failure, frustration and satisfaction.

He didn't know if leaving Olivia had been a good call, but it was too late now.

He woke up early after a particularly bad night on his camp bed, but he welcomed the sunlight streaming through the windows. It was the kind of beautiful spring morning that had seemed out of reach in March. He got dressed and struck off down the road to his neighbor's house.

Beyond that, he didn't know anything.

Olivia was out brushing off a window screen. He grinned at her. "What did you do, lock the windows and discover a dusty screen?"

"A bat in the screen."

He had a feeling she might be telling the truth. "I thought you might like to go on a picnic."

"To Quabbin?"

"That's right. I thought we could check out the pond Grace mentioned."

"And I get to pack the picnic?"

"I'll pack it," he said, approaching her with a wink. "You just have to provide the food."

Twenty minutes later, they set off on foot down the road and onto Quabbin land. Countless old roads, lanes and trails laced the protected watershed. Streams that once wound their way into the Swift River now emptied into the reservoir. Stone walls and cellar holes were reminders of the valley's past. Dylan focused on the great weather and scenery and the attractive woman beside him. The unmarked trail to Carriage Hill Pond wasn't easy to find, just a narrow, overgrown footpath that led deep into the dense woods. They followed it over a stream, then up and down a relatively shallow ravine, until finally the woods opened up and he and

Olivia came to a small pond and, across the still water, glimmering in the spring sunshine, a freshwater marsh.

She stood on a boulder at the water's edge. "If I were injured and on the run with stolen jewels, I'd hide out here. I'd heal here."

Dylan shrugged off his hip pack. "What would this area have been like in 1938?"

"Different. This part of the valley had a number of summer cabins. Most of the ponds and lakes are under Quabbin water now. We went over one of them yesterday in the boat." Olivia squinted out at ducks on the opposite bank, almost into the marsh. "I didn't find anything in the library that suggested the police searched for the jewelry robber this far west of Boston. I don't know how a robber would even know about the work on the reservoir."

"Coincidence. He—or she—heads west to escape the police and discovers a massive reservoir is under construction."

"Dylan, are you sure your father never mentioned Knights Bridge?"

"He wasn't big on talking."

"He was a man of action," Olivia said.

Dylan noticed a trio of deer standing stock-still in a stand of white pine. The deer jumped, leaping through the woods and disappearing. He didn't want to talk about a decades-old jewelry robbery, or his father. "It couldn't have been easy for Grace to leave this place." He turned to Olivia. "Let's find a sunny spot and have lunch."

Chapter 19

I knew I should tell Gran and Daddy about Philip but I didn't. He was my secret, and he was healing quickly and regaining his strength day by day. I kept expecting to come to the cabin and find him gone. I wasn't permitted to spend time with the out-of-town workers hired by the state to construct the dam, raze the houses and cut down the trees. We called the tree cutters "woodpeckers," a derogatory term for men hired in Boston under political cronyism to clear the valley. Most didn't know one end of an ax from the other. It was the ultimate insult in those days of high unemployment for the work of dismantling our towns to go to the people who would benefit from the waters of the reservoir and not the ones who were losing so much.

One afternoon, Philip helped me pick blackberries and make a cobbler on the old kitchen stove. We ate it *steaming, fresh out of the oven, with cream I'd bought from a friend who still had a cow. She wanted to know where my hideout was, but I wouldn't tell her.*

After the cobbler, Philip and I sat in the shade together and this time he read to me. I loved his English accent. He would tease me about my swashbucklers but tell me that I'd make a great teacher.

The next day was brutally hot and humid, and I caught him swimming in the pond. I could tell he wasn't wearing anything and tossed him a threadbare towel. He made me turn around while he dried off. Then he gave me the all clear, but when I turned back around, I saw that he wasn't wearing a shirt or socks and shoes. The effect was startling. I don't mind saying that Philip Rankin was the handsomest man I ever knew.

He'd finally told me his full name. Philip Rankin. It was a good name. He said he was from a village outside London, but it seemed as far away to me as the moon.

I remember how he laughed at my shock at his bare chest. I could tell he was a man who liked to laugh and I wanted to ask him why he didn't more often.

He was healed. I felt a jolt of panic at the thought that he might leave. But we were all leaving the valley, weren't we? Our time there was running out.

I left him reading by the pond and went inside. I found the jewels a little while later, while I was sweeping out the cabin. My broom hit something hard under the cot. I knew it wasn't a book. I got down on my hands and knees, then on my belly as I reached under the cot all the way to the wall.

It was a cookie tin, one I didn't recognize. "Biscuits," the lid read. I hadn't put it there. I'd never seen it before.

I opened it up and gasped when I saw a red velvet bag instead of cookies. I didn't need to open the bag to know what the contents were. I knew the stolen Ashworth jewels were inside.

The screen door banged open. "What are you doing?"

I spun around. I had no protection. Philip could kill me with his bare hands if he wanted to, or he could grab a rock or a garden hoe and hit me on the head. But I knew he wouldn't. I just knew, and I wasn't afraid. "Where did you get these?"

"They're nothing, Gracie, love. Nothing for you to worry about at all."

"You don't have to protect me. You just have to tell me the truth."

He kissed me then, for the first time. I went weak at my knees. I'd been dreaming about what it might be like. "It's a long story," he said.

"Tell it to me."

"Not now. Go home. Go to your father and your grandmother." He held my hands closely. "Take them blackberries and tell them you lost track of time."

"How old are you?"

He seemed surprised at my question. "Twenty-eight," he said.

"You're barely ten years older than I am. That's not so bad. I'm not a child."

"We come from different worlds. Go home, Grace."

I set the tin on the foot of the cot. "Do you have a wife in England?"

He stared at me, not the tin with the jewels. "I did."

My heart beat rapidly. He was older and more experienced, and he'd seen beyond the Swift River Valley.

"You'll tell me what happened," I said firmly. "Not today, maybe, but one day you'll tell me why you have these jewels and how you ended up here on Carriage Hill Pond."

I ran back through the woods and fields and got home just as thunderstorms hit, breaking the grip of the heat and humidity. My father was furious with me for being out on my own in such conditions, but Gran was there to stop him from getting the switch, as if I were still a small child. I knew he was afraid for me. He wanted to protect me from a future he couldn't see.

Gran came to my room after I changed into dry clothes. "The daughter of one of the women in our study club is engaged to a Quabbin worker. No one blames her. We want the best for everyone. We have to go forward. We have no choice. We have to."

"I never want to think of another place as home again, if it can just be taken from me."

"People are suffering far worse fates now than we are. Let us count our blessings, Grace."

"I'm not sneaking off to see one of the workers. I picked blackberries. I studied."

"You'll make a good teacher."

"What if I don't want to stay here? What if I want to leave and start a new life?"

"Where?"

That was Gran. Always pragmatic. I thrust out my chin. "England."

The next day was unbearably hot and steamy. The storms the day before hadn't brought in a cold front. I'd dreamed about scoundrels and thieves, and about a fortune in diamonds, gold and sapphires—enough for me to run away forever. I didn't have to stay and watch *the valley die. I didn't have to watch it fill with water for other people to drink.*

I ran all the way out to the cabin without stopping. I was terrified that Philip had taken the tin of jewels and gone. Why risk my returning with the police?

He was sitting on a rock in the shade above the pond, eating leftover cobbler as if nothing had changed. He was as handsome as ever.

"You're a thief," I said.

He nodded. "I am."

"I hate you."

"Good. That's good, Grace. You should hate me."

Chapter 20

Olivia stopped at the mill in the morning. Her mother was quiet. Too quiet. "What's wrong, Mom?"

"Nothing. I'm just thinking. You're going to Boston?"

"Just for the day. I have to see two clients. I'd like to cut back on freelance work, but I can't just yet."

"You'll get there. Everyone in town's talking about Carriage Hill. Your mother-daughter tea was a hit. Liv…" Her mother swiveled around in the chair and looked up at her elder daughter. "I've booked our flights."

"To California?"

"We're flying into Los Angeles in late August. I want to go before we get too busy with fall. You know we're always nuts here then."

"What about Dad?"

"I bought a ticket for him but I'm going, with or without him."

Olivia noticed her father in the doorway. He obviously hadn't overheard anything. He walked into the office. He glanced at the large piece of paper on the desk, a few colorful dots floating in the middle. "Working on more dots, Louise? I'm not on the page anymore? What's your therapist say about that?"

She scowled at him. "I changed you to dark blue, because of your eyes."

"Ah. I'm right there with you. I guess that's good."

Olivia smiled with relief. Her mother's good-humored openness about the dots was a surprise, but Randy Frost, the rock of Knights Bridge, the man everyone counted on, had finally figured out that his wife was seeing a therapist—or she'd told him. Either way, he didn't seem shocked or upset.

"I finished with the therapist," she said. "It's up to me now. My doctor can give me a prescription for antianxiety meds, just as a backup. I've learned to pay attention to how I talk to myself. The therapy wasn't about getting rid of fear altogether. It really was learning when to and when not to listen to the fear, understanding where it's coming from and carrying on in spite of it."

Olivia watched as her father tapped a thick finger on the map of California. "What about this trip makes you afraid?" he asked.

"I worry about being so far away from home. I've calculated how far it is from each of our stops and how long it would take us to get back here. It's not that bad. Information and planning help how I talk to myself about going." She glanced up at Olivia. "My therapist put me in touch with a pilot. My fear of flying has more to do with being away from home than with the mechanics of an airplane, but he asked me to imagine a model plane suspended in Jell-O and explained that's what it's like with a real plane flying at high speeds. He also said to remember that the plane wants to fly."

"I hope it wants to land, too," Olivia muttered.

"You two," her father said. "We could always drive to California."

Her mother shook her head. "We're flying."

"Buy the tickets, then."

It was half challenge, half protectiveness. She thrust out her chin. "Bastard. I already did."

Olivia laughed and headed out. Her own problems with flying had little to do with fear of being in the air but in a confined space, unable to get out if she wanted to. She wasn't claustrophobic in every setting, but the thought of flying brought on a crawling sense of panic. Jess was convinced Olivia was taking on their mother's anxieties.

Jess, who couldn't wait to go on an adventure but never did.

Dylan was at Smith's when Olivia stopped for a coffee to-go. "I'm at a loose end," he said, sliding off his stool at the counter and easing next to her. "I can go to Boston with you."

"What if you're not invited?"

"Am I not invited, Olivia?"

She couldn't resist a smile. He was so damn sexy. And he knew it. She sighed. "You can come with me, but I'm driving."

Dylan, of course, invited himself into Olivia's former design studio and charmed Jacqui Ackerman. When

Marilyn emerged from her office for a guilty hello, Dylan charmed her, too. Marilyn, who already knew he was an ex-NHL player and partners with Noah Kendrick in NAK, Inc., couldn't resist an opportunity. "I'd love to get out to Knights Bridge and see Carriage Hill. It sounds idyllic. Olivia's design skills must come in handy. The change seems to be working for her. She looks so relaxed."

"She has family and good friends in Knights Bridge," Dylan said.

"In Boston, too," Marilyn said. "A support system is critical. I've only been in town a short time. Before that I was in Providence, but Olivia and I have been friends for several years. I'm excited about working with her, even if she's just freelancing now."

Olivia was happy to pretend not to hear Marilyn and left her with Dylan, joining Jacqui in her office. "I appreciate the offer, Jacqui," Olivia said immediately, "but I'm not coming back full-time. I just can't right now."

Jacqui nodded as she sat at her desk. "I understand, especially now that I've met Dylan McCaffrey."

"Dylan's not a factor in my decision."

"No?" Jacqui smiled. "That's too bad."

They chatted about freelance jobs for a few more minutes. On her way back to the conference room, Olivia ran into Marilyn, ducking into her office. "It's so good to see you, Liv, but not in a million years would I have guessed you'd walk in here with Dylan McCaffrey. You never were a big hockey fan, but I remember him as a player." Marilyn paused in the hallway. "How did he end up in Knights Bridge?"

"It's a long story—"

"Why don't we have lunch together and catch up? Dylan can join us."

Six months ago, Olivia would have accepted the invitation without hesitation. Even now, her first inclination was to say yes. Despite Marilyn's behavior the past few months, Olivia still found herself wanting to reconnect with her. They'd been such good friends, and she hated to give up on a friendship.

Dylan appeared just down the hall. "Parking meter's running out."

There was no parking meter. They'd parked in a garage. He just wanted to get out of there, or to get Olivia out. She smiled at Marilyn. "Thanks, but another time."

Instead, she and Dylan walked over to Newbury Street for lunch at her favorite restaurant, her first visit since running into Marilyn and Roger Bailey there. Dylan looked just as at ease in the restaurant as he had in his leaking kitchen in Knights Bridge. Olivia expected it would be the same at NAK headquarters or on the ice.

They sat across from each other at a small table. "I almost asked Marilyn to join us," she said.

"From the freezer to lunch."

"I'm not proud of that, you know."

"Why not?" He leaned back, studying her. "You want her to like you."

"I don't care—"

"You care. It's okay. Confrontation isn't easy for everyone, and you don't have to confront her. You just can't trust her. She's got crazy-bitch eyes."

Olivia had no idea if he was serious. "Crazy-bitch eyes, Dylan?"

"Yeah. You can see her scheming behind those eyes."

"You're prejudiced because you found her in my freezer."

He leaned forward, his eyes narrowed, intense. "I'm prejudiced because she did you wrong."

Olivia felt a surge of warmth at his solidarity and protectiveness and realized that by keeping Marilyn's betrayal to herself for so long, she had also isolated herself. Her family and real friends couldn't offer their support because they didn't know anything was wrong. As Dylan continued to watch her, she squirmed, the warm, good feeling about him turning to physical desire—which, she suspected, he could tell.

She changed the subject. "How did you make the transition from hockey player to working with Noah Kendrick?"

"I was injured and eventually cut. It's not something I expected, but I knew it could happen. The idea is to save your money."

She eyed him. "But you didn't."

"Not enough. I was never one of the big-money players. I kept thinking I'd be one. A lot of people believed in me, but it just didn't happen. Then it didn't matter. I loved the game, and I had a great run."

"That's a good attitude."

"It didn't come naturally. I worked at it. I think certain people bring out the best in us, or we allow them to. I was with the wrong team for a while but then I got with the right team. I know a lot of guys who would have given their eyeteeth for the opportunity I had."

"Regrets?"

"Yeah, sure, but I had a good time. I worked hard. I always focused on improving my skills. I had a few tough injuries."

"Were you smart about the game?"

"Yes, and I had a great team and coaches the last couple years. I still got cut, though. That's life. I didn't want to tell anyone I'd blown most of my money. I pretended all was well with my folks. My father wanted me to start an adventure travel company with him, but we never got to it."

"How did you and Noah end up working together?"

"He asked me to help him. I was sleeping in my car out on Coronado and he knocked on my window. He needed a right-hand man. Someone to watch his back, basically. I accepted, and everything took off once he was able to focus and get rid of some of the loons around him. Banging around the NHL gave me good insights into people, and I learned not to stick with the crazies. You can find all kinds of reasons to stick with someone but sometimes what you have to do is cut them loose and move on."

Olivia noticed his penetrating gaze and knew he was talking about her, too. "It can be easier than letting them cut you loose. So you're loyal to Noah?"

"Yes. It's not like you and this Marilyn woman. She used your energy, talents and goodwill to get what was good for her. She was never a friend. That's key in my philosophy."

"Would you have seen through her?"

"I didn't have anything she needs. I deal with people who want access to Noah. You are who you are. Don't beat yourself up over what you did to help Marilyn. Would you be happier if you hadn't helped her, and she was still your struggling friend?"

Olivia considered his words. "It doesn't matter anymore, does it? What's done is done. I'm mad at her for what she did but we had some good times together."

"Olivia, I don't want you to be anyone but who you are. You'd never have written to me about the junk in my yard if you hadn't caught her and your big client together. It was here, wasn't it?"

"My favorite restaurant."

He made a face. "Think she worried you might walk in?"

"I don't think she gave it a moment's thought. She liked the restaurant and she wanted to impress a client, so she brought him here."

"There's where you and I are different. You're nicer. I think she knew. I think she was eaten alive with envy when you were doing well and she wasn't, and she loved the chance to stick it to you."

"That can't be an easy way to live."

"Her choice. Yours is to allow her to be who she is and let her go."

"How did you get to be so philosophical?"

"I'm not. I'm just watching my language. It's a little restaurant, and people know you here." He winked at her. "Users and fakes bug the hell out of me."

After lunch Olivia debated walking down to her apartment with him. She wasn't self-conscious about showing it to a man who could afford to buy half the block, but it was time to give it up. Her landlord had a prospective tenant. Olivia had promised to borrow her sister's truck and pack up the last of her stuff. When she explained the situation, Dylan offered to help. The man was worth a fortune, and he was willing to load a truck.

He was right, she realized. He was straightforward,

and he wasn't one to flinch. What people saw was what people got with him.

"Let's go have a look at the building where Lord Ashworth was robbed," she said.

They walked down Newbury to Arlington Street and an attractive, seven-story brick building, a former luxury hotel that had been converted into condos.

"Lord Ashworth's suite probably faced the park." Dylan glanced across the busy street at Boston Public Garden, lush with spring flowers and greenery. "He stayed here for a week in early September of 1938."

Olivia looked up at the elegant 1920s building. "That wasn't an easy year, or an easy month. War was brewing, the Depression was full on. The worst hurricane ever to hit New England struck a few weeks after the robbery. There was massive damage. Hundreds of people were killed. Why was Lord Ashworth in Boston?"

"Apparently no one knows," Dylan said. "I've done more research but there's not a lot to add. Ashworth wanted the United Kingdom to avoid war with Hitler at all costs. He might have been meeting with like-minded people here."

"Why take a fortune in jewels with him? Was he married?"

"Not then."

Olivia frowned. "Did he have a woman with him in Boston?"

"It's possible, but it looks as if he came alone."

"I wonder who our thief could have been. An American? A Brit? It's hard to imagine, standing here all these years later, that Ashworth or the thief had anything to do with Knights Bridge."

"What about Grace? Did she have any ties to Boston back then?"

"I don't know. I doubt it."

He took her hand suddenly. "Let's forget this for a while. Want to show me the Public Garden?"

She pictured walking with him among the spring flowers and winding paths of the Victorian botanical garden and smiled. "I'd love to."

Jess stopped at Rivendell after work and ran into her grandmother coming in from bird-watching. "I'm glad you're here, Jess. I want another opinion. I don't know if it's just Grace being Grace or if she's acting weird. Will you go see her? She's in the sunroom."

"Sure, Grandma."

She insisted Jess go alone. Her presence would be a distraction, and Grace was already annoyed with her friend for "hovering." Jess didn't argue and headed down to the sunroom. She found Grace settled in a chair in front of the wall of windows. "Hey, Grace," Jess said cheerfully. "Beautiful day, isn't it?"

Grace barely gave her visitor a glance before she turned back to the windows. "The birds are quiet today. They're finding food elsewhere with the warm weather. That's good. They'll be back at the feeders this winter." She put down her binoculars. "I know Audrey put you up to coming in here."

"You two are lucky to have each other. You've been friends forever."

She softened slightly. "I don't take a good friend for granted." She stared out at the empty bird feeders, then said, "Tell me about Olivia and Dylan McCaffrey."

It wasn't what Jess expected. "Olivia got him to clean

up the yard at your old house. It was an eyesore. That's all I know."

"It's not all you suspect."

"Grace," Jess said, firm but amused, "I'm not spying on my sister. If anything is going on with her and Dylan, she'll tell me in her own good time."

"No, she won't. She's a Frost. You're all close-mouthed about certain things." Grace tilted her head back and frowned up at Jess. "What's on your mind?"

"I'm not here about me—"

"But something's on your mind. I can tell. I was a teacher for many years, Jess. Here, sit. Talk to me." Grace waved a bony hand toward the windows. "Even my cardinal's deserted me."

Jess figured she didn't have much choice and sat on a cushioned rocker. "You've lived in Knights Bridge most of your life, but you're educated, and you're sophisticated in so many ways. Did you ever feel constrained living here?"

"This area is my home, and I didn't have the choices you have now. I was a young woman during the Depression and World War Two. After that..." She was thoughtful, serious. "I had my life here. I had a job, and I'd made friends in Knights Bridge. Once my grandmother and my father were gone, I had no one else. I had to be practical."

"Did you ever go anywhere? Have adventures?"

"I loved to take long walks, and friends would invite me to their lake houses and sea cottages. Cape Cod—"

"I don't mean in New England."

"Ah. I went to Europe once, after my grandmother died. I went to London, Amsterdam and Paris, and I spent some time in the English countryside. I was gone most of one summer. My grandmother had left me a cookie jar of money, and that's what I decided to do. I didn't have children. I was doing all right financially as a teacher, and I didn't want any more property. I gave a little to the church, and I went on a trip."

"Did you enjoy it?"

"Every minute."

"I want to see Paris," Jess whispered.

"Then go," Grace said. "If you can afford to, just go. Flights are easier nowadays. There's so much information. Go if that's what you want."

"My mother—"

"Your mother will be fine. Jessica, your mother doesn't want you not to live your life because she's afraid of living hers."

Jess's eyes widened in shock.

"I'm old," Grace said with satisfaction, "but I'm not unaware of what's going on. Your parents' marriage isn't in danger. Your mother's happiness with herself is."

"What about Olivia?"

But Grace had drifted off, and Jess reported back to her grandmother before heading home to her saw-mill apartment.

Mark was sitting out by the dam. Jess stood over him, her hands on her hips. "I'm going to Paris."

"I know you are."

"Then I'm going to other places. Vancouver, San Francisco, Prague, London, Ireland. You have Irish ancestors. Don't you want to go to Ireland?"

"My Irish ancestors are all dead."

"Mark!"

She realized he was kidding, yet he also had no real love of traveling. He was a workaholic, and he enjoyed hiking. His vision as an architect wasn't limited because of his limited desire to travel. She wasn't going to make this about him, or try to talk him into liking something he didn't like. But she was going to Paris.

"I don't think you're boring," she said. "I won't get tired of you even if you won't go to Paris. Even if you go just for me but don't like it. We can go hiking in the Alps. I want to see them, too."

"What about Knights Bridge?"

"It's home. I can love other places and still want to be home."

Chapter 21

Dylan paced in Grace Webster's former dining room and dialed Loretta's cell phone. Olivia had dropped him off at his car and disappeared, mumbling about needing to get home and walk her dog. He suspected she was just as restless as he was after their day together.

He didn't wait for Loretta to say hello before he pounced. "Did my father ever mention the Frosts? Did he go to Boston? Did he check out the old hotel where Lord Ashworth was robbed?"

Loretta sighed. "No, I don't know and I don't know."

"What aren't you telling me, Loretta?"

"How's Knights Bridge? Snow melted?"

He immediately thought of walking hand-in-hand with Olivia in Boston but refused to let Loretta divert him. "I deal with people who want to hide things from me all the time. I'm not saying you're being dishonest. I am saying you haven't told me everything."

"What else do you want, Dylan? Any other questions? Some of us have to work for a living."

The tart response was just a cover. Dylan took no offense. He was dealing with a savvy lawyer. She'd stall and all but lie. He had to be smart if not patient. "All right, then. Let me rephrase. What do you suspect and not necessarily know for sure that you're not telling me?"

She sighed, hesitating longer this time. "Nothing I can grab hold of. I *am* a lawyer, Dylan, and I try to deal in facts and not get carried away with speculation."

"When you do have facts, you'll tell me."

"No promises."

No promises? The woman had backbone, Dylan gave her that. "I'm still trying to figure out why my father thought there might be a connection between the Ashworth jewelry robbery and Knights Bridge."

"I understand your curiosity, Dylan."

Another careful answer. "I haven't told you yet. I also found an article about the robbery torn out of a newspaper, with *Isaiah Webster* and *Knights Bridge* handwritten on the edge."

There was silence on the other end. "I have to go."

Dylan didn't pressure her. Whatever she wasn't telling him—he'd get it out of her eventually.

He sat at the old English teacher's table with a pad of paper and put everything he knew about 1938 in chronological order. His father had been an interesting, often frustrating mix of impulsiveness and careful calculation. He could easily have lined up the same set of facts and, instead of analyzing them, went with whatever his gut told him.

He'd left a message with his mother in Los Angeles. She finally called him back, and he asked her the same questions he'd asked Loretta. She had nothing to add to what she'd already told him—until she said, "Your father did mention wanting to see Boston after his mother died. That was a long time ago."

"What did Boston have to do with his mother?"

"She grew up there. She left after she married your grandfather. They lived in New York City before they moved west after he was born. I think that's right. Dylan, I hate to tell you this, but the blunt truth is that your father wasn't a big part of my life—except for you."

"I know. It is what it is."

"I love you, and I know he loved you."

"That's not what this is about."

"Then what is it about?"

Olivia Frost, but he said, "Curiosity."

His mother laughed, as Dylan knew she would. "Now you sound just like your father," she said as she hung up.

There was no internet connection in the house. If he planned on staying in Knights Bridge much longer, he had to hook up Wi-Fi.

Who was he kidding? He wasn't going to stay. He didn't belong here. He would only end up breaking Olivia's heart.

Or his own, he thought as he considered his options. In his years playing hockey and then operating in Noah's cutthroat business world, he'd learned to act decisively, but Knights Bridge was different. The stakes were different. Losing a game, losing money—they mattered, but they weren't the same as dealing with the people in a close-knit community and their dreams and secrets.

He had to think. He had food in his little fridge. The weather was good, so leaks weren't an issue for the moment.

He could take his time.

Loretta Wrentham settled into the comfortable, ergonomic chair at her desk in her La Jolla home office and contemplated the situation in Knights Bridge on the other side of the country. She remembered Duncan McCaffrey walking into this room on a stormy afternoon two years ago. "You get a few drops of rain in Southern California, and people suddenly forget how to drive. They all talk about the oil buildup on the roads, but I think they just can't deal with rain."

She'd smiled at him. "Come back and live here awhile, and you'll remember."

"You're my son's lawyer."

"Yes, I am. What can I do for you?"

"Nothing. Just…" He hadn't wanted to tell her anything but finally relented. "I'm leaving everything to Dylan except for what I'm giving to a foundation that specializes in historical archaeology."

"Are you ill?"

Duncan hadn't looked shocked or dismayed. He had seemed, in fact, amused and pleased by her bluntness. "I'm not ready to croak yet. Soon, maybe. I've never expected to live to a ripe old age. No, Lori—"

"Loretta," she'd supplied.

"Loretta. That's a pretty name."

She couldn't swear to it, but she suspected she'd blushed. "Thank you."

"Loretta, I'm on a treasure hunt that might lead me somewhere I shouldn't go. Not that I don't want to, but shouldn't. If I die before it's complete, I'll have left Dylan a few clues. It's up to him if he doesn't do anything with them. It's up to him if he even looks at a thing I've left him."

"All right."

"I know you represent him and not me, but I want that to be clear. I don't want to reach out from the grave and screw up his life for him."

"It's about this treasure?"

"Yeah. If he inherits a house in a little town in New England called Knights Bridge, then you know I didn't finish."

"Knights as in knights in armor or nights as in—"

"Armor. I think the Knights were a family in the area. Who the hell knows."

"You know more than you're saying."

He grinned at her. "Yeah, I do, but not as much as you think."

"Why did you buy this house? Does it have to do with this reluctant treasure hunt?"

"What would you do if you thought someone close to you had been involved with a long-ago crime?"

"Depends on the statute of limitations and the type of crime. Mr. McCaffrey—"

"Duncan. Anyway, I'm not telling you the details. The less you know, the better."

"Did this crime involve murder? There's no statute of limitations on murder."

"No murder. I'm not out to unearth people's secrets. We all deserve our secrets, don't we?"

Loretta didn't know how it happened, but they'd ended up in bed together. In his early seventies, Duncan had been a vigorous lover. She'd known there'd been a long string of women before her and it was meant to be a momentary interlude. She'd given herself up to the night. He had seemed complex, a man who loved life and knew who he was and yet was lost, didn't know where he belonged. When he left in the morning, she had a feeling she would never see him again.

And she didn't.

Being with him had rekindled a desire for love, and sex, in her life. She had started dating again. There'd been no repeat of such a one-night stand—she wasn't the type and had never run into another Duncan McCaffrey—and she had no interest in letting his son know, or even hinting to him, that they'd been intimate.

She'd done what Duncan had asked and had simply paid the bills on the house in Knights Bridge; until Dylan started asking questions. Now the questions included a 1938 robbery involving a British aristocrat and jewels going back to Queen Victoria.

The treasure hunt, obviously, that had absorbed Dylan's father.

In her view, Duncan had spoken with her under the assumption he had attorney-client privilege, but it wouldn't have mattered.

"I'm not out to unearth people's secrets."

Loretta told herself that unless there was an urgent reason to do otherwise, she needed to respect Duncan's secrets.

Plus, she realized he'd wanted his son to carry on the hunt on his own, without any goading from her.

Whatever was going on in Knights Bridge was meant for father and son.

Chapter 22

Olivia was both pleased and surprised when her mother came out to Carriage Hill on her own. It was early—she was taking the morning off and didn't have to be at the mill until noon. Just as well, Olivia thought, that she'd stayed home last night and painted and worked instead of inviting Dylan over for soup or knocking on his door. Figuring out what was going on between them was complicated enough without the added complication of explaining his presence to her mother at eight o'clock in the morning.

There was no question in her mind that if she'd seen him last night, he'd be at her house right now.

She made coffee and brought it out to the terrace. Her mother brushed her fingertips over the lavender in the backyard. "It smells so nice already. Everyone in town is talking about this place, Liv."

"Good talk, I hope."

"All good." Her mother stood straight. "I divided perennials at the house. I brought a bunch over here. They're in the car. You don't have to take any but I thought—"

"Are you kidding? This is great. I have tons of space yet to fill."

They headed out to her mother's car and loaded up the wheelbarrow with daylilies, astilbe, cranesbill geraniums, yarrow—Olivia was thrilled. She pushed the wheelbarrow back to the terrace, dumped it out and started sorting the plants. Her mother hadn't labeled any of them. She recognized them on sight.

"I don't want to get too far ahead of myself," Olivia said, pausing her plant-sorting to help herself to coffee, "but I keep thinking about getting into artisan soap-making. Maggie's mother has goats now. I could do goat's milk soap scented with herbs and flowers from my own garden."

"The Farm at Carriage Hill Soaps," her mother said, sitting at the table and eyeing the plants she'd brought. "I like that."

"I even have a design in mind for the packaging."

"You're bursting with ideas these days, aren't you? I know from work at the mill that some will prove to be profitable and worth the effort, and some won't. We learned early on that we can't compete with the large manufacturers. We had to focus on quality custom mill-work."

Olivia nodded, appreciating her mother's insights. "Artisan soaps fit with my plans for a getaway and small shop. I wouldn't want to get into selling soaps over the internet but focus instead on small batches, almost as a premium for guests." She set her coffee on the terrace and knelt back down among the dirt and plants—plants that now needed homes in her backyard. "It's all fun to think about."

"Do you think you'll start your own design studio or keep freelancing for your old boss?"

"I don't know yet. It depends on finances, I suppose."

"Liv…" Her mother stood up, stretching her lower back. "You left Boston sooner than you thought you would, didn't you? There were problems."

Olivia sighed, reaching for a daylily that could be further divided. "There were, yes, but they're sorted out now."

"You're happy here?"

"I am, yes, Mom."

"Dylan McCaffrey—"

Olivia quickly changed the subject. "What do you know about Grace's book? I asked Dad and Grandma, but they don't know much."

"I don't, either. I think writing helped her to cope with selling her house."

"Has anyone read it?"

"Not that I know of. She says she doesn't want anyone to read it until after she's gone."

"I know, but I was hoping she let someone read at least parts of it. Think she has secrets?"

"I can't imagine what they'd be, or why she'd want to tell them in a book and not just take them to the grave with her. I think it's just the story of her life."

"Maybe there's more drama to her life than any of us realize. I'd love to get my hands on a copy of this book. She'd never know."

"Olivia, shame on you!"

She grinned. "I'd never do it, Mom. You know that. Doesn't mean I wouldn't want to."

"What about Dylan? Does he know about Grace's book? Is he putting you up to sneaking a copy of it?"

"I don't know what he wants, but he's not putting me up to anything."

"There's something you're not telling me."

"There's a lot I'm not telling you, Mom."

"I should be glad?"

"Ha, I wish my life were that interesting." Olivia grinned, sidestepping her mother's questions, and separated the roots of the daylily. The weather was warmer than she'd expected, and she wished she hadn't bothered with a long-sleeve shirt never mind a sweater.

She and her mother worked comfortably together through most of the morning, plotting where to put the perennials, dragging fertilizer and garden tools from the shed, digging and planting.

"It's good to have you back here, Liv," her mother said as she started for her car. "So long as you're happy."

"I am happy, Mom."

After her mother left, Olivia wandered through the upstairs of her two-hundred-year-old house. Mark could help expand the rooms and add bathrooms, whatever was needed for an overnight getaway, but right now she had to concentrate on daylong events. A local walking group had just booked their annual meeting there in June. They planned to hike up Carriage Hill.

Olivia looked out her bedroom window at the view behind her house. Wildflowers were starting to blossom in the fields. She loved this place. She couldn't let this opportunity slip through her fingers. She couldn't imagine what she'd do if The Farm at Carriage Hill failed. Go back to Boston and work for Marilyn? Find a place for herself in her family's millwork business?

"I won't fail," she said aloud.

She headed back downstairs and out to the front yard to plant the last of her mother's perennials. Buster followed her and flopped in the shade, dutifully staying out of her flowerbed.

Five minutes later, Dylan showed up and found her elbow-deep in the dirt. He struck Olivia as preoccupied if not distant. "What's on your mind?" she asked, settling back on her heels as she looked up at him.

He tugged a maple leaf off a low-hanging branch. "I'm not here to screw up your life, or this town."

She narrowed her gaze on him. "What have you found out?"

"Lord Ashworth's sister was Lady Helena Ashworth." Dylan tossed the leaf down to Buster. "Lady Helena married a British flyer named Philip Rankin, but she died before the war. I'm still digging, but it looks as if the jewels actually belonged to Lady Helena—she inherited them from her grandmother."

"So why did the brother have them?"

"When she died, apparently he ended up with them instead of her husband."

"Helena and Philip didn't have any children?"

"A daughter, Philippa."

"Is she still alive? What about Philip? What happened to him? Did your father—"

"I have no idea what my father knew and didn't know," Dylan said, more with frustration than impatience. "I'm still gathering information on the Rankins."

Olivia got stiffly to her feet, dusting the dirt off her

hands and forearms. "You think Philip stole the jewels from his brother-in-law," she said finally.

"The police never had a local suspect. Any suspect, for that matter."

"Was Philip in Boston in September, 1938?"

"You ask good questions." Dylan smiled, relaxing slightly. "You could keep the bastards away from Noah Kendrick."

"I wish I could keep them out of my own life. Was Lord Ashworth a bastard?"

"Hard to say, but I doubt he and Philip Rankin played by the same rules."

Olivia brushed more dirt off her hands but realized it'd take a good scrubbing to get it all. She hadn't bothered with gloves. She could feel Dylan's eyes on her and wondered what her life would be like now if Grace hadn't sold her house to Duncan McCaffrey but was still there, watching birds, managing with home care and friends.

Dylan touched her cheek with a curved finger. "You've got a smudge of dirt on your face. Olivia…" He paused, moving his finger across her cheek to her hair, tucking a few strands behind her ear. "If you're not busy right now, I'll grab my files and you can see what you think."

"I'm not doing anything that can't wait."

Olivia watched him walk back up the one-lane road, as pensive as she'd ever seen him. She put away her garden tools in the shed out back and glanced around her yard. It was taking shape, and she could imagine sharing it with people, looked forward to having a full schedule of events. She reminded herself that the mystery of Dylan's house in Knights Bridge involved a father he'd lost less than two years ago. Her own problems suddenly seemed insignificant in comparison. She was excited about being back in her hometown, even if she'd taken a bumpy emotional and professional road in getting there.

When he arrived back at her house with a file folder in hand, the temperature had dropped, and she struck a match to the kindling and rolled-up newspapers she already had set up in the fireplace in the living room. Dylan sat on the floor, leaning back against the couch, his legs stretched out as Buster wandered in from the kitchen. Olivia felt her breath catch in her throat at the homey image, but she had never witnessed Dylan in action in San Diego, or at his home on Coronado—or in pads and skates on the ice. She'd seen pictures of him in his hockey uniform. Could she say, really, that she knew this man?

He explained that he had been to the library and used its computer since there was no Wi-Fi at his house. He had printed out what he could find on Lord Charles Ashworth and his sister, Lady Helena Ashworth. He handed Olivia a printout of a black-and-white photograph of a man and a woman standing in front of a mansion. "It's the only photograph I could find of either of them," he said. "It was taken in 1932. I found it on a site about the British aristocracy."

"She's lovely," Olivia said. "He's a bit watery."

Dylan withdrew another printout from his file. "This one's from 1912. Their grandmother sat for this portrait. Note the ring she's wearing. It fits the description of the diamond ring that's missing."

The grandmother bore a strong resemblance to Lady

Helena. Olivia peered closely at the ring. "It's some-thing, isn't it? It'd make my wrist hurt."

"Not much on baubles, are you?"

"Depends on the baubles, but I have no desire to own a ring worth millions." Olivia studied the photograph again. "None of this was in your father's trunk?"

"Not that I found, no."

"You can hide a ring anywhere. If our British flyer stole the jewels and hid them in Quabbin and meant to come back, there's not much hope of ever finding them. More than likely they're under water now. It'd have to be like Gollum stumbling on Sauron's ring."

"Is that what you think this is? A dark quest?"

"I don't know what it is. The daughter would be in her seventies now. She could have children and grand-children of her own. Would she want to know her father was a thief? Her uncle was a bastard?"

"Maybe she already knows."

"Anyway, it doesn't make sense that he would end up out here. There's just no reason."

"To hide and to heal."

His eyes held hers and Olivia realized he wasn't talk-ing about the Brits and the jewels. He was talking about her. "This is my home."

"I know, but you think you're here to hide and to heal."

"I think I'm here to survive."

"Maybe that's the same thing."

"To live, then."

He smiled. "Better."

"What about you? You're not here to hide or to heal—or to live. You're here to finish your father's trea-sure hunt. Maybe it'll help you understand him, make your peace with him. Then what? Leave Knights Bridge and never return? Go back to your life in San Diego?"

"Olivia—"

Olivia touched his lips, silencing him. "I know you can't answer that right now."

"I'll quit this treasure hunt right here and now."

"I'd never ask that, and I don't want you to." She smiled. "I'm curious about the missing Ashworth jewels now, too."

Dylan kissed her fingertips, and she knew she was lost. "I can make love to you here in front of the fire," he said, "or we can go upstairs. If you want to get rid of me, say so in no uncertain terms. Otherwise, I'm not going anywhere. You could fall down the damn stairs this time, and I swear I'd just pick you up and carry you to bed."

"That sounds downright tempting, but I won't fall."

And she didn't. She got all the way up the stairs to her bedroom before she faked a swoon and collapsed into his arms. He swept her up and laid her on the bed. "I can't promise I won't tear off buttons getting these clothes off you." His voice was low, teasing, deliberately sexy. "I suppose, though, if you can grow herbs, paint furniture and make soap, you can sew on buttons."

"Grandma Frost taught me herself."

"Grandma Frost." He cupped her hips and eased her pants lower. "Please let's not mention her for a while, okay?"

Olivia laughed, but Dylan was intent on one thing and one thing only and it had nothing to do with sewing. Her pants disappeared, and she helped with the rest of her clothes. By the time it was his turn, her hands were shaking with so much anticipation that she fumbled unclasping his belt.

He put his hand over hers. "Olivia. I'll do it."

"No, I want to."

She tried again, succeeding this time, and when she loosened his belt and lowered his jeans, she heard him take in a sharp breath. For a moment, she thought he was about to tell her he'd come to his senses and needed to get out of there, fast. But it wasn't that kind of breath. It was the kind of breath that said he was at his limit and wasn't going to torture himself with more delays.

Which was good, Olivia thought, because she was in the same place.

When his clothes were scattered on the floor with hers, she knew that would be her last coherent thought for a while. He rolled onto her, whispering her name as he slid a hand between her legs, kissing her, his tongue and fingers sharing the same rhythm. She cried out his name and grabbed his hips, and in the next second, he'd pulled away his hand and was driving himself into her.

That was just the beginning.

It was a clawing, nipping, wild lovemaking, with nothing held back, nothing denied. Olivia took, demanded, gave and surrendered, throwing her arms over her head as he lifted his chest off her, his eyes locking with hers as he thrust deeply into her, again and again. Finally she was spinning, spiraling, coming with such abandon and ferocity that she thought she might wear him down, but then he was pounding into her, bringing her again to a peak and keeping her there until she couldn't breathe. She gasped, screaming his name as he drove into her once more.

Afterward, they held each other, hearts still racing.

Olivia smiled, rolling onto her side and tracing a fingertip across his chest. "It's going to be a long night, isn't it?"

"Uh-huh," he said, taking her hand. "We're just getting started."

Chapter 23

I was in despair. My home was gone, finally razed by state workers. After days and days of rain, the valley once filled with life was now a muddy, barren wasteland. The relentless work on the reservoir proceeded. I hitched a ride with a young couple also displaced by Quabbin and visited the new cemetery where the bodies were being taken. It was a beautiful spot, just like Gran said, and great care had been taken with relocating the graves, but I threw up. I couldn't bear to think about my mother getting dug up, and my grandparents, and Gran's babies.

The Websters had arrived in the Swift River Valley two hundred years ago, but Gran reminded me they'd come from somewhere else. They hadn't been wealthy. They'd fled famine, disease, persecution, poverty. Some had come as indentured servants who had to work off debts. They'd begun a new life in a new place, and that's what we had to do.

I'd fallen in love with a man who wasn't what I wanted him to be. He wasn't an aristocrat. He wasn't a Scarlet Pimpernel. He was what he'd told me he was that first day: a scoundrel.

A thief.

I would never live in a castle. I would never have stately gardens and wear pretty jewels.

There was talk of world events. Another war in Europe.

I asked the couple to drop me off at our old house. It wasn't there anymore, of course, but the land around it hadn't been cleared yet. The air was oppressively hot and humid for late September. The light was green. I blamed the work going on in the valley. I knew that before long the spot where I was standing would be flooded forever.

No one would ever stand here again.

It was as if the rivers were rising already. I knew it would take years for the reservoir to fill to capacity. It wouldn't be like a flash flood. Yet as I stood on that scraped, exposed land on that dismal summer day in 1938, that last day of our last summer in the valley, I could feel the waters rising. I looked up at the clouds and saw nothing but water, water too deep for me to swim to the surface before I ran out of air.

I couldn't breathe. I was drowning there on the edge of a cellar hole, all that was left of Gran's old house and our lives there. The elms and maples and chestnuts had been cut down and chopped up. The rosebushes, the lilacs, the white irises. All were gone. The tire swing and the white picket fence and the lanes...gone, gone, gone.

I gasped for air but I knew there was no one to save me.

If I was to survive, I had to save myself. Gran was from another time. She didn't know if she would live to see what the valley would become. Daddy had a new job in Knights Bridge but he was angry and bitter, and for him the valley would always be what it had been. Only the past was good. There was no hope in his world for the future.

One of the stones on the edge of the foundation dislodged, and I slipped but regained my balance before I fell. If I did, who would ever find me in that old cellar hole?

"No," I said aloud. "I'm not going to die here. I'm going to live."

I ran and ran and ran. The green sky darkened and opened up with rain and wind like I'd never experienced before. I knew I couldn't stop. If I did, I'd drown for sure. Raindrops pelted me. The wind ripped at my dress. My wet shoes came off in a muddy puddle and I ran on, barefoot.

I don't know how I made it to my hideaway cabin, but I did. I didn't want to go inside. I knew Philip would be gone and I was terrified that the howling wind would tear apart the cabin.

The air smelled of the ocean, and I knew then that I was in the middle of a hurricane.

And I was alone.

"Grace!"

A tree down by the pond cracked and fell onto the boulder where I liked to sit and read. I didn't know if I'd turned the wind into a voice calling my name.

"Grace! Grace, where are you?"

Philip.

Now I knew I was losing my mind, making things up. I couldn't stand up straight in the wind. I couldn't get to the cabin now. Soaked, my skin raw from the pounding rain and wind, I huddled against my boulder, putting its hard granite between me and the direction of the storm. I grabbed sodden field grass and dug my fingers into the mud, searching for something firmer to grasp—tree roots, anything.

I felt strong arms around me. "Grace. Gracie, love, it's Philip. I won't hurt you. I will never hurt you."

He carried me to the cabin and dried me off. I wasn't cold. I just wanted the storm to end.

"It's a hurricane," *I said.*

"I know. It's a bad one."

"I thought you were gone..."

He didn't answer. He pulled me close to him, and we clung to each other as the wind howled and roared. The cabin was in a protected area, and it held. I was terrified, but I felt safe with Philip's arms around me.

Never before and never again would I feel as safe as in the middle of that raging, vicious hurricane.

Chapter 24

Jess banged on Olivia's front door at noon the next day. "Grace Webster borrowed Grandma's car this morning and hasn't come back. It's been three hours, Liv." Her sister gulped in a breath. "Grace hardly ever drives but she still has her license. She told Grandma she was going to the library."

"You checked there?"

"Phoebe O'Dunn said Grace went up to the stacks— to the same files Duncan McCaffrey asked about and then you asked about. I don't know how she managed the stairs. She stayed a few minutes, then she left. That was more than two hours ago."

Dylan eased in behind Olivia. "I'll get my car. I can look for her."

"I'll go with you," she said. "We should start out

here. Grace lived on this road for more than seventy years."

Jess nodded. "Sounds good. Keep me posted and I'll do the same. I have my cell phone. Mom's beside herself. She doesn't want us going off half-cocked. You know the drill."

"We'll be careful, Jess. I'll see you later." As her sister left, Olivia turned to Dylan. "We can take my car. I'll grab the keys."

"I didn't hear a car on the road this morning. Did you?"

"No, but…" She didn't finish. No way would either of them have noticed a car, but she knew what he was getting at. "Dylan, if Grace decided to return to the site of her old cabin, she's in way over her head. You saw what it's like out there."

He gave a grim nod. "Let's go."

They drove the short distance to the end of the road. Olivia took in a sharp breath when she saw her grandmother's twelve-year-old Volvo parked under the trees by the Quabbin gate. She managed to get two bars on her cell phone and texted Jess about the car. Jess would inform the police and they would get a search team out here. In the meantime, Olivia ducked under the gate. Dylan had already started on foot down the worn, narrow road that had once served the lost towns.

"How's Grace's health?" Dylan asked.

Olivia kept up with him. "She's old and frail—"

"Heart disease, high blood pressure, diabetes, dementia?"

"As far as I know she's fine mentally. Anything else—I wouldn't know."

They maintained a brisk pace through the woods,

veering off onto the unmarked trail to the pond. "This was mostly open farmland when Quabbin was built. It'll look different than what Grace remembers from when she was a teenager."

"She knows that, even if she hasn't been back to the pond since then."

"None of this is your fault, if that's what you're thinking," Olivia said. "Grace isn't a child. She knew what she was doing when she borrowed my grandmother's car. No matter what happens, she wouldn't want us to think otherwise."

"Let's just find her."

They crossed a stream, no sign of Grace's footprints on the muddy bank. When they reached the pond, Olivia scanned the woods, looking for anything that could suggest a cabin had once been there. An old lilac, a bit of myrtle, a well, a cellar hole—any visible remnants of the lives of the people who had lived here.

She glanced at Dylan. "This must have been an idyllic spot a hundred years ago."

"Yeah. Must have."

"Dylan…"

He stepped closer to the water. "Grace! Grace!" His voice was strong, forceful.

Olivia stood on a small boulder and scanned the immediate area. Grace had to be there. Where else could she be? Olivia pushed back the worst-case scenario answers that swarmed into her head and focused on finding her.

Dylan crouched by a trio of white pines close to the water. Across the pond, a family of ducks emerged from the marsh grasses, as if they, too, were searching for Grace.

"Do you see anything?" Olivia asked.

"The grass is matted here. Someone must have gone through. Whether it was Grace…" He grimaced, stood up. "She has to be here."

Olivia jumped down from the boulder and stopped abruptly, thinking she'd heard a moan in the pines. She saw that Dylan had heard it, too. Athlete that he was, he reacted immediately, springing to his feet, moving fast as he pushed back pine branches. Olivia followed him, catching the branches as they swept back toward her.

She heard another moan.

Whoever was there was alive.

She and Dylan emerged from the pines, onto a wet spot a few feet from the shore of the pond. Just ahead, Grace was sitting on a rock, staring at the water, a book clutched in her hand. A gentle breeze caught the ends of her white hair. She wore a hooded gray sweatshirt, knit pants and sturdy shoes with lightweight wool socks. A half-dozen mosquitoes buzzed around her but she didn't seem to notice them.

Dylan eased in close to her. He gently took the book from Grace and handed it back to Olivia. She saw that it was a ragged copy of *The Scarlet Pimpernel*.

"Grace," Dylan said softly, touching her trembling hand.

She looked up at him, tears in her eyes. "I knew you'd come, Philip. I knew you'd come."

Chapter 25

I thought it was my last night on this earth. I could see from Philip's expression that he did, too, but the only words he spoke were ones of reassurance. When the wind and rain calmed, I knew enough about hurricanes to realize we were in the eye of this monster. At that moment, nothing seemed more natural than reaching out to another person for love and comfort.

The Hurricane of 1938 swept over Long Island and churned up the Connecticut River, killing more than seven hundred people and leaving a path of catastrophic destruction. In the Swift River Valley, the newly finished Winsor Dam and Goodnough Dike held.

I knew none of that as Philip and I held each other in the eye of the storm. Then, I only knew that I wasn't alone. I was with the only man I would ever love.

I didn't care about the stolen jewels.

"I love you, Gracie Webster," Philip whispered in that eerie calm.

I knew that everything he said, everything we did together through that long, terrible storm, would remain embedded in my heart for the rest of my days.

Even now, as I watch the birds and look out at Quabbin as an old woman, I can hear his voice and feel his touch.

The calm of the eye gave way to more ferocious wind and rain. We reached for each other, and only when it was quiet and still, when a cool breeze touched our overheated skin, did Philip tell me what I had already guessed.

"My wife died of a fever almost three years ago. I have a daughter in England."

"How old is she?" I asked.

"She's three. Her name is Philippa. She's with my parents right now." He was as serious as I'd ever seen him, a mature father and lover, not the rakish thief who'd stolen jewels from a British lord, not the amused and irreverent swashbuckler of my fantasies. "I'm a pilot with the British Royal Air Force. I have to go home, Gracie. There'll be war with Hitler. If I live—"

"You'll live! You have to live! You have a child."

"And I have you. I'll come back to you, Gracie. I promise you."

The next day, after the hurricane, I had to go back to our new home in Knights Bridge. Gran and Daddy would be terrified I'd been swept away by the hurricane. I knew that Philip couldn't go with me, but I ached at having to leave him.

I remember his eyes as I left him. "I love you, Gracie," he said over and over, until he was out of sight as I climbed over fallen trees and branches on my way to Knights Bridge on the other side of Carriage Hill.

With all the damage and disruption in the aftermath of the hurricane, I couldn't return to my hideaway cabin for several days. I sat on my rock by the pond just in case Philip would call my name, but he didn't. This time, he really was gone.

The state finally came for the cabin. They didn't expect to find anyone there, but I talked a worker into letting me clear out my things. I packed my books and my blankets and drawings. As I folded up the cot, a small royal-red velvet bag fell onto the floor. It must have been tucked under the mattress.

I swear my heart stopped beating, but I recovered myself, swept up the bag and faked a little laugh. "I almost forgot I had this."

"What is it?" the worker, a portly man in his forties, asked me.

"Would you believe a gift from the queen of England?"

He laughed, too.

Only later did I understand that Philip had left the jewels with me because he didn't dare take them with him to England and risk being branded a thief. He would make peace with his brother-in-law, and then he would come back for the jewels, and for me.

Chapter 26

Dylan stood back as the search-and-rescue team took over and strapped Grace Webster to a stretcher. She was dehydrated and suffering from mild hypothermia, but she was already rallying, arguing with the paramedics. She wanted to walk back to her friend's car. "If I could walk out here on my own," she said, "I can certainly walk back on my own. I've done it many, many times."

"When you were a teenager," Olivia reminded her, then glanced at Dylan. "I'll walk a little ways with her and then come back."

"Take your time."

She was obviously relieved that Grace was alive, even if she was showing a little of the stern Latin and English teacher of old. Dylan was relieved, too. He saw her off with the rescue team and then walked back down to the pond. He stood on Grace's rock, looking out at the quiet water, the ducks, the marsh, the seemingly endless wilderness, and he wondered if his father had ever made it out here.

In a few minutes, Olivia joined him. "Why did Grace come back here now?"

Dylan could see she already knew the answer, but he said, "Because of me."

"She figured out you knew about the missing Ashworth jewels and realized that was what your father was after." Olivia walked closer to the water, her shoes sinking into the soft ground; she looked back at him. "I have a feeling Grace fell for this scoundrel British jewel thief."

"Maybe he wasn't such a scoundrel."

"What are you thinking?"

Dylan winked at her. "I'm thinking today has worked out all right." He hopped off the rock, slipped his arms around Olivia and held her close. "And some things are just meant to be."

"They're all nuts," Mark Flanagan said as he and Dylan surveyed the exterior of his house in Knights Bridge, getting a sense of the possibilities—or, more likely, the extent of the problems. "Jess, Olivia, their mother. Randy, too. I don't know if I'm coming or going half the time."

Dylan grinned at him. It had been twenty-four hours since he and Olivia had found Grace Webster, and she hadn't died in the woods, and it was a beautiful day. "Could be because you're besotted," he said lightly.

"Besotted? What the hell?" Mark laughed in surprise. "You've been listening to Grace, or living here has started to affect you." He pulled back a bush of some kind and checked what appeared to be a section of rotted wall just above the foundation of the old house. "You're right, though. I just can't figure out what Jess wants. She's never wanted to live anywhere but Knights Bridge, but she's planning a trip to Paris and who knows where else."

"The two aren't mutually exclusive."

"What if she gets to Paris and decides not to come back?"

"You're going with her, aren't you?"

"Yeah, but I have to come back. My work's here."

"Her work's here, too," Dylan said. "So is her family. This isn't about Jess, is it?"

"Maybe not." Mark paused a moment, considering, then shook his head. "I'm not going to be tempted to leave Knights Bridge. Not again. I don't care if anyone thinks I'm boring."

"Boring? What's that about? You're a successful architect—"

"I was engaged in my early twenties for about ten minutes. It didn't work out for a lot of reasons, but basically she thought I was a bore."

"I don't think Jess thinks you're a bore, Mark. I think she just wants to go to Paris."

He replaced the bush back in front of the wall. "Hides that mess."

"It's a problem?"

"One of many problems. This house isn't in good shape."

"So it looks run-down because it is run-down."

"I've discovered in my work that not all old houses can or should be saved. I've said for a long time this one should probably be condemned." He looked up at the second-floor window above him, grimaced and then turned back to Dylan. "Olivia doesn't have Jess's wanderlust. She wants to make this getaway of hers work. It's off to a good start. She has a real chance. Is she why you have me out here?"

"I have to figure out what to do with this place," Dylan said, deliberately keeping his answer vague.

Mark shook his head. "No, you don't. You're rich. You could go back to San Diego and do whatever you've been doing for the past two years." He started around to the back of the house. "You need something to do, Dylan. You're not one to be idle. Any chance of moving Noah Kendrick out here?"

Dylan realized Mark was joking. Just about the last place in the country anyone ever would expect to see Noah Kendrick was little Knights Bridge. Noah knew Boston from his MIT days and appreciated New England, but moving out here?

Dylan smiled. It was even crazier than him moving out here.

Mark stopped at the back steps and just shook his head at more rot. "This isn't good. In fact, Dylan, this is really bad."

"Wrecking ball time?"

"Past time."

"All right. Tell me more about what kind of house you could design here that would blend in with the surroundings."

"Blend in with The Farm at Carriage Hill, you mean?"

"I wouldn't want to create another eyesore," Dylan said with a smile.

Mark shifted his attention from the house to Dylan.

"I was away from Knights Bridge for a long time. I never thought I'd come back. This isn't San Diego, Dylan. Don't talk yourself into thinking it is. It's a pretty little town and I'm glad I came back, but it's not a city."

Dylan had the feeling Mark's words had more to do with him and Jess Frost than anything else. Mark grew silent and edgy and left abruptly, as if he understood himself what he'd been getting at. Maybe he knew what he had to do now, Dylan thought, and headed back inside.

He looked at the old maps and Grace's musty books, and he realized that Mark Flanagan wasn't the only one who had to figure out what he had to do.

Dylan picked up one of the Latin primers. He'd never studied Latin. He'd never even remotely wanted to study Latin. He imagined Grace Webster here as a young teacher, a young woman who had figured out early in life that she had to rely on herself.

He knew what he had to do.

The truth might change Knights Bridge—and him—forever, but he couldn't run from it.

He was halfway to the village when Loretta called him. "I've been trying to reach you," she said.

He pulled over. "Lousy cell service."

"Your kind of place," she said sarcastically. "I don't know if there are rocks you don't want me to turn over. Tell me what you don't want to hear."

"I want everything, Loretta. The good, the bad and the ugly."

"I did some digging. Philip Rankin died early in the war. He was a fighter pilot with the Royal Air Force. He went down during the Battle of Britain."

Dylan noticed a few drops of rain on his windshield. The information wasn't a surprise and yet he felt a sense of loss. "The jewels?"

"You were right. There's no report that they were ever recovered. It's hard to say if the police or anyone else suspected or had any evidence that Philip stole them, but I imagine there was talk. His wife—Lady Helena—died before the war, but you have that. Their daughter's alive, still in England. She has a grown son and daughter and several grandchildren. A granddaughter's in London. Alexandra Rankin Hunt. She's a clothing designer, of all things. She plays up the mystique of the missing jewels."

"What else, Loretta?"

Loretta hesitated. "What do you mean, 'what else?' Never mind. I have to go."

"Loretta—"

She'd already disconnected. Dylan tossed the phone onto the seat and continued on through the village. The rain picked up. He turned on the wipers, noting how green the landscape was now, so different from his first day in Knights Bridge.

Audrey Frost had forgiven Grace her adventure with her car and joined her and Olivia for afternoon tea at Grace's apartment at Rivendell. Olivia had made scones and brought them over with her. Afterward, she cleaned up the kitchen area while the two older women discussed their plans for the week. Grace had recovered fully but she was more subdued than usual, and her friend finally left, promising to see her tomorrow at yoga class.

"Come, Olivia," Grace said. "Walk with me to the sunroom. It's my favorite spot in this place."

"You're happy here, aren't you, Grace?"

"Yes, I am. I truly am." When they reached the sunroom, she grabbed Olivia's hand, an intimate, emotional gesture for such a starchy woman. "He's a handsome man, this Dylan McCaffrey."

Olivia smiled. "He is."

Grace squeezed her hand, then released it as she settled into a high-backed chair. "You've fallen for him, have you?"

The question startled her but Olivia answered, "I don't mind saying that I have. Grace, the spot where we found you—"

"I spent many happy days there the last summer we lived in the valley." She looked out at the rain. "It was my hideout from a world that was changing around me."

She drifted, lost in her own thoughts. Olivia wasn't sure whether to leave or to stay awhile longer. Then Dylan arrived, and Grace sat up, wide-awake. She turned to Olivia. "A moment, dear."

Dylan remained on his feet after Olivia had left the room and glanced out the floor-to-ceiling window as a gray squirrel raced up a pine tree. The rain had stopped, but everything was still dripping, shrouded in fog. He was aware of Grace watching him from her chair. "You saved me yesterday, just as another man saved me all those years ago." She spoke quietly, her voice steady, as if she'd guessed he would come. "You remind me of him."

"When did you know?" Dylan asked, turning to her.

He could see she knew exactly what he was asking. "The moment I laid eyes on you."

Chapter 27

*G*ran was the first to suspect. I think she knew before I did. *"You'll get through this. I will be there with you. You'll do what's best for the baby. We all will."*

"Gran, I'm not... I don't know what you're thinking."

"You are, and I'm thinking about your future, and this baby's future."

We kept it from Daddy for as long as we could. He raged and cried and I knew I had to tell him everything—about my cabin, about Philip, about how Philip was on the run from the police. I could see that the baby was one more thing that reminded Daddy that the world as he knew it was ending. He was already desperate, and now here I was, pregnant.

I walked out to the pond. Only a few stones of the foundation of my hideaway cabin remained. I sat on my boulder and stared at the water, and I knew I would never come here again.

Daddy had searched my room, looking for any remnants of my time with Philip. "You're to have nothing of that man's near you. Do you understand me, Grace? Tell me you understand."

"I don't understand," I said, "but I know what you're saying."

"It's for your sake."

I knew that he was terrified if anyone discovered that Philip stole the Ashworth jewels, I'd be accused of harboring a criminal, even of complicity in the robbery.

A few months later, when it was obvious that I was expecting, he told people I was visiting a friend who owned a farm in upstate New York and hid me in my room in Knights Bridge. Daddy and Gran took good care of me in those last cold, lonely months. Gran kept thinking of alternatives to giving up my baby, but Daddy had everything arranged.

"A childless couple who used to summer on one of the lakes in the Swift River Valley will adopt the baby," he said. "They're good people. They've wanted a child for years. They'll give the baby a life we can't. This way, you'll both have a chance."

I had no choice. I had to do what he wanted me to do. By spring, I knew Philip wasn't coming back. Not that he didn't want to. He couldn't. I read everything I could about the war that was erupting in Europe and what was going on in Great Britain. I read about the Royal Air Force. Once, I tried to run away to England. I got as far as Boston before Daddy found me. He was alone. Gran wasn't with him, and I thought he would do something terrible. Instead, he looked at me with tears in his eyes. "Do you think I want to give up what could be my only grandchild? It's what's best, Grace," he said, his voice cracking. "It's what's best."

"What if Philip comes back after the war? What if I wait and care for our child—"

"Does he know about the baby?"

I could tell that my father knew the answer already, but I shook my head. "He's a good man, Dad," I whispered.

"I believe you, Grace. I believe he's a good man. I believe he would come back for you if he could."

"Are you just saying that to keep me from killing myself after you take my baby from me?"

"I'm saying that because this man was the love of your life. I can see it in your eyes."

"Is, Daddy. He is the love of my life."

"Grace. Ah, Grace."

As my due date came closer, Daddy and Gran drove me to a small, private lying-in hospital near Boston. He'd packed some of my books. "You'll make a fine teacher, Grace. Maybe one day..." He didn't finish but I knew what he wanted to say: Maybe one day I would find another man.

I went into labor two days later. I wasn't allowed to hold my baby, or to be told if I'd had a boy or a girl. I woke up alone, and it was done. My baby was gone.

I always knew I had a boy. Even now, decades later, I can still remember the feeling of him moving inside me. My father said he didn't know whether I'd had a boy or a girl, but I could tell he was lying—to spare me, to help me forget when we both knew I would never forget.

We resumed our new lives in Knights Bridge. Eventually I got a job as a teacher. I loved my work, and I looked forward to each day. It would be easy to say that I never looked back to that long-ago summer, but I did.

I looked back all the time.

Chapter 28

Dylan wasn't sure at first, but then it was obvious that Grace wanted to talk, and that she had the strength and the capacity after her ordeal at Carriage Hill Pond. Otherwise he wouldn't have stayed. He wasn't there to upset her.

She made him pull up a chair and sit down. The wind had picked up, blowing out the last of the rain, the fog, the clouds. He could see patches of blue sky. He didn't argue with Grace. He suspected most people didn't argue with her, but he knew he would never forget finding her out in the Quabbin woods.

When she looked at him, she had the eyes of a teenager...of a young woman in love.

"The day you walked in here with Olivia," she said, "it was as if Philip had come back to Knights Bridge.

I thought I was losing my mind. Finally I realized that you're his grandson."

And her grandson, Dylan thought. "You didn't recognize my father?"

"Not then. Now…" She fixed her gaze on the view out the windows. "I see now that he bore a strong resemblance to my father."

"This story's all in your book?"

"It's all there. At first I thought I was writing it in case my son found his way to Knights Bridge and wanted to know about his roots. Then I realized I was writing it for myself, and for Philip. So that people would know who we were and what we meant to each other."

"You never told anyone about him?"

"Gran and Daddy knew but I never told another soul, not even my closest friends. I buried that summer very deep. I never spoke about it again after I came home from the hospital. I knew Gran and Daddy wanted to pretend it never happened. They thought that would be best for me."

"Did you find out what happened to Philip?"

She took a shallow breath and nodded. "He died early in the war. He was a fighter pilot—a hero. I only found out years later, but I knew he was gone, because I never heard from him again."

Dylan leaned in close to her. "I'm sorry, Grace."

"If he'd come back, what would he have thought of me?" Her voice was a whisper now, and her face was pale. "How could I have told him I gave up his child?"

"He'd have understood."

Grace looked at him as if he were channeling the man she'd loved. "I hope so. I think so."

"There was a war on. The circumstances..." Dylan tried to picture what their lives must have been like. "He'd have wanted what was best for you and his son."

His son. Dylan's throat caught.

"Philip was..." Grace raised a hand and pushed back her hair, and for a fleeting moment, she might have been a teenager again. "He was a good man, Dylan. Your grandfather was a good man."

"Did you ever search for the couple who adopted your baby?"

"I never did. My son—your father—belonged with them. They were his parents."

"They were decent people, Grace. My father loved them." Dylan reached over and put his hand on hers. "I think he knew. I think you're the reason he came here."

"Not the jewels?"

"Well, nothing like throwing a fortune in lost jewels into the mix. What happened—was Lord Ashworth planning to sell the jewels in Boston and then claim they'd been stolen?"

"Something like that," Grace said. "He was broke, or at least by his standards he was. He also resented his sister for having inherited the jewels. Philip followed him to Boston and..." Grace shrugged her bony shoulders. "You know the rest."

"He knocked his brother-in-law on the head, grabbed the jewels and ran. Ashworth didn't tell the police the whole story because he'd look bad, and Philip didn't because who'd believe him?"

"And because Lord Ashworth was his dead wife's brother, and his daughter's uncle," Grace said quietly.

"Hell of a treasure hunt." Dylan rose and kissed her

on the cheek. "You're a good woman. I'm proud to know you. I'm proud to be your grandson."

"I wanted my baby to have a good life." Her voice faltered. "Did he?"

"He did, and he died the way he would have wanted, just too soon." Dylan grinned, thinking of his father. "He'd have liked it that I'm here with you."

"He'd have liked for you to find those jewels, too, wouldn't he?"

Dylan laughed. "No doubt. Now get some rest, okay? I hope you'll reconsider keeping that book of yours in the vault until after you're gone. I imagine I'm not the only one who doesn't want to wait to read it. You say it's all in there, huh? Your whole life story? Everything, Grace?"

She gave him a mischievous smile. "Well, maybe not quite everything."

He started to ask her if she knew what happened to the Ashworth jewels, but she was asleep. He left, driving straight to Carriage Hill and Olivia. He found her out back in her ever-expanding herb garden. "Noah was right. My presence here has changed everything. I have to go back to San Diego. I have someone I need to talk to—Loretta Wrentham, the woman who told me about Grace's house. She's my lawyer. We're friends."

"She knows something?"

"More than she's admitted," he said, certain he was right.

"Do you think Philip took the jewels back to England with him?"

"And risk getting caught with them?" Dylan shook his head. "No. I think he left them here. He expected to come back for them—"

"And for Grace," Olivia said.

"And for Grace," he repeated, picturing her as a teenager, saying farewell to the man she loved. He took Olivia into his arms and kissed her, knowing he'd be back, that he'd make love to her again. "Olivia…"

She smiled. "I'll see you soon."

He drove up the road to the house he'd inherited from his father. It felt different now. He saw a young woman starting a new life here with her bitter father and her stoic grandmother, facing more than they had ever anticipated having to face—eviction from their hometown, its removal from the map, a devastating hurricane, the onset of war and, most of all, giving up a baby to other people to raise.

Maybe the story wasn't unique, but it was their story.

And it was his story, Dylan thought.

He got back in his car and drove to Logan Airport and was on his way to San Diego by nightfall.

The day after Dylan left for San Diego, Olivia's parents, sister and grandmother all descended. Olivia brought them out to the terrace. Mark showed up, and Jess eyed him in that neutral, repressed way she sometimes had. Since Dylan's abrupt departure, Olivia had gone crazy working on designs for everything that went with artisan soaps—packaging, bags, cards explaining the ingredients—and then went crazy in the kitchen, throwing together a pot of soup and digging out her grandmother's recipe for molasses cookies.

She sat restlessly with her family on what had turned into the most beautiful day yet that spring. They were still absorbing Grace's reasons for taking off to Carriage Hill Pond. At Grace's request, Olivia had told her parents and sister what she knew about Philip Rankin and the summer of 1938.

Her father sighed. "Your grandma was a co-conspirator in getting Grace out of Rivendell."

"She wanted to borrow my car," Audrey Frost said. "What was I going to do? Tell her no?"

He didn't hesitate. "Yes."

She waved a hand in dismissal. "No one tells Grace Webster no. Not these days, anyway."

Her son kept his gaze on her. "Did you know about this jewel thief?"

"No."

"But you suspected something?"

"She's older than I am. We didn't get to be friends until later."

Olivia could see her father wasn't buying that one. He leaned forward. "You're being evasive, Ma."

She picked up a warm molasses cookie. "I haven't made these in years. They smell wonderful, don't they?" She took a bite, then sighed. "I always had a feeling Grace had a transforming experience that summer. It was before I knew her."

"A transforming experience?" Randy grinned, sitting back in his chair. "What do you old ladies talk about while you're playing canasta?"

"We're journaling."

"Journaling?"

"Watch out," she said, eating more of her cookie. "I might write my own book."

Jess laughed, and Mark patted her knee, a subtle gesture that Olivia didn't think anyone else noticed. He belonged in Knights Bridge, with Jess. Olivia pictured Dylan at a Frost gathering but wondered if he'd let himself belong anywhere.

She put the thought out of her mind. "If you stole a fortune in jewels and didn't want to take them back to England with you, where would you stash them?"

Her father winced. "Don't let that get around. We'd have every idiot in the universe here with a metal detector."

"I didn't think about a metal detector," Olivia said.

Her mother helped herself to a cookie and sat back in her chair in the shade. "You could spend the next twenty years scouring the Quabbin woods and not get anywhere."

Jess smiled at Mark. "Lost treasure. Stolen jewels. Do you really think I'd ever be bored here? No wonder Dylan McCaffrey decided to clean up his yard himself."

Olivia noticed a bee buzzing in the lavender. "Dylan didn't know until I wrote to him that his father had bought Grace's house. I think they both came here looking for answers."

"Some secrets are best taken to the grave," her mother said.

"Not Grace's," Olivia said. "That's why she wrote her book. She wanted her secrets to come out and for us to know that she'd loved a man, and she'd had a child and had the strength to give him up and to carry on with her life."

Olivia bolted up out of her chair and down a mulched path, past lady's mantle and catmint to a rosebush she was nursing along. She'd wanted her family there, but she'd thought she could talk objectively about Duncan and Dylan McCaffrey, the decades-old jewelry robbery and Grace Webster's secret past. But she couldn't.

Her mother joined her. "I moved up our trip to California. We're going next week. If I wait for everything to be perfect here, for us both to have time, I'll never go. I'll have my cell phone and email."

Olivia realized her mother's statement wasn't as much of a non sequitur as she'd thought at first. "Mom…"

She took a deep breath. "You and Jess will be fine. We all have our own lives, even if we all live right here in Knights Bridge."

"Dylan McCaffrey doesn't belong here. At least that's what he believes."

"Is that why he left?"

"He said he had business in San Diego, but I also think he needed time."

Olivia noticed that her mother had gone quiet. Finally she said, "I waited and waited to get up the nerve to make this trip to California. Then I decided to take action, and that's when the fear and second-guessing eased. I can't say they went away and I don't have my bags packed and I'm not on the plane yet, but deciding, acting—they've helped."

"I can't just wait for Dylan to figure things out, can I?"

Her mother gave a little shrug, and smiled. "I'd never interfere."

Mark left first, then her parents and grandmother. Jess stayed behind, helping herself to a bottle of chilled chardonnay and bringing two glasses out to the terrace with her. She filled the glasses and handed one to Olivia. "I want to get married here at Carriage Hill."

"Then you and Mark—"

"No ring yet, no. I'm just saying that I want to get

married here. Mark won't care. He'd get married in a shed if it's what I wanted. He can be...inert." Jess grinned and sat down with her own glass of wine. "But I love him."

"What about Paris?"

"I'm going to Paris. Then I'm coming home."

Olivia lifted her wineglass and clinked it against Jess's. "I'd love for you to have your wedding here." She smiled, trying her wine. "Just not tomorrow, I hope. I have more work to do before I can put on a wedding."

Jess drank more of her wine, then said, "Do you think Mom will get on that plane to Los Angeles?"

"Yes, I do, Jess. She's determined."

"Will you worry?"

Olivia swallowed and set down her glass. "Mom can't not go because of me, but I'll be fine."

"Dad says you probably have some kind of herb here we can chew on if we get nuts."

"I do, actually."

Jess grinned, but her humor didn't last. "This thing with the missing jewels and Grace and the McCaffreys feels unfinished. I think you need to find the jewels. I can help look for them."

"Thanks, Jess."

They chatted for a few more minutes, and after Jess left, Olivia patted Buster and got him up for a walk. "I wish you could find the Ashworth jewels."

An offhand comment Mark had made at Olivia's house had been bugging Jess. She finally put her finger on it and confronted him when she found him out at the pond by the old sawmill. "You were engaged once?"

"I was twenty-two. It didn't work out. We'd only known each other for a couple months."

"Why didn't you tell me?"

He shrugged. "I didn't think it mattered. I've known you for as long as I can remember. Hell, Jess, we used to jump in this pond together as kids. Remember?"

"You tried to drown me."

"You and the drama." He grinned and drew her into his arms. "Jess, I love you. You're a romantic at heart. I'm... I can be a rock head."

"So can I. We're kindred spirits in that way."

He laughed, then withdrew a small, navy-blue case from his jacket pocket. He opened it up to a sparkling diamond ring and got down on one knee. "Jessica Frost, I love you, and I want to marry you. I want to be with you for the rest of our lives." He took her hand. "Jess, will you marry me?"

"Oh, Mark. Yes, yes, yes. I love you so much."

He slid the ring onto her finger and swept her into his arms as he rose. He had tickets to Paris and hotel reservations, with more adventures to come.

Jess saw that her parents had arrived back at the mill. She and Mark went up and told them the news, and Jess showed them her ring. Her mother laughed and hugged her. "I'm so happy for you, Jess—for both you and Mark."

Her father sighed. "Finally. I thought I was going to have to get my shotgun."

He didn't own a shotgun. Jess rolled her eyes. "Honestly, Dad." She grinned at him, then was serious. "Are you two really going to California?"

"We're going," her mother said.

* * *

His daughters needed them. Randy Frost could see that same thought running through Louise's mind after Jess left. Jess was excited about her wedding and would start making plans. And Olivia… Randy grimaced. His elder daughter had missing British jewels and a rich Californian on her mind, and she didn't have a steady paycheck.

Louise turned from the map of California tacked to her wall. "Jess and Louise will be fine without us. It's hard to believe sometimes, but they're grown now." Her voice was steady but not loud, as if she were repeating words she wanted to be true rather than she was certain were true.

"It's not flying and driving that get to you," Randy said. "It's not having your chicks in the nest. It's worrying about them."

"I remind myself that it's a big piece of paper." She shut her eyes a moment, as if imagining those dots of hers, then smiled at him. "There's enough room for us all to live our lives and still be together."

Randy slung an arm over his wife's shoulders. He saw that she'd added a couple more colored pushpins marking the places they'd stop on their trip. "Jess and Olivia live in Knights Bridge because they love it and they want to be here. They have lives here. If that changes, they'll move on. They're not here because you've held them back."

"They're so independent. I never wanted to stifle that."

"You didn't and you don't. Maybe I did a little— maybe we both did a little, but not enough to do any damage." He paused, cleared his throat. "Maybe I stifled you, just from wanting to protect you."

"You're my rock, Randy."

"Yeah, but not because you're weak. I'd crush you if you were weak, and you're not." He pulled her close to him and groaned. "Damn, Louise. Now I'm sounding like I've been seeing a therapist."

"I'd support you if you did. It's a good thing, Randy."

Looking at his wife now, he couldn't disagree. "Being independent doesn't mean Liv and Jess have to move a thousand miles from us. It doesn't mean that they don't want us in their lives. Too bad if it does, because we're not going anywhere." Randy grinned. "Except to freaking California."

Louise smiled back at him. "I can't wait."

"Good, because those rich nuts out there have arranged for a car for us and a suite at the Beverly Hills Hotel for the first two nights. Just until we get over jet lag."

"Dylan McCaffrey?"

"He and Noah Kendrick."

Louise's eyes widened. "You've been in touch?"

"Yep."

Randy liked that he could still surprise her. He thought of the two of them heading off together, then coming home together, and he knew he was the luckiest man in the world.

Chapter 29

Dylan looked out at San Diego from his office windows, aware of Noah Kendrick behind him. "Olivia would love San Diego," Noah said. "I can see her at your place on Coronado. She'd paint all the walls. She'd liven up that cappuccino-and-white look of yours."

"She hates to fly."

"I hate to fly. I do it all the time."

"Helps to have your own plane."

"Helps to have a good Scotch handy."

Dylan knew Noah was kidding. He might dislike flying, but flying was like driving to both of them. Just something they did to get to where they were going. "I don't know what's going to happen, Noah."

"Your father complicated your life by buying that place, but his life was complicated, too. I took your lawyer to dinner. Straightened out what was attorney-client privilege and what I needed to know."

"As my boss."

"I've never been your boss, Dylan. Hell. You know that. We're business partners. More than that, we're friends. I wanted to know as your friend."

"Don't tell me Loretta and my father—"

"I'm not telling you anything. Your father couldn't settle down, even if he wanted to. He had a restless soul. If he found those jewels, what would he have done with them?"

"I don't know."

"Yeah, you do. He wasn't an easy man but he was a decent one." Noah gazed out the window. He was in an expensive black shirt and jeans today, as if to make a statement. "It's been an intense few months, Dylan. You've been a big help. You always are."

"If you ever need me, you know I'm there."

"I know. Same here. I figure it's time for us to get into venture capital. My role here is changing. Anyway, that's for the future. This adventure travel thing of yours will only take up so much time. We'll talk." He turned to his friend. "Right now, you have a plane to catch. Mine. Go."

Dylan raised his eyebrows. "Noah, what have you done?"

"I'm meeting Randy and Louise Frost in Beverly Hills. I want to make sure you're in good hands with these people, plus I have some millwork I need done for my winery." Noah settled back on his heels, a little hyper but also pleased with himself. "It's time I had your back, Dylan."

"You always have. Noah—"

"Just go, will you? Pack, lock the doors and take off."

Dylan headed out. He found Loretta Wrentham on

his front porch. She held up a hand before he could say a word. "I adored your father but I knew the score. I found out he was adopted. He suspected but he didn't know for sure. His parents never told him—that wasn't as uncommon then as it is now. He found that newspaper article in his mother's belongings after she died. I think she meant for him to find it, so that it could be his choice to pursue answers or just let them be."

"She tore the article out of the newspaper herself?"

"Right. It's not Grace Webster's handwriting in the margin. It's your Grandmother McCaffrey's handwriting. Maybe she thought Isaiah Webster was the jewel thief, foiled somehow since he never did have money, but, personally, I think she suspected that the jewel thief was her son's biological father. Your father stuck it in that trunk of his and didn't think about it again for years. Then two years ago he decided to check out Knights Bridge. He assumed everyone concerned would be dead by then."

"Grace—his birth mother—wasn't dead."

"That's right. And your father wasn't going to upset her or do anything that would reveal her secret. Not for anything, Dylan. I see that now. I didn't know. I've tried to put him behind me. I could have spared you a lot of pain."

"Pain?" He grinned at her. "No pain, Loretta. It's been a hell of a treasure hunt, exactly what he'd have wanted."

She looked relieved. "I'm sorry I didn't tell you sooner."

"No. You did what you promised to do. That's enough. Now if you'll excuse me—"

"Go, go." Loretta gave him a quick smile. "The treasure hunt isn't over."

He laughed and headed inside to pack for his flight east.

Grace summoned Olivia to Rivendell and asked her to come to the sunroom. She was alone, a shawl wrapped over her thin shoulders as she stood at the windows. "I checked the copies of my book. I'd just had them printed when Duncan McCaffrey visited." She paused, her eyes pinned on the view of the bird feeders and, in the distance, Quabbin. "One wasn't in pristine condition. Someone had obviously borrowed it, read it and returned it."

"Duncan?"

"That rogue. I remember now that I had the books out when he was here. They'd just come back from the printer. I'm not as young as I used to be, Olivia. I never let students put one over on me back in the day. Duncan, though…"

"You're glad he purloined a copy of your book."

"He had a chance to read it before he died." Grace stared out the window, then took a breath and continued without looking at Olivia. "There was a hand-dug well behind my cabin. It might have caved in by now. I used to worry it would get covered up by leaves and someone would fall into it. I mention it in my book, in passing."

A well. Olivia studied the older woman. "Grace… did you tell Dylan about this well?"

She smiled, a spark of mischief in her eyes. "Thirty minutes ago."

"He's here? He's in Knights Bridge?" Olivia couldn't

hide her surprise. "Has he gone out to Carriage Hill Pond to look for this well?"

Grace sat in her seat and arranged her shawl around her, then lifted her binoculars. "Look, Olivia. A blue-bird."

Olivia found Dylan at the pond, tossing a stick into the quiet water, and she wondered if all those years ago young Grace had responded to her jewel thief the same way, with a breathless gasp and a sense that this man was the only man she would ever want to be with.

He grinned at her. "Think I just stole millions in missing British jewels?"

"You wouldn't be standing here throwing sticks if you had." Olivia pushed through ferns to him. "I didn't know you were back."

"I rolled into town this morning. I had this unfinished business to settle before I saw you."

"Looking for Grace's well. I have a feeling your father got a shot of his wanderlust from her." Olivia felt a welcome breeze on what had turned into a warm spring day. "I have something I want to tell you." She pushed back a flutter of anxiety. "Before we go treasure hunting."

He stepped up onto Grace's rock. "All right. What's up?"

Olivia faced the water so she wouldn't be distracted by her reaction to him. "My sister and I were in a car accident when we were teenagers. I was driving. We were on our way to pick fiddlehead ferns." She held up a hand before Dylan could ask. "Fiddleheads are like wild asparagus. You eat them. Jess and I were a one-lane road that dead-ended at Quabbin. It's a lot like our road. Hardly anyone's ever on it."

"Except that day," he said quietly.

Olivia nodded. "A car came straight at us out of nowhere, going way too fast. I swerved and went off the road."

"The other car?"

"I'm not sure the driver even realized we'd gone off the road. I remember Jess screaming, 'Car, car,' and—well, we careened between two trees, down a hill and into a stone wall. We were lucky. We weren't seriously injured—bumps, and a few scrapes—and we never lost consciousness, but we couldn't get out." Olivia paused, focused on the rustling of the trees in the light breeze, the rich smells of the damp ground and greenery around her. Finally she continued, "We were wedged in tight. We couldn't open our doors. We couldn't climb into the back and get out that way. We could barely move. I remember…" She took a shallow breath. "I remember thinking we'd die of thirst."

"How did you get out?" Dylan asked.

"My mother found us. She and my father were in separate cars, driving all over town looking for us. She noticed a tire mark on the road and investigated. When she saw our car, she thought Jess and I were dead. She scrambled down the hill…." Olivia forced herself to take a few breaths before she went on. "I've never seen her so pale, but she didn't cry or scream or anything once she realized we were alive. But she couldn't get us out, either. She had to wait for my father to get there with the fire department."

"That had to be tough for all of you."

"We were fine, though. As I said, we were lucky. My

mother was always a worrier, but she had a hard time after the accident. After a while, we thought things were better, but I realize now we all adjusted to doing what we could to keep her from having to worry."

Dylan toed a stone loose from the mud. "And you don't like feeling trapped."

"Like on an airplane," she said. "It doesn't do any good to tell myself it could have been so much worse that day. It was what it was, and I didn't like being stuck in that damn car, with my sister in pain and upset, knowing my parents were crazed with worry. I don't play that moment back as much as I used to, but the end result is that I don't like to fly."

"It was go into the ditch or have a head-on collision?"

Olivia nodded.

"Habits of thinking and reacting can be hard to break. You did good, Olivia. You survived, but you weren't uninjured."

"Jess says we suffered a traumatic stress injury. I say we were lucky."

"Maybe you're both right. A guy I know took a hard hit in hockey and was permanently disabled. He was 'lucky' because he wasn't paralyzed, but he'll walk with a limp for the rest of his life and he had to give up his dream of being in the NHL. It was one of those unintentional hits that went wrong. I wasn't involved, but I watched him get hit. I was sure he'd never walk again. I got stuck in that moment for a while. I held back because of it. I wasn't all in. I had to rearrange my thinking in order to get back to the game."

"Did your family attend your games?"

"Some. Not always. They had their own lives. I wasn't living out their fantasies."

"But you felt supported?"

Dylan grinned suddenly, sexily. "Yeah, sure."

Olivia smiled. "We can go treasure hunting now."

They found the well by an old stone wall in the woods behind the spot where Grace's cabin had once stood. The opening was covered in wet, rotted leaves, mud, twigs and cobwebs. A beetle scurried past Dylan's foot, and he saw a fat, brown slug oozing through the muck.

He grinned at Olivia. "I'm not that big on slugs. I've lived in a dry climate for a long time."

"They're gross but at least they're harmless."

He got down on his hands and knees at the edge of the well, then angled a look up at her. "Do you want to dig in first?"

"No way. Whatever's in this well has nothing to do with me. Grace, Philip Rankin, your father—these are your people, my friend."

He grabbed a fistful of sodden leaves and tossed it onto the ground next to him. "Right. My people."

Olivia knelt on the opposite side of the well, wishing she'd brought work gloves. She dug in, and in a matter of minutes, she and Dylan had uncovered the top section of the well's stone-lined interior.

He looked across the opening at her. "I suppose you don't want to stick your hand in there, either?"

"Nope. You're the son of the treasure hunter. You go right ahead."

With a grimace, he reached into the well, leaning forward as he lowered his arm past his elbow, deep into the dark muck.

"It's a long shot that the jewels are still there," Olivia

said, suddenly wanting to dip her hand in there after all and see what she could find.

Thirty seconds later, Dylan lifted out a dented, rusted, filthy tin box. "It was embedded in the stones about ten inches into the well. I didn't have to stick my arm in so damn deep."

He took a breath and set the tin on the ground, then shook off some of the mud that had collected on his arm. Not that it did much good. Mud had splattered on his face and soaked into his jeans. Olivia knew she wasn't in much better shape.

"It's a biscuit tin," she said, staying focused on their discovery. "British."

Dylan managed to open the tin's stiff, creaky lid.

Inside was a small package wrapped in dark oilskin. He lifted it out of the tin and set it on a path of dry ground, carefully unrolling the oilskin, exposing the remains of a royal-red velvet drawstring bag.

He handed the bag to Olivia. "You open it."

"Dylan—"

"Go ahead. You've known Grace all your life."

Olivia loosened the frayed gold drawstrings and emptied the contents onto the oilcloth.

Three rings and a necklace, perfect, caught the afternoon sun gleaming through the trees.

She sat back on her heels. "Grace knew the biscuit tin was in the well. Did she hide the jewels herself?"

"I imagine she did," Dylan said.

"With Philip gone, with their baby gone, with no way to prove how she came by the jewels, with no way to clear Philip's name, she left them here and never came back." Olivia held back tears. "All these years, Dylan. She kept these secrets…."

"They were her secrets to keep. No one else's." He frowned down at the tin, his eyes narrowed. "Hold on."

With the pads of two fingers, he lifted out a tiny metal replica of a sword that might have belonged to Porthos, Aramis or Athos, or one of the other swashbucklers on Grace's bookshelves.

Dylan laughed. "I'll be damned."

Olivia shook her head in amazement. "Your father got here before we did."

"Leave it to Duncan McCaffrey, treasure hunter."

"Grace suspected he'd sneaked a copy of her book."

Dylan held up the sword to the sunlight. "He must have done a little late-night reading about her life and times. Even if she doesn't say she hid the jewels in the well, it's the only intact structure out here. He'd have figured it out."

Olivia carefully returned the jewels to the worn bag, then rolled them back up in the oilcloth and handed them back to Dylan. He placed them in the tin with the toy sword and got to his feet.

She brushed mud off her hands and stood. "You're not going to put the tin back in the well, are you?"

He didn't answer. Instead, he started back through the woods with the tin. After a moment, Olivia followed him, found him standing on the rock where they'd found Grace with her copy of *The Scarlet Pimpernel*.

More than seventy years ago, a teenage Grace Webster had come upon a swashbuckler of her own, out here on Carriage Hill Pond.

Olivia stood with her toes almost in the still, clear water. "You know what you have to do."

He nodded. "Yeah. I do."

She smiled past the twist of anxiety in her gut.

"Nothing like having a private jet at your disposal if you're smuggling a fortune in stolen jewels."

He winked at her, and they walked back through the woods to the Quabbin gate. Olivia watched him climb into his expensive rented car. First Duncan McCaffrey, then Dylan McCaffrey. Their presence in Knights Bridge had changed her little hometown forever.

And me, too, she thought, climbing into her beat-up Subaru.

She brushed mud off her hands and noticed a mosquito had followed her inside. She rolled down her window and ushered it back into the wilderness. She blew Dylan a kiss as she rolled up her window again.

The man she loved blew her a kiss back, then grinned and drove up their quiet one-lane road, off to finish the mission his grandfather had started so long ago.

Chapter 30

"**I**'m not that wild about Beverly Hills," Randy Frost told his older daughter; it was his first call to her since he and his wife of thirty-plus years had left for the airport. "We drove past where they filmed the opening to the *Beverly Hillbillies*. I feel a little like Jed Clampett myself. Next we're having brunch at the Polo Lounge."

"Sounds fun," Olivia said as she put down her paintbrush in the back room, the last of her collection of cast-off tables and chairs almost finished. "How's Mom?"

"Wondering why she didn't run away from home at eighteen."

Olivia laughed. "It's like a second honeymoon."

"It's like a first honeymoon. We went to Cape Cod for the weekend for our first honeymoon. How are you, kid?"

"I'm on my way to England." Olivia liked the confidence she heard in her voice. "Don't tell Mom. I don't want her to worry."

"I'm not playing that game anymore, Liv. She worries about you so you don't have to worry about yourself and blah, blah, blah. My head starts to spin. Go to damn London. I assume it's got something to do with Dylan and those missing British jewels. Have a great time."

"Where are you and Mom off to next?"

"Leaving Beverly Hills behind and starting our drive up the coastal highway. Your mother has a notebook of things for us to do. We'll see you when we get back. How long will you be in London?"

"I don't know," Olivia said truthfully. She hadn't thought past finding Dylan. "Jess and Mark say they can hold down the fort here."

"Good. Your mother and I have flights back home in two weeks, but who knows."

Randy Frost watched the faint worry in Louise's eyes dissipate as she smiled from the plush chair in their room at the Beverly Hills Hotel. Noah Kendrick, Dylan's friend, was taking good care of them. He was different, but Randy liked him. His wife stood and took his hand. "I'm glad I didn't wait any longer for this trip."

He grunted. "I wouldn't have wanted you to make it as a widow."

What he heard from her next was genuine laughter, not laced with anxiety, not faked just so he wouldn't feel like a heel. The woman, he thought, was having the time of her life.

"This is all good," he said. "The hotel, the scenery, everything. You've planned a hell of a trip, and we're having a fine time for ourselves, but there's only one thing in this world I want, Louise, and that's to be with you."

"Randy…"

He slung his arms around her and grinned. "I want to be the last dot on that damn page with you."

Chapter 31

Olivia went through her carry-on bag twice to make sure she didn't have any liquids she'd forgotten to put into a clear plastic bag, anything in general that might trigger closer scrutiny. Not that she was hiding anything, like stolen jewels. She just didn't want to give herself any excuse to turn around and go back home to Knights Bridge. She had to act fast, before she could change her mind. She put her vial of calming herbal drops into a clear plastic bag and threw in some eye drops and hand cream because she didn't want it to look as if she might go crazy on the plane, not that the TSA workers would even notice. She made sure any liquids were under the three-ounce limit.

Dylan would come back to Knights Bridge, but it wouldn't be the same if she didn't do this. For her sake. On her own.

Jess saw her off, arriving at Carriage Hill in her truck. "You're flying to London, alone," she said, clearly keeping her shock at bay.

Olivia tossed her carry-on into the back of her car. "I've memorized the airport. I have my route planned. Logan's big but I've been there enough times to pick up and drop off people."

"I can drive you over there."

"No. I have to do this myself. Start to finish."

"You're sure Dylan's there and not back in San Diego?"

"Pretending we don't exist? I'm sure, Jess."

Her confidence in her own judgment and herself in general was back to full strength. She had time before things got busy at Carriage Hill. She would have to hire a staff. She wanted to take the risk. She wanted the freedom to do things.

To do things with Dylan, she amended.

She climbed in behind the wheel, started the car and waved to her sister.

She'd printed out her boarding pass at home. She arrived at Logan without incident, parked and got through airport security with no issues.

She had chosen a window seat, as close to the front of the plane as possible. She wanted to see the scenery—even if it was just clouds or darkness—and she wanted as quick an exit as she could manage without traveling first-class. She figured she would do what she could to prevent a panic attack.

Settling into her seat, pulling on her seat belt, she debated telling the flight attendant that she hadn't flown in a while and didn't like to fly at all, but she opted to keep her situation to herself.

A businessman sat next to her. He was, to her eye, the classic bored, experienced flyer. Perfect, she thought. He yawned and tore open his plastic-encased blanket. "Where you headed?" he asked her.

"To visit a friend just outside London. You?"

"A few days in London and then on to Switzerland."

"Switzerland. I'd love to go to Switzerland one day." Olivia thought she sounded like a twelve-year-old. Apparently so did he from the look he gave her. She smiled. "I've never flown overseas."

"Ah."

"I'll be fine. I won't freak out on you or anything."

He laughed. "That's good. Where you from?"

"A little town on the edge of the Quabbin Reservoir. Have you heard of Quabbin?"

"That's where we get our water, isn't it?"

"Yes, it is. It was built in the 1930s. Four towns…" She stopped herself. "I won't talk the whole trip. Promise."

"It's okay. I fly so much, I forget what it's like to be new to it. Nervous?"

"Excited," she said. She pointed to her eyes. "I have a happy place I go to if I start to get nervous."

"Where's your happy place?"

"I'm in the woods, following a rock-strewn stream on a hot summer day. I'm barefoot, jumping from rock to rock." She didn't say that Dylan McCaffrey was with her.

"That's a good happy place."

"Do you have one?"

"I've never thought about it. I don't think mine would be in the woods. I'd be on the golf course. Yeah, I like that."

Olivia fell asleep after dinner. She wasn't interested in movies or reading. She put on eye shades and her iPod, with the range of music she'd chosen to help her relax.

The big adventurer, she thought with a smile.

The flight was smooth and not as interminable as she'd expected, and soon the lights were on, orange juice, tea and scones were being served and then they were landing.

She'd figured out money and a taxi. She wasn't going to rent a car and try to drive herself. She'd arranged to arrive early at a small hotel in the Mayfair section of London and checked in. She showered, changed and had breakfast, then walked to an address she had found in her own research on Philip Rankin.

She came to a small shop owned by a young clothing designer, Alexandra Rankin Hunt. Alexandra was at a frosted-glass counter. She was a slim, angular, attractive woman in her late twenties, the great-granddaughter of Lady Helena Ashworth and Philip Rankin, Grace Webster's jewel thief.

Alexandra greeted Olivia with a warm smile. "You're Olivia Frost." She noted Olivia's surprise. "Dylan McCaffrey was here earlier. He's gone to see my mother and my grandmother. I'll take you."

"I don't want to inconvenience you."

"You aren't. Dylan said to expect you, and I offered. Please. No arguing. I'm delighted to meet you."

Dylan said to expect her? The man did have his nerve, Olivia thought, amused and, she admitted, pleased. He'd known she'd get on a plane and come to London. No one had told him.

She drove with Alexandra out a twisting, scenic road

to a graceful brick house in the green and scenic countryside. Alexandra—the granddaughter of Duncan McCaffrey's half sister—led the way to the back of the house and a flower garden, one of the most beautiful gardens Olivia had ever seen. Dylan was there with two older women, Philippa Rankin Hunt and her daughter, Elizabeth.

Philippa remembered her father as a fighter pilot and hero. When the war started, she went to live with the Ashworths, her mother's family, although she never got along well with her uncle Charles. Olivia couldn't guess what Philip Rankin had planned for, hoped for all those years ago, but he must have wondered if he'd die in the war. Had he dreamed of bringing Grace to England? Of moving with his small daughter to New England?

"I was only three, but I can remember my father coming home from America. My aunt always said he was a different man. I realize now that he wasn't sad." Philippa smiled, tears shining in her deep blue eyes. "He was in love."

Olivia saw Dylan withdraw a new, red velvet bag from his jacket and set it on a small table on the veranda, next to a silver tea service. Lady Helena had inherited the Ashworth jewels from her grandmother. They were meant for her daughter. Philip had known that, and in whatever grip of grief and anger he'd been in that September of 1938, he'd done what he could to make it happen.

The rest was for Philippa Rankin Hunt and her daughter and granddaughter to sort out.

After tea and a pleasant visit, Dylan walked around to the front of the house with Olivia. He, of course, had rented a shiny, expensive car. He grinned at her. "I see, despite all your careful planning, you don't have a way back to London."

"I figured I'd wing it and call a cab if it came to it."

"It'd cost you a fortune. Where are you staying?"

"A little hotel. It's charming. I read reviews on the internet."

"Of course you did."

"Where are you staying, Buckingham Palace?"

"That's Noah. I don't have a place for tonight. I didn't plan that far ahead."

"I didn't plan past tomorrow." She grinned at him. "I figure I'm due for an adventure."

"Good. Let's see what happens."

The next morning Dylan spirited Olivia away to a cottage on the Cornish coast that Noah had found for them. "It's perfect," she said, her eyes shining with excitement.

"Olivia…" Dylan looked at her, amazed at how much his life had changed. "We're going to have such a life together."

Her breath caught. He thought he said his name but couldn't be sure.

"Noah's fine. He knows he doesn't need me all the time anymore, and he knows I'll slay any dragons he needs me to slay. We've got some venture capital projects in mind. In the meantime, I want to paint old furniture, make basil soap, coach small-town hockey and try my hand at adventure travel."

"You'd be happy in Knights Bridge?"

He didn't hesitate. "Yes. I've started talking to Mark about how you and I could combine our two properties—" He stopped, angling her a look as he noticed her smile. "What?"

"I've talked to Mark, too."

"Imagine that. I figure Knights Bridge has been waiting for the better part of a century for me to show up and just didn't know it."

"Dylan… I'd move to San Diego or England or anywhere else to be with you."

"I know you would."

"That confident, are you?" She took his hand. "When I saw you standing in the freezing rain with Buster that night…"

"I thought he was going to chew my leg off. Where is Buster?"

"He's staying with Jess. Dylan—"

He squeezed her hand. "Me first. I love you, Olivia. I love you for who you are, and I belong with you, wherever you are."

"That's what I was going to say." She smiled. "I'm a little jet-lagged, but let me try. I love you, Dylan. I love you for who you are, and I belong with you, wherever you are."

He lifted her off her feet. "Do you know where you are now?"

"England."

"Olivia…"

She threw back her head, laughing, teasing him. "I'm in your arms, right where I'll always want to be."

Chapter 32

On a warm early summer morning, Grace Webster sat in her favorite chair in the sunroom and listened to the birds through the screen. She had just received an invitation, designed by Olivia Frost, to the autumn wedding of Jessica Frost and Mark Flanagan at The Farm at Carriage Hill.

According to Audrey Frost, Olivia and Dylan were planning a Christmas wedding.

Dylan...my grandson...

Audrey and the rest of the residents at Rivendell still weren't over the shock of that one. Grace smiled, thinking not just of their shock but their support and love.

Everyone has their secrets, she thought.

Louise and Randy Frost were planning a trip to Tuscany next spring, after the weddings.

Grace knew that her traveling days were long past, but Olivia and her friend Maggie O'Dunn had asked her and Audrey to teach them all they knew about old-time soap-making. They'd looked at each other and figured, well, why not?

A breeze floated into the sunroom, bringing with it the scent of mowed grass and summer flowers. Grace took out a pad of yellow-lined paper and the fountain pen she'd bought for her journaling class, and she wrote in wavering but clear script:

"As I write this, I am dressed for a bridal shower for Jessica Frost at The Farm at Carriage Hill. I'm taking a moment to add this postscript to my book. So far every night this beautiful summer, I've dreamed about that long-ago summer when I lost my town, my valley, my home and very nearly myself...when I fell in love for the first and only time of my long life.

If Philip had come back to me, I'd have gone with him anywhere. I know that. We would have raised his daughter and our son together. But he didn't come back, and I stayed on the path I was always on... I became a teacher, a woman destined never to marry but to have a full, good life and to keep her secrets close.

All these years, I thought I'd lost my son, but I never did. He had his own path in this life, and at the end, he brought Dylan to us all here in Knights Bridge.

My grandson is a swashbuckler of a man, and he and Olivia are so much in love.

My story is their story now.

Ah. I see an eagle flying high over Quabbin. I'll put my pen down now, and I'll sit here a moment and let myself be a girl again, snapping beans on a summer afternoon with my grandmother, dreaming of romance and adventure.

* * * * *

Author's Note

Thank you for reading *Secrets of the Lost Summer*! I hope you enjoyed the story. Knights Bridge and the Websters are fictional, but the Swift River Valley is a real place, a beautiful place in West-Central Massachusetts where I grew up. My family home, a former eighteenth-century carriage house, is on the western edge of the Quabbin Reservoir. No doubt being so close to that vast "forbidden" wilderness fueled my storyteller's imagination.

For help with research, I want to thank my mother, M. Florine Neggers, and her friends at the Stone House Museum in Belchertown, Massachusetts. It's a "must visit" if you're in the area, as are the Swift River Valley Historical Society in New Salem and the Quabbin Visitors Center. During the research for this book, I enjoyed revisiting and exploring many of the trails and old roads of Quabbin that are open to the public.

I also appreciate the detailed and fascinating histories of Quabbin by J. R. Greene; *Quabbin: A History and Explorers Guide* by Michael Tougias; *Quabbin Valley People and Places* by Elizabeth Peirce; and the many websites with photographs and information on Quabbin. The photography of Les Campbell opened my eyes as a teenager to the beauty of the area right outside my door; his work and his talent are as amazing as ever.

I want to pay tribute to the people my family and I knew who gave up their homes and livelihoods in this idyllic valley to provide pure, safe drinking water to millions. I especially remember Eleanor Griswold Schmidt, who once called the lost town of Prescott home. Her well-known quote says it all: "Now I have two beauties; one to remember and one to enjoy."

For more information, please visit my website, www.carlaneggers.com.

Thanks again, and happy reading!

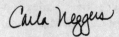

New York Times bestselling author

CARLA NEGGERS

celebrates the joy and romance of Christmas in New England with a brand-new holiday tale in her *Swift River Valley* series.

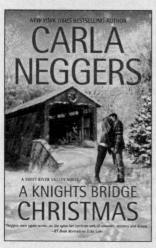

Clare Morgan is ready for a fresh start in Knights Bridge, Massachusetts. Widowed for six years, Clare settles into her job as the town's new librarian and a slow-paced life with her young son, Owen.

Then Clare meets Logan Farrell, a Boston ER doctor in town to help his elderly grandmother settle into assisted living. *Slow* isn't a word Logan understands, and he doesn't plan to stick around for long. But Daisy Farrell has other ideas. She enlists her grandson to decorate her house one last time—and Logan looks to Clare for help.

What neither of them expects to find is an attraction to the other. But they both know firsthand the crazy things that can happen in life, and everything about Knights Bridge and this magical season invites them to open themselves to new possibilities…and new love.

Available now, wherever books are sold!

Be sure to connect with us at:
Harlequin.com/Newsletters
Facebook.com/HarlequinBooks
Twitter.com/HarlequinBooks

www.MIRABooks.com

MCN1759

CARLA NEGGERS